BRANDI C

firebrand

BOOK ONE OF THE HEROINE SERIES

Firebrand

Book One of the Heroine Series

Brandi Gann

This book is a work of fiction. The names, characters, and events in this book are the products of the author's imagination or used fictiously. Any similarity to real persons living or dead is coincidental and not intended by the author.

© 2021 Brandi Gann-Teller of Tales

Editor: Nikki Wright

Cover Design: Heidi Wilson

A CIP record for this book is available from the Library of Congress Cataloging-in-Publication Data

ISBN: 978-1-7366763-1-8

Printed in USA

For Jonathan.

Thank you for encouraging me to dream

these whimsical dreams.

For Griffin.

In hopes one day, you follow your own.

Contents:

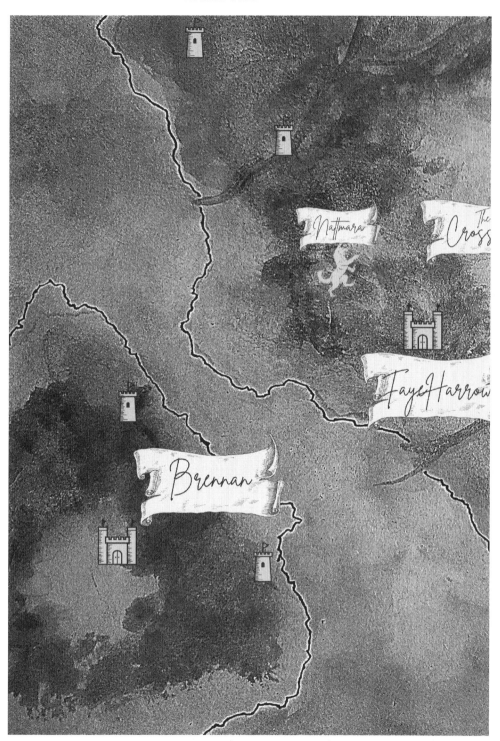

Rimheld

Wimborne

The Human Realm

7

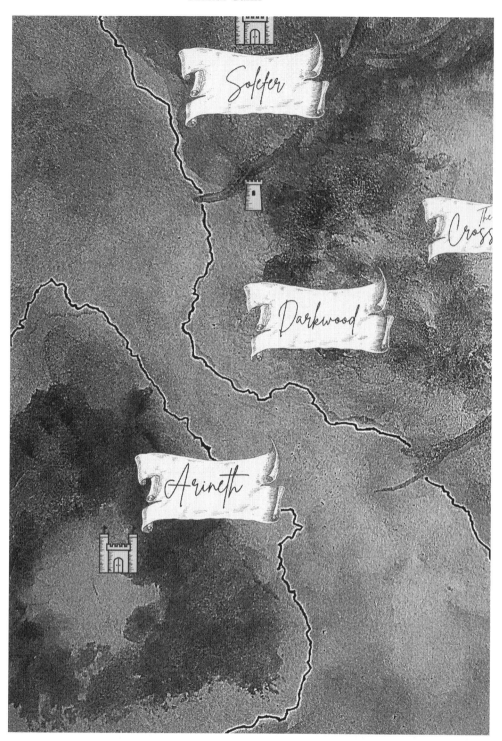

Aleria

"Again!" Aleria shouted. The young man across from her gave her a long-suffering glare, then sighed. A smile teased her lips as she crossed her arms over her chest. The girlishness of her voice was a vivid contrast to the wicked pull of her smirk.

"Oh, come on, Dray. Not scared of a girl, are you?"

Draven huffed and rolled his eyes as he broadened his stance, squaring his shoulders, and preparing himself for her next attack.

"Good," she thought as her own body sank into a ready position.

It was typical for soldiers under her father's employ to try and take it easy on her during sparring lessons. Draven was the only exception. Even though it was his goal to become the Knight Protector to her Lady of Fayeharrow, he never pulled his punches. Dray was always the one to push her to be the kind of ruler she wanted to be. Swords, knowledge, and kindness. A powerful mixture gifted to her by her parents in both blood and breeding.

Being the sole heir warranted the occasional over-protective behavior, but still, she hated the fact that she was treated with kid gloves most of the time.

Aleria barely had time to swing before Draven's practice sword came slamming down on hers with a reverberating crack. She hissed between her teeth as she looked up at her best friend. A teasing chuckle slid from her mouth.

"Oh-ho. There you are, Lion of Edlind," Aleria teased.

Draven snarled playfully at her, pushing back and disentangling their weapons. Aleria knew her cousin both loathed and loved the nickname that testified to his prowess on the battlefield, as well as the thick shock of auburn waves that encircled his face like a mane.

"Yeah, yeah. What was it they were calling *you* after the festival two years ago?"

The two were circling each other once again in a slow prowl.

"Winner?" She nonchalantly flipped her sword in her hand before narrowing the blade in his direction.

He snorted through his nose in a way that reminded her of his namesake.

"Green-Eyed Witch," he huffed. "Though I have heard some rhyming variations with the last wor-."

The wind rushed from his lungs as Aleria took the opportunity to fly at him, snapping her legs around his waist and flipping him to the ground in one smooth move.

With a flurry of curses, Draven drove his elbow into her hip, prompting his immediate release. He rolled to his feet, readying his weapon again.

"You can't fool me, Ali. I know why you're so desperate to pick a fight today."

Her smile disappeared in a blink. A pinprick pierced her heart, and she had to fight the urge to place her hand over it to soothe the invisible wound. He was right. She was desperate to start a fight, and though it wasn't fair to be taking out her frustration on him, it also wasn't fair of him to make her face the realities of the day to come.

"That was low of you, Draven Edlind," she said quietly as she walked off the practice field. His apologies and explanations followed her the entire way back to the weapons shed.

That Creator forsaken weapons shed.

It had taken her an entire year after MyKhal left before Aleria could even set foot through its dilapidated door frame. She cursed the memory of him as she slammed her sword on the rack.

MyKhal.

His name had been banned from her thoughts, but it echoed now and again in the dust of places like this. Looking around the wooden building, she shook her head as if she could shake away the ghost of the memories that haunted this room. Their first kiss was here, as was the moment he whispered promises of their future together. Her hand drifted over her heart again to rub at the phantom injury long since scarred over. It wasn't fair that nearly three years later, he still had such a hold over it.

"It kills me too, you know."

Draven's whisper cut through the silence loud enough to make her flinch.

"I know," was all she could bring herself to say, lacking the emotional fortitude to look him in the eye.

Draven and MyKhal were thick as thieves from the first moment her cousin arrived after his father's death. When MyKhal left her, he must have known where Draven's allegiance resided. The loss was painful for Draven too, even if it was a different kind of hurt.

At first, two of them had feared the worst when no word had come. They had even planned to take a ship to Brennan to make sure MyKhal was alright. When they discussed it with her father, they were met with a pitiful look and a letter from Lord Anwir, MyKhal's father and a longtime family friend. The letter had mentioned nothing of MyKhal's intentions towards her, nothing of their courtship, and not a word of his intended return. It did mention his remarkable adventures, rigorous training, and rumors of his "sewing of wild oats." That night, Aleria had torn a practice dummy into such ragged pieces it nearly matched her ravaged pride and shattered heart.

She still remembered the conviction in MyKhal's voice as he told his father of his plans to court her. He had no idea she was listening through one of the castle's secret passageways as his father raged his refusal.

"I have raised you to be a ruler, not to wed one!" The crack of a signet ring on bone still made her stomach churn. She wondered if the scar on the top of his right cheek remained or if it had faded like his affections.

Today would be the first time in two years that she would have to entertain the Anwir family. The first time in years she had to look into the eyes of the man who sent his son away "for training" when the real truth of the matter was that he sent him away from the *"entirely too willful Edlind girl."*

With a deep breath, she turned from the weapons rack and looked at her cousin. His face was grim, but his Edlind-green eyes were pleading with her.

"I forgive you," she sighed, "but I expect you to not leave my side tonight. We face him like we do everything else: together."

Draven's mouth turned up slightly in the corners before he nodded in agreement.

"Together then, but could you take a shower first? You smell like you tumbled into a tub of offal."

Aleria tilted her head down to sniff herself, then shrugged before throwing her arms wide and chasing after him. "Was that a hidden plea for a big hug, cousin? I think it was."

His faked girlish squeal nearly made her choke on her laughter.

Thankfully, her bathing time had wasted enough of the afternoon that she was allowed to skip formal welcomes and tastefully displayed hors d'oeuvres in the main hall. When she finally deigned to grace the celebration with her presence, Draven was waiting for her with a mouth full of what she could only assume was pastry by the crumbs dusting his lapel. Even with the smattering of pastry pieces, her cousin knew how to clean up well. His wild auburn waves were slicked back into a low, perfectly-messy bun. A few wild tendrils danced across the angular planes of his freckled cheeks. All these years in her father's service had honed him from a gangly, young cub into the young, slightly scruffy man before her. There was no one she would be more honored to have at her side as her protector, advisor, and friend for the rest of her days.

"You're thinking too much," Draven interrupted, offering his arm.

"How could you tell?"

His eyebrows raised slightly. "Besides being able to read you like a book, you worry your bottom lip until it's raw. Remind me to never let you play cards - on my team at least." Her elbow connected to his ribs, making him cough out a laugh. "You look lovely," Draven whispered as a way of an apology. "And I'm not the only one to have noticed."

He nodded his head towards the rest of the room, indicating the crowd gathered there. Some whispered among themselves; others blatantly stared.

"I'm making a statement," she whispered back, as her fingers ghosted over the dark velvet of her gown. The rich ebony fabric reflected in the flickering candlelight like deep, dark emeralds. The wide neck of the gown hung precariously on her shoulders before plunging into a revealing drape in the back. Her golden blonde waves had been tied up with a matching velvet ribbon, exposing the lightly freckled column of her neck, except for a few stray pieces that refused to be tamed. She was the picture of modesty and sin, propriety and wildness, the contradictions that reflected how she lived.

When Lord Anwir looked her way and narrowed his gaze at her, Draven bristled at her side.

"Such a bell-end," Dray groaned before he begrudgingly announced her presence. Aleria nearly snorted at her cousin, but composed herself, dipping low in a flawless curtsey before offering her hand to Lord Anwir. She glanced at her father before turning her attention back to him.

"A dubious pleasure seeing you again after all this time, Lord Anwir."

Her father nearly choked on his drink. A slow, sly smirk stretched across her cousin's lips, but Aleria's face remained neutrally uninterested.

Anwir attempted a smile, but it looked more like a sneer. "Oh, come now, kitten. You can't still be angry with me," he purred as he plucked a goblet of wine from a passing servant's tray. "You know as well as I do that the training was necessary. The boy had gotten far too...soft...to be a proper successor."

He was taunting her, and she knew it. Aleria slid her eyes to her father's and searched for some kind of clue as to what words would be too far when her saint of a mother crossed the room with her hands outstretched.

Looping her hand through her husband's arm, she sighed, "Dearest, I need you. Ansel is in a fit again over the soup, and I need you to assure her it is perfectly satisfactory." She glanced Aleria's way before tugging her husband off in the direction of the kitchens. "Please do carry on," her mother added with a graceful sweep of her hand.

With a fake smile, Aleria turned her attention back to Anwir.

"I'm sorry. Where were we? Ah, yes. You were confusing the word 'soft' with the word 'kind.' Do continue," she waved him on.

He raised his glass to her. "You know, you are a lovely little thing, kitten. You would have made such a healthy breeding mare for my family line. Too bad my son couldn't break you with a good riding like all the others. A pity."

Draven's shoulders went taut as a bowstring. "Mind your tongue, milord," he growled, "or you will find yourself missing it."

Aleria smiled softly and placed her hand on his arm. "Your son was quite a proficient rider, but our preferences were quite different. His was a bit too easy, too fast, and over so quickly. I prefer long rides, a bit more treacherous. I feel it makes the trek all the more satisfying in the end. Wouldn't you agree, milord?"

Draven nearly choked.

Anwir scoffed, lowering his wine from his lips.

At that moment, her father returned, leaning down to place a kiss on Aleria's temple. His red-gold hair shimmered in the candlelight.

"What did I miss?" A slight challenge hung in the air, ringing in the deep timbre of her father's voice.

"Aleria's riding preferences," Draven said, shooting her a look. She shrugged.

"You are blessed to have such a lady as a successor. Well ridden - I'm sorry - written. With such class and grace. I'm sure my son would be quite put out to see what he is missing."

Aleria felt every word from him like a backhanded slap, but Philip Edlind, Earl of Fayeharrow smiled. An equally wondrous and fearsome thing.

"Dear Lord Anwir," she said, "you must be joking. Who would dare miss the fabled Green-Eyed Witch?"

Her father let out a boisterous laugh that made a real smile tug at her lips. His laugh was infectious. He was always the life of the party with stories, humorous anecdotes, and all-around gracious nature. A perfect example of what a leader should look like. Aleria hoped in her heart of hearts that her leadership would mirror his in every way.

"You are no witch, daughter," her father narrowed his gaze, seriousness in his tone. "You are a firebrand. You refine the fires of those around you. You are an ignitor of passions. And you can and will spark change."

His words reverberated in her heart like that of a prophecy. She almost forgot where she was at that moment. If it weren't for the cheer coming from her right, she would have probably gazed in loving awe at her father for a few moments longer. She jumped to her tiptoes and threw her arms around his neck. To the nethers with propriety. With a loud, smacking kiss to her father's cheek and a whisper of love and gratitude, she bounded off towards the center of the room. Grabbing a glass of cider, she raised it high.

"To igniting passions and sparking change!"

A toast ricocheted off the stone walls, echoed by her father and Draven before the strike of a cittern filled the room with the magic of song. Aleria chuckled as she mockingly bowed to Anwir and joined the merriment. Couples young and old began filing in and spinning round to the rambunctious tempo of an old fairy folk song.

Do not trust a fairy, child.
Don't bend unto their whims,
Though their kiss be like the sweetest wines,
They get more than they give.

The words echoed in her head, and she couldn't help but huff at the irony as her dance partner lifted her playfully into the air. Perhaps MyKhal was her fairytale prince. After all, he certainly got more than he gave.

Her father and mother joined in dance in a loving embrace that made her heart squeeze. Aleria sighed as the song came to an end, but her parents dawdled a bit longer, swaying to music all their own. Flirting even after all these years.

To have that kind of love was a song her heart longed to sing along to, but for now, she took the offered hand of one of her father's soldiers and danced and flirted without a care in the world. Occasionally, she felt the heavy weight of Anwir's stare on her back, but at that moment, she could not deign herself to care. Let him write to his son about this moment. Perhaps she would do the same. MyKhal hadn't written her a single letter. Another broken promise. She had written to him every day for the first year, and when no reply came, she wrote less and less until she had nothing left to say. At least not until now.

After the merriment died down, people made their way to their rooms with full bellies and red faces. Aleria loaded her bag with a piece of paper, ink, and a blanket before saddling her horse and riding off in the direction of the place this letter should be written: Fayeharrow Coast.

Fayeharrow's coastline was hugged in black sand and the crashing waves of the Whispering Sea. During hot summer days, the sand was sole scorching, but at night, it remained blissfully warm, a breathtaking contrast to the cool seawater. The coast was one of her favorite places in all of Fayeharrow until the day MyKhal left. It was on this beach he spoke vows to her that she believed would last a lifetime. She was a fool to have believed him.

Aleria

Fayeharrow: Nearly three years ago.

The four months since their betrothal were the hardest Aleria had ever had to endure. Four excruciating months without MyKhal. She had missed him desperately and positively ached to be in his arms once more. She smiled into the mirror. Appeased with her final look, she tucked an errant strand of blonde hair behind her ear and dabbed some beeswax on her smiling lips. With one final perusal and twirl, she took a deep calming breath. The sound of horses drawing near brought a squeal past her lips, wrecking her attempt at remaining calm. In the blink of an eye, she flew downstairs, blowing past her cousin who was shamelessly flirting with one of the laundresses.

He told her not to be in a rush, that Khal would be here for the next two weeks. She ignored him. What did he know? He wasn't the one in love.

Aleria nearly stumbled as she slid into the grand hall and down to where her parents waited, ready to welcome their guests. Brushing the same ever-wild strand of hair from her face, she looked up through her lashes at MyKhal as he entered. Creator's beating heart, he was so handsome: tall, lithe, and those eyes…Those honey-brown eyes rendered her incapable of cohesive thought. She had daydreamed of running her fingers through his dark tresses, brushing her lips over his tawny skin, the slight scrape of his stubble against her throat. Creator save her, it took everything she had not to run headlong into his arms and kiss him senseless.

MyKhal greeted her parents with a cold voice. He didn't smile. He didn't look at her. His lips were pressed so tightly together; they looked like chiseled, cold marble. Something was wrong, very wrong, and it sent a chill down her spine.

"Hello, young Lord Anwir," Aleria said, trying to gain his attention. He looked over in her direction, giving her a nod and a light smile. The smile didn't quite reach his eyes though, and her excitement guttered.

As their families stood together making small talk, Aleria crossed the stone floor of the receiving room to stand next to MyKhal. She leaned in close enough that he could hear her whisper. "I see distance has not made your heart grow fonder." When he didn't reply she added, "Creator, Khal, you sure know how to make a girl feel missed."

He leaned in and gave her a small peck on the cheek before pulling away just as quickly. His closeness, his warmth gone. He warily turned his gaze to his father. Her stomach turned to lead; her heart sank to meet it. Putting on a cheerful, angelic façade, she turned to her father.

"Father? May MyKhal escort me to the stables? I think he'd appreciate the new stallion you found for me. We will be certain to be back in time for dinner this evening." It was unlikely they would have a chance to talk soon if she didn't excuse them now, especially because Khal didn't give any indication he was eager to do just that. The anxiety that lodged itself in her stomach became overwhelming, and she needed to find out what was wrong with him.

Her father agreed, then gave his typical warnings to be careful with his girl, though they both knew all too well her ability to throttle the young Lord if necessary. Given the situation, she was very likely to do just that.

The only sounds between them were pebbles crunching beneath their feet, the hustle and bustle of the courtyard, and the whinny of horses as they inched closer to the stables. Aleria's hands balled tightly into fists, the sting of tears pricking her eyes.

"Didn't you miss me at all?" she blurted out. "I have been counting the moments until I would see you again. I haven't slept in days...I just..."

He pulled her into his arms none too gently and sealed her mouth with a desperate kiss. His fingers tangled into her hair and pulled her so close to him it was like he was trying to breathe her in. Aleria's words died on her lips as tears of panic turned to tears of relief and streamed down her face. "Khal, I love you, but don't ever scare me like that aga-"

His eyes locked on hers, and the pain there, the desperation in the way his fingers tips clung to her...

"He's sending me away."

Aleria's heart stopped in her chest. Her throat was suddenly so tight she could scarcely breathe. "What?" she exhaled. "If you're joking, I'll never forgive you." She hoped it was a joke, but she also saw the proof in the watery brown depths of his eyes.

"No... no, no, no," she stammered. "Why? What happened? And all of a sudden? I don't understand. He can't. We are..."

MyKhal took her in his arms and held her tightly against his chest. "I'm sorry, love," he whispered into her hair, brushing his lips against her temple. "I'm so sorry. I don't want to leave you."

Trembling and gasping for air, she couldn't keep her mind from racing, searching desperately for a solution, something...anything to cling to.

"Where is he sending you?"

He tensed. "Father wants me to squire for a friend of his in Brennan," he said hollowly, bracing for her reaction.

She pushed back from him, a frown creasing her forehead. "Brennan? Across the Sea? But he agreed to our marriage."

A thought formed in her mind. Desperate, unreasonable. But it was there, and she couldn't shake it. MyKhal shook his head, but she caught his face in her hands.

"Run away with me."

She knew the implications of what she was saying, but her ravaged heart was killing her. She couldn't imagine being without him. Not now, not ever.

A long moment passed. MyKhal took her trembling hands in his, and with a brush of his lips across her knuckles, he gave her a heartbroken smile.

"You know we can't do that, Ali."

Tears fell fresh as she shook her head. He was right, curse him. As much as she wished otherwise, she had obligations that only she could fill, and so did he. They both knew that. But still, thoughts of all the possible hurdles they now had to cross raced through her mind.

Casting her eyes down at her feet, she murmured.

"I hear the women there are quite beautiful..."

"Aleria-" MyKhal sighed, sliding his finger beneath her chin and tilting it up to meet her eyes.

"Khal, what if you change your mind? What if you fall in love with someone else?"

"Never." His fingers brushed over her jaw. "You hear me, Ali? Never. Not in a thousand years. I'll come back to you, and then, we'll get married, and no one will come between us."

She felt as if she were going to shatter like glass in his arms.

His thumb brushed away a stray tear running down her cheek. They had yet to reach the stables; the conversation had stopped them right outside the large doors. The sound of soldiers in the training yard and the movement of animals felt like a mockery to this moment. Everything and everyone else was going on as if her world wasn't asunder. Hearts broke every day. But this moment was more like bleeding out than breaking. A stable hand walked past, and Aleria wiped at her face, forcing a smile for him. Sniffling, she turned to MyKhal.

"Promise me you'll wait," he whispered. "Promise me you'll be my wife."

Aleria knew if someone else made an offer...

"I promise," she swore against his lips. The kiss was more than inappropriate for prying eyes. Their hands and lips sought to be as close as possible.

Breathless and between kisses, she whispered, "Father will kill us if he sees -," MyKhal growled a little and pulled back.

"I'm sorry -"

Aleria swallowed his apology with her lips, shaking her head. "Shush! Follow me."

The weapons shed was only a quick jog from the stables. With the morning regimen in full swing, it wouldn't be used for at least another hour. Pushing the rickety door open, she yanked him inside. Stumbling a bit, she pressed herself against the wooden wall and tugged at the front of his shirt. He smiled at her, overwhelmed with awe and desire, but still somehow, closing the distance between them.

Khal's hand tangled in her hair as the other stroked a heated path down her neck, her chest. His fingers trailed down the dip of her waist before gripping her arse as he pulled her flush against him. Aleria gasped, and he swallowed the sound, deepening the kiss in the most sinful ways.

He plundered her neck with his lips, and she burned against him. Until Khal was jerked back by his collar. Draven slammed his fist into MyKhal's face. MyKhal stumbled back, crashing into the weapons rack. The wooden swords clattered to the ground. There was only a breath before Draven was upon him again, tackling him back to the ground.

"Draven Edlind, you stop it right now!" Her cousin's temperament was accurate to the stereotypical depiction of ginger boys. Rage and wrath were his first response when someone was in the wrong, and he caught his best friend groping his cousin in a shed, which would most likely be on his list of things that validated murder.

"Go inside, Aleria. You're betrothed." Each of his words staccato and hissed through gritted teeth as each of them fought for control. "And I need to have a little chat about indecent behavior and how a proper gentleman should be treating the future Lady Edlind." Draven pinned MyKhal down with his legs and slammed his fist his face again. Aleria shouted, running over to pull him off. "I am not a child you can order around. If anything, I should be the one giving the orders."

Draven flinched, and MyKhal's eyes went wide. Her words hit their mark.

"When you start acting like the Lady of Fayeharrow and not the town whore, I'll consider it," Draven hissed. At that, MyKhal let his fist fly for the first time. A sickening crack echoed in the tiny shed, followed by the thud of Draven hitting the floor. MyKhal stepped over his unconscious body and cursed, shaking out his stinging fist.

Aleria crouched down to Draven, pity warring with anger. "He's going to be furious when he wakes up," she said. "You deserved it though, you raging oaf." MyKhal had yet to move from his spot and was still bleeding from his lower lip. Aleria reached for him with whispered apologies. He hissed as her fingers grazed his busted lip.

"He's right," MyKhal said. "I shouldn't have put you in such a compromising position."

Aleria rolled her eyes at him. "Chivalrous as always, love, but I'll have you know that if I didn't agree with everything we were doing here -"

"Yes, yes, you would hand all my most cherished parts back to me in pieces. You forget I'm the one who suggested you carry that blade at your thigh in the first place." He chuckled with a devilish smirk, inching his hand down her hip. She slapped it off just as kittenish.

"Chivalrous indeed," she quipped looking over at her cousin again.

MyKhal cupped the side of her face. "You should go. This is something I have to work out with Dray alone."

Aleria sighed and kissed his cheek before heading to the door. She wouldn't win this argument; it would be better for them both if she simply acquiesced.

"I love you. You know that, don't you?"

She paused, bracing herself on the doorframe of the shed. She couldn't help but sigh, resigned when those fathomless eyes met hers.

"I love you too."

Ping.

Pop.

An incessant noise woke her from her sleep. One, then another, before a shower of what sounded like a fist full of tiny stones smattered against her window. Drearily rolling off the side of her bed, she stumbled her way over to the window and gave it a shove. A shriek jumped from her throat as she was pelted with a handful of pebbles. A curse echoed from below, and she leaned out into the warm night. A breeze drifted over her face, whipping her hair about. Squinting, she looked out into the moon-drenched castle grounds for the source of the ruckus.

"What in the infernal regions is going on here?" she hissed. When her eyes settled on the man below, she cursed her rumpled appearance and bed-addled braid.

MyKhal tried to whisper, but it came out more like a hushed shout. "My lady! Join me for a walk in the moonlight."

"Shh! Creator, MyKhal, are you insane? If anyone sees you here..."

"Then, end my misery and join me down here. We are young and so is the night," he shouted, swaying a bit on his feet. The rational part of him was left somewhere in the bottom of an empty glass. Aleria frowned down at him and pursed her lips in disapproval.

"What exactly have you and my cousin been doing all evening?" she groaned.

MyKhal was having none of her trying to dampen his high spirits. "Woman, stop questioning me and get down here before I climb up and get you."

Aleria shook her head. "Don't do anything foolish. I'll be down in a moment."

MyKhal scoffed. "An Aleria moment or a real one?"

"Shut it, you," she called out the window with a foul gesture. His chuckle followed her as she grabbed her cape and rushed to the hidden passage in her room.

Sneaking around the corner, all she saw was darkness. Frowning, she turned to leave when strong arms wrapped around her waist and whiskey scented lips began kissing the exposed part of her neck. She drew her shoulder up in a reflexive defense and stifled a giggle. With a smirk full of wicked intentions, he pulled her in the direction of the stables. When she saw he already had a horse saddled and ready, Aleria crossed her arms over her chest and raised an unbelieving brow at it.

"Khal, you are swaying on your feet. How in the world do you expect to lead a horse? You're going to get both of us killed."

"My lady, drunk or no, I can deal with any stubborn thing that comes my way." He grinned at her like a wolf about to devour its prey and grabbed a handful of her curved behind. She gasped and swatted at him, trying to keep the smile from her face.

"How about you let me lead?" she whispered sweetly with a kiss to his cheek.

With a playful smirk, his mouth graced hers with a teasing kiss. "Mmm. I love a woman who knows how to take the reins and ride."

Aleria rolled her eyes, sliding into the saddle. "You're a deplorable drunk and a cad," she teased him. When he slid behind her and nuzzled his face into her neck, she couldn't help but laugh at how easy it was to manipulate him.

Before long, they had reached Black Sands. She and Draven spent nearly every summer evening there when they were younger. Midnight shores and sapphire waves. It was pure magic.

He offered her a sweet but sad smile and his hand. "I want to show you something," he said gently. "Take off your shoes."

Her hand pressed into the warmth of his as he pulled her towards the shoreline. The sapphire waves tickled her toes and beckoned her to walk into the water's embrace. The stars mirrored themselves in the calmer parts of the water like a shimmering kiss of the heavens to the earth. She was helplessly enthralled by the beauty of it all.

"The Whispering Sea touches both the shores of Fayeharrow and the shores of the Brennan." He ran his hands down the length of her arms entangling his calloused fingers with hers. "When you're lonely, when you're sad, when you miss me, come here." His lips brushed her ear with every word. "I will be sending you my love on the waves."

A gentle breeze danced across the water, making her hair flutter across her face, and with a loving smile, he turned her towards him and tucked the stray strand behind her ear. "When the wind blows your hair back, that's because I'm longing to see your beautiful face." His eyes sparkled with unshed tears in the moonlight as he spoke more of his poetry to her soul.

"When the current pulls at you, it's because I'm trying desperately to bring you closer to me."

Hot tears began streaming down Aleria's cheeks, and she pulled herself closer to him. "Khal…"

Present

Rain splattered the last words penned on the letter, making the ink run much like the tears streaming down her cheeks. Banishing the memories back to the dark recesses of her heart, she walked the black sands to the water's edge to make vows of her own.

Sliding off her shoes and taking a deep steadying breath, she walked into the churning pull of the waves. The wind whipped her face, snatching hair from her ribbon as her verdant eyes glared in the direction of Brennan.

"I hope you hear these words," she shouted into the wind. "I hope the spray of the sea reminds you of the tears you've caused." Her voice swelled over the crashing of the waves.

"I pray a storm racks your shores so you feel my pain! My rage!"

In the distance, lightning split the skies like a promise of her words. With a ragged breath, she screamed over the sound of the approaching storm.

"From this moment on, I will not waste another moment loving you!"

The current pulled her so hard, she nearly fell to her knees. It was as if the sea were begging her to reconsider. Tears and rain washed over her face as she staggered back to the shore on trembling legs, the letter falling from her fingers into the churning waters.

Draven waited at the edge, his hair whipping like a fiery beacon. Her cousin. Her best friend. Her Knight Protector. He didn't need to say a word, and neither did she as they walked back to their saddled horses. In this storm and all others, they would walk through it together.

Aleria

Light rain fell on Aleria and Dray as they left Black Sands behind. The storm left as quickly as it came, but not without leaving them both thoroughly soaked.

Their achingly slow trudge was reflective of how wrung dry Aleria felt despite her drenched and now horribly heavy velvet gown. She longed for a blanket and the hearth fire in her room. Perhaps the heat would sink bone-deep and release the cold clutching her heart.

"Aleria!" The alarm in Draven's voice halted her.

In the distance, an ominous aura lit the countryside. Her stomach leaped to her throat as she watched the red and orange dance through the dense fog.

Fire.

Without a word, Aleria and Draven took off like lighting across the fog-drenched countryside. Towards her blazing home.

Before even reaching the courtyard, she could taste the ash on her tongue and feel the backdraft of heat coming from the west wing of the castle. The smell of ash and something acrid turned her stomach as she and Draven ran towards the large double doors. At first, she couldn't make out much through the thick smoke, only the eerie cast of shadows and wavering flickers of light. No alarms were being raised. No attempts at putting out the flames. The silence was haunting, and it didn't take long for Aleria to understand.

This was not an accidental fire.

A scream echoed within the castle walls. Aleria stumbled a little and glanced down at the stone walkway where rainwater and blood swirled around her feet. Trembling, her hands clapped over her mouth, and she walked towards the bodies littering the ground. She knew their faces, knew every position they held. Soldier. Midwife. Laundress. Her people. Sobbing, she looked towards Draven, whose shock and anguish echoed her own. Without a second thought, she grabbed the sword off a fallen guard and raced through the blood and ash-covered courtyard, Draven on her heels.

"Aleria, stop!" he shouted, but she paid him no heed. Her parents were in there. They could be hurt. Creator help her, they could be…

Her mind raced with the half-arsed formation of a plan. She would have to enter through the main doors and work her way through the halls that had not yet been touched by fire. She had to make it to her parents' chambers.

"Aleria!" Draven shouted, grabbing her shoulders and yanking her to face him. "Listen to me." His voice was raw from running after her in the smoke. "We have to make a choice here. I know you want to wage war, but we don't know how many there are. If your parents are - you could be all that is left, and I will not allow you to be the next body to burn!"

Aleria shrugged off his grasp, but Draven grabbed her again, cupping her face in his hands

"I love them too," he said. "You know that I do, but we have to be smart about this." His eyes glistened with pain and a fear she never knew the Lion of Edlind could possess.

"You would risk anything to save your parents, Dray," she whispered as desperate tears ran down her cheeks. "Please, don't fight against me on this. Fight with me."

He stared at her for a long harrowing moment before nodding solemnly and looking around them. "How well do you remember those passageways we use to play in?" His tone was hard, determined.

"Well enough."

She took his hand and pulled him in the direction of an old tapestry. Fumbling beneath it, Aleria ran her fingers over the rough stone until the sound of a click echoed through the eerily silent corridor. She didn't dare think of why it was so quiet as she pulled Draven into the pitch blackness. Moving through the passage in complete darkness made their task tedious and dangerous. Neither of them dared to light a lamp or torch for fear of revealing their location to anyone who was still raiding the castle walls.

Damp stones scraped her fingers as she traced the path in as straight a line as she could. Each step was measured, each breath quiet. Her hand pressed over her frantically pounding heart, afraid that it could be heard over the stillness. Draven kept his fingers at the hem of her shirt, using it as a guide as she felt her way along the walls.

A scream tore through the air. With a gasp, her hand lept to the hilt of her sword, the other clutched to her chest. Raucous laughter followed by another scream sent shivers of disgust down her spine. Creeping towards the small crack of light at the edge of the tunnel, she carefully peeked through and saw the familiar decor of the kitchens. Her mother would always bring her there when she was upset, saying there was nothing that cookies couldn't fix. This was one of those few and far between moments that her mother was wrong. She said a prayer to the Creator, begging him to be with her and with her family. With a shuddering breath, she turned to face Draven.

"You with me?"

Draven huffed his response as he pressed in close behind her. "Quick. No mercy, Aleria."

The words almost made her cringe. No mercy. Though she had been trained for battle, she had never had to land a real killing blow on another human. She had never felt blood on her hands, apart from accidents and helping in the infirmary when there was a shortage of hands. The only thing that brought her any peace was the knowledge that it was killed or be killed.

"No mercy." Steeling herself, she took a deep breath and pushed the hidden door slightly ajar. Scanning the room through the tiniest of cracks, she assessed what they were up against. Five men in dark cloaks and black leathers. Two by the door, two doing Creator knows what to the poor girl across the room, and one pilfering whatever he could find from the cabinets. Holding out her hand to Draven, she signaled whom he would advance on first.

Aleria took on the first soldier, being that he was too involved in his raiding to notice her slipping behind him like a wraith. There was no other sound besides the sickening gurgle that came after. It made her face go sallow, but she knew to stop now would mean certain death. Draven slid behind the two who had pinned the screaming woman to the prep table. Her pleas struck a chord of rage that wound him so tightly he was trembling with it. He barely made a sound as he cut the throat of one and shoved the other off the terrified girl. Three strikes, feign, strike again, and the soldier was splayed open like the sacks of flour hanging from the larder.

The element of surprise gave them a leg up, but the other two guards were running towards them, swords out and raging over their fallen comrades. Moving together, Aleria struck low, and Draven went high, slicing at the same soldier. His blood spattered the walls. Aleira panted as she slung the remaining gore from her sword. In her peripheral vision, she caught the final man trying to make his escape through the open door.

Coward! These men were nothing but cowards to attack in the night like this. To prey on defenseless women. To run when they were losing. What kind of demons were these men, and more importantly, who was the puppet master calling the shots? Aleria hissed and took off towards the guard trying to make his escape. Before he could even round the corner, Aleria snatched him by the collar and slammed him into the stone wall. Her blade pressed to his throat none too gently.

"What? Don't want to play now that the girl has a sword?" The blade sank in hard enough that blood started to trickle down the shaft. Anger and adrenaline filled her as she took in the man's appearance. He was young, no older than twenty, but the cruelty in his eyes made her stomach churn. What in the world could have made a man so young so cruel in such a short time? She wouldn't kill him. There were answers she needed first.

"Who sent you here?" she growled as the boy's gaze grew colder. When he didn't say a word, she silently threatened him with a wriggle of the blade. "Live or die by your words."

The young man dared to smirk at her. "You're the one who's going to die here...Edlind."

Aleria snarled, but before she could respond, a presence slid in beside her. The boy's eyes widened as his full weight slumped in her hold. Draven ripped his sword from the man's rib cage and shot her a look.

"Never let your guard down, Aleria. What if that had been the other man and not me? You'd be dead," he chided her as he pulled her away from the body and looked her over. "Are you alright?"

"I was trying to figure out who sent them -"

Draven held out his hand. A torn piece of garb with an embroidered emblem shone up at her. Her eyebrows knit together as she held the cloth up to the lantern still lighting the hall. There in its signature red and gold was a crest she knew far too well. The crossing swords of gold. Recognition and disgust hit her like a physical punch to the gut. Betrayal glimmered in her eyes as she looked up at Draven.

"How? How could he..." she choked. "Do you think MyKhal..."

"No," Draven said, shaking his head. "Creator, I want to say no and let it be that, Aleria, but to be honest...I don't know."

"We have to find my parents," she whispered, her voice hard behind her gritted teeth. "The girl?"

"Shaken, but safe. She went out the way we came in," he assured her as he leaned down to grab the dead soldier's sword belt. "Armor up as best as you can. We don't know what else we will find or what will find us."

Doing as she was told, she tried her best to focus her anger on a weapon instead of letting her fear and despair cripple her. If she were angry, then she couldn't be afraid. If she were angry, then she couldn't fall apart. If she were angry, she could still put one foot in front of the other. Her thoughts drifted to the cloth in her hand. She let that anger consume her as she stared at the Anwir family crest.

Lord Anwir was a monster. A power-hungry monster who would likely spin a tale that made him the hero in all of this. What would MyKhal do when he found out? Or did he already know? Was she just a pawn in his father's game of chess? She swore to herself at that moment that her family name would not burn out here. This would not be her ending.

Armed with enemy weapons, Aleria and Draven made their way to her parents' quarters. She prayed that the fires had not yet reached this far and that the way would be clear. Fumbling along with the stones and trying to remember where she was in the dark was disorienting, but if she were remembering correctly, they weren't too far from the entry point of the High Quarters.

"Almost there -" Her whisper was clipped with an *oomph* as she nearly tumbled over something blocking her path. If not for Draven grabbing hold of her, she would have fallen flat on her face. Her hands came down to steady herself on whatever it was blocking her path, but she quickly pulled them back and away when something wet and sticky clung to her fingers.

Quickly wiping the liquid on her dress, she carefully stepped over the obstacle and towards the sliver of light marking their destination. Her heart was beating out of her chest as she pressed her ear to the door, hoping that she could hear if anyone were left within the room. The only sound that echoed was cracking wood, hissing embers, and nothing else. Maybe they had made it after all.

Aleria reached back to squeeze Draven's hand as if to ask if he were ready. When he squeezed back, she slowly inched the door open. The creak that answered was too loud in the dead silence of the room. Light from the fireplace blinded her. Wiping the bleariness with her hands, she blinked the room into focus. The harrowing image before hit her so hard, she staggered to brace herself on the wall.

One. Three. Seven. Nine. Twelve. She counted twelve bodies littering the floor in splashes of crimson that soaked her mother's favorite rug. The copper tang of blood scented the air so heavily; she clapped a trembling hand over her mouth to keep in the gag she knew was coming. Somehow, her wobbly legs took her further into the horror. She prayed that there would not be a familiar face among the bodies. Draven took a few steps in front of her, checking the room for possible dangers. When he stopped in his tracks and turned back to her, she knew her prayers had gone unanswered.

It was as if time had stopped, and everything began moving in slow motion. She was running towards where Draven stood, tears already pouring down her cheeks. He stopped her, wrapping his arms around her waist tightly, trying to bar her path. She screamed and kicked, but he locked his arms around her tighter.

"Ali, please. You can't unsee it." His voice desperate and pleading as he clung to her despite how she fought him, completely unhinged.

"Let me go, Dray!" Draven's arms slowly and hesitantly released her. Stumbling past him, her legs barely holding herself, she came to the place her father had made his final stand. Every memory she held with him flashed before her eyes as she took in the image of his broken body. The first time he taught her to hold a sword. Racing him on horseback in a field of poppies. Crawling into his lap when a thunderstorm would hit, and she couldn't sleep. All of those memories became drenched in the deep red color of his life's blood.

With a soul-splitting cry, she fell to her knees, next to her father's ravaged body. She didn't know where to touch first, as if the slightest brush of her hand could hurt him more. As she reached out to brush a blood-stained lock of hair from his temple, she gasped, noticing her trembling hands were already covered in dark red stains. She held them up to Draven in alarm.

"Where…" she started. Realization and horror passed over his features, and he turned towards the passageway. A curse flew from him, swallowed in the darkness. Aleria couldn't bring herself to look away from the hole in the wall.

A hollowness deepened in her stomach as Draven emerged from the dark, carrying her mother in his arms. Tears glistened at the corners of his eyes. Draven gently laid the body down on the blood-soaked bed. Her father must have told her to run and defended her until his dying breath.

"I'm going to kill him," Draven growled through clenched teeth. "I swear it, Ali."

His hands drifted over her mother's face, closing her eyes for the last time.

Her gaze slid towards her father. Fingers brushing back the matted hair on his face as she rasped, "I will avenge you."

The words hung in the air for a few moments before the promise was drowned out by shouts echoing down the hallway. Draven's eyes shot to the door, and with a curse, he ran to it, slamming it closed.

"We have to go," he said sternly, reaching to help her off the ground.

Aleria brushed his hands off. "I can't leave them like this." Her eyes still locked on her father's face. "We have to do something…"

"We don't have time, Ali." His expression held all the agony she felt, but still, he reached to yank her up again. "We have to!"

Draven cursed again as he guided her towards the passageway. "Go! Now!" He shoved her hard into the darkness, making her trip and land on her hands and knees. She turned back as Draven slammed the door shut behind her. Her eyes widened. Panic, unlike anything she had felt before, shook her to her bones. Sobbing against the barred door, she screamed,

"Draven! You can't do this! Please! Don't leave me! Let me help you!" Her fingers dug at the opening until her nails cracked.

"Ali." His voice was soft, resigned through the door. "This is what I've trained for my entire life. I am your Knight, and I will protect you."

Aleria wailed as she heard voices begin filling the room. A crack. The sound of the bedroom door giving way. "Dray!" she rasped, pleading one last time.

"Live, cousin!" His words nearly drowned out with the ring of steel on steel.

Larkin

"On your left," Larkin hissed, pressing his back against a towering oak. The forest in the human realm was as thick and overgrown as Glair, but it lacked the serenity and magic found within every branch of his home. A pity, he thought as he focused again on the task at hand.

He and his comrades had gave chase from the borders of Glair. They passed through the crossing and into the lush forest of the Human Realm. The scent of wet dog and the unnatural sickly sweet scent of fresh Fae blood permeated the air. It was so thick he could almost see it.

The Nattmara would pay for the lives they severed, for every scar inflicted on his kin. Leaning around the tree, he checked everyone's positions.

Zander ducked behind a massive rock formation. He smirked as he flicked his wrist lackadaisically, a ball of flame lighting up in his palm.

Larkin shot his brother a glare that only made Zander chuckle as he snuffed out the flame. He and his younger brother had very few things in common. The snowy hair, the cut of their jaw, and competitive nature were enough to prove their relationship. Though their temperaments and general view on life couldn't be more opposite. Both of their giftings were chaotic. But whereas Larkin was the cool calm of an autumn breeze, Zander was a forest fire in squelching summer heat.

Now was not the time for Zander's messing about. Three of their kin had fallen to the curse before they could administer the restorative. Two of which escaped with their new...pack. The one remaining died of blood loss before the transformation took hold. This was the case more often than not when attacks happened. The beasts' claws and teeth could shred the bones of even the most powerful of Fae.

Larkin glanced over his shoulder in the direction of one of the other four members of his group. The ebony-haired male was staring off into the distance as if he were seeing something they all could not. Nox's ability to call upon his senses was unrivaled among the Fae. He could feel other be-ings, their emotional and physical states.

Larkin had opened his mouth to question him when Thea raised a hand to stop him. Her looks and giftings a stark comparison to her brother. White hair tied, dusky golden skin near luminous in the moonlight. She was the other side of the coin.

After a long moment, Nox finally spoke.

"The moon is nearly at its peak. The blood lust is..." He whispered almost in a trance,"If we don't engage now..." His glassy eyes blinked a few times as if trying to focus on something new that came into his line of sight. Nox hissed, his wide eyes moving about. "Humans. A group of them chasing after...I can't tell..It's like...It's like I'm blocked."

"What do you mean blocked?" Zander chimed in, but Nox only shook his head, rubbing at his temples in frustration.

"That's the only way I can describe it. Something's there, but it's like everything's underwater. Garbled. I've never felt something like it before."

Larkin shifted his attention to Ruke, his second in command. "Humans will make a good distraction. The Nattmara will be so focused on feeding they won't see us coming. Ruke, Zander, fan out and form a barrier. Thea, you're with me. Nox…," he started, but Nox raised a hand and growled.

"You act as if I've never done this before." His ability, though helpful, wasn't made for battle. They had learned the hard way not to let him into the fray. The feelings alone could incapacitate him. That didn't keep him from loading a bow and being their long-range source of attack.

Larkin flicked his head in the direction of the clearing, and his elite band of warriors disappeared like shadows through the trees. He and Thea kept to the edge of the clearing, waiting for the others to herd the Nattmara towards them.

Taking a deep breath, Larkin focused on drinking deep from the Mother's Well of Magic. The spark of that eternal vein of power fluttered in his lungs before prickling along his tongue. A prayer of thanks and devotion rumbled low in the ancients' dialect as he sought to dive deeper. Larkin's fingers began to move at his side as if they were plucking the strings of an imaginary instrument, his magic pooling between his fingers. With the slow lift of his hand, fog began seeping up and flooding the forest ground. He would consider such a trap to be overkill, but there were too many uncertain variables to take any chances. Their end would be swift before he purged the area of the filth that would remain.

As if on cue, the pack of Nattmara wandered into the clearing, sniffing the air like the overgrown dogs they were. Their hulking bodies slunk through overgrown wood. All claws and teeth. A swift and brutal death on two legs.

With the full moon approaching, there was no doubt in his mind that the beasts could see and smell them. The air became thick with tension. They readied themselves for an attack; every member of the Huldra wound and ready to strike at his cue. His magic crackled with lightning around his fingertip, ready to signal. Just as he began to form the words, the moment was stolen by a scream that tore through the tension like a hot blade.

At the edge of the wood, a frantic young woman tumbled over the slope. She crashed to the ground in a way that made him wince. He swore he could hear his brother's voice in the distance, barking out a curse followed by a snort of laughter. Mother help them. The temporary comedy of the situation cut short when he saw the young woman find herself staring up at a beast that would make a full-grown male wet himself. The same curse that flew from Zander's mouth moments earlier echoed in hers.

The Nattmara released an ear-splitting scream in her face.

A strange chill shivered down Larkin's spine, his magic reacting instinctively. Lightning ricocheted from his fingertips and towards the beast. Its jaws snapped dangerously close to the girl's throat. If not for her swift dodge, the creature would have already wrapped its maw around her throat.

It was sheer chaos all around him; human warriors poured over the hill and into the fray. Larkin rolled his eyes when he heard the shrieks of men as they saw the Nattmara. A few of the cowards ran, but the battle had already begun. Zander and Ruke's perimeter of flame and fissures barred any hope of escape. It was fight or die, and most were not on the lucky end of that choice. To his surprise, the golden-haired young woman stumbled to her feet. She grabbed a discarded weapon and was holding her own against the beast in front of her. Who was this bruised and battered woman that twenty men were after her, and yet, she stood there with a stronger constitution than the lot of them? He had never seen a creature so small seem so...

His curiosity transfixed his attention to her so tightly that he almost missed the massive claws slicing towards him. His magic didn't have enough time to react, but he was fast enough to keep from getting impaled. The barest tip of the claw caught his arm, slicing a wicked cut from his elbow to the wrist. Rage shook his entire being as the sting of his wound pounded. Honing all that rage into a concentrated ball of lightning in his hand, he unleashed it upon the Nattmara that struck him. The creature jolted and roared before falling to the ground in a lump of steaming gore.

Thunder rumbled around them as his anger continued to make itself known. A torrent of rain saturated the killing field. His power pounding beneath his skin, begging for release. It was foolish to get distracted. The girl was human, nothing more. She was finite. Dust in the wind. He was a Fae Prince, charged with protecting his people and destroying these monsters.

Controlled fury pinpointed his focus. The twang of Nox's bow blended with the spark of Zander's flame became a cadence in his ears, uniting with Ruke's rumbling earth and the dead silence around Thea. The thrum of battle. With a deep breath, he reached over his head to the two long swords strapped to his back. Larkin unsheathed them with a roar that echoed like a clap of thunder. Unquenchable fire blazed, and the ground rumbled beneath his feet in answer. Bursting with power, he tore across the field like the storm he held within his veins.

The Nattmara was powerful and required all the magic and swordsmanship he could muster. Their flesh was thick and impenetrable unless you were aware of the softer spots. Even worse still, while in wolf form, they were much more resistant to magic. Larkin's swords met claws as he whipped wind around himself to speed his blade. The creature roared its fury before pummeling him to the ground. The sheer force knocked the wind from his lungs. Massive claws struck at him with enough force to skewer him to the forest floor. But in a quick move, he jabbed his swords upward, aiming for the Nattmarra's sensitive underbelly. The creature roared like the sound of metal on sharpened bones and screeched in protest. Electricity crackled across his skin as he yanked his swords back and struck again. Teeth and claws matched him blow for blow until the creature yelped, its back arching in a death throw before slumping to the ground. Behind it, stood the young woman. Her ebony gown was in tatters, flaxen hair matted to her head with blood and gore.

Those wide unblinking eyes, pinned him to his spot, and a shudder ran deep into his bones.

Shock and something else he didn't dare name flashed, echoed by thunder and lightning. He was immediately under the spell of those watery green eyes. His instant reaction was to rage against whatever strange magic was pulling at him. The siren's call beckoning him to come hither. She had to be an enchantress to have bewitched and transfixed him so. With a quick move of his bloodied hand, he gripped her around the throat. To the girl's credit, she didn't scream. She only flinched and tried to pry his long fingers from her throat. It would take one twist, one flip of his wrist to snap her neck, but something was holding him back. Something screaming from deep inside his being that this was wrong.

"Who are you?"

Blood from his gashed forearm, dripping off his skin, and patting in fat droplets onto her chest. A matching wound lay splayed open there. He loosened his chokehold on her for long enough to let her speak.

"Aleria Edlind, Lady of Fayeharrow."

He didn't have time to respond before a wave of power exploded between them in a rush of energy and sound. A connection formed between them, ruling and dynamic. His eyes instinctively closed at the shock of power. When he opened them, the remaining Nattmara stood before them, Fae, like him, but bare from head to toe. For a moment, the entire killing field froze, shock anchoring them to the ground. Larkin's hand tightened on her throat as he shouted to the Huldra,

"Attack now!"

Shouts of the wide-eyed retreat came from the Nattmara Alpha as they tucked their nonexistent tails and ran. Larkin dared not take his eyes off the young woman as his companions began to make chase. The only one who joined his side was Nox, who was looking at Aleria as if she were some sort of miracle.

"What are you?" Larkin growled.

The blonde-haired enigma blinked up at him before swaying on her feet. The wound on her chest was still seeping blood. "What are you?"

"She's the thing I couldn't get a read on," Nox said circling the human with unabashed curiosity. "Are you afraid?" The girl's posture rose. "Fascinating."

"I'm glad I...that I - " but her words cut short as her eyelids fluttered and rolled back into her skull. Her small body went limp. By instinct alone, Larkin caught her and hoisted her up in his arms. Nox's eyebrows nearly raised into his hairline as a shocked look passed over his features.

"Not a word," Larkin growled, but Nox grinned up at him with wicked acknowledgement.

"A word about what?" Zander's voice cut in as he, Ruke, and Thea rejoined them. Larkin ignored his younger brother and shot a look at Ruke.

"Report," he snapped as he adjusted the girl's body in his hold. Ruke cast a glance at the limp form in his arms, but Thea stepped closer with obvious interest.

"Two hundred paces north they returned to their forms. We took down four, but the rest kept their pace. I suppose they were as shocked as we were when…" His eyes wandered to the human lying limp in Larkin's arms.

"When that human girl used some sort of magic to turn the Nattmara," Zander finished the sentence with a conspirator's smirk. Leaning forward, he sniffed at the girl. "She smells human, no scent of magic."

Larkin nodded in agreement. Under the coppery tang of blood, sweat, and Nattmara gore, there was only the scent of a human.

"It is a mystery to me how I can't sense her though. I can't get a single flicker from her," Nox whispered in awe as he stepped towards the girl, reaching out a tentative hand to touch her. A territorial snarl tried to rumble up from somewhere deep inside him. He clamped down on it. Anger and frustration immediately took its place instead.

What was it about this girl?

Theories and scenarios raced through his mind as he began formulating a plan of action. No matter what she was, it didn't matter. All that mattered was what she could do. Taking her back to Glair could help fortify them for the next attack. There had to be someone who could figure out how they could use her to their advantage. She could be the key to set their kind free from this curse laid upon them hundreds of years ago.

Before he placed any hopes in her though, he needed to see how far her abilities stretched. Was it only Nox who couldn't affect her? Or did she have the power of immunity against them all? Knowing the extent of her power was the only way he could justify putting his kin in possible danger. He wasn't sure his grandfather, the sovereign ruler of the Fae, wouldn't kill him on sight for even attempting it. Nonetheless, the reward far outweighed the risk.

"She is somehow immune to Nox, but what about us? Brother, come here. I'd like to test something," he said, bringing the young woman over to a large slab of rock left over from Ruke's barrier. After gently laying her down on the stone, he lifted her hand and held it in Zander's direction

"Burn it," he said matter of fact.

"What?" Zander, Ruke, and Thea echoed in unison to his command. Nox only raised a curious eyebrow at him.

"She's immune to you. What if she is immune to us? Zander's flame is the most controlled, and the most humane to use as a test. Unless you would like me to hit her with lightning or Thea to…"

"No," Thea interrupted. "No, you're right. A burn is much more humane." Her fingers tugged at her long-sleeves as Zander snapped his fingers and held a small flame in his palm.

Sliding Aleria's hand over Zander's flame, he grimaced and waited. Part of him would feel guilty, but the fact that she was unconscious made him feel a bit better, but only a bit. With that in mind, Larkin flipped over Aleria's hand over after only a few breaths and checked for burns. Nothing. Not even a warm spot. His eyebrows crinkled in confusion.

"Burn hotter," he whispered, and Zander wiggled his fingers as the flame grew larger and deepened its shades. Larkin held her by her wrist and quickly placed her hand over the flame. The heat licking at his fingertips was enough to make him flinch a little. After a full moment, he pulled her hand back. Any other human would have a severe burn and limited use of the hand. His fingers touched the fevered, but not scorched palm of her hand. He chuckled a little in shock and disbelief. "You're losing your touch, baby brother."

Zander frowned and tilted his head to the side before taking a deep breath. Slamming his hand into a fist, it glowed with a glittering blue flame. He rarely saw his brother use that particular flame in battle. It took a massive amount of stamina and control to maintain it. A flame that hot could melt steel.

Larkin gave him a look that warned him to proceed with caution.

He didn't want to maim the girl. Zander wrapped his flames around Aleria's dainty wrist. Larkin could only watch in amazement as the skin barely turned pink. Zander yanked his hand back and stared slack-jawed at the pink marks. A curse tumbled from his gaping mouth, and Larkin looked up at Nox for any sense of pain from her.

"So not completely immune, but resistant," Larkin said. The excitement was short-lived when he saw Nox froze wide-eyed. Tears pricking his eyes.

"What are you sensing from her?" Thea whispered, bracing her brother with gentle hands.

"Pain. So much pain," he murmured, taking a step towards her. "Asleep, she...Her guard is down...She's bleeding out. She's...been through terrible things."

Nox reached a trembling hand to touch her, sympathy written all over his face. "Suaimhneas." He whispered peace over her, stroking her matted blonde locks from her face.

"Nox -," Thea's voice held a gentle warning.

He shot her an annoyed look. "Don't, Thea. She's in pain."

Nox lived by a strict code when it came to his magic. No one deserved to be in pain. There were even moments where he would take the pain of the Nattmarra who returned to the Mother's side. He said that their brethren did not choose this path, and thus, deserved to be gently returned to her embrace. That was not always the case in battle, but Larkin allowed it whenever he could. Part of him still wondered and worried that his father and uncle were among those they had fallen.

"So what now?" Zander whispered as he moved over to where he had lain the human.

"We will bring her to Glair and see what we can make of all this. If she is somehow the key to our Nattmara problem, it's worth a try."

"Larkin, your grandfather won't -," Thea started, but Larkin cut her off.

"For now, we make camp, tend to our injuries and hers, then see what happens when she wakes."

"And if she resists?" Zander asked.

"She's resistant to magic. Not impervious. The best part about it is that she most likely doesn't know," Larkin said with a conspiratorial smirk. Zander chuckled and patted him on the shoulder.

"Don't worry, brother. We all know I spark female desire as well as I do flames." Thea made a gagging noise, and Zander sparked a small fire beside her foot. At her squeal, Ruke opened the ground and swallowed the flame whole. Larkin laughed as he slapped Zander on the back a little harder than necessary.

"Set up camp, hothead. Nox and Thea, with me please. Ruke?" He nodded his head in the direction of the area where their human was still unconscious. Ruke nodded as a low rumbling hum came from deep within him. The ground beneath them rattled, and rock formations began to enclose around them. The building had four walls and a simple stone fireplace. Soft, mossy ground sprung up beneath their feet and atop the stone seats. The makeshift bed, a slab of rock covered in spongy moss, had a stone basin formed next to it.

Thea threw her pack next to the girl. She fumbled through it, then handed Nox the gauze to tear.

"This would be much easier if you could sense where the pain is coming from," he said to Nox with a rueful smile and a snarl of his nose. "I suppose we have to go about it the old fashioned way."

The temperature in the room dropped as the smell of rain and the power of magic filled his senses. With a press of his hand, water filled up the stone basin. He noted that his wound had healed already, and only a small line of scabbed blood remained. His thoughts drifted to that of this mortal's wounds. How long did it take for humans to heal? How could something so small, so delicate emit as much power as she had in that clearing? With a sword in her hand, she was a force of nature. If he had seen her in this state though, he would have never known. His grandfather had always spoken of humans like dogs. Seeing this mess of a creature in front of him, he could see why. She reminded him of when his pup would come home after a hunt covered in mud and blood and stinking to high heaven. An effective hunter, but difficult to house train.

"Let's clean her as best we can and dress her wounds. Perhaps she will choose to bathe herself when she wakes. If not, there are some hot springs we can accidentally toss her into on the way back."

Thea breathed a laugh, and Nox's expression was pitiful. After a few moments of only the dripping sounds of rags being cleaned, Larkin spoke.

"Her name is Aleria."

"The human woman," Nox corrected him without looking up.

"Yes, the human woman," Larkin amended. He enjoyed the feeling of her foreign name rolling strangely around on his tongue. "Aleria. She's had a hard life?" he asked as a way to glean at least a little bit of information from him. Nox shook his head no as he took out a knife and began cutting away Aleria's tattered gown. "Her gown seems to be of fine make. She must have been quite wealthy." Observations that required a simple yes or no answer seemed to be the way to go. Nox shook his head yes this time. "Why would a rich young human be running from a group of soldiers?" Larkin asked, but Thea rolled her head towards him and gave him a look that said it was the wrong question.

Thea pulled the torn fabric away. Aleria was bare apart from a delicate set of underthings. Mother, those things were not of Fae make. That was for certain. There was a charm to them that had him wanting to ask her why humans made underthings more lovely than outer things.

His eyes slid over her slight form. Something about her seemed much more breakable than the Fae standing next to him. Her musculature depicted someone who had trained in the art of battle. But even so, she still maintained a softness that was unlike other female bodies he had known. The momentary curiosity and comparison had him examining her closely.

The gash along her upper chest was particularly nasty and had already begun to set up with an infection.

"This needs a few stitches," he said as he moved up to her shoulder. He was certain he saw bloodstains on her back as well. When he lifted her to access the wound, a curse flew from his mouth, and adrenaline set his heart to racing. Nox, sensing his panic, stopped cleaning and peaked at the wound.

"There's a claw broken off in her shoulder," Larkin said, running over to his pack. The clang of glass and metal objects filled the tense silence before he pulled out a vial of shimmering, iridescent liquid; a knife; a needle; and thread.

Thea and Nox both knew this process like the back of their identical hands. They had trained and experienced moments like this too many times to count. Thankfully, it was a claw and not a fang. A fang would hold enough venom to transition a Fae or kill a human.

Nox tilted Aleria's head back as Larkin poured the contents of the healing vial down her throat. Aleria's occasional cough gave him pause, but only long enough to be sure she was drinking enough of it. The three of them then rolled her to her side, sliced open her shoulder, and removed the remnants of the claw. Then, they set to cleaning and treating the wound. Larkin's steady hand stitched up the hole in her shoulder and the wound on her chest.

"All we can do now is treat everything else and wait." Tenison tightened Larkin's voice. If she died of her injuries, so would the hope her gifting had bloomed in his heart. Thea placed a hand on his shoulder.

"The Mother would not have led her to us to take her away." Her words were a soothing balm to his scarred heart. "She's in good hands with us both. We will heal her. Just begin to think of how you'll convince her to stay once she wakes."

Larkin huffed a deflated laugh.

"Didn't you hear? Zander's going to seduce her into staying with us."

"That would give your grandfather even more reason to throttle us all," Nox mumbled as his hands joined Thea's, cleaning the unconscious girl's wounds. "Speaking of...do you think this is wise? Your grandfather... has harsh beliefs when it comes to humans. What makes you think he won't kill her on sight?" The splash of water from the basin was the only sound as Larkin considered his words.

"He has to listen. We all want this Nattmara threat to end. We all have lost loved ones to this curse. And if there is a possibility that we can get those loved ones back…" His jaw clenched. "I'll make him listen."

Thea reached out to touch his shoulder. "I know you will."

A slight whimper from their patient drew both of their attention in an instant.

"Nox and I can finish up here if you want to check on Ruke." The look in Thea's eyes betrayed her eagerness to do just that. With a nod in the direction of the door, he released her to fret over her lover.

"Nox will make sure whatever Zander is cooking this evening is edible?" Nox chuckled and rinsed his hands in the basin as he mumbled something about trying his best.

Larkin finished tending to the patchwork of other injuries on Aleria's body. Though he had healed many wounded soldiers, this felt different for some reason. Curiosity and cautious awe filled him as the rag unearthed new details of her person.

Humans were like Fae in general anatomy. Same body parts, musculature, and smatterings of body hair. The only stark difference seemed to be that of the human's less pointed teeth and ears. There were other imperfections, like blemishes, pink undertones of scars, and dots of varying shapes and sizes. Aleria was a human who had little of the first two flaws, but the spots all over her body were numerous. Some clustered together along her shoulders. Others were singular and in the strangest places, like the dip of her hip or center of her ankle. The Fae would see these markings as birth defects. Their skin was the picture of perfection amongst the magical folk. But Larkin found himself staring at the strange markings as if they were a mystery to be solved.

Larkin traced the patterns he recognized with the series of dots on her shoulder. He smirked when he recognized some of the star patterns he learned as a sprig. The tea-colored spots like stars smattering her fair skin. A whimper from the girl's lips snapped him out of his musings and into immediate embarrassment. He snatched his hands back as if she had burned him and ran both of them through his hair. What is the Mother's name was he doing?

"What am I getting myself into?"

Aleria

Pain.

The searing pain was her first and most prevalent feeling as she fought to open her eyes. The crackle of a fire and the gentle hum of someone's voice tickled her ears as she drifted in and out of consciousness. How much of the images playing through her mind were a dream, and how much were a world-shattering reality? For a long time, she laid there assessing her surroundings. Beneath her was something soft and damp. Spongy like moss. Where in the world was she?

Flashes of memory assailed her mind, foggy and blurred.

Sprinting through the woods. Breathless. Fearful and a maze of trees. Shouts and clanging of armor. The sense of falling down, down. Rocks and branches stabbing and slicing into her skin. Smacking the ground so hard it drove what little breath she had from her lungs. Forcing herself to stand on wobbly legs. The one thing she remembered as clear as day was coming face to face with a hideous creature. A being from nightmares, stories, and folktales that children would tell to scare each other. Creator above, it was real. In the woods, there were wolfish beasts the size of a man with claws as sharp as blades.

And she had fought one.

She obviously didn't fight it very well due to the amount of pain she was currently in. Still, grief and fear must have given her the fortitude to even try. Or it was what her father had once said about fighting or flying. Creator, she was sick of flying. Flying away from Anwir's men, from despairing over her parent's death, from the guilt of Draven sacrificing himself. Being fed up made her fight.

Panic began to creep its way to the surface as images hit her one after the other. Her father's blood on her hands, her mother's limp body in Draven's arms, Draven's voice echoing over and over: Live, Cousin!

Forcing back the feelings that tried to overwhelm her, she attempted to open her eyes. This was not the time to lose herself to the pain. If she were to do as Draven commanded, she couldn't let panic overcome her. Instead, she focused on the one thing that gave her any sense of steadiness. Rage. A cold calm draped over her like a blanket. She snapped her eyes open and tried to assess her surroundings through the blurry haze.

Stone walls surrounded her. Nothing fancy, but incredibly thick, which could be the reason why she felt so warm despite the size of the room. The eerie silence interrupted by the unsettling pop and crack of a hearth fire nearly burned out. One window and an oddly formed, large fireplace sat anchored in the corner. It was there that four bedrolls circled amongst each other. She wondered who filled them.

Four people.

Better than the twenty who chased her down the incline, but with some luck, she wouldn't have to run this time. Perhaps the Creator was finally taking pity on her, and she could escape while the group slept. It was foolish of them to not have a watch set up for the night. They must have thought she was almost dead or were simply careless. Either way, she wouldn't look a gift horse in the mouth.

With all the strength she could muster, she rose from the stone bed. Whatever bandages they used were pinching her. It almost made her yelp as they pressed into her injuries. Clenching her jaw to choke back her cries, she managed to get on her feet. That's when she noticed she was in nothing but her undergarments. No shoes, no dress, only her small clothes - that and the strips of cloth that seemed to be covering a good fifty percent of her body. A plethora of profanities ran through her mind as she weighed her options. Not one seemed like a good idea at the moment.

"The sleeping beauty wakes." A smooth voice rumbled from the only exit in the building.

"Sard," she thought.

Her eyes connected with a strange almost glowing pair of ethereal eyes. This was not the man she had last seen in the woods. No, this one was younger, and by the slight lean of his posture and quirk of his mouth, arrogant too. He brushed his short silvery hair back off his face in a way that made her think it was intentional. Then, he dared to wink at her. Narrowing her gaze, her mouth drew down into a frown.

"I'm Zander. A pleasure," he purred as eyes did a quick perusal that made her want to roll her own, but she had dealt with boys like him before. With a slow sensuous smile, she took a step towards him.

"Pleasure, huh? I bet you know a lot about that."

Drinking up the compliment, he matched her slow pace forwards. An impish smirk stretched across his handsome face. His body moved with a controlled grace as he stepped in front of her. He was only a hair's breadth away from pressing fully against her. Rage still simmered beneath her skin, fueling the calculated calm of her countenance.

"I do," he whispered, reaching up to brush away a strand of hair that had fallen across her face.

As a lady of the court, she was taught many useful things. One of which was that not all weapons were made from metal. A soft, flirty smile pulled at the corner of her mouth before she bit down on her bottom lip suggestively.

"You know what I know a lot about?" Her voice a silky purr as she leaned in close to his ear. His appreciative hum of response almost made her laugh as she walked her fingers down his chest and to his belt. "Guess."

He took a breath to voice his reply, but as quick as a blink, she grabbed the pommel of his short sword and pressed it to his throat with a growl.

"Pain. You arrogant prat."

His answering chuckle was as infuriating as his smile, now a full cat-like grin. She pressed the blade harder, causing a slight trickle of blood to drip across the shaft.

"Literal point taken, love." The tip of his finger carefully directed the blade from his throat.

"Obviously not, since you seem to believe that I won't split you where you stand."

A couple of whispers came from where the bedrolls had been set up. Five to one. Not great odds. An amused laugh rumbled from the male at the center of the group, the firelight casting him in silhouette and dancing shadows. Laughter still rang in his voice as he spoke.

"I'll say it again, baby brother. You're losing your touch."

"She didn't let me get that far," Zander huffed as the shadowed silhouette turned to face her.

The man standing before her was the prettiest male she had ever seen. He reminded her of snow on a mountain top. All alabaster and sharp angles, with eyes like molten silver in the firelight. At that moment, she was gobsmacked.

"Let me apologize on behalf of Zander. He's a bit of a firestarter," the stranger said as he stepped towards her. His tone and posture were like that of someone who was trying to calm a skittish horse. Powerful, but cautious. He was the type who was used to holding the reins. "As much as you are a living, breathing fantasy standing there half-clothed and dangerous, would you please put the weapon down? No one's going to harm you."

Aleria weighed his words, but kept her defenses up. "I will drop my weapon if I deem you as harmless as you claim to be." Pointing her blade at the group, she sidestepped towards the doorway. The cold ground beneath her bare feet, a stark reminder of her current state of vulnerability.

"Come sit with us by the fire, and I will answer whatever questions you have. I find it's best to tell a person's intentions when you can see their face."

Aleria's brow scrunched as she scrutinized him. What kind of game were they playing? Amiable kidnappers were too much to hope for. Unfortunately, her knees took that moment to begin trembling beneath her. The adrenaline fueling her willpower began to concede to her pain. Did he know how weak she was right now, or did he assume from her wounds that she would be? Either way, he was right, and taking a seat was better than showing weakness by passing out.

One slow step at a time, she circled to where the other four were sitting on the floor by the fireplace. Three men and one woman. One of the males had shoulder-length brown curly hair and the build of someone who lifted stones for a living. His arm was wrapped protectively around the waist of a tall, lithe female with waist-length ivory hair. The female stared at her in a way that made Aleria feel as if the woman could see right through her. Next to her was another male with obsidian tresses that cascaded down his chest and back. His face was hauntingly lovely to look at, but something about him made her hyper-aware. His gaze almost like a comforting touch as he gave her a disarming smile.

Her slow assessment finally brought her to the male who took a prominent seat in front of the rest, the leader then and Zander's older brother. Her throat tightened as a bundle of nerves coiled up in her stomach.

He was tall, at least six feet if not more. His broad, muscular chest on display from the low dip of his black tunic. Layered leather and stone necklaces followed the defined line of muscle, drawing her eyes downward. Realizing she was full-on ogling him, she snapped her eyes back to his face. The man's hair was the same shade of light silvery blonde as his brother's. The only difference was it was long with braids and leather ties woven in. Part of her delirium-addled brain began imagining what it would be like to run her fingers through the silky strands. But the warrior within her cursed and chided her in response to the foolish notion. She was already beginning to look weak in her hesitation. Now was not the time for girlish feelings. These people could still want to kill her or worse, and she was being distracted by how pretty they all were. Idiot.

Swallowing hard, she became keenly aware again of the fact that nothing but small scraps of fabric and bandages were covering her body. Bringing her arms up over her chest, she whispered, "As much as I am thankful for the bandages, could I get something else to wear?"

It felt odd asking them something so trivial when there were much bigger issues to discuss. That and she hated the way his head tipped to the side as if it were a curious request. Were they not as uncomfortable as she was about her near nakedness? Before she could say something about it, a warm woolen blanket draped over her shoulders.

"You're welcome," the younger brother said with a smirk as he returned to his post by the door. Aleria straightened her posture and shot him a look that said not in a million years. Snuggling beneath the warmth of the soft blanket, she fought the urge to throw out an insult. Her courtly manners rose first though with a simple "Thank you."

The leader tilted his head yet again as he seemed to consider her. It was as if she were something he was trying to figure out, and each word from her mouth was another clue. For a long moment, they were embroiled in some kind of staring contest. Each sizing up the other, each weighing what words to say first. It reminded her so much of court that she wondered if he were not of royal descent. It was all over his posture, his practiced calm, his easy decorum and control. Things that were ingrained in her since birth. Things that she found herself to be sorely lacking at the moment.

The battle of wills and tense silence thoroughly irked her. At least until her eyes landed on something off in his otherwise unfairly perfect features. There, at the side of his head, the tips of his ears came to sharp angular points. It was her turn to tilt her head to the side in confusion. Then, another series of images hit her like a torrential flood. Rain, fire, earthquakes, pointed ears, and pointed canines. Creator save her.

Gripping her sword so tightly her knuckles turned white, she croaked, "What are you?" The leader only smiled, revealing those beautifully white, horribly sharp teeth.

"I am Larkin, and this is my Huldra. Ruke, Thea, Nox, and you've met Zander. You stumbled upon us in the woods while we were about to engage a creature called Nattmara -"

"I didn't say who. I said what." She knew how rude that sounded, but she wasn't able to give a care at the moment. If they were keeping her alive only to eat her, she would rather know sooner than later. Were they going to eat her? She would die before she let them eat her. Well, at least she hoped she would be dead before they ate her.

Stop it.

She couldn't allow those thoughts to betray the fear looming inside her.

"You did, didn't you?" The man said with a little smirk. "Well, our race is Faerie - though, there are many that fall within that category. I suppose, what you would call us is High Fae. Have you never heard of the Fairy race?" His tone was so cavalier that it made her want to punch him in his smug, controlled face.

Yes, good. Rage. Focus on that. You want to punch that far too pretty face. "And what is it you want with me, High Fae?"

That amused smile tugged deeper at the corner of his perfect mouth. The overwhelming desire to throttle him grew a little more.

"Direct. I like that. You may call me Larkin. Aleria, correct?" he asked as if he were offering her tea and not blowing the entire framework of her world apart.

"Yes. Aleria Edilind. Daughter to the House of Edlind. Entirely human and wholly confused at what in the world is happening right now."

A twinkle of humor and mischief sparkled in his icy blue-grey gaze. It infuriated her all the more.

"I know this must be strange for you but -"

"Strange?!" A manic laugh bubbled up from her panicked insanity. "No, strange is setting your tea down in one place and finding it in another."

"Pixies," a smooth, lyrical voice interrupted from behind Larkin.

Aleria stared as Larkin cut a look towards the fairer one. The female spoke with a soft smile. "Pixies are tricksters. Their magic makes them unseen unless they want to be seen. That would explain the movement of your teacup. Or you moved it unknowingly. Not everything has a faerie influence, but most things do." Aleria's jaw dropped as she felt herself slip further into lunacy.

"Not helping, Thea," Larkin sighed, as he crossed the room to take a knee in front of Aleria. "You should sit back down." She hadn't even realized she had stood up in the first place. Plopping back down, she covered her face with her hands and took a few deep calming breaths. This was complete and utter madness. Was she dead? Was she still unconscious and dreaming about this?

"Are you alright?" He was being gentle as if his words alone could shatter her like glass. Lifting her head, she found his eyes searching hers in a way that made the dam holding back her emotions crack. A single traitorous tear rolled down her cheek. His eyes widened as he cautiously reached out to wipe away the drop. Rubbing it between his fingers, he asked, "Are you in pain?"

Wiping a few more stray tears off her cheeks and clearing her throat, she looked up at him with a cold stare. From what she knew from Fairytales, fairy folk were tricksters, obsessed with pretty things, and had magical powers. All of which would not work in her favor.

"Stop beating around the bush and tell me why you deigned to save me. Is this some Faerie curse? A life debt I'm bound to for all eternity?" At this point, it wouldn't surprise her.

"Fair enough. What did you do out there to make the Nattmarra change back into their Fae forms?" His voice has taken a hard, serious tone.

"I didn't do anything."

"You don't have to lie," Zander piped in. "Listen, I get that you smell human, but we've been around magic folk long enough to know that what happened was some sort of -"

"Smell human? Are you part dog? That explains a lot…" Aleria quipped at him with a snarky scowl. What did she have to gain by lying?

She realized she may have gone a little too far when the amber of Zanders's eyes flashed like a wicked flame. Sparks began dancing across his arms and down to his fingertips. Aleria cursed and shot to her feet. Fire. He had fire shooting from his hands. Did all Fae have fire? Merciful Creator, they could flambe her before eating her.

Before she could react or pass out, Larkin stepped in front of her. "She didn't mean it that way. Calm down." Zander's flames sparked again as a low growl rumbled behind his clenched teeth. Larkin hissed something in a language she didn't understand. All the while, a mist began settling between them. Aleria stepped back until her back pressed against the hard stone of the building. She was not about to step into a standoff between two creatures of their ilk. When Zander's flames guttered, and his harsh breathing became deep and even, she looked towards Larkin. He slowly turned to face her in a way that more than suggested his patience had run thin.

"I have answered all your questions, Aleria Edlind. It is time you answered mine."

Looking up at him with the same cold resolve in her eyes, she shook her head. "I have no idea what you are talking about. I have been human for nineteen years. If I had any kind of magic, I can guarantee you I would not be here." Her eyes locked on his stormy glare as he weighed her answers. Gooseflesh rippled along her entire body, and the air around them seemed to change. A tension, much like the calm before a storm, rippled through the small room, making the hair on her arms stand up.

"Then, there is more to you than you know." His words cut through the tension like a blade leaving her bare and even more confused. A cold wind began whipping at her skin, making her cling tighter to the woolen blanket.

"What is it that you want from me, High Fae?" Her voice trembled a bit as she faced the bubbling wrath of whatever he was conjuring up. The question was only a formality. She knew if they wanted something from her, they had the power to take it by force. What hope did she have against five creatures from another world? The wind around them began to die down as Larkin took a deep breath and released it slowly. His glare softened into something more vulnerable that made her heart prick.

"Your help."

Mykhal

He was in Fayeharrow.

He had imagined this moment in meticulous detail ever since the day he landed on the shores of Brennan three years ago. In his mind, the day would be warm with flowers blooming everywhere. And she would be the most beautiful wildflower of them all.

His girl.

His Aleria, smelling like honeysuckle and wearing flowers in her hair. He'd imagined her waiting at the gates of the castle for him. He knew that before he'd even pass the guard stand, she would be flying across the courtyard. Her skirts and golden locks blowing in the wind like a banner of green and gold. At least, he'd hoped she'd wear that green dress he'd always loved. Its make was that of the softest cotton that never failed to bring out the fierce green of her eyes.

As she ran, his arms would already be open wide and waiting for her to throw her own around his neck. Her hair would fall around the two of them like a curtain of silk as she whispered her words of welcome. He would laugh a real and true sound. Then, he'd tell her how unladylike it was to throw herself at a man like that, and she would promptly tell him to put his mouth to better use. He would, of course, acquiesce to the command with great enthusiasm and promptly kiss her senseless.

But that was before things had gone straight to the infernal regions.

Instead of the bright, sunny skies he had dreamt of, the weather was bleak. The skies black from torrential rains. The weather followed him from Brennan to Fayeharrow's harbor. Though he still had a year left to squire abroad, the news of the Edlinds' fate had him buying a one-way passage back.

When the letter had reached him, recounting the horrific actions of Phillip Edlind, he could scarcely believe it. Phillip, Aleria's father, had been the kindest, most inspiring man he had ever known. That he could do something so vile made him heartsick. He knew how war could take its toll on a man's mind, but that Lord Edlind would murder his wife in cold blood seemed unreal. MyKhal's father had yet to mention how Aleria and Draven were holding up. He could assume it wasn't well, considering the circumstances.

Creator, he was dreading that reunion more than anything else. No matter how he pictured the conversation in his head, it always turned out disastrous. MyKhal knew when he started a relationship with Aleria that Dray would always choose her. That had been alright with him then because he loved Aleria and would have chosen her as well. It was too bad she never had intentions of choosing him.

His father had told him of her many suitors coming to call after his departure. Tales of scandal after scandal that made him sick and beyond furious. He lost it once, slamming his fist into a wall, wishing it were one of her lover's faces. The loss of control earned him a broken hand and a month's worth of shoveling offal. After that, he requested that his father never mention her name to him again.

He pinched the bridge of his nose, feeling a headache coming on as he passed the guard stand. The smell of ash still hung heavy in the air, even with the rain that should have washed away most of the stink. He entered the courtyard and trudged up the rain-slicked steps to the large oak double doors. There were too few people outside. It could be the rain that drove them all indoors, but still, it made the place feel abandoned. Farrowharrow Castle was full of such joy and lightheartedness. Now, it was like something from a nightmare. Even the stone lions looked as if they were weeping as rain dribbled down their maws.

A sick feeling clutched at his stomach as he rested his hand on the large metal handle. With a deep breath, he laid his forehead against the wood. Things would never be the same here, and he had to come to grips with that and soon. If his time in Brennan had taught him anything, it was that the world was cruel. Only those who could both handle cruelty and know how to deal it out themselves would survive it. His father was the epitome of such dire sentiments.

Swinging the heavy door wide, the first thing that hit him was a rush of heat. The oversized fireplaces lining the receiving room greeting him like an old friend. Creator, it had seemed like years since he had been warm. Between the barracks, the hunts, missions, and training, he felt that warmth was a luxury that was past due. Part of him wanted to throw off his sodden boots and lounge by the fire for a week straight, but that wasn't why he was here. No, he was here for a whole other kind of torture.

Seeing to it that his ex-lover and an ex-best friend were sound of mind. That, and, to assess their ability (or willingness) to run the largest Lordship in Rimeheld. At least, that was his understanding of his father's letter. His father mentioned that his occupancy of Fayeharrow was to help rebuild and keep order.

Part of him wondered if either of the Edlinds would even be able to rule in the estate their family died in. He wouldn't be able to stomach it. No matter his feelings towards them, he would do his duty as a neighboring Lord to help them get back on their feet.

Wimborne and Fayeharrow had long since been trading partners. Each dependent on the other for goods, travel, and mercantile routes. All those businesses would fall if someone wasn't in temporary control of things. His father had mentioned allowing him to run Wimborne while he handled things. Still, there was no real guarantee his father would relinquish such power to him yet. If anything, he expected his father to run both and make him his vassal for everything else.

Looking around the hall, there was something strange about the goings-on. None of the servants were familiar. The Edlinds were very particular about their staff. They'd had many of the same people employed for decades. Perhaps the murder made them resign their positions out of grief. Maybe the fires claimed more victims than his father had let on. These servants moved quickly and quietly from the room. Their eyes remained cast down. Their hands were always full or busy doing something. The scene reminded him too much of Wimborne. The servants there were much the same. Afraid to make the master angry with them for fear of his wrath. The sight seemed so out of place for him in the castle of the family he had once admired. The Edlinds were what he would imagine being the perfect family. He supposed this was only further proof that the world was cruel, and people weren't always what they seemed to be.

Reaching out, he grabbed a maid by the shoulder as she passed. The girl flinched as if bracing for a blow, but when she saw his face she relaxed, but only a bit.

"Could you announce my arrival to Lord Anwir, Lady Edlind, and Knight Protector Edlind? I am MyKhal Anwir." His voice was curt, but not unkind. Still, the girl flinched again and bit her bottom lip.

"Ye-yes, m'lord. Ri-right away, sire." Dropping into a clumsy curtsy, the girl ran from the room as if nether-hounds were snapping at her heels. Sighing, he plopped down in front of the fireplace to wait for his announcement. MyKhal hoped it would be quick and that soon he could sink into a steaming bath.

A disapproving throat clear from behind him had him shooting to his feet. He hadn't realized he had dozed off.

"You look like a drowned rat." The snide comment echoed off the stone walls of the receiving room like a slap.

"That happens when you ride in a monsoon for two days straight." MyKhal quipped back at him, his sleep-addled mind not having a proper reign on his tongue. He knew it was coming even before he felt the back-handed slap send jolts of pain rocketing through his jaw. He'd had worse and knew he deserved it for loosening his tongue. The same hand that had struck him before reached out to grip his jaw forcing him to look up.

"Good to see that Brennan gave a bit of a backbone, Son." The grip of his fingers tightened to the point of pain, but MyKhal refused to show any weakness by flinching. This, like every "lesson" his father doled out, was a test of will. His brown eyes went cold as he met his father's.

"It did. Thank you, Father."

It was difficult to keep his tone from shifting to something more sarcastic. His father released his face. MyKhal's body remained stiff as Lord Awir began circling him much like a hawk ready to swoop down on its prey. Brennan had done many things for him. It had taught him discipline and fortitude. It had shaped his body and soul into that of a warrior. It had mentally scarred him until his skin was as thick as boar's hide. Even his father couldn't pierce through it with his attempted fear-mongering now. Something for which he was thankful.

His father scrutinized every piece of him. When he found nothing else offensive to name, he finally spoke.

"Get cleaned up. There is much work to do, and it's about time you start pulling your weight." The finality in his voice was an obvious dismissal.

Still, MyKhal had to ask, "The remaining Edlinds, they are still not faring well then?"

His father paused and let out a deep, exasperated sigh.

"I hate to be the bearer of bad news, my boy. And I would have rather waited until you were well-rested before you found out."

MyKhal's stomach rolled painfully at the words. Balling his hands into fists, he braced for whatever his father would say next.

"Aleria has fled the castle, and no one has seen her since the death of her parents. There are rumors of her finally feeling free to run off with some pirate she met while...Well, you don't want to know the gory details, I'm sure." It took everything inside MyKhal not to ram his fist through something. How could she leave her home in such chaos? He had always thought she was better than that, that she had more pride. A tickle of unease made itself known at the back of his consciousness. The Aleria he had known would have never left this way. He may have been unsure of her feelings, but of this, he was more than certain.

"And have you sent out search parties for her?"

Trying not to sound frantic was harder than he imagined it would be.

"And Draven? What did he say about it? He knows her better than anyone. You as well as I know how rumors can be." The patronizing sneer that tugged at his father's mouth made him realize he had made a mistake

"Oh, don't tell me you are still pining for her? Creator help you, Son. I thought you had left such pathetic notions behind years ago. She is not a lady; she is a whore who has done as whores do: take you for what you are worth and leave." The notion to knock his head off nearly overwhelmed him. He was not still pining for her. The rumors and unreturned letters were enough to cure him of that pathetic whim. No matter her choices in her love life, she was still a woman whom he believed to have pride in her role as a Lady. He had trained in the field with her, watched her study tirelessly. There were times when she had shared her hopes and dreams with him. All were about being the next great leader of Fayeharrow and an example in the court of Rimeheld. He knew she wouldn't up and leave like this.

Ignoring his father's jab completely, he continued, "What does Draven say about all this? Surely, he has mounted a search?" His father had avoided the topic of Draven on two occasions now, and he wanted to know why.

"Again, I hate to tell you this," he began as if the trouble were nothing but a pebble in his shoe, "Draven was the one who came across the bodies first, and he hasn't been in his right mind ever since."

"Where is he now?"

"He attacked the men who were trying to help evacuate the castle, so I've had him jailed until he comes to his senses." Anger and disgust tore at him at the thought of Draven being in the dungeons on top of everything else. He would see for himself how out of his mind the Lion of Edlind was. The tickle of unease became a bell of warning. It rang so loud that it was hard to ignore it long enough to put on a passive facade.

"I will see to it the problem is dealt with, Father. One way or another," he said, hoping the coldness in his tone was believable enough to lend no second guesses. MyKhal bowed his head and took a step towards the direction of the guest quarters.

"I will take my leave if you grant it. The road has been long, and as you pointed out, I am soaked."

His father waved a dismissive hand at him with a roll of his eyes and a muttered insult he didn't quite catch. The warning bells were ringing in his mind, demanding he get to the bottom of things quickly. Closing his eyes for a moment, he listened. The rain still beat against the glass pane of the window at the end of the hall. There were no other sounds besides the occasional quick shuffling of servants' feet.

"Good," he thought.

Ducking into a familiar alcove, he ran his fingers along the stones. His fingers fumbled around for the mechanism that released the passageway door. A rush of memories brought a smile of distant joy and ongoing sorrow. Sixteen-year-old Aleria sneaking down the hallway in her flowing nightgown. His hiding here in this very spot, waiting to grab her as she ran by. Giggles, kisses, the familiar sound of the passageway opening. A game of hide and seek that always ended up with his winning in one way or another. The sound of a click and the cracking of the stone door opening brought him back to the present.

He finally found the hidden entrance to the castle dungeons. MyKhal was more familiar with how to get from Aleria's room to his own and back, rather than to the dungeons. He was glad Draven had shown him around the entire estate a few times. The thought of his friend, long lost or no, chained down here like a criminal made him miserable.

The dungeons were dank, dripping with excess rainwater runoff and slick with mold. The shiver that skated through him made him regret not going for a change of clothes. Only a few sconces flickered with half lit flames casting eerie shadows about the room. One dark shadow though didn't flicker and move when the light bounced across it. The body of a man hunched over with his head in his hands.

Draven.

For a long moment, MyKhal stared, afraid to move any closer. Not finding the words to say, Draven broke the silence first.

"Now you show up?" His voice was brittle and raw, either from not speaking at all or screaming too much. Part of him hoped it was the former, but when Draven lifted his head, MyKhal clenched his fists. Creator's Mercy. What had his father done? Draven snorted and shook his head when MyKhal still couldn't find the words to say.

"Come to finish your daddy's dirty work?" he said, glaring at him through swollen eyes. His face was so bloodied and bruised that if it weren't for the fire-orange hair, MyKhal wouldn't have recognized him.

"No" was the only way he could think to respond. So many questions filled his mind that he couldn't land on only one.

"No? That's all you're going to say?" Draven pushed up from his cot and gripped the bars so hard his bloodied knuckles cracked and broke open again.

"Well, I have buttload more to say to you," he said through clenched teeth. All MyKhal could do was a gesture for him to go ahead. Draven growled again and punched the bars.

"Where in the infernal depths have you been while your father destroyed everything and everyone I love?!? People you claimed to love!" He punched the bars again, and MyKhal stepped forward. The sick feeling in his stomach roiling. What did his father have to do with this? "What did you do when you walked in that door, huh? Kiss your daddy's boots and thank him for expanding your future reign? Did you shed a sodding tear when you heard about my uncle? My aunt?" He choked as he spat the words, and tears ran down his blood speckled cheeks. "Did Ali even…," he started choking harder on his tears. "Did she even make it, or is her body rotting out there in the woods?!?"

MyKhal felt the wind rush from his lungs at the words. None of this made sense. What Draven was saying was not lining up. He reached out to grab the keys to Draven's cell off the wall.

"It was unfortunate what happened to your uncle and your aunt. I never would have thought him to be a murderer," he said as gently as he could, but immediately, Draven's eyes widened, and the tears therein ran cold.

"A what?" His whisper more of a hiss in the silence. Reaching for the lock, MyKhal met his gaze.

"Your uncle murdered your aunt in cold blood," he repeated his father's words almost verbatim. Draven began trembling as a manic laugh bubbled up from somewhere deep within him. The malice in that laugh made him think that perhaps Draven was as mad as his father implied. When the laughing stopped, Draven's voice turned into something much colder, something filled with pity and disdain.

"You are an idiot, aren't you?" Draven rested his head against the bars and looked him in the eyes. "Your father had hundreds of men sack our home and murder my family."

MyKhal froze as the words hit him like a physical blow. Something in him cracked as the warnings in his mind became so deafening he had to fight the urge to cover his ears.

"They tried to kill Philip and Erica in their chambers, twelve to one. Erica made it into the passageways and died there. Aleria and I found them both." Silver lined his eyes. MyKhal's hands balled into fists so tight he could feel the crescents of his nails break the skin of his palms.

"I told Aleria to run and fought off as many as I could. I don't know if she made it. Tell me that she made it." His voice broke, and MyKhal's heart along with it.

"I don't know." That was all he could say as warring realities ripped him apart from the inside.

"My father said...she...she had run away. That she had run away with some pirate lover she met on the coast." Draven's hoarse burst of laughter made him shrug in confusion.

"Did you hear the bollocks that came from your mouth?" Leaning his back against the bars of the cell, he continued, "Aleria Edlind, Pirate Queen. You're kidding me, right? I swear if your father told you the sky was green, you'd believe him and call it grass." He turned back to him, narrowing his gaze at him through the bars.

"I'm behind bars, my family is dead, and it's you I feel sorry for," he groaned, covering his face with his hands.

MyKhal bristled at the insult, but kept his mouth shut. He felt dizzy and so sick he thought he may wretch at any moment. His mind whirled with everything Draven had told him. There was no way his father would stoop so low. No way he would murder the Edlinds as a power play. There had to be something else. Some reason he would -

No.

There had to be sound reasoning for this. Though everything since he arrived echoed a certain truth. The tension he felt upon entering the estate. The way the servants acted. The constant itching of unease in his subconscious. Panic and shame flooded him as he shook away the thoughts and turned to leave. He had to figure out what in the hell was going on in this castle. Before he could get far, Draven's voice carried to him, echoing off the stones like a ghost.

"How does it feel knowing your father might have murdered the girl you loved?"

The words hit him so hard he reached for the wall to steady himself. He knew Draven had meant to cause a reaction, and Creator curse him, it did. Deeper and more brutal than he knew how to deal with at the moment. What he needed right now was proof. Not emotion or gut feelings that could lead him astray. Proof that either Draven or his father was lying to him.

"I will send a healer to tend to you and bring you fresh food and water" was the only condolence he was willing to offer at the moment. The slew of profanities that followed him out of the room was enough to make him flinch, but he couldn't let his emotions cloud his judgment. There was too much at stake for everyone.

Aleria

Warm spring water splashed around Aleria as she cupped handfuls over her skin. Each pinch or jolt of pain was a stark reminder that this was all horrifically real. As were the blue and purple bruises spreading between slashes of broken skin. Her broken, ragged nails were a painful recollection of having to leave Draven behind. The deep wound on her shoulder and gashes in her chest were proof that she had fought a beast of nightmares. The only reason she survived was because of the hidden agenda of fairytale creatures. Beautiful, dangerous, fairytale creatures.

A hiss slipped from her lips as she ran a bar of soap over her wounds, the herbs stinging while they healed. The blood and gore were still tangled in her hair and under her nails. It was a kindness the group of Fae had afforded her to be able to bathe, even if she wasn't allowed to be completely alone.

Alone.

The word echoed in her mind like that of a curse as tears began to form in the corners of her eyes. Her mother, her father, her cousin, her only family, gone in the span of one evening. She was utterly and achingly alone in this world. A world that had changed into something even more terrifying than she had ever known it could be. Beasts were roaming in her backyard for Creator knows how long, and now, she had to face them alone. Clutching the soap to her chest, she tried to get a hold of herself. Each breath was coming harder and faster, her heart pounding so hard it felt like a mallet in her chest. The tears she had been suppressing in favor of rage finally won out, and they began pouring down her cheeks in earnest.

Ducking beneath the water, she let out a scream that had been fighting to get free since she found her parents. For one achingly vulnerable moment, she thought about breathing in the spring water. She wondered what it would feel like to sink into the peacefulness of the stone floor below. To give up.

"Live, Cousin."

Draven's words were the only thing that brought her back to the surface. She stared at her haggard and distorted reflection in the water. It was her duty to honor his sacrifice. To live. To honor him and her parents. To seek her revenge on their behalf. Purpose flooded through her. Her mind raced with adrenaline and the half-arsed formation of a plan as she came to the water's edge.

Pushing herself up on slick rock, she climbed out and grabbed the spare leggings and tunic Thea had gifted her. Not bothering to dry off she yanked on leggings and a loose-fitting top and stomped barefoot into the center of the Huldra's camp. Thea, who was her assigned guard while she bathed, trailed behind her.

"Don't you dare try to use magic on me," Aleria warned.

Thea immediately lifted her hands in a sort of surrender.

"Trust me when I say you do not wish to feel my power, and you would certainly know if I had." The warning was clear, as was the instinctual clenching of her gut that made the Fae woman's words ring true.

The threat didn't deter her as she strode to where Larkin was sitting by the fire. A ridiculously sharp sword was draped across his lap. He was sharpening it. Aleria swallowed nervously, but stepped up to him as if she were not. The other three men looked up. Ruke and Thea shared a look as Aleria blurted her thoughts out to Larkin.

"I will help you under the stipulation that you help me in return." Larkin looked up from his work with a raised eyebrow. "Once I help you find a solution to your Nattmara problem, you and your companions will help me take back my home."

"How was your home taken?"

"There are monsters in my world too. One of them murdered my family."

Aleria held her breath. He was weighing his words. A high born noble, with politics ingrained in him, unwilling to make a promise he may or may not be able to keep. Something seemed to flicker in his eyes for a moment. Pity? Maybe even guilt? But it was gone as soon as it came. He only stared at her in a way that made her feel as if she were being weighed and measured, yet again. He must not have found her wanting because his reply was curt and to the point.

"Is it restoration or revenge you want?"

"Both," she answered without a second thought. She wanted her home back. She wanted Anwir to pay for what he did. His head on a pike after he's drawn and quartered should fit the bill.

Something like understanding seemed to pass over his countenance. He looked to his companions who didn't oppose him, but a sense of wariness clung to their countenance.

"Agreed. Our restoration and revenge in exchange for your own. I give you my oath," he said, placing his hand over his heart and inclining his head towards her.

"That's not enough," she dared to say as she took a tentative step forward. Part of her knew she was pushing it, but what was a Fae oath to her? There was a modicum of trust between them. Just because they had yet to kill her wasn't enough to build a matchstick house upon, much less a belief in oaths.

"My people make blood oaths as a pact between one another to solidify a contract that cannot be broken. A blood oath." She slid her hand along the sword he had polished to a dazzling shine, marring it with a splash of blood from her palm. She hid her wince of pain as blood began to bloom and pool in her hand, and she waited for him to reciprocate the gesture. His shocked expression was quickly replaced by a wicked grin.

"You continue to surprise me, human. Keep it up, and I may come to like you," he said, slicing his hand in the same manner before holding it out for her to grasp. With a small smile of her own, she pressed her hand to his and started to speak her oath. Instead, a gasp escaped her lips as something akin to adrenaline rushed through her veins. Her entire body felt as if it were alight and burning brighter and hotter than any flame. An ethereal voice echoed in her mind in words she couldn't understand. It took her a moment to draw her mind back. Snatching her hand, she broke the connection between them.

Panting a little, she shot him a glare.

"What were you doing to me?"

Larkin glared back, winded. His eyes still danced with whatever energy flowed through the two of them.

"I've only felt that once before. I have no clue," he growled, pulling out a rag to wipe the excess blood off his palm.

"You're the ones with magic. Figure it out," she said with no little amount of annoyance and sarcasm. Larkin's gaze darkened as he looked up from his bloody palm and towards her again.

"I don't know how humans speak to their superiors, but consider this a final warning of how you will address me. You will not speak to me as if I am serving you. You're no princess here, and if you want to keep your tongue long enough to order around your subjects, I would suggest you watch it."

The reprimand landed like a blow. As much as she wanted to retaliate with a verbal lashing, she knew it would do little good. Larkin was right on one account. She was no princess, and if she were to survive she had to play the game in the same manner as if she were at court. No one was to be trusted in court, and no one was to be trusted here.

"Sorry," she said after a long, tense moment with no reply. Larkin sighed and ran his fingers through his hair.

"Good. Now…" He walked over to a bag and tossed it her way. "If you are to fall in line with us, you must bring something to the table besides snark and pomp." Aleria glared at him, but he smiled back in a way that all too easily got beneath her skin. Sharp, perfectly white teeth...shapely lips, and was that a dimple? Sard. She began forming a list in her mind as a way of diverting her anger and that niggling bit of unbidden attraction.

You're arrogant. You're cocky. You're annoying.

A smile tugged at the corner of her mouth as she wondered if he were thinking similar thoughts about her.

"Do you hunt?" He went on, tossing her a bow

"Bet I'm a better shot than you," she challenged with a raised brow and an impish smirk. "Said with the utmost respect, of course."

A couple of good-natured "Ooos" came from Ruke and Zander, but Nox and Thea looked at each other and grimaced.

Larkin narrowed his gaze at her and grabbed his bow, then stepped so close he was nose to nose with her. The stormy gray of his eyes seemed to crackle with electricity as he stared down into hers. Being this close to him made static dance across her skin, every bit of her aware of the unnatural power radiating in her direction. What was wrong with her? Why was it that she couldn't keep her smart mouth shut? A shiver ran down her spine as he leaned in close enough that she could feel his breath on her face. He was trying to intimidate her. Though it was working, she did her best to keep her challenging smirk in its place.

"Has anyone ever told you how brash you are?"

A burst of laughter exploded, making her stumble a few times on her words before she could respond.

"I have heard the phrase before about myself, yes." Still choking on her laughter, she thought, "Have you?". Larkin seemed as if he were fighting a smile as he nodded towards the woods.

"Let's see if your shot is as quick and efficient as your wit, human, " he challenged her right back. She couldn't help but give him a toothy grin in response.

Nock.

Draw.

Aim.

Release.

Just as MyKhal had taught her.

Steady.

Breathe.

Unwanted thoughts of MyKhal and his lessons made their way to the forefront of her mind. The first time she held a bow. How his fingers pressed against her hips. His warm fire and citrus scent filling her senses and driving her mad. Swallowing hard, she fought the urge to allow her mind to linger upon him. The way he used to make her feel...

She had to focus on the task at hand. If she could prove her salt to these beings, maybe she could at least earn their respect. Trust was too much to ask for from either party, but respect could be just as valuable.

Drenched in the muted tones of dusk, it wouldn't be long before the forest grew so dark she couldn't see. They had to make this quick if they were to bring back something to camp. It wasn't helping that Larkin was watching her with an intensity that made the pressure to perform increase tenfold. Still, she had never backed down from a challenge before, and she wouldn't start now.

Relying on everything her father taught her about tracking, she looked for signs of a quarry.

"Double almonds. Follow the points," she thought to herself as she studied the ground around them. Larkin leaned over her shoulder to take a look at the tracks she had found. His quiet contemplation was grating her nerves. Instead of lashing out, she walked in the direction the tracks had indicated. If hunting didn't call for utter and absolute silence, she would have struck up some sort of small talk. So, what is it like to be Fae? Do you have any more special powers? What's your favorite food?

Creator, she was an idiot.

Crack.

The sound of movement in the distance snapped her attention. As quick as a blink, her bow was up, nocked, and aimed in the direction of the sound. What she hadn't considered were her wounds. At the pull of the bowstring, pain ripped through her, making her gasp and unintentionally release the arrow into the void. An ear-piercing shriek shot fear down her spine. It didn't bode well that Larkin let out what she assumed was a curse in his native tongue as he reached for the long sword on his back.

"What in the Creator's name was that?" She groaned, pressing her hand to her aching affliction. The borrowed tunic had already started to speckle with blood from her reopened wound. Larkin stared off into the distance and sniffed the air.

"Sluagh," he murmured along with the ring of steel unsheathed. Aleria looked towards where her arrow flew and saw it thrashing about wildly in mid-air. Merciful heavens, she had hit something invisible.

"What is a Sluagh? How do we kill it?" she panic-rambled. She released her injury and grabbed for the borrowed sword at her side.

"Trouble. Stay behind me." He answered in perfect succession to her questions. An ear-splitting scream rattled her to her core. Fear and helplessness filled her as she watched him brace for an attack she could not see.

The fog began rolling in around them, thick and low lying on the forest floor. If she hadn't known where it was coming from, she might have panicked with the eeriness of it all. It was still so surreal to see this sort of magic happening before her eyes, to watch as electricity sparked down his skin and thunder echoed in the skies. Part of her felt a strange sense of awe and wonder followed by gratefulness that such a creature was on her side.

Her thrashing arrow, lodged in the still invisible Sluagh, moved towards them as if it were being pulled back to her in reverse. The swing of Larkin's blade drew out another shriek and sickening squelch. The blade met its mark with enough force to splatter what she imagined to be the creature's blood all over her. She only had a moment to be disgusted before she was yanked to the ground and thrown on her back. She couldn't see anything, a weight pressed down. Something was sitting atop her chest. Sharp appendages trailed down her face, accompanied by a crackling sort of cackle. Frantic and panicked, she blindly stabbed her blade upward. Spatters of more black ichor dropped onto her tunic as she scrambled to get away. A clawed grip clasped around her ankle and dragged her back across the misted grass. Though she hated playing the damsel in distress, she also knew, in this case, she was outmatched.

"Larkin!" she screeched as a last resort. The creature yanked her leg so hard she was afraid it might sever it from her body. She screamed in pain as her hip felt like it was brutally ripped from its socket. Her fingernails clawed frantically into the mossy ground, trying to get away. Suddenly, the pulling stopped. The only sounds were the chirping of crickets and the rustling of the wind blowing through the trees. She fought to stand, but the pain in her leg was so much she only fell back down on her hands and knees. Larkin had dropped to his knees beside her.

"I am not used to the fragility of humans," Larkin whispered in a soothing, compassionate tone.

Larkin lowered himself to her level. His hand rested gently on her lower back as he tried to pat her in the same way one would calm an injured pup. She had to fight the urge not to growl and snap at him.

"Wasn't...your...fault...," Aleria hissed between pained gasping breaths. Larkin gritted his teeth as guilt sketched itself in his features.

"In a way...it was." Aleria couldn't bring herself to look him in the eyes. "I can smell what I'm hunting from a mile away. I can hear the rustling before it even registers in your...tiny ears. I can hit a vital organ on the first draw. I wanted to see if your bravado held up."

Aleria stayed quiet as embarrassment made her tear-stained cheeks flush. She was an idiot.

"I suppose I proved one thing...," she choked as his hands moved in gentle massaging motions along her injured hip and up to where it had felt like it dislocated. "I'm still a pretty decent shot to hit something I can't even see." Her grin was too wobbly to be taken as anything but false bravado. But to her surprise, he humored her.

"That you are," he whispered with a soft smile that made her think she had not seen a real one until now. The severe angular lines of his face softened, and the pull of his full lips revealed a dimple in his left cheek. It seemed out of place and entirely unfair to have something so sweet on the face of someone so dangerous.

"My apologies for before and -" Before she could protest or even say a word, he pressed one hand on her dislodged hip and the other on her shoulder, yanking down in one hard, fluid motion. A sharp snap of pain and a grotesque pop made spots dance before her eyes. The little food in her stomach rocketed out of her mouth onto the forest floor. Something between a roar and sob spilled from her lips with the last of her vomit. "For that," he finished, patting her on the back as she sputtered and sobbed.

Would her humiliation ever end? Using the back of her hand to wipe off her mouth, she pushed up off the mossy ground and onto her feet. Her knees wobbled as she tried to find purchase on the uneven ground. Every part of her was screaming in some sort of pain. She knew she had no right to be angry with him. If she were in his place, she might have tried something just the same. It was harmless until her unfortunate luck made the situation take a turn for the worse. Still, he had apologized, and that alone left her mystified.

"Can you walk, or should I carry you?" he asked. There was a hint of mirth hidden behind the compassionate intent of his words. Crossing her arms over her chest, she glared at him. Was he really this obtuse, or was he getting some sort of sick enjoyment from torturing her? She couldn't think of a more humiliating way to return to camp. Well, it would be even more embarrassing if she died. At least she wouldn't have to suffer the indignation of being carried like a princess.

You're no princess. His words from before taunted her as they stood there locked in another staring match. She wondered if the irony was lost on him or if he was honestly trying to annoy her.

"Are all humans this stubborn, or is it just you?" he huffed mimicking her stance and her glare. She hated that he was right and that his offer was the only possible way she was making it back to camp. There was no way she would be able to manage the terrain with her injuries. Much less manage to not break her neck in the darkness that was slowly enveloping them. With an over-dramatic roll of her eyes, she let out a sigh of resignation and lifted her arms towards him like a petulant child.

So. This was what rock bottom felt like. To his credit, he didn't mock her. Instead, he swept her up as if she weighed nothing at all. After a few awkward adjustments, he settled her into the cradle of his arms and began the walk back to camp.

At first, Aleria refused to let more of her than necessary press against him. She let her arms hang loose at her sides in the only form of protest she could offer. The awkwardness of that mixed with the tense silence eventually broke her resolve. She decided to try to help him by wrapping her arms around his neck in an attempt to relieve some of the weight. He only pressed his lips together in a thin line and stared straight ahead. It wasn't long before she started to acknowledge how good it felt. Though she loathed admitting it, part of her longed for comfort in all the most human ways. She wished for a moment she didn't have to be strong, that she could lay her head on his shoulder and cry until she was hoarse, that he would stroke her hair and tell her everything was going to be alright, even if it were a lie.

His scent of fresh rain, the soft brush off his silken hair, and the warmth of his body began to lull her. So she gave in, just a little, and laid her head upon his shoulder. He stiffened momentarily, turning his head towards hers curiously. After a moment, he relaxed and resumed his pace through the darkened woods.

She had almost given in to the draw of sleep when the deep timbre of his voice cut through the silence.

"I know you do not trust me," he started, keeping his eyes focused on the path in front of him. "I know you have no reason to believe the words coming from my mouth, but I'm hoping at the very least you believe this." A new sort of tension filled the space between them. "In this world, there is always a balance. You may see us as godlike…" Aleria couldn't help but scoff at the description.

Larkin sighed exasperatedly before continuing, "But there is and will always be a counterbalance to power."

Aleria looked up at him. "And yours is?"

"We cannot lie."

Aleria stared at him with her mouth agape. "You can't expect me to believe that."

"It's true. I can't lie and have not lied to you."

Aleria considered his words for a long moment before offering for him to continue. "Let's say I believe you. What other balances are there?" He readjusted her in his arms as he stepped gracefully onto a large rock, most likely to keep his boots from getting wet in what sounded like a small stream.

"Our vows are binding," he added, stopping to look down at her. "We cannot lie, and we cannot break a sworn vow unless both parties wish it so."

Her eyes connected with his as the knowledge sank in. He couldn't betray her. He could kill her though. If she were dead, he wouldn't have to fulfill his side of the vow.

"Why are you telling me this?" Her eyes were still locked on the icy grey of his that seemed to glow in the faint moonlight. His embrace tightened on her. For a moment, his mouth opened and closed as if he were momentarily looking for the right words.

"I will keep you alive, even though it seems like death stalks you like a scorned lover. If you will break the curse, I give you my vow that I will return you to your home and make it safe for you and yours, Aleria."

His words shimmered through her in rippling waves of magic and settled in her veins. She felt the pull of his words, this strange binding of his vows to her. It was enough to ignite a spark of hope in her battered heart.

"There is no magic to my vows, but I swear to keep them just the same. I will help you to the utmost of my ability. I swear to you."

He nodded his head and pulled his gaze from hers and back towards the darkness. For the first time in the past few days, she felt as if she could breathe a little easier. Perhaps this was the start of trust, binding magic, or no.

As the camp came into view in the distance, she grimaced up at him. Though their newfound understanding was more than she could have hoped for, still, she decided to press her luck further.

"You can put me down now," Aleria said, hoping to be able to hide her limp enough that no one would ask questions.

"And why would I do that? You're injured," he huffed as she tried to wriggle out of his grasp.

Aleria glared up at him and tried again to wriggle free of his hold. "You do love playing the savior, don't you?" she hissed crossing her arms over her chest in defiance, though she still could not get herself free of him. His answering grin and that infuriating dimple was all the answer she needed. "Well, let's get this straight. I am not a damsel. I do not need rescuing. Now, put me the sard down. Now."

Without preamble, he dropped her to her feet, shaking his head as he watched her put pressure on her injury. She didn't dare wince under the weight of his gaze.

"I would never call you a damsel," he said, offering her his hand instead. She stared at it as if it would bite her. He rolled his eyes and dropped his hand to his side when she refused his help, yet again. "Words I would use are foolish, childish, stubborn, oblivious to your mortality, and -"

"Oh, really, and? Please continue. Your flattery is positively swoon-worthy."

"Intriguing."

Her eyes met his, and she wondered if that keen hearing could pick up on the sudden racing of her heart. She wanted to curse herself for how easily she allowed him to agitate her. Years of court politics, and one kind word from him flustered her.

She was never flustered.

Taking a deep breath, she feigned disinterest and turned towards the camp.

"Have I stunned you silent?" he teased. She would not let him bait her this time.

"No, I was simply raised that if I didn't have something nice to say, I shouldn't say anything at all." She stopped to glare at him over her shoulder. "And I have nothing nice to say about you. Who knows? Maybe one day, you'll do something that strikes my fancy." She had to resist the urge to stick her tongue out at him.

His low chuckle did that funny thing to her stomach as he matched her slow pace. "Then, I will be sure to do my best to strike such fancy."

"Liar," she huffed, shooting him a glare.

"I can't lie, remember?" His answering grin was positively ruthless.

Mykhal

Neither the warmth of the tub, the fireplace, nor his bedding could do anything for the bitter cold that permeated his heart and soul. Not with the warring stories in his mind, battling for dominance with no sure footing to stand on.

Either his father was a murderer, or his best friend had gone insane from trauma. How was he to sleep with such horrors hanging over his head? He threw off the blankets and stalked over to the chifferobe across the room. As he tugged the wooden door open, the smell of honeysuckle and vanilla tickled his nose.

His favorite scent. Hers.

Creator, he loved and loathed that scent. It made him wonder if she came to this room when she missed him.

Pulling out a white cotton shirt, he breathed in the rush of memories and closed his eyes. It was almost as if he could imagine her standing beside him, her golden hair unbound and cascading around her slim shoulders... her almond-shaped eyes gazing upon him with so much weight it felt like a physical touch. In moments like these, her memory was more like a ghost, haunting him.

Pulling the shirt over his bare shoulders and bracing himself in the closet, in his anguish, he spoke the words he had refused to say for the past two years, words he had bottled up like a poison, embittering him to the point of rotting him from the inside out.

"You never wrote."

The ghost did not reply, but he felt the weight of her stare as if she were real. He could imagine how she would tilt her head to the side when she was considering something, how her teeth would worry her bottom lip until it was cherry red. The little things about her that he remembered like it was yesterday. If she were here, he would ask her the question that still loomed so heavy over his battered pride and wounded heart.

"Did you ever love me as I loved you?"

The memory of her opened her mouth as if to speak, but a knock at his door broke whatever hold his imagination held over him. Aleria disappeared like smoke on a breeze. Shaking his head, he thought that maybe it was him who was slowly descending into madness.

Sliding a pair of breeches over his thighs and lacing them up, he barked a "Hold on!" to whomever came to call. When he opened the door, the sight in front of him nearly sent him to his knees.

"Noona Lee!" he shouted, throwing his arms around the plump older woman's shoulders, squeezing tightly.

"Aye. It be me, boyo. Now, calm yerself before som'em sees."

Without a word, he yanked the woman into his room and quickly arranged a place for her to sit down.

"Now, don't ya fret over me. Let me get a look at cha." With rough leathery hands, she pinched his cheeks, mussed his hair, and squeezed each muscled arm with an impressed harumph. "Looks like all tha time out there did ya body good. How's yer mind holdin' up tho? All this musta been a shock, huh? Broke my heart too, ya know? The Edlinds, Creator bless em', they was good folk."

MyKhal nodded and took her hands in his. If anyone could give him any clarity and peace at this moment, it was her. Noona had been like his mother since his mother died during his birth. Though she had children and grandchildren of her own, she treated him the same, sneaking him treats, holding him when he couldn't sleep, things he was missing from his father as a child. Without her influence in his life, he was sure he would have turned out much different. His joy was tempered by the ever-present questions holding his thoughts captive.

"Noona," his fingers brushing over her work-worn hands, "Do you think...do you think Philip killed Erika? And that Ali..." His voice cracked a little. "That Ali ran off with someone?"

The elderly woman looked up at him with pity in her eyes and a tight-lipped smile.

"I wasn't here when it all happened, boyo. I got nothin' to tell you there, but..." She looked down to her apron and back at the door nervously. "I do got somethin' that's rightfully yours." Sticking her hand inside her deep pockets, she pulled out a stack of letters tied together with a red string. He looked at her curiously as she placed the pile in his hands. In whispered tones, she explained,"Ias cleanin' the master's office and gatherin' the things he needed when I foun' these. They're writ to you. There's a whole stack more where that came from, but I didn' wan' him to notice em' missin'."

His fingers ran over the script in shock at the words written in scrawling black ink.

To: MyKhal Anwir

From: Your future wife

The words stole his breath from his lungs and made his heart shudder. Confusion and panic bombarded him like a herd of wild stallions. He couldn't decide if he wanted to rip the thing open and read it or throw it in the fire. Swallowing hard and not taking his eyes from the letters, he spoke.

"These were in my father's study?" Though he knew she had already said so, he had to hear it again.

"Aye, darlin'. They were." Kneeling in front of him, she gently placed her hands on top of his.

"Yer father never approved of 'er. But I did. Ya wanna know why?"

He nodded his head, trying to fight back the anger and emotions threatening to explode at any moment.

"'Cause she made ya better. She made ya stand up for whatcha wanted. She pushed ya, but most of all, she made ya smile," she said, patting his cheeks lovingly. "I know them smiles were rare roun' here, but when she was roun', them smiles were a permanent fixture." Tilting his head up to meet her eyes, she smiled sadly.

"A girl who writes dis much to ya ain't running away with nobody. Pirate king or no." MyKhal looked at her with a raised eyebrow. "Oh, hush, you know I got an ear out in all the gossip roun' here. Now, get yourself back in bed. I'ma go launder yer clothes."

He huffed a laugh. Noona was rushing about the room. She picked up all his clothes strewn about and those still in his pack. After tossing another log on the fire, she was about to take her leave when he called out to her. His eyes still on the letters like they were a snake about to bite him.

"Noona?" he whispered as she reached the door, loaded to the gills with laundry.

She paused and waited, but there was a tension there that made him worry.

"Keep a good distance from him...and me. I won't see you harmed. No more risky moves, no matter how good-natured."

Putting her free hand on her hip, she harrumphed at him. "Have those three years gone made ya lose yer mind?" Her voice had gone hard and full of sass."I'll do what I see fit. My path is my own, and you'll do good to member that." Without another word, she slammed the door closed behind her. MyKhal couldn't help but smile, though it slid from his lips as he gazed back down at the pile of cream-colored envelopes still laying in his hands.

His fingers traced over the delicate, feminine script. There was no doubt in his mind that this was Aleria's handwriting. It was typical for the two of them to write during the months their families spent apart. His summer holidays were spent in Fayeharrow, and her winter ones were spent in Wimborne. In the beginning, their parents would use the opportunity as trial runs for their future diplomatic letters. They practiced their penmanship with trivial writings of the weather and general nonsense. It was all so droll. That was until one day Aleria sent him a hilariously sarcastic anecdote of the goings-on in Fayeharrow. He remembered laughing so hard his stomach ached. From that point, real and true communication began.

It started with stories and jokes, but before long, it became more of a diary between the two of them. They spoke of their dreams, their hopes, and their goals as sole heirs to their families' estates. It was odd at first when they would come together after all the intimate things they shared in those letters. The writing was one thing, but being face to face with the person who held all your secrets was another. When he turned eighteen, she was only fifteen at the time. He expressed to her that maybe it wasn't such a good idea that they write to each other anymore. He had begun seeing a young woman in Wimborne and didn't think it fair to continue to have such a...confusing friendship with Aleria. There wasn't even a reply to that foolish letter, and he had immediately regretted it.

The following winter was the coldest he could ever remember. No one in Rimeheld could give a cold shoulder like Aleria Edlind. His fling with the girl in Wimborne only lasted a season. Aleria's coldness towards him lasted an entire year. Then, he lost his mind, let her kick his behind in Fayeharrow's Tourney, and well, he had gone and kissed her. After that, his entire world had changed, and she had become the center of it.

He had a feeling today would be another moment where his world would change. Yet again, Aleria Edlind would be the cause. With trembling fingers, he pulled the string binding the letters together, reaching for the first one. Cautiously, he slid his finger beneath the seal, and with a deep breath, popped it open. His stomach clenched as he unfolded the delicate piece of parchment that still smelled like her. As if the scent was some sort of summons, the memory of her stood before him again. He flinched in shock at the sudden appearance, but then, he rolled his eyes.

"This is hard enough without you standing there, watching me," he growled, but the vision gestured for him to continue. He stared at the specter for a moment longer, expecting another disappearing act. Instead, she crawled up onto the bed and sat cross-legged across from him. He was losing his mind. Was it guilt that manifested this apparition? The most plausible option was something he couldn't bring himself to believe...not yet. When Aleria raised her eyebrows and waved him on again, he looked down at the folded letter in his hand, opened it, and began to read.

My dearest MyKhal,

I hope this letter finds you well, safe, and missing me as much as I miss you. I went to the beach today to be close to you. It was cold, but it was nothing compared to the loss of the warmth of your arms around me. You have ruined me to the kiss of sunshine because nothing compares to how your kisses warm me.

The words filled him with such grief and longing; he had to fight the urge to rip the paper to shreds. Instead, he took out another letter from the pile and began reading.

My dearest MyKhal,

It has been one hundred and twenty-five sunsets since I have last seen your face or heard your voice. I keep writing in hopes that these are being compiled for you somewhere. That they will give you some solace when you are settled and have time to reply. Draven told me you have yet to return his letters as well, but for me not to worry. It takes time to settle into a new place.

Three months. He had waited all that time in that horrible place for a single word from her. Some sort of hope that she was still his no matter the distance, and unbeknownst to him, she had been. Tears pooled in his eyes as he moved from letter to letter.

My love,

Draven and I are worried about you. That is why we have asked my father if we can make the trip to Brennan to visit you and make sure you are well. I'm coming to see you, love. Please don't give up on us. I know that distance is hard, but I'm certain if we try, we can make it.

Bitter tears were falling freely now as a pained growl rumbled low in his throat. He hadn't even realized he had begun pacing the room like a caged animal. What had stopped the two of them from coming? Everything would have been clear if they had followed through. Shoving the letter into his pocket, he headed to the one place he knew would have the answers he was desperate for.

MyKhal was less cautious this time as he ran through the passageways to get to the dungeons. He was glad to see that a servant had followed his command about making Draven's stay down here more comfortable. His cell looked closer to the barracks.

Without even announcing his presence, he shouted, "Why didn't you come?!?" Waking from a dead sleep, Draven lifted his head from the blankets and glared at him.

"If you haven't noticed, I'm currently detained and not able to come anywhere you call, your highness." The drawl of his voice was both mocking and full of disdain.

MyKhal growled and pulled the letter from his pocket and shoved it between the bars. "No, a year or so ago. Why didn't you and Aleria come to Brennan as this letter said you intended to?"

Draven took the crumpled piece of paper and held it up to his face before a scowl wrinkled his forehead. Slowly, he rose to his feet and glared between the metal bars.

"The better question is if you have this letter, why did you never respond?"

"I just received this Creator forsaken letter! All the letters, every sarding letter!" he screamed, slamming his hands against the bars. Draven didn't flinch.

"Tell me. Why did the letters stop here? Why did the two of you not come?" he rasped brokenly. Draven considered him coldly for a moment before opening his mouth to reply. His mind seemed to be making all the same connections MyKhal didn't want to believe.

"Your father told us you had written to him. You were having the time of your life in Brennan, sewing your wild oats and making a name for yourself across the sea. You've never been one for conflict, Khal. I realized it was your way of…," he choked a little and clenched his teeth. "Your way of ending things with Aleria without having some dramatic blow up."

The words were like a physical blow. That his best friend would think so little of him burned like coals beneath his skin. The burning bubbled into a furious rage as he flew towards the bars.

"I LOVED HER! I loved her with everything I am, and you let her believe I would dismiss her so easily! I ought to kill you!" he roared through the bars. "You, you of all people know me well enough to at least think I had some modicum of pride! Did you think so little of me? Creators, what did I do to deserve such mistrust?!? Did you think I was such a coward?!?"

Draven inched up to the bars before quickly slamming his fist through the opening and into MyKhal's face. The sickening crack of bone on bone echoed through the stone dungeon. MyKhal staggered backward. His cheek was already beginning to bruise.

"You left!" Draven screamed back at him. "Left us both to fulfill whatever purpose your father willed you to! It's always been about him! You're a daddy's boy on all accounts. Don't dare deny it. We all were second fiddle. She even knew it too; she just…"

"Just what?" he started, but shook his head. His father again was the root of all this. Where all the mistrust came from.

"She hoped her love would be more precious to you than his."
MyKhal froze as the brutal words hit their mark. "I'm guessing he wrote to
you too, hm? What did dear old daddy say? What could he have possibly
said to make you doubt her? Did you not trust her?" Draven said in a mocking tone. "Or were you relieved? If she didn't want you, that made you a
free man."

MyKhal roared as he snatched the keys off the wall and flew to
unlock Draven's cell. He knew it was unwise to release him, but his patience
had run dry, and he wanted to settle this in the same way they had as boys.
Draven grinned like a cat about to swallow a canary as he waited for the cell
door to open.

"About time you -" Before he could finish the taunt, MyKhal had
slung the door open and tackled him to the floor. Landing the first punch to
Draven's ribs, MyKhal shouted.

"You were my best friend! You should have trusted me. You should
have known!" he said, landing another blow to Draven's ribs as they wres-
tled on the floor of the small space. Draven resisted, rolling until MyKhal
was behind him, grappling him into submission. With a quick twist of his
waist, he raised his elbow and slammed it into the side of MyKhal's face.
The move sent him flying into the metal bars with a clang.

"You were mine, and you should have stayed! There were more
options for you, and you know it!" He launched himself back at MyKhal,
pinning him to the bars.

"My father's word is the law!" he screamed at him, landing another
blow that made Draven wince, but his hold remained firm.

"That's bull, and you know it! Your father's approval is all that mattered to you! Not Ali, not me. Him. It's always been him above all! And how
does he repay that loyalty, huh?"

"Shut up," MyKhal hissed as Draven's emotional assault continued.

"He beats you like an insolent pup."

"Shut up!" he screamed, slamming him into the other side of the cell.

"You were still not cruel enough, not callous enough, so he did what
cruel masters do." MyKhal tried to land another hit, but Draven dodged the

swing and pushed him back.

"He took away your toys, isolated you, and shipped you off for proper training." MyKhal seethed and panted as he waited for the next blow, but it didn't come in a physical sense.

"And here you are now, his lap dog. Well trained and waiting for his whistle."

Angry, bitter tears lined his eyes as he stood there in shock and barely contained fury. Draven's words were echoing off the stones like some curse. If that is what he thought about him, then maybe, that's what he should be. What he was always destined to be. A coldness began to spread through him, wrapping his heart in a vice of bitterness and despair. Without warning, Aleria's memory was standing beside Draven with tears on her cheeks. Her appearance was so shocking that for a moment, he gaped at her slack-jawed. He could never stand seeing her cry.

"What do you want from me?" he whispered to the spirit, but it was Draven who tilted his head to the side in consideration. He looked at him for a long while, a softness creeping across his features.

The two Edlinds spoke simultaneously. "I want you to see what has happened here, and I want you to do the right thing." MyKhal just stood there, knowing that Draven was right about him, about his father. About everything. He knew even without any more proof that his father was a cruel, sadistic man, who took what he wanted no matter the cost. Tears of hatred and pain begin dripping off his cheeks and onto the stone floor. His breathing was rough as he cleared his throat to force out the words, and his face was an impassive stone mask.

"I have, and I will," he finally rasped, leaving the cell door wide open. Draven's eyes drifted to the opening he was giving him. He could tell he was weighing the option of running with the option of killing him where he stood. With a half-smirk full of wicked intent, he offered him another option.

"Or you can help me make this right."

Mykhal

Sleep had finally and blissfully pulled him under moments after his head hit the pillow. He and Draven had spent most of the wee hours of the night formulating the beginnings of a plan of attack. The goal was to gather all the proof and information they could find. Then, they would then bring it to Rimeheld's sovereign ruler King Gawayne Richart. If the King knew what had happened here, he would surely arrest his father and put him on trial for his crimes.

The Edlinds were dear friends of the crown. To have committed such a crime against them would most likely end in the harshest of punishments. MyKhal was aware that his inheritance could be the boon in which the king could demand punishment, but it was a price he would willingly pay to see the wrongs his father had committed rectified. It took a lot to convince Draven to let the courts enact justice instead of killing his father in cold blood. What finally won him to his side was the fact that if he did, he would be the exact kind of monster his father was.

When Khal was sure that Draven would follow along with the plan, he slipped him some coin and told him to go to The Laughing Griffin. It was one of the less reputable pubs in Fayeharrow. At least the people there wouldn't know him, and he could keep a relatively low profile. MyKhal wasn't quite sure how his father was going to react when he found Dray missing from the dungeons. This would at least put him a safe distance away until MyKhal could gather what he needed from here. The surest way to keep what had happened a secret would be to rid the estate of all witnesses. It made sense why he replaced the long-time servants in favor of some of his own.

MyKhal's father was a careful man. A cautious man. So there had to be something he wanted from Draven. It was no secret that Draven had become one of the most formidable warriors in the land. But there had to be more to it than that.

After a quick rinse, he grabbed a traveling bag and packed a few of his things: some coins, the letters, and any weapons he could find. He hid it in the passageway in case things went badly before he expected it. Donning his worn leathers in favor of more courtly attire, he made his way from his room and father's office to the one place the bastard would be sure to desecrate first, Phillip's weapons room.

Phillip Eldlind had one of the most awe-inspiring weapon-rooms in Rimeheld. Large, carved, double wooden doors added to the anticipation of what magnanimous weaponry would be inside. Every warrior from here to the capital would have died for a chance to gaze upon such craftsmanship.

Weapons from foreign lands with spikes and swirling blades. Wooden weapons with the sacred etchings and designs that were said to increase a person's swing or stamina. Some of the artifacts seemed almost as if they could have been magical at some point in time. His favorite was an ancient-looking recurve bow made from golden thorn trees. The shaft of the bow was snowy white. In its grains, something like liquid gold pooled, twisted around like veins of magic. That one, in particular, was something he had his eye on since he was a little boy, barely able to draw the string.

Once, Phillip had caught him eyeing it and took it off its mount to let him give it a try. MyKhal didn't have the strength to pull it back. With disappointment written all over his face, he had handed it back to Phillip. The lord only smiled a gentle smile at him. MyKhal had expected a taunt or a reminder of how he was insufficient, but Phillip Edlind was not his like father. Instead, the great and kind Lord Edlind ruffled his hair and patted him on the back.

"You now know how hard you must work to get what you want. The only question is are you willing to do so?"

Those words had forever been an inspiration to how he lived his life. If he wanted something that could not yet be his, he was and would always be willing to do the hard work to get it. Aleria had noted his love for the bow and had sworn to make it his wedding gift. The thought filled him again with a longing he still wasn't sure he could bear.

His love had not forgotten him, but instead, thought that he had betrayed her. He still couldn't stand to consider that he would never have the chance to tell her otherwise.

Swallowing the emotions that threatened to cripple him, he opened the large wooden doors to the stolen study. The room that once held such fondness for him now felt like an homage to murder. A slap in the face of the warrior who curated it. If his father had met Phillip head-on in battle, he would have lost. Instead, his father had taken the most deplorable route a man could take, coming like a thief in darkness with no honor. Fighting the scowl on his face was difficult as he presented himself to the man who'd both given him life and yet taken the lives of so many others.

"Father," he said with a bow, hating the idea of playing this part so well. Draven's words echoed in the back of his mind about him being an obedient pup, waiting for his father's whistle. Shame and disgust washed over him. He had been that pup for far longer than he'd like to admit, and he would have to appear to be such for a while longer.

"Son," Lord Anwir answered without looking up from his papers. "I have a list of duties for you today." Pushing a piece of parchment towards him, he continued, "How well you complete them will tell me if you are ready and able to run the day to day of Wimborne. I have intentions to send you there within the week as I continue to run things here. Do you think you can manage this?" The words would have been thrilling if not for the plans he had to unravel everything at the seams. Still, going to Wimborne could work in his favor and give them more time to build a case against his father.

"You honor me, Father. It would be my greatest achievement to be able to take care of our home and our people," he said in all truth. It was all he ever wanted, that and Aleria.

"Very well then. See to it." He dismissed him with a wave of his hand, but before MyKhal could reach the door, he called back to him, "Oh, before you go...," he said, walking over to the wall and grabbing the golden thorn bow. MyKhal's breath hitched in his throat as panic began welling up inside him. Was he going to ask him to sell it? Destroy it? How did he know the piece even meant anything to him? Carefully schooling his features, MyKahl waited for his father to continue.

"I have been settling Lord Edlind's will, and it seems that you are the rightful owner of this piece," he said with an impressed smile as he placed the bow in his hands. "It seems he thought a great deal of your bowmanship to give you such a fine weapon."

Keeping his hands from trembling, he nodded his agreement. There were no words for how such a gift made him feel, but the first one that came to mind was "unworthy."

"I am humbled and will put it to good use, sir." His voice choked up a bit. "He was a good man," MyKhal added, knowing that he was towing a thin line.

His father's eyes grew sad as he nodded his head.

"Indeed. He will be missed. They all will."

Bile churned in his stomach, twisting him in knots. How could he speak of the Edlinds with such fondness after what he had done? How could he say the words with such grief, knowing he was the cause?

"Ali, she may not be…and Draven. You talk as if they are truly gone as well. Are you sure we can't mount a search for her? Maybe that would help Draven too."

His father looked at him with a pitying expression and shook his head.

"We will talk about this later, Son. For now, there are more pressing issues. Rebuilding efforts have begun, trade routes need to be secured, and the guard needs restructuring. There seems to have been an outbreak of animal attacks along the woods on King's Road. Part of your job is to enlist some local hunters and trackers, so we can better secure the routes. Perhaps on your way back to Wimborne, you will get the chance to use that magnificent bow of yours. Now, off with you."

MyKhal did as he always had and acquiesced without another word. Excusing himself, he nodded his head and clutched the bow to his heart. He did not deserve such a gift, but he would not let it go to waste. Without a second thought and with all his heart, he swore his fealty to the Edlind line. He'd renounce any gift or title his father bestowed upon him. Instead, he would devote his life to seeking justice in the name of the people who had shown him the truth, that goodness and kindness were far more precious than anything money or power could buy.

The ride into town was full of thoughts of the Edlinds, but moreover, how foolish he had been to spend his life vying for his father's approval. Especially when everything he had ever wanted was there all along. He could have married Aleria without his father's approval. They could have ruled Fayeharrow and Wimborne together. It was his pride and desire to please that took the opportunity from him, and he would never forgive himself. Perhaps if he had stayed, then things would not have turned out this way. He had yet to give up on the hope that Aleria had survived all this and was hiding away, formulating some plan of action. Knowing her, she was already five steps ahead of them and in Rimeheld's capital, rousing an army to aid her cause.

A small smile tugged at his cheek at the thought of it. As soon as he and Draven had the proof they needed, they would seek her out. He wouldn't believe her to be gone until there was undeniable proof. Though, if the day ever came that proved him wrong, he wasn't sure what he would do.

Upon reaching The Laughing Griffin, he found a message waiting for him at the bar.

There is a servant who survived and is willing to give a written account. The only problem is he can't read or write. I'll be taking the testimony down and getting a few signatures. Wait for me here.

-Lion

That was one step in the right direction at least. It seemed Draven was already busy and rightfully so. In the meantime, he didn't mind waiting here. The Griffin was a good place to find the hunters and trackers his father had requested.

It was as simple as asking the barkeep who was whom and paying for a couple of rounds of ale. It was as simple as offering a better ale and a bit more coin for the trackers to sign up. He knew very few men who would turn down such an offer and expected a few of them to show by the early afternoon. Grabbing a pint of his own, he sat in a corner booth and decided to watch people pass the time. He watched as barmaids flirted to guarantee a tip, and then, roll their eyes when a patron slapped their behind. He would never for the life of him understand how some men treated the women they were interested in. The thought of laying his hands on a woman who wasn't consenting made his stomach churn.

The scene and the setting brought him back to a memory from another pub here in Fayeharrow. Three years ago. The Silver Sparrow. A higher-brow drinking establishment for nobles and their ilk. Three years and the tourney to decide Fayeharrow's Champion.

Three Years Ago. Laugher and merrymaking filled the halls of the Silver Sparrow.

Lords, Ladies, Knights, and Soldiers alike devouring their fill of food and wine. MyKhal was sitting in his normal booth with a few of the other competitors from the tourney. Most were good-naturedly grumbling about how the contest was rigged. The Edlind girl was technically a cheat for not entering from the beginning. They were sore losers and would never get up the gall to say such things to her face, though. In truth, he didn't blame her for entering. It was a good opportunity to show her strength, to prove her ability, to hold her own as a future heir. That and to claim her right to kiss whoever she pleased. Though, he would be lying to himself if he didn't admit he was a bit disappointed to have not won that prize. He shook the thoughts away and took a deep swig of his ale.

That was a foolish notion.

She was like a little sister to him. A friend and nothing more. He made sure of that with his bone-headed request that they quit writing to each other nearly a year ago. At least she seemed a tad bit less miffed to see him this summer than she had the previous winter. It seemed the sun and time away had thawed at least a little of her chilly attitude towards him.

If he were being truthful though, it was not enough. A pleasant hello or a passing nod was not enough for him anymore. He missed her. He missed her humor and her smart mouth. He missed her fire and passionate talk of her dreams. He missed the comfortable companionship. The trust they had built over the years, but he had dug his grave, and pride would not allow him to go groveling at her feet.

He took another long drink of his ale and nearly choked on it as Aleria entered the bar with no small amount of fanfare. She smirked and blushed, waving her hands dismissively for them to stop their hooting and hollering. At her side, Draven was eating up the attention whether it was good-natured humiliation or he was just ridiculously proud of his cousin. Most likely both. He watched as Draven grabbed an ale and climbed onto the nearest table. Shouting to the crowd, he lifted his tankard in the air.

"Who among you would hear the tale of Fayeharrow's newest champion?"

Cheers and laughter exploded through the room. Aleria covered her face in sheer and utter embarrassment. He couldn't hear the words she was shouting up at Draven, but it more than likely had a few curses mingled in. Adding his cheer to the mix, he lifted his glass in agreement, grinning towards her. Her death glare landed on him, and he tilted his glass towards her in salute. He was a sad sack indeed; he'd rather have her ire than her indifference.

"Eh, then, settle in, friends, and I'll tell you a tale of a lady fair whose kiss is prized more than silver or gold," Draven began in a voice that sounded something between a pirate and a fortune teller. With an eye roll and a deep pull of whatever the drink was in her hand, she begrudgingly gave in. Always such a good sport.

Draven recanted the tourney's bouts one by one with grand flourishes and dramatics that were only slightly embellished. He had the entire room hanging on his every word in no time at all. The patrons cheered at each telling of victory and defeat. Anticipation and dread alike filled him as he waited for the part of the story that featured him.

"Through all the bouts, one brave young Lord rose above the rest," he said, jumping from table to table until he was standing right in front of MyKhal.

Creator help him.

"The brooding, the beastial, the breaker of hearts, young Lord

MyKhal Anwir of Wimborne!"

Cheers and jeers echoed across the room as MyKhal stood up and flourished a bow followed by a wink in Aleria's general direction. She hated it when someone winked flirtatiously at her, which gave him all the more reason to do it.

"And with that, the only son of Anwir gave his all and bested the villainous Lord Luther of Quent!" Luther was not a villain. He was a prat and an arrogant one at that, but villainous seemed a bit much. The only truth of the story was that he had indeed bested him. It was hard-fought. His ribs were still sore from a particularly hard blow he received, but he had won. They would have named him champion were it not for the next part of Draven's story.

"But!" Draven said in a way that built tension in the room.

"Our fair Lady found nothing swoon-worthy about Lord MyKhal the Broody and refused to let him win the day."

Awes and chuckles responded in kind to the sad part of the tale, and MyKhal played along and grabbed his chest as if the words had been a direct hit to his heart.

"Sorry, Friend. I mean, I think you're quite handsome. Don't you lot agree? I mean, look at him," he said, rousing the cheers and wolf whistles of the crowd. MyKhal raised his glass in thanks for the compliment, hardly able to keep the grin off his face. Aleria's cheeks had flushed pink as she took another deep pull from her tankard.

"But this wasn't about him. No, this was about honor, about pride, and no one taking her very first kiss."

Aleria's face grew five shades deeper as she covered it with her hands. MyKhal's brows rose at the idea that she had yet to be kissed. That explained the ferocity in which she fought him. That and perhaps she was letting out all that pent up anger and frustration towards him. Either way, she was a hellcat on that field. Fast, cunning, and as deadly as any man he had the honor of fighting. They had matched each other blow for blow until something in her eyes threw him off. Desperation, pain, and a rim of frustrated tears gave him pause. He would have never given her the dishonor of pulling his punches or throwing the match, but he would be lying if he didn't say what he saw in her eyes distracted him enough for her to put a blade to his neck.

"And with a grand show of dexterity, our Lady Fair had him by the throat. The arena collectively gasped as we watched what might happen next. But being the gentleman and good sport we all know MyKhal to be, he admitted his defeat and bowed to your new Champion Of Fayeharrow." With a sweeping bow, he added,   "Aleria Edlind!"

The crowd went wild with cheers and a few boos as Draven made his way back to Aleria's side. She punched him hard in the arm and murmured what he assumed were threats and promises on his life. Draven laughed and raised his glass again.

"Now, who will be buying the Lady's next round, hm? Perhaps you'll curry her favor and that coveted kiss!"

Aleria counter offered to the crowd. "Or the kiss of my steel. Which might not be worth the risk." Laughs and offers of marriage were thrown about, and Aleria turned down each one with a smile.

The night wore on, and drinks were plenty, but his mood had soured from watching her. Each lad that made a pass at her made his blood boil. Each smile or drink poured to earn her favor made him wish he had been the one to offer it.

When she mentioned needing some air and walked out towards the alleyway, he had half a mind to chase after her, but he was not the only one. Luther, of all people, headed out the door and in the same direction as Aleria. He knew she would have no interest in a man like that, all brute strength and no brains. Still, the idea of it irked him.

Moments came and went, and yet, she hadn't returned. His blood was pounding under his skin, threatening to burst if he sat idle any longer. With one last gulp of ale, he stomped towards the door. He didn't care if he caught them snogging in the alleyway. Perhaps that would finally douse whatever it was burning him alive from the inside out. Steeling himself and looking as casual as possible, he made his way to the alley.

There, pressing Aleria into the stone of the pub, was Luther, and he had his tongue down her throat. The sick feeling that hit like a bucking bronco nearly brought him to his knees, but the jealous rage that quickly took its place kept him standing firm. A tinkling bell of warning rang under the raging fog of jealousy as he stared a bit longer. Aleria wasn't pulling him towards her...she was...

"Ah! You bloody - !" Luther spat as he pulled back from her bloodied face. "You bit me! Oh, you're gonna pay for that." He grabbed her by the throat and pulled out a small blade. Aleria choked on a scream as he slid the blade down the side of her dress. MyKhal didn't understand what was happening, why she wasn't fighting back until the sound of fabric ripping hit his ears. She was unarmed, wearing a dress her mother probably forced her into for the evening. Rage like none he had felt before tore out from him in almost visible waves as he moved like a wraith behind the brute.

"Care if I interrupt?" MyKhal's tone was as sharp and lethal as the blade he had pressed to Luther's ribs. Luther froze but did not remove his hands or his blade.

"Nothing to see here, Anwir. Keep moving," he slurred in hot breaths Aleria could no doubt smell as much as feel. Drunk or no, there would be a reckoning.

"I've seen enough. If you don't want the people in the Sparrow seeing your entrails spattered down this alleyway, release Lady Edlind and make yourself scarce." The silver of MyKhal's blades refracted the light like a deadly promise. Luther slowly began backing away.

"Come on, Anwir. I was just having a bit of fun."

"Fun? Excuse me, my lady, but were you having fun?" The pitiful look on Aleria's face broke his heart into pieces and stoked the fires of fury simmering low in his belly. "Seems you have been playing with an unwilling participant. Care to play with me next?"

Luther sneered at him before more forcefully than was necessary pushing Aleria back into the wall. It took everything in him not to snap his neck or run him through. As Luther turned to leave, MyKhal moved as quick as a breath, pressing the point to his blade between Luther's ribs.

"Oh, before you go," MyKhal hissed, "if I see you anywhere near her again, you will lose more than a tournament. I'll be starting with the bell-end," he explained as he moved his blade to the target to make his point. "Maybe then, you'd be able to think with your brain instead." Slowly lowering his sword, he shoved Luther away from the two of them and focused his attention on the girl in front of him. On the field, she was a spitfire. All energy and calculated moves as she danced with her opponent. Sometimes, when he watched her, he forgot about her age, her youth, her naivety, and saw only a warrior. What he saw now was a frightened sixteen-year-old girl who had gotten her first taste of how ugly men could be.

She tried to push herself off the wall to stand, but her legs were trembling. As slowly and as gently as he could, he offered his hand to her. "I've got you. You're safe with me," he whispered, feeling more helpless than he had ever felt before.

Her shaking fingers tentatively reached out and clasped his hand. The tense silence broke with her choked sobs and frantic rationalizations.

"He was going to...I told mother I needed a blade...She said...She said I had Dray. Why did I need a blade? I should have protected myself. Why? Why couldn't I?!?" she screamed at him as desperate tears ran down her cheeks.

"Because you were ill-prepared and out-matched in size. Aleria, the real world is not a tourney with rules and judges. It's life and death, and one wrong move -," he cut himself short when he saw her countenance drop further into despair. The poor thing didn't need a lecture right now. She needed a cup of tea, some treatments for her wounds, and a listening ear. With a sigh, he pulled her closer and tucked her under his arm.

"I'm sorry. I'm not scolding you. Let's get you home, alright? I'll duck in and tell Dray I have you. Will you be alright for a moment?"

Nodding solemnly, she wrapped her arms around herself and shivered. As quickly as he could, he popped in and told Draven of his plan to escort Aleria home under the guise that she might have a sour stomach. He was well into his pints and easily convinced that all was well. If he found out what had happened, Luther would be face down in a ditch somewhere, and Draven would be on trial for murder. Two things Aleria shouldn't have to deal with on top of everything else that happened tonight.

When he returned, she was standing exactly where he left her. The lamplight shining from above made her image far more startling than it was in the dark. Her soft grey dress was torn from her hip to her knee where Luther's knife had slid through. Dark patches of red had spotted along the line; he had cut skin along with fabric. Her blonde hair hung around her cheeks where a bruise was beginning to appear, and blood was still smeared across her lips. He swore he could hear an audible crack as his heart splintered at the sight of her.

"Come on, Ali. Let's get you fixed up," he whispered as she tucked herself back into the safety of his arms.

The walk back to Fayeharrow was full of tense quiet until from the corner of his eye, MyKhal noted her staring at him. He raised an eyebrow at her curiously.

"Is there something on my face?" he asked half-serious. Aleria only blushed and quickly shifted her gaze downward, shaking her head no. "Hey, look at me," he whispered as he gently tilted her chin up to meet his gaze. "Creator, Aleria, your face looks horrible." A frown creased her features, and he realized too late how tactless it sounded.

"What I mean is, let's stop by the training yard. I know they keep some medical supplies in the equipment building." Aleria nodded her agreement, but it was odd for her to be so compliant. It was almost as if all the fight he had so admired had been drained right out of her. Once inside the building, MyKhal fumbled around until he found a lantern. The flame reflected against the armor and weapons, bathing the room in warm light. Dusting off a table near the medical supplies, he motioned for her to come closer. When she was within reach, he scooped her up in one swift motion and sat her down facing him. Grabbing a jar of ointment and dipping two fingers into the milky-white substance, he started rubbing it between his hands to warm it up.

"Ready?" he asked her before gently applying the foul-smelling remedy on her face. Her answering hiss of pain made him chuckle a little. "Suck it up, Edlind. It's not that bad," he teased her to lighten the mood.

"How about I hit you, so you can see how it feels?"

Part of him felt a small bit of victory at having brought back some of her sass. "You'd think a lady would be much more appreciative of her savior," he said, feigning indignation and half-smiling up at her. Aleria scoffed.

"Oh, so should I start calling you 'my hero' now?"

"That's what a lady would do, but then again, you don't strike me as that kind of Lady," he said absentmindedly as he began looking over the rest of her for injuries.

"I have a feeling I should be offended."

"You shouldn't be. All I'm saying is that most ladies don't wield any weapons apart from salacious gossip and torrid stares. You, my lady, have always been a breath of fresh air. "

She went quiet then, and for a moment, he thought he had said something wrong. An apology was ready and waiting on his lips when she finally spoke.

"Thank you, Khal." Blinking up at her, he couldn't help but lift one eyebrow in question. "I know things have been strained between us, and I should have been more considerate of your feelings. I mean, if I were in your girl's shoes, I wouldn't want you writing to another woman either. It just...hurt. Sometimes, it still does," she whispered, looking at her hands playing nervously with her skirts.

He didn't know what to say to that besides how much of an idiot he was and how it hurt him too. But instead, he took the coward's way out again.

"You needn't worry about her shoes anymore. Her affections lasted about a season before she and I both were ready to part ways," he said with a smile before moving his attention to tending the wound on her thigh.

"Oh," she whispered as she watched him intently.

Soaking a rag in a bit of alcohol, he looked up at her. "May I?" he asked, and when she nodded, he began cleaning the shallow wound. It was a struggle to not notice the perfect tone of her thigh or the smoothness of her milky white skin there. It was nearly painful to ignore how his touch raised goosebumps on her skin.   He swore he wouldn't read too much into the way she was staring. Or how they both were holding their breath for some unknown reason. When he finished dressing the wound, he dared to look and found pitiful tears rolling down her cheeks.

"I'm so sorry. Did I hurt you?" he whispered, stroking the tears away with gentle fingers. Seeing her cry was something he could never handle well. Even as children, he always felt the urge to fight whatever dragon or demon had invoked them. She shook her head and took his hands in hers, seemingly trying to find words to say.

"I wish I had never entered the tourney. I wish I had let you win." Her head hung low as her fingers restlessly stroked over his. The shock left him speechless for only a moment before he reached for her chin, tilting it up to make her look at him again.

"Why in the world would you say that?" He caressed her jawline and up to her cheek before pushing her hair back from her face and tucking it behind her ear.

"Then, my first kiss wouldn't have been...It wouldn't have this memory hanging over it...The feel of him my only..." She shook her head as if she could shake the memory of what happened away. MyKhal rested his forehead against hers, tangling his fingers with her restless ones.

"Ali...," he whispered, fighting the urge to take her in his arms and kiss her until her only thought was of him, until his kisses washed away the fear with passion and his touch soothed all her ills. But that wasn't an option right now. She had been through a trauma, and the last thing she needed was him pawing and slobbering all over her. At least that's what he told himself as he begrudgingly pulled back and patted her hands.

"That kiss was not your first." His smile was soft as she looked up at him in bewilderment.

"Yes, it..."

"No. A real kiss requires two willing partners. What he did to you was not a kiss, but an attack, and like all wounds, it will heal with the right cure."

"What is the cure?" she whispered hopefully, as if she could find it within this very room.

"It's different for everyone. It could be talking about it or beating a dummy to a pulp. It could be time or prayer. It may forever be scary when it pops into your mind, but you are Aleria Edlind, and no opponent you face stands a chance, right?"

Sitting up a little straighter, she nodded her agreement.

"Listen to me, Aleria Edlind, Champion of Fayeharrow. One day there will be someone who wants nothing more than to kiss you. Not because of your beauty, which you have in spades, but because he loves everything about you. Your fire, your spunk, your humor, and even your wicked temper. All of it will drive him to near insanity with the intensity of his love for you." Her eyes widened in rapt attention as he ran his fingers through the tangled parts of her hair, gently righting it again. "And if you love him back, he will kiss you in a way that erases all other kisses but his. Unless he's an utter dolt who has no idea how to kiss a woman, but even then, you won't care because you love him and -"

"Khal," she interrupted, placing her fingers to his mouth to stop his ramblings. Something in her eyes had changed as she looked at him more deeply than she ever had before. It was almost as if she could see him down to his very soul. "Don't break my heart again," she whispered as the tension between them pulled like a tether.

"Never again. I'm so sorry, Ali. I was a fool, but you were so young and -" Her fingers came to his lips again as she shook her head.

"There are far better uses for your mouth right now."

A breathy chuckle escaped him as he nodded his agreement and allowed that invisible tether to tighten between them. For a moment, there was a pause, a question still hanging in the air between them. Her breathing slowed and then stopped completely as she held her breath in anticipation. The sweetness of the moment was not lost on him as he made the first move. A slight brush of his lips against hers. Her shaky gasp made a satisfied smirk ghost across his lips before he finally closed the distance between them and stole what was left of her breath.

MyKhal was so lost in the memory that he jumped a bit when Draven plopped himself down across from him.

"On edge, Anwir?" Draven asked, waving over a barmaid and signaling that MyKhal would be paying his bill.

"I was thinking about Ali," he said solemnly as Draven slumped and reached for the tankard the barmaid had returned with.

"She's alive. I don't know how I know it, but I feel it in my bones. She's alive, Khal. You and I are going to restore to her what is hers," he said, brokering no argument.

"I hope so, Dray. I do. I'd suffer whatever wrath she had waiting for me just to see her again. Though, Creator knows, it would be hellish enough for me to eat my own words." His smile was rueful.

"You're sarding right. It would be well deserved," Draven added with a swig of ale and a stinging punch to his arm. MyKhal tried for a laugh, but it sounded half-hearted at best.

"Father wants me to go to Wimborne by week's end. That gives us four days to get what we need here and the freedom to search the estate for more. The only thing is your escape hasn't been found out, so you need to continue to lay low until we can get out of here. Be careful who you speak with. My father could have spies everywhere."

"We can do this, Khal. Four more days, then Wimborne," Draven said, tilting his glass towards MyKhal's for a toast.

"Then, the capitol." The sound of their glasses clinking together in agreement rang like a promise.

Larkin

Much to the chagrin of their human companion, the road to Glair was a full day's hike. The mountain passageways and rocky terrain were not an easy trek. At first, the human's stubbornness won out yet again, and she refused to be carried through the woods by anyone in the group. Her tune swiftly changed when a gnarled tree root caught her foot and sent her tumbling to her knees. He would have chuckled, if not for the low whimper that had broken through her clenched jaw.

Something about her had created a soft spot in his otherwise guarded heart. Perhaps it was her stubbornness and pride that echoed so like his own. Or it was her willingness to do whatever it took to regain her home. He could relate to that too. Those things had won her some respect in his eyes, but the softness of his heart was harder to explain. His mind kept referring back to the moment in the clearing. How she was swinging that blade with such violence, such precision. The way her blood and ash matted hair had blown in the wind and rain that he had unleashed around them. A cacophony of chaos, the two of them.

Her blade had even stopped a potential killing blow on his behalf when she could have run. This human girl Aleria was skilled, but moreover, she was brave. It was her bravery that made him curious to know more about her. Such bravery, despite her weakness as a human, was a marvel to behold. Though she could play the damsel in distress, she seemed to have full intent of saving herself.

Without preamble, Ruke picked her up and threw her over his shoulder. Aleria fought him like a wild beast before he pinned her flailing legs down to keep her from kicking at him.

"If you do not stop, girl, I will make good on your assumptions and eat you. You're lean enough to taste pretty good with a char. Eh, Z?"

Zander sparked a flame in his hand and winked at her.

Her momentary freeze of panic was enough to send the rest of the group into fits of laughter at her expense. Ruke patted her on the backside as one would an irritated child. "Nice fatty piece right here. Would make a good roast with potatoes," he added with a playful smirk. Larkin laughed and shook his head as Aleria murmured a curse, but didn't fight back anymore.

Much like a child, Aleria fought sleep until slowly her head lulled to the side, finding purchase on Ruke's shoulder, eyes drifting closed. A frown creased Larkin's brow as a tiny nagging feeling wormed its way into that soft spot. The niggling little part wished that he had been the one she had fallen asleep on.

"Something has changed." Nox's well-timed interruption was a welcome distraction.

"You know you and your sister are the mind readers. If you wish me to comment further, you'll have to be more specific," Larkin quipped. Nox frowned as the two of them watched the girl sleep.

"Do not get close to her," he warned him in a tone that signaled finality.

"I'm not," Larkin snapped almost too quickly. Nox gave him a blank stare.

"If breaking the curse required all her life-blood at this very moment, what would you do?" Larkin flinched at the idea, a sick feeling churning his stomach. Nox looked to Thea.

Unbidden and unwelcome, images of Aleria strapped to an altar assaulted Larkin's mind. He could only stand there while she screamed in agony as his grandfather flayed open each arm, pouring her blood into golden offering bowls.

"Stop," he whispered to the images and to the Fae woman who was spinning them. Thea continued to switch the images around, each one more horrific than the last, until he felt his knees buckle beneath him.

"Stop!" he commanded, shoving them back with a roar of thunder and a burst of wind. "You've made your point. Just stop," he rasped, glaring at Nox and trying to catch his breath, as the wind around them began to die down. Sometimes, he forgot how powerful his companions were. By now, everyone had turned around to see what was happening. Thea looked at him with pity. Zander and Ruke simply glanced between the two of them as if waiting for a fistfight to break out. Aleria was snoring softly, the sound tugging a tiny snort of laughter from him.

"We all have things at stake here, Highness. Do not let your emotions rule you. You may have a difficult choice ahead...if your grandfather even allows you to make one," Nox said.

Talk of his grandfather immediately sobered him, and he nodded. As much as he hated the idea of it, Nox was right. Bringing a human into Glair could spell disaster for them all if his grandfather wasn't in a listening mood. Still, he couldn't let that small hope go. He would gladly pay whatever price he had to if it meant saving his people.

Nox was right. There was more at stake here than he could risk by getting close to this girl. With sadness in her eyes, Thea met his gaze. She more than any knew what it was like to be alone. Her powers were the most volatile he had ever seen. A slip of control, whether in passion or anger, could mean death. She had learned that the hard way. Ruke was the only one brave enough to face the odds with her. He wondered for the first time in a long time what it would be like to have someone to brave the world with.

The cavern passage was muggy and sticky in the midday heat. A typical cave might be damp and chilly, but this one was lined with hot springs. The warm, bubbling water filled the space with a thick, rolling fog. Sweat dampened his skin, making his hair and thin cotton shirt stick to every part of him. The only thing that kept him from stripping away the layers was that Aleria was still asleep, and he didn't want her to wake thinking the worst of them. Besides, he would be taking part in the purification rite soon anyway.

The crossing, hidden behind a fall of water, was the gateway between his home and that of the human realm. The Elysian, a celestial being charged with keeping the balance between worlds, guarded the entry day and night. There were always checks and balances to their world, and the Celestial creature kept the balances check.

The Natmarra were the only creatures who were allowed to come and go as they please. An oddity that had been plaguing him all these years. In truth, he wasn't sure how many, if any, humans have tried to pass through the crossing before. Or if it would even be allowed.

His companions were already preparing by ritualistically purifying themselves in the hot springs. Taking a moment to reflect and meditate before passing through the barrier. He wasn't sure when the purification rite had begun, but it, like the Elysian, always had been and always would be.

Aleria was the only variable he was not sure of. Ruke had passed her sleeping form off to him, and it took all his self-control not to stare too long at her. It was such a dynamic contrast to when she was awake. The fire in her eyes, the readiness and pride in her stance, the warrior girl full of power and passion melted away in the throws of sleep. In his arms was a delicate woman, achingly soft. He begrudgingly noticed how lovely her mouth was... at least when it wasn't attempting to spear him with words. With a rueful smirk, he began gently patting her cheeks, beckoning her to rouse.

"We've arrived," he whispered, so as not to frighten her. A dreamy smile graced her features, as she snuggled deeper into his arms with a contented sigh.

Crack.

The wall around his heart took a slight hit. He steeled himself with a curse and patted her face again a little harder.

"Khal?" she whispered drowsily up at him, blinking away the fog of sleep.

Khal?

Who was Khal, and why was she whispering his name in her sleep? A sudden wash of feeling ran over him as he mentally chided himself. She could have a mate. She could have someone who...Of course, she would have someone who...*Mother take him.*

Why was he even thinking about her having a mate in the first place? It was foolish. He was foolish, and this was not going to distract him.

"I do not know a Khal," he said matter of factly as he tried to set her down on her feet. He wasn't sure if it were the pain of her walking again or the shock that he was not whom she had wished for, but she startled. Her eyes blinked wide and looked around for something, a weapon most likely. When her wild eyes settled on him, she relaxed slightly.

"Larkin, I'm sorry. Where...where am I? Where are the others?" Larkin held up a hand to stop her delirious ramblings.

"They have already passed through The Crossing. I stayed behind to explain to you what will most likely happen when you do." Or what he assumed would happen, but she didn't need to know how uncertain he was. By the look on her face, he could tell she echoed his feelings. Her teeth began worrying her bottom lip as she picked at her nails.

"Tell me what I need to do." Her posture was rigid as she looked into the living blackness before her. "I know I have little choice here, so just prepare me as best you can."

So brave.

"There is a being within who will see you to your innermost. It will decide if you are allowed to enter. It is not a malevolent spirit, so it should do you no harm. It will either grant you entrance or push you right back out here."

She nodded and took another step forward, but he held her back yet.

"You must purify yourself in the hot springs before stepping through," he said, not expecting the bright flush that began spreading from her neck to up to the soft curve of her ears.

"You're kidding," she groaned, but when he only stared back at her blankly, she sighed and shook her head. "You're not kidding," she whispered, running her fingers through her hair before starting to unlace her trousers. Noticing he was still watching her, she shot him a look that he didn't quite understand. With a twirl of her finger, he understood why. "Turn around, then."

Larkin couldn't help but laugh, but that only made her glare turn to ice and narrow on him further.

"You're kidding," he parroted her previous words. When she gave him a deadpan expression and stopped moving her trousers down her hips, he finished in the same way. "You're not kidding." Acquiescing to her odd request to avoid a fight with her, he added as he turned, "I hope you are aware that I am the one who dressed your wounds, and so I've -"

"That's different," she snapped from behind him.

"I don't see how this is any different. It's not as if I'll be leering at you or expecting -"

She cut him off again, but this time by throwing a boot at the back of his head. "I don't care. You'll stay turned around, or you'll get worse than that."

Rubbing the back of his head he doubted for a moment if dealing with her was even worth the trouble.

"You may be surprised to find that creatures in our world do not view clothing as much a necessity as you do here. It is protection against the elements, against the sword. On warm days like today, it is very common to see children and adults alike completely bare."

The sounds of water splashing and her sigh of pleasure were enough of a cue that she at least was following through with the rite. After a few more splashes and groans, she finally replied.

"I will respect your customs and not gape at your people, but that does not mean that I have to participate or shy away from my customs. All I ask is that you show me the same respect."

He pondered that thought as he heard her step from the water and back into her clothes. The sounds of her grumbling and cursing as she tried to slide her wet skin into the dry garments distracted his train of thought. Profanity never sounded so adorable.

So much for meditation.

With a chuckle, he thought again about her request. It was fair and honest, and something seemingly easy to agree to. Though, he wasn't sure she could resist the gaping bit when it came to people of his world. Nonetheless, when she permitted him to turn around, he stepped close to her.

"I will respect your customs as you respect mine," he said, reaching his hand towards her to clasp it in a warrior embrace. She seemed to not understand, offering her hand instead. The brush of his fingertips against hers sparked a tremor that shimmered from his hand and down his spine. Her large green irises focused intently on him, their hands remaining clasped. The way her damp, glittering lashes framed the emeralds therein was mesmerizing. What spellbound him further was the smattering of those dots across the high points of her cheeks and nose.

"Speaking of humans," he whispered completely entranced. He released her hand only to brush his fingers across the constellations of warm brown speckles. "What do you call this?"

Her intake of breath made him think for a moment that he may have hurt her, but when her eyes betrayed no pain, a masculine sort of pride and smugness filled him.

"A face? Nose?" she breathed, obviously confused and just as flustered. Larkin shook his head.

"No, the dots," he said, pointing at them one by one, making her pull back a step and clear her throat.

"Oh, freckles? Do Fae not have them?" she asked as she turned towards the glassy black darkness. He found it astounding that he had embarrassed her enough that she would face horrible unsettling darkness, rather than look him in the eye.

"No, we do not. Faerie bodies are perfect. We would consider such spots as a birth defect." Though his intention was not to be cruel, he could immediately see how it landed. He wished he could put the words back to his mouth.

"Well, then," she bristled, obviously struck so hard that she couldn't find something sassy to throw back at him. For the first time in his life, he felt embarrassed as he struggled for the words that could smooth things over.

"I see constellations," he blurted out and felt even more foolish for it. Aleria's eyebrows rose in confusion, but she still looked as if she'd tasted something foul. Clearing his throat, he took a deep calming breath before speaking again. "What I mean is I don't see them as flaws. I see stars. Constellations more exactly. Your freckles are...intriguing to look at."

Aleria's posture relaxed a bit, but her defenses were still in place. Her arms crossed over her chest. "Better than comparing my face to a birth defect, I suppose." She gave him no time to reply before pointing to the blackness of the crossing and saying, "So are we going to do this or not?"

Nodding his head, he came to stand beside her and placed a hand on her back. "Go. I'll be in right after you."

Walking over to the softly churning water of the hot springs, he began unlacing his boots. It was good that he had this time to think, to shake off the way she made him feel. So off-kilter. He had never been the type of man to stumble over his words. But with her, sometimes, it felt as if he could never say the right ones. Taking a deep breath, he calmed himself, releasing all thoughts of her into the peace of the rite. The steady sound of his breathing and the gurgle of the spring echoed in the cavern as he slid off his shirt.

A gut-wrenching scream tore through the silence. Fear ripped away all thoughts except for those of her as he ran barefoot into the darkness.

Blood and agony tainted the air so thickly he could almost taste the coppery tang of it. Death was all around him, and Aleria was at its center. The room was pitch black apart from streams of light shining down on three humans, drenched in blood. A sharp pang of pity hit him as he watched Aleria beg from her knees on the ground.

"Leave me be please. Leave me be..."

The voices whispered in unison something he could not hear. Whatever they said made Aleria wail and clutch her stomach as if she were in physical pain. He beheld the Elysian with its seeing but unseeing white eyes as it hovered close to her. Swathed in flowing sheer robes, it's hauntingly lovely femine form circled her. It's nearly translucent hand lifted her jaw to make her look at three bloodied humans. Their dead eyes stared back at her. Though the Elysian was not inherently cruel, its methods for getting to the heart of a person were not always gentle. Aleria closed her eyes, refusing to look upon the people, fighting the will of the Elysian as if it were any other enemy on the battlefield. Larkin knew that if she did not at least bend, she would either be held here until she did or not permitted access to the other side.

The Elysian floated around Aleria with all the slow ethereal grace of the other world, whispering things only she could hear. Each word pulled another wracking sob from her until she was panting on her hands and knees. The sheer fabric draping its form billowed in a windless breeze, teasing across her skin like a lover's caress. A contradiction to the chaos it was unleashing inside of her. Protectiveness roared beneath his skin as he dared to go to her.

As soon as Larkin stepped closer, the Elysian's eyeless face snapped in his direction, hissing a warning.

"You are unclean," it growled in layered tones.

"Forgive me," Larkin replied bowing low. "Allow me your grace, Elysian, and allow me to extend my own to the human girl."

The creature's haunting feminine face creased in a frown. It's bone-thin limbs stretched, reaching for him, waving a delicate hand over his face and invading his mind. From this close, he could see the dark pits where the creature's eyes should be, swirling with magic.

The creature balked, and with a curious smile that bordered on menacing, it gestured for him to pass. As he settled in beside her, she did not open her eyes. Her fingers digging into the hard ground of the cave.

"The Elysian simply wants you to acknowledge your pain, Aleria," he whispered, but she shook her head.

"I can't. If I do...I will break. I can't break, Larkin. I can't be weak," she sobbed between clenched teeth and ragged breaths. If she only knew how much he understood her.

"Acknowledgment of pain is not weakness; running from it is." His voice was stern, but not unkind. "Acknowledge it and let it strengthen your resolve. Mourn, then be brave enough to feel joy. If I've learned anything of you in our time together, it's that you have bravery ingrained into your very being. Bravery and enough stubbornness to rival even mine."

He wasn't sure if it was a sob or a scoff that burst from her throat. He itched to lend her his strength, but he wasn't sure how. His fingers began to tingle, reminding him of their touch only a few moments before. Taking his own advice, he accessed his bravery and twined his tingling fingers with hers.

"Be brave and know I am here to help share your burden."

For a moment, her hand hung limp in his. But then, with a sniffle, she closed her calloused fingers around his and slowly opened her eyes. The humans in front of her collapsed on the floor and tears fell afresh down her cheeks. Her grip tightened on his as she spoke.

"I couldn't save you, but I will avenge you. I swear it."

He had once uttered those very same words, and the irony that she would be the one to help him make them a reality was not lost on him. A powerful wind began to gust as the bodies disappeared and lightning cracked.

"Are you doing this?!?" Aleria shouted over the chaos, her hand still clinging tightly to his.

"No...this has never..." But his words were cut off by the sudden appearance of the Elysian. It's flowing garments whipped around in the brutal winds. It's mouth opened, a woman's voice, clear and echoing even above the storm surrounded them.

"One and one. Two of the same.
Blood by blood. Taste and claim.
Peace, come soothe the hunger pangs.
Peace, love, know we are the same."

Lightning flashed again, and before he knew what was happening, the Elysian was smiling and shoved them roughly out of the gate. He hit the grassy earth with a thud. Aleria's full body weight crashed into him, knocking the wind from his lungs. The two of them gasped and choked, trying to catch their breath as the Huldra surrounded them.

"What in the Mother's heavenly underthings happened?" Zander swore as he and Ruke bent down to help them up. Larkin stared at Aleria, awestruck with hope so fierce that if he had Zander's gift, he would be on fire.

"I think we heard the original curse."

Aleria

One and one, Two of the same.
The words of the Elysian echoed over and over in her mind.
Blood by blood, Taste, and claim.
She shivered at what that could mean... Her mind wandered as Larkin prepped whatever beast he had shot and cleaned in the wood. They had decided to stop and make camp for the night not far from the crossing in the shelter of an overhang. Zander lit up a flame that kissed the cold from her

skin. It surprised her that it didn't scare her. Moreover, she welcomed the warmth that drove away the residual chill in her bones.

She was also surprised that so far Glair did not look much different than her world. Though, perhaps it was the same as it had been with the Sluagh, and she could not see the true nature of it. Without thinking twice, she asked Larkin the question warring in her mind.

"Do Fae drink the blood of humans? Like the folktale of the Sanguinarian?"

Larkin chuckled under his breath as he placed some meat on the spit hanging over the campfire.

"Still thinking we're going to eat you, Aleria? I had thought we'd gotten past that."

Thea chuckled, and Rook grinned wide, flashing his beautiful, deadly teeth.

"Don't let the curse scare you," Zander piped in. "If I had to guess, 'taste and claim' has something to do with The Claiming." Larkin shot him a dark look, but Zander smirked in response. "Don't you think, big brother?" The flame wielder's smirk was positively simmering. Larkin looked as if he might throttle his brother where he stood, but Aleria drew his attention back to her.

"What's The Claiming?" Her question brought out a wide variety of responses from the group. Thea's reaction was the first as her cheeks burned bright pink, the color creeping to the tips of her ears. Ruke then took the opportunity to lean down, whispering something that turned her scarlet. Zander chuckled as Larkin and Nox shared a weighted look that she didn't quite understand.

"Larkin? You said you wouldn't lie to me." In truth, he told her he couldn't lie to her, but she wasn't sure he'd told them all that he'd shared such a secret with her. The thought of that night still made a warm feeling of hope permeate her heart. Larkin sighed, but said nothing. "Come on. Out with it," she huffed, crossing her arms over her chest. A low growl rumbled from Larkin's throat as he deadpanned at her.

"When the Fae find their mate, they take part in a ritual called The

Claiming."

Aleria shrugged her shoulders as if he had told her the current state of the weather.

"We have something similar. It's called marriage. We pledge ourselves, body, soul, and earthly belongings to another person. Sometimes it's for wealth or power, but it sounds like what you're talking about."

Larkin sighed again as if she knew nothing of the world, and it was his unfortunate task to teach her. "Though the idea is similar, to claim someone is...deeper. More of a commitment."

Aleria's forehead wrinkled, "What could be more of a commitment than marriage?"

It was Ruke who replied, "We share more than our possessions and our love when we claim each other. Our blood becomes mingled, and we share each other. Our power, our fates are forever woven together." He looked at Thea with a roguish half-smirk. The heat in his gaze made even Aleria feel flush.

Taking Thea's hand, he continued, "Our lives, our thoughts, our fears, we bare it as one." From the way, Thea's stare darkened, she could tell there was a history behind the words and what the two of them shared. The idea of it was strange, but so was magic itself. In a way, she found the whole thing the ultimate picture of what love should be.

"In our ceremonies, we say, 'Until the creator parts us by death'," Aleria whispered.

"Even death does not part us," Thea replied, tracing her fingers over Ruke's cheek. Aleria felt a slight pang in her chest, looking at the love the two of them shared.

"So...the two of you..."

"Are claimed," Ruke offered, not taking his eyes off Thea as he pulled her close and pressed his lips to hers. The kiss was all fire and passion. It made her remember all those same feelings from years ago...with MyKhal. Blinking away the feeling, she changed the subject.

"So how does one go about claiming the other? Is it mutual, or can someone claim someone else apart from their will?" An immediate tension filled the small group as everyone froze at her words. The tense silence was answer enough. Larkin looked at her with eyes clouded over with something she didn't quite understand.

"It is an abomination for the act to be non-consensual and usually leads to death in one way or another."

Aleria shivered at the thought of being forced to share a life with someone she didn't love. To have her every thought invaded, her very soul tied to someone who forced her to be there. "I can't imagine," she whispered almost to herself. Zander laid a hand on her shoulder with a smirk.

"Luckily, you won't have to. It is against our laws to claim a human. Humans are…" A sudden gust of wind blew Zander back, Larkin was glaring daggers at him. "She's going to find out eventually. Might as well be now," Zander added, holding his hands up in surrender. Aleria's stomach dropped as she looked between the two brothers.

"Humans are what?" she said quietly, stepping between them. Her ire grew by the second as the two of them had a silent pissing match. "Humans are what!?!" she demanded, shoving Larkin in the chest. The bulk of him didn't move nor take his eyes from his brother as he spoke the words.

"Humans are not allowed in Glair," he said through gritted teeth, and Aleria backed up a few steps, tension springing to her muscles, readying her to attack or run, whatever the moment called for it.

"And what is done to them if they are found here?" she hissed through gritted teeth.

"They're executed," Thea said simply.

Aleria felt her blood boil over as something inside her snapped, and she flew at Larkin. Her rage was such a shock to him that when she grabbed his blade from his scabbard, he didn't react in time to stop her.

"Liar!" she screamed at him, as she pressed the blade against his throat. Larkin's shock soon turned to anger, and he placed his hand against the pommel of the blade. She knew he could overwhelm her in a hundred ways, but she would not die like this. She would not die in these lands and be forever separated from her parent's souls. "If you knew bringing me here would mean my death, your oath was a lie," she growled, pressing the blade harder. Feeling the presence of someone at her back, she growled again. "Tell your brother to back off, or I swear I will spill your blood and not think twice." Larkin gave her a look and held up his hand for his brother to step back.

"I trusted you," Aleria whispered as frustrated tears pricked her eyes. A curse slipped from her lips as a rogue tear fell on her cheek. Larkin's eyes went wide as he blinked up at her.

"I stand by my oath. I will not let you die here, Aleria," Larkin whispered through gritted teeth. They stared at each other for a long moment. Her eyes locked on his, searching for any deception in his words. He didn't back down, didn't flinch, or avert his eyes. Aleria pushed away, but still kept the blade up in defense.

"And how do you plan on doing that, hm?" Her hands were trembling when she felt the soft touch of long delicate fingers wrap around her free hand. Nox had appeared like a wraith beside her. Her shock and anger suddenly slipped at the kindness in his dark eyes.

"It's going to be alright," he whispered, his voice echoing in her ears like it would in a large empty room, beautiful, ethereal. She dropped her guard. Her fingers grasped his and squeezed gently as a slow wash of feeling began to envelop her.

Peace, like none she had felt in years, flooded her mind and heart as she slowly relaxed. Creator in heaven, she could get used to this. Why had she not allowed it before? Somewhere in the forefront of her perception, she heard voices shouting, the spark of flame, and crack of lightning, but her senses remained wrapped like her fingers around Nox's.

"You've been through a lot," Nox said, his eyes connecting with hers, seeing deeper than anyone ever had.

"Yeah, it hurts," she whispered, feeling her mental walls wanting to gate themselves.

"I can help with that," Nox whispered as a deep sense of calm and euphoria blew through her veins. A gasp slid from her open mouth, and the feeling drew her deeper. Creator, all she wanted was to cuddle up in a warm bed and sleep. Even better if it were accompanied by a warm body...with strong arms.

Images and sensations of the times MyKhal had snuck into her room at night just to lay with her made her cheeks heat. Her heart fluttered. She missed that. Missed him. The ache that accompanied the thought slammed the doors to her mind. With a gasp, she ripped her hand away from Nox and pressed it against her heart.

"What did you -"

"You allowed me to," he said with a shrug. "With anyone else, I wouldn't even have to touch them. With you, however, you have to accept it. You have to let me in. It's the strangest thing I've ever come across. Though, to be fair, I have not come across many humans in my time. Still…," he said with a smirk, "I believe you are a rarity."

The warm, fuzzy feeling still buzzed in her blood as she remembered where she was and why she was so angry in the first place. Though, the fire within her had turned to nothing more than the lulling flicker of a candle flame. Turning to Larkin, who looked a tumbled mess, a bruise blooming on his cheek, she raised an eyebrow.

"Did I hit you?"

Larkin huffed a laugh and nodded towards Zander who was wiping blood off his split lip.

"No. A little brotherly sparring session seemed in order," he said, working his jaw bit. "A healthy disagreement, but we worked it out, right, baby brother?" Zander threw up a vulgar gesture and sulked over to plop down beside Ruke. The beast of a Fae ruffled Zander's hair, then handed him an amber bottle. The liquid inside sparkled burnt umber in the glow of the firelight. From the hissing sound Zander made after pulling deep from the bottle, she guessed it was alcohol.

"Speaking of a disagreement," his tone shifted from playful to serious as he tilted her chin up to make her eyes meet his, "I am sorry. I did not keep you in the dark to hurt you or because I intended to break our deal. I simply did not want you to fear what is to come. My grandfather…," he started, but then shook his head. "He is a difficult person. Old, set in his ways, and obstinate at best…spiteful at his worst," he said with a humorless chuckle. "But he has ruled Glair for over five hundred years. We are a prosperous and safe nation because of him. I know that he will do what is best for his people. Ending this curse would be something that could sway him. I have to believe that to be true. There is no other course of action in my mind." She hadn't realized that his fingers still rested along her jawline until he pulled them back. Clearing his throat, he closed his hand as her skin had burned him.

"My people are dying, Aleria. Whether by an attack or by being turned, they are in danger. The Nattmara are growing in numbers. Their attacks are smart, well planned. Not everyone is equipped to fight them, and an entire battalion of our warriors was turned. Trained, skilled warriors. The people do not stand a chance against them, and I will not see more suffer and die when I can do something. When we can do something."

Aleria couldn't help but let out a deep exasperated sigh. It would be cowardly to turn back now, and if she were honest, and the table was turned, she would have done the same. Though the two of them were from completely different worlds, they were so very much alike. She knew that desperation, that drive to uphold duty and calling. She also knew that this was the only way she could return to her own home with enough backing to take it back. A nod of agreement was the only acknowledgment she allowed herself.

"Never lie to me again. Even by omission. If I am going to risk my life for your people, I deserve to know the whole truth of things." Her finger pressed into his chest for emphasis. He looked down at her finger and then back up to her. Shock and then amusement sparkled in his eyes.

"Done," he said. Though, his mouth pulled upward, revealing that annoyingly attractive dimple.

Snorting through her nose, she huffed a growl, "Why are you smirking at me?"

He shook his head, but the twitch in his mouth was a dead giveaway. Creator, this man was infuriating. And devastatingly handsome, which was even more annoying. If he weren't so pretty, perhaps he would be much less disarming. One smile from his perfect mouth, and her brain strayed to wildly inappropriate thoughts.

It didn't help that he was kind and that he apologized when he made a mistake. All she had ever known were proud, obstinate, men who would rather choke on their tongues than admit fault. Draven, MyKhal, and even at times her father were extremely proud men, unable to admit or accept defeat in anything. So for him to look at her like that, like her trust mattered, like he expected her to fight back, to push him, it made her feel...

No. No, she refused to entertain the thought.

"Has anyone ever told you how devastating lovely you are when you're angry?" His smile was positively impish.

"Has anyone ever told you that you're infuriating?" she said when she could finally find the words to quip. His low chuckle did strange things to her stomach.

"Yes," a unanimous sound of agreement came from those around the fire. Thea and Ruke chuckled. Zander grinned, and Nox hid his smile behind a bottle of whatever drink they were passing around.

"Some friends you have," she teased. Their easy nature around each other warmed her heart and made her ache for those she had lost. Larkin tilted his head to the side as if he were studying a piece of artwork. "What?" she snapped, feeling a blush creep to her cheeks. Curse her open book features and her girlish feelings.

"You smile so easy, and yet, it slips away as quickly as it appears."

Was she so transparent, or was he too perceptive?

"I thought Nox was the one who dealt with emotions." A weak deflection, but perhaps it would work.

"You don't have to have that gift to see what's written on your face. I wonder what it would take to keep that smile in place before whatever ghosts that haunt you frighten it away."

Aleria balked, wide-eyed, the blood rushing to her face, making her a little dizzy.

"Why?" she choked a little and cursed herself. "Why do you care if I'm smiling or not?"

Larking started to open his mouth, but Zander answered from across the way.

"Fae adore lovely things, and while your scowl is charming in its own way, your smile is lovely. Stunning really. Wouldn't you say so, big brother?" he asked with an impish grin of his own.

Larkin rolled his eyes and mumbled something in that language she didn't understand. Zander replied in the same language followed by a vulgar gesture. Thea, Nox, and Ruke nearly spit their drinks out as they laughed. Aleria pressed her hands to her flaming cheeks. Creator, she needed a drink. Narrowing her eyes at Zander, she walked across the campsite and yanked the bottle from his hands. Before anyone could stop her, she tipped it back and took a long pull.

It was a mistake.

A huge, fiery, burning mistake from the pits of the nether regions.

Larkin

This girl was...unexpected.

Well, unexpected was the smallest fraction of what he could use to describe her. When she snatched the bottle of Fuisce from Zander and proceeded to take a large gulp, he couldn't contain the shocked laugh that burst from his mouth. Especially when her flushed cheeks burned brighter as she tried her best to swallow it.

To say that Fuisce is strong was an understatement. They didn't call it "Dragon's Piss" for nothing. It was pure liquid fire in your veins. For magic folk, it worked to heal occasional fatigue or the pulsing build of unreleased magic. Its purpose was to relax the power that pushed and pulled beneath their skin all the hours of the day and night. What it would do to a non-magic user, he had no clue, but it seemed as if they were about to find out.

A very unladylike word croaked from her mouth as she stared at the bottle as if it were a snake that had just bitten her.

"What in the Creator's name is this?" Her voice sounded like it had been raked over hot coals.

"Fuisce," Larkin said, choking down his laugh as the rest of his party chuckled and hooted at her. "Fae alcohol, and it's incredibly potent."

Aleria stared at the bottle again as if she were squaring off against an opponent. "Sard it." With a deep breath, she placed the bottle to her lips again and pulled in a deep swig followed by another hiss.

"Oh! Eh! Atta girl," Ruke shouted with a burly laugh! Thea slugged him on the shoulder.

"Don't encourage her. This is a horrible idea," she said, looking towards Nox who shrugged.

"It is, but let her be," he replied.

"Oh, this is going to be fun," Zander snickered, stretching his legs out and reclining against a tree.

"I agree with Thea. This is a bad idea," Larkin added as he took a step towards Aleria and reached for the bottle. "That's enough." But before he could grab the bottle, she held it away from him.

"You're not the boss-a-me, good sir," she said with a lopsided grin. "Some of this should help me sleep good. Sleep well. Well...sleep, ya know?"

He couldn't help but chuckle at how fast the liquor took hold of her human constitution.

"Uh-huh, I know," he said, reaching for the bottle again. This time, she cradled it against her chest like a child would a toy. Larkin snorted. She was adorable with that obstinate pose and slightly off-balanced stance. Gone was the rigid female with a sharp tongue and even sharper wit. In her place was a young woman with stars in her eyes and a sloppy grin. "Fine, but don't say I didn't warn you. You're going to regret this in the morning."

"Cheers to tha-mornin' then, darlin'," she proclaimed, raising the bottle to her lips once more and barely grimacing this time as she took a deep pull. Blinking her eyes and swaying a little on her feet, she giggled.

"Fairies do good drinks. There's gotta be magic in thi-sh. I feel like, well, I feel like I could fly." She turned a pointed look to Larkin and proceeded to make her way behind him. "Do you Fairies have wings? Like to fly with? That's what the stories say." Her fingers probed his back in a way that made a shiver of something tingle down his spine. Even though a part of him bristled at her comparison to lower Fae.

"We are not Fairies. We are Fae. High Fae to be exact. Fairies are much smaller. Some have wings; some do not. There are many different races of Fae, not all of them live in Glair."

"Oh," she replied. Her hands slid over his shoulder, and she walked around the fire to where Nox was sitting. He smiled at her curiously and scooted over to make room on his stone seat.

"Are you coming to check me for wings too?" he joked, turning his back to her to show her the proof that he was wingless. She giggled. Actually giggled, and it was enchanting.

"Nope. I want you to make me feel good," she purred, laying her head in his lap like a pup asking for a scratch behind the ears. "Will you make me feel good, Nox?" The wording and the fact she was laying in his lap made the warmth drain from him and a tempest took its place. Nox looked up at Larkin helplessly, feeling an onslaught of everyone's reactions at once. Zander, Ruke, and Thea were in various fits of laughter.

"Go on, Nox. You heard the girl. Make her feel good," Zander teased, holding his stomach and nearly choking on his snort. The images that danced through Larkin's mind made him want to roar. His magic beneath his veins bucking and writhing with his emotions. He needed to get away before he did something stupid.

"Thea," he snapped, feeling bad for his misplaced anger. "Would you mind sharing a tent with Aleria tonight?" A knowing look passed between her and Ruke before she came to collect Aleria, who was already slipping into unconsciousness. Nox made certain not to touch her as Thea scooped the human into her arms and whisked her in the direction of her tent. Ruke and Zander shared a look before heading off towards their tent. Nox stayed, his eyes locked on Larkin's. The tension in the air crackled like the magic beneath his skin. He had to release it or…

A rush of calm hit him from Nox's direction. His coiled muscles untightened; his body and his mind slowly melted into relaxation. The pulse beneath his skin more like the push and pull of a tide instead of the raw chaos of a tempest.

"I'm sorry," he finally whispered in Nox's direction. "Thank you for that. I don't know what came over me."

Nox gave him a long hard look before tying his long onyx hair back in a leather tie.

"I do, and it's unwise, Prince."

Larkin cringed a bit at his friend's use of his formal title. It was a reminder. A line drawn in the sand. A moniker, who he was and where his allegiances lied. This...infatuation, or was it simply fascination? Either way, it shouldn't be. He should have more control than that.

"She is…"

"Not for you."

"I know that," Larkin sighed. "We've already had this discussion."

"And yet, you reacted as a Claimed Male might. You know as well as I that your Claiming has been planned since your birth. Do you want your grandfather to have all the more reason to kill her?"

"No." The idea of that kind of wrath poured upon Aleria churned his stomach.

"And what would Oliva think?" The tone in his voice shifted into something more teasing.

"Mother help me. Do you have to bring her up?"

"Well, she is your betrothed."

Larkin growled and rolled his eyes.

"When we break the curse, and my father returns, there will not be a betrothed. I'll get to choose for myself as he did with my mother."

"The chaos that broke loose at that pairing was of epic proportions," Nox said with a chuckle.

"He loved her. He would have endured all manner of chaos to have her."

"Would you? For the human?" Nox asked, all jest gone from his voice.

"I…," Larkin started, but thought about it for a moment. "I don't know. How could I answer that when I barely know her?"

"Exactly, not to mention the issue of her humanity...and your immortality. How would that work?"

"The Claiming," Larkin said without thinking twice. "There have been tales of Fae joining with humans. Perhaps, the Claiming…," Nox shook his head as he stoked the fire.

"You've thought too much about this already. You're infatuated with her, attracted to her. You want her...so...why don't you just lay with her and get all this out of your system? You've had lovers before. None of them have stuck for longer than a fleeting romp."

"What are you trying to say?"

Thea was the one who answered as she stepped outside of the tent where he could hear Aleria snoring softly.

"He's saying you are a hunter, and you enjoy the chase. You have scented your quarry, and now, you need to attack. It's the only way to satisfy the blood lust."

"You've spent too much time with Ruke. I don't like how he's rubbing off on you."

"I quite like all the rubbing he does." A chuckle echoed from Ruke's tent.

"That is something I could have gone all my existence without knowing."

"That's payback for putting me on guard duty tonight instead of enjoying said rubbing."

Larkin smirked. "Would you have rather I pair her with Zander?"

A unanimous no came from the two of them. Then, a third from Ruke and Zander's tent. Zander was the only one who replied with, "Yes."

"She would most likely wake and try to castrate him," Thea joked.

"I wouldn't put it past her," Nox added.

"Neither would I," Larkin said as he moved towards the fire. "I'll take the first watch. The two of you go to sleep. Ruke will relieve me in a couple of hours which is another reason I separated the two of you. To let him get some sleep." Thea stuck her tongue out at him as she made her way back to the tent.

In truth, Larkin was glad that Thea and Ruke were claimed. Thea had been like a sister to him. She needed someone lighthearted and full of joy to balance out the darkness of her power. Ruke has always been the type to thrill at the idea of something dangerous, which was exactly why Thea was the perfect match for him. Very few Fae would allow such intimacy from the likes with her powers. She was a Spirit Breaker, a Mind Bender, and some considered her love no better than that of a succubus. Ruke said he craved the danger of her like a free fall from a cliff into the sea, that loving her was exhilaration like no other. Knowing that only her control over herself was what kept him from possible death. He was insane of course, but Thea deserved such mad devotion. It was commonplace for Ruke to say that she was his goddess. He would gladly worship at her feet for however many days he had left of his immortality. If he died bringing her pleasure, then, he would consider it his greatest offering. Again, he was insane.

Part of him envied that kind of affection. That mad sort of devotion that bordered on insanity. His mind immediately drifted to what amount of insanity led him to Aleria. Not that he was in love with her. No, he would describe it as fierce infatuation. Maybe deep admiration or simply mind-altering attraction. The attraction bit was as surprising to him as it was to everyone else. She was human. By comparison to Fae women, she would fall short in every aspect of beauty. Where Fae women were long and lean, Aleria was much shorter, but with curves that made his eyes dance up and down her form. Her waist was much smaller in proportion to her hips and rounded out at her backside.

He chided himself for even thinking of her backside when he shouldn't be thinking about her at all. Thea and Nox were wrong though; he couldn't have only one night with her and be done. Something about her pulled him in, made him desperate to know more about her. Being with her would only open his world to even more curiosities. Entertaining such thoughts was inviting disaster. Still, flirting with her felt too good to stop.

As if his thoughts alone had summoned her, Aleria stumbled from the tent. She only made it a few steps before falling to her knees and violently tossing her insides onto the forest floor. He grimaced, then sprinted to her side, pulling the hair back from her face as she heaved pitifully.

"I told you that you would regret it, and here you are," he said with a chuckle.

"Don't gloat," she moaned between retching.

"Just making my point. You should consider listening to someone older and wiser than you," he teased her.

"You've had hundreds of years to make mistakes. I only get a few," she groaned, sitting back on her haunches and wiping at her mouth with her shirt. "You were right. I was wrong. Happy now?"

"Believe it or not, your misery does not bring me joy," he said with a smirk.

Larkin reached for a rag and soaked it with an accumulation of rain water into his hand. Gently, he wiped the rag over her brow, her cheeks, her mouth. A slight moan of delirium was his only clue that she was still conscious. For a long while, the crackling fire and slight whisper of wind through the trees was the only sound until her voice filled the comfortable silence between them.

"What would make you happy, Prince Larkin?" she asked, leaning her head closer to his. The honest curiosity in her gaze made his heart do something strange in his chest.

"Breaking the curse. My freedom for just a little while longer," he whispered the words he had yet to tell anyone else.

"What would you do with that freedom?" she asked almost as if she were in a dreamy trance, her fingers drifting up to play with the leather binding at the ends of his hair. The movement felt so intimate, such a gentle gesture of affection. He heard himself whisper the words before he could think twice.

"I would do something disastrous."

Aleria snapped her gaze up to his, her fingers stilling - no, they were wrapping around the length of his hair. His heart kicked up as she used the strands to tug him closer.

"What would make you happy, Aleria?" he whispered as the distance closed between them.

"I haven't been happy for a long time. I'm not sure I know what it feels like anymore." Her nose brushed his, and he felt as if he were about to burst from his skin. "Larkin," she whispered, but then a strange noise came from her throat. Shoving his face away from hers, she vomited onto his breeches. A curse slipped from his mouth as he sighed and stroked her back.

"That's alright. Get it all out," he chuckled lightly, looking towards his pack. With a magic breeze, he tumbled his bag next to them and found a rag and a waterskin.

"Let's get you cleaned up and back in bed, hm?" Aleria's only answer was a pained moan as Larkin lifted her into his arms and walked her back to her shared tent. After a quick wipe down with a rag and a change of her tunic, he had her cleaned up and laid back in the pallet next to Thea.

A few hours later, Ruke rolled out from his sleeping arrangements and joined him by the fire. Ever the reliable second.

"You smell like vomit and Dragon Piss," Ruke sniffed in his direction.

"Aleria woke up," he said with a shrug.

"Ah, didn't even last till morning. I thought she was tougher than that," he joked, throwing another log on the flame.

"She's only human," Larkin said as he headed towards where Ruke had come from, but to his surprise, Thea exited her shared tent.

"She's having some nightmares," she said uncomfortably. While Thea was kind, her gift and the fear that was ingrained in her made comforting others difficult.

Larkin looked towards Aleria's tent. He told himself he would only stay to soothe her for a moment and then return to his own. As he ducked beneath the fold, what he saw made every part of him wish he had Nox's gifting instead of his own. Aleria was curled in a tight ball, clutching her blanket to her chest, shaking and sobbing. Her face was blotchy and streaked in tears. Dropping to his knees, he shook her gently, calling her name and wiping at the tear stains. Her eyes popped open, and she gasped.

"Larkin?" Her voice wavering as she tried to come to herself. "Will you -" But she wouldn't continue the question. Instead, she folded in on herself again, burying her face in the fur-lined quilt. Her form trembled and shook as her fingers dug into the blanket, and his heart cracked wide open. Slowly, he made a decision. An offering. Laying himself down beside her, he waited. Steady, cautious, open to whatever she would ask of him. At first, he thought she would not move. Her hiccuping breaths the only noise between them. He reached a hand to hers, a barely-there touch of his fingers. A question and permission. With a pitiful sob, she threaded her fingers with his and inched closer. He opened his arms and let her settle within them. The wetness of her tears soaked his shirt and pulled at a part of him he thought he had lost.

"You're safe with me. I won't let you go."

And he was shocked at how deeply he wished for that to be true.

Mykhal

Meetings.

Budgetary plans, rebuilding funds, staffing, mercantile, and trade discussions. Guards dispatched to investigate the series of robberies and murders. All the things a good Lord's Son would take care of while his father was doing Creator knows what. All the things he would have done were he to have married Aleria instead of going to Brennan.

If there wasn't all manner of bollocks to deal with outside of the day to day, he would have found joy in the mundane of this life. In the thought of running not only a Lordship, but a home. After Brennan, anything stable, warm, and not covered with blood and mud suited him just fine. His squiring was nothing more than mercenary work under the guise of soldiering. It was brutal, unforgiving, and full of despicable and horrendous acts that haunted his thoughts day and night.

Even with the circumstances as they were, he found himself falling into his position. He donned it like a second skin. The only skin that was not hardened and scarred. Here, there was only the specter of death and not the bright red of it that seemed to coat his hands. Here was a remnant of warmth left by those who had made this place home.

A warmth that had been burned to ash, he reminded himself as he found his way to Phillip's invaded study. His father had set up shop there now. His desk piled with missives, books, and ledgers both of Fayeharrow and Wimborne. Laying his notes from the meetings down on the large mahogany desk, MyKhal reached for the pile of open missives. His fingers couldn't move fast enough as he rifled through the letters and documents. There had to be something here, something with undeniable proof of what his father had done.

Part of him knew it wouldn't be that easy. His father was a careful man, and to leave such things out in the open was far too risky. Dropping the pile where he found it, he began moving about the war room. He tried to think of any clue to where his father might keep such evidence. A till, a receipt of payment, travel papers, anything to prove he was on the move the night of the attack. Bracing his hands on the desk, he stared across the room and into the smoldering fireplace. The crack and hiss of logs echoed, sparking a thought that made him want to punch through the old, well-loved wood.

Bloody nethers.

There would be no proof here. His father would have burned it all the same night he burned the castle. All his hopes in discovering anything were now in whatever was in Wimborne.

The noon bells tolled, pulling him out of his thoughts. He sighed a curse. He was going to be late meeting Draven at The Griffin. Apart from his nerves being constantly stretched thin, he at least had Dray. There were still a few touchy subjects that neither of them had broached. The subject of Ali was still sensitive, especially when Draven had come up empty-handed on clues to where she might have gone. The two of them had mounted their own search through the woods. He was glad they came up empty-handed. The thought of finding something made his heart constrict painfully. Flashes of her decaying body mingled with those he had seen in Brennan...Bodies desecrated, unburned, and left for carrion to pick clean. If someone had left her to such a state...

Shouts and crashes echoed down the corridor. The commotion snapped him away from his dark thoughts. The clang of weaponry and shouting making him break into a full sprint. Curses and groans of pain echoed down the halls in a symphony of chaos that beckoned him towards the throne room.

"What in the Creator's name is - "

The words froze on his tongue at the sight before him. There was

Draven amidst twenty men, slicing them up like dummies on a practice field. His shoulder-length auburn hair spattered in blood. His Edlind green eyes shining with blood lust and unhinged wrath. Time slowed as he caught sight of the archers in the shadows, noticing their arrows. His father stood in front of the Edlind's throne, watching the chaos unfold, cold calculation in his eyes. He was going to let this happen.

No.

He would not let another Edlind's blood spatter these stones.

"Hold!" MyKhal shouted. He lifted his hand, running into the fray and commanding the archers. They held. The soldiers stilled their blades. Even Draven, who looked more feral beast than man, halted at his command.

His father dared to smile.

MyKhal stood in the line of fire between his father, his father's men, and Draven, not knowing who would initiate the next bloodshed.

"Leave us," Lord Anwir finally spoke. The guardsmen who were still standing balked and began to protest, but Anwir silenced them with a look.

"Tend to your wounded," MyKhal said. His eyes looked towards Draven who was glaring up at Lord Anwir with murderous intent. Before everyone could clear out, Draven made his slow ascent to the raised platform where his father stared down at the two of them, haughty confidence radiating in waves.

"You lying, murderous, son of a - "

"Yes, I am all that, but before you run me through, there are some things you need to know." Anwir's gaze shifted to MyKhal. "Things you both need to know before you run off to tell the king of my deeds."

A cold sort of fury settled in his bones. His father knew of their plans.

"You set this up." The words echoed, snapping Draven's attention away from his father and to him instead. "You knew I would release him. You knew he would tell me what happened." Fury and a deep sense of betrayal welled up inside him, threatening to burst, as one word slipped from his lips: "Why?"

"Because I knew neither you nor he would hear me out without the other. Draven is an asset to this lordship, to the task I have been assigned. It would have been a waste to have such talents destroyed."

Draven hissed a slew of profanities that would make even a sailor cringe, but Mykal pressed on.

"What assignment?"

With a stone face, his father reached for the trunk beside the throne and slowly began unlocking it. "Phillip Edlind would not act. He thought my theories were folklore and childish fantasies."

"How dare you speak his name?!?" Draven spat as he rushed the throne, but MyKhal held him back. Anwir clicked the lock and pulled a bloodied burlap bag from within. The sight froze MyKhal to his spot. His grip tightened on Draven as he watched his father toss the bag in their direction. It bounced and rolled, revealing what was inside. The head of some abomination stared up at them through milky eyes. A creature with half humanoid features, one pointed ear, and the other half of its face was some sort of mutated, mutilated wolf. Bile rose in his throat at the sight of the half decomposed monster. Draven snarled as he leaned over to take a closer look.

"What in the bloody nethers is this?" Draven hissed, rolling the head with the tip of his blood-stained boot.

"This is what has been stealing cattle and horses between our lands. This explains the disappearances along the King's Road. And this is what Phillip said was nonsense."

MyKhal stared at the remains of the creature in shock and disgust. The idea that whatever this was had been roaming their lands for Creator knows how long sent shivers down his spine. What were they, and how in the world did this one end up with its head in his father's hands?

"Where did you find this?" MyKhal's mouth was dry as cotton.

"When my men mounted a search for Aleria Edlind."

"You told me she ran away with a pirate," MyKhal said slowly, carefully while Draven scoffed. Lord Anwir's face fell as he shook his head.

"You can't blame a father for trying to protect his son's tender heart." MyKhal couldn't help but laugh bitterly at the notion. He shook his head and looked at his father with barely veiled contempt.

"Like you did with the letters?" He knew he was being bold, but his father was spouting such heresy, he couldn't help it. Lord Anwir looked regretful, but shook his head as if MyKhal were a toddler who understood nothing of the world.

"Do not pretend that Aleria Edlind was not your reason for being. Do not pretend that her being here, blossoming and beautiful, while you trained would not have shaken your resolve to stay. The two of you knew nothing apart from each other, nothing apart from the world you built around yourselves. It was for your future that I stopped communication between you."

"That should not have been my choice!" MyKhal shouted, trembling with barely checked rage. "Don't dare spit upon my feelings by saying our separation was for my good. You and I both know there was more to it than that. You hated her, and you did it to break us both. It was cruelty. Do not pretend otherwise!"

"I understand you do not see it that way, but look at what you have grown into. Tell me, if she and young Draven had come for you, would you have not left everything and begged me to return?" Draven looked at him and rolled his eyes; they both knew the truth. He would have. He would have come home whether his father gave his permission or not. Anything to stop the pain of being separated from her.

"As I thought," Anwir said, reaching towards the trunk again. MyKhal braced himself for whatever horror his father planned on pulling out next. Draven, beside him, stiffened as something changed in the air. Sinking dread.

"The two of you are the most capable soldiers in all Rimeheld. The two of you would bleed and die for your people. Your blood runs for this land." Anwir's voice began to crack as he lifted out another burlap bag. "I need you to help find the beasts ravaging this land, the beasts Phillip Edlind would not fight at my side. Believe me when I say that Aleria and Erica were never supposed to be casualties. There was no other way to face what was to come, united by one goal."

Searing hate filled him as he debated wrapping his hands around his father's throat, if only to get him to shut up, but then, he pulled an ebony fabric from that same box, and Draven fell to his knees. He didn't understand at first as his father took a few more steps and handed the fabric over to Draven. The words he spoke made MyKhal's world tip and shatter.

"This was with the creature's remains. I am sorry. I truly am," he said in a tone that was more gentle than he believed his father was even capable of. Draven's hands began shaking as he pulled the bloody velvet of Aleria's gown close to his face. His fingers ran over the fabric as gently as he would have an injured pup. A sob broke free, followed by a scream of anger and agony that echoed in the near-empty throne room.

Aleria.

MyKhal couldn't breathe, and he turned away from the sight in front of him. Creator in heaven, no! No, it couldn't be. His feet were like lead as he turned to walk...somewhere...anywhere. He only made it to a support beam before the sick feeling in his stomach was too much to contain, and in a violent rush, he emptied his guts on the stone floor. Draven's roaring agony was still shaking the walls. It mirrored his own, but all he could do was sob into the rough wood of the beam. His fingernails clung to the pillar as if it were the only thing keeping him from falling into his darkness. It could be hours that he poured his sorrows into that wood. Time didn't seem to matter anymore. He sank to the floor in a boneless heap of raw anguish and heartbreak.

The ting of glass on stone drew his attention away. He slowly turned his gaze around to watch his father lay down two bottles of his best brandy.

"I am sorry, son. If I had known...," his voice caught, but he cleared it quickly. "I have never claimed to be a man with no faults, but the Edlind woman's blood will forever be a stain upon my hands."

MyKhal glared up at him through bleary eyes and uttered curses he had never dared to say. He didn't care. There wasn't much more pain his father could put him through, and he bloody didn't care what the repercussions would be. He did not wait for a reply, but instead, grabbed both bottles and made his way to Draven's side. His blood brother had curled up in a ball on top of the soiled fabric and was still weeping quietly. Reaching down under his arm with one hand, he lifted him to his feet and led him in the direction of his rooms. There were a thousand other places he would rather be, but his rooms were the closest, and Draven couldn't make it much further than that.

The splash of brandy against glass was the only sound apart from the crackle of the dying fire in his room. They were both soon three glasses in, and still, neither of them had said a word. As he poured them both a fourth, Draven broke the silence with a whispered rasp.

"I should have been with her. I should have gone with her." His voice sounded like it had been raked over hot coals.

MyKhal couldn't bring himself to look up at his friend. He only stared into the dark amber of the liquid that promised sweet and utter numbness. It had not proven itself yet, so he would pour another and another until it did.

"I should have come home. I could have...maybe...We would have married and run away together. She would be alive and...," he shook his head again as he took a deep pull of the fiery drink.

"Yeah, you should have," Draven agreed, mirroring his deep gulp. Running his hands through his still blood-stained hair, he looked up at him.

"She let you go that night," he said, sloshing the liquid around in his glass. "Your father said some asinine things to her, and it was the last straw. I watched her scream her heart out to you on the shores of Fayeharrow, and you know what I thought?"

"That you wanted to run me through?" MyKhal said with a self-deprecating, weak smile. Draven huffed and held his glass to his lips.

"That I hoped I would never fall in love like that."

MyKhal flinched as Draven laid his glass down and stared into it as if he were seeing something far away.

"Then, something hit me, and I thought of how her face would light up when you entered a room. How you would laugh so freely around her even after your father had roughed you up. How she seemed to heal parts of you that my friendship could never touch. You could push without breaking her, and she would rise to your every challenge. It wasn't puppy love between the two of you," he said, pouring himself another glass. "I've never been convinced of anything more than the idea that the two of you were soul mates," Draven whispered sadly as he took another drink.

MyKhal felt as if a lead brick were sitting in his stomach as he listened to every word. He couldn't have agreed more, and he knew it from the moment she fought him in Fayeharrow's tourney three years ago. She was his match in every way. Hearing Draven speak the words made an emptiness he had been ignoring for years make itself known. MyKhal lifted his glass as the room turned to a soft blur of warmth and utter emptiness.

"To the missing half of my soul, may she find peace and somehow know how much I loved her in this life. I will fight forever to find her again in the next." Draven lifted his glass to clink againt his in a toast. The silence stretched on for a while longer before Draven spoke again.

"I will not aid your father. I will not be his sword." His eyelids grew heavier and heavier. "But I will be yours, Khal. Whatever monsters you chose to fight, be it him, or be it them, I will remain at your side." Tilting to the side, he reached for a blanket laying on a nearby chair and wrapped it around himself. "If she knew everythin', that's what she'd wan' me to do," Draven slurred as he laid down near the fireplace.

MyKhal took one last swig of his drink before joining his friend on the floor. "When the new monsters are all slain...then, we'll take care of the old one," he promised as his eyes drifted close.

Aleria

Good, merciful Creator, she felt like she was thrown from a cliff and caught by the sea. The only solace was that she was incredibly warm. Bundled deep within blankets of furs and the softest suede and burying herself deeper in the warmth, she groaned and pressed her fingers to her aching skull. Larkin was right. She regretted ever taking a sip of that...What did they call it? Dragon Piss. The name certainly deserved the title. It tasted like fire and burned like acid. What had she been thinking?

Ah.

She remembered.

Larkin spoke about her smile. He listened. He apologized. He was making her feel things that she should not. Things she hadn't felt since... Well, since MyKhal left. Creator help her, she wanted to feel such things again. But this, this was a terrible choice. He was a creature of lore and magic, and she was just a human. They were the most beautiful creatures she had ever seen. If Thea was any sign of what Fae women looked like, she was certain he would have no interest in her.

Not to mention, he was a prince. The bloody prince of this world she never knew existed. While the twelve-year-old girl Aleria had always wished for a "Prince Charming" to come and sweep her off her feet, that was a fantasy. This was all too real - as was the new information that humans are not allowed in Glair by penalty of death. Yes, this was foolish. She was foolish. In her mind, she allowed herself to admit that she indeed had a bit of a crush on The Fae Prince, but it was just that. A fleeting attraction. A silly infatuation. Nothing more. She could deal with that and maybe allow herself to flirt a bit. Nothing would come of it. It was a distraction from the heaviness around them. A devastatingly beautiful distraction.

With a deep sigh and a stretch, she tried to turn over on her side but realized something was off. Something was keeping her pinned down. Her hands slid down to untangle whatever blanket had wrapped around her midsection when a sound jolted her. No, not a sound. A voice.

"Are you going to get sick again? If so, please warn me this time."

She froze at the deep rumbling voice mere inches from her. The breath of each word tickled her neck and made her skin pebble in the most intimate of ways.

Sard. Sarding, Sard, Sard. She didn't. Oh, Creator save her. She didn't! Looking over her shoulder, she clamped down on the gasp that barreled through her at the sight of Larkin. How in the world was she going to deal with this one? Should she ask what they had done? Should she pretend she knew? She reached down and touched her chest, feeling a tunic still there, and sighed.

Okay, not naked. Good. That's a good clue.

Larkin's chuckle was low and sleepy behind her as he removed his arm from around her waist.

"You are certainly full of surprises," he purred with a wicked smile, propping up on his elbow to look at her.

Oh, no.

"I didn't know what to expect when you invited me to your bed last night…"

Oh, sard. She didn't remember that.

The violence of her embarrassment made her feel a bit lightheaded as she cursed herself. A wanton, debaucherous part of herself hated that she didn't remember it.

"To think that you would beg for such interesting things was a shock, even to a debaucherous Fae like myself. Are all humans quite so enthusiastically depraved?" he asked with a roguish smile.

"Excuse me? What?!? What did we - ? What did I - ? You. You - ," she started, ready to smack him across the face. He had taken advantage of her. Oh, Creator. She was an idiot for thinking -

"Nothing happened, Aleria." With an impish grin, he added, "I'm teasing you."

Relief and embarrassment flooded her. Her body went limp in relief before she shot back up and smacked him hard on the arm. It hurt her more than him.

"You prat! Oh, I will get you back. I can't believe you would - Ow." A splitting headache raged, silencing her and sending her back down. "Does anyone do hangover magic?" she whimpered, flopping back onto the bed-roll.

"Afraid not," Larkin said, standing up and walking out of the tent.

"Hey! Where are you going? I was talking to you!" She started to chase after him, but was stopped by his head poking back into the tent flaps.

"I have spent a whole evening being a gentleman. I need a cold dunk in the river. Unless that is, you would like me to stay and teach you a few of those depraved things."

Her mouth dropped open, but she had realized by now that he was toying with her. "Alright, off with your trousers then." She called his bluff.

He raised an eyebrow, then a wicked smirk pulled across his face that made her realize her plan had backfired. When his hands went to the laces of his breeches, she squeaked and covered her eyes.

"Pervert," she huffed when her mind could form a coherent thought.

"Vixen," he laughed, turning to leave again. "I am quite the gentle-man after having resisted the charms of a beautiful woman all night."

Aleria rolled her eyes. "Don't patronize me." He was still teasing her, and she would be lying if she didn't say her pride felt pricked. Larkin turned, narrowing his gaze on her. An entire flutter of butterflies took flight beneath her skin as his eyes met hers. The heat there could rival the sun.

"Believe me, I'm not."

Swallowing hard, she stammered for another comeback.

"You're - "

"Handsome? Delightful? Witty?"

"A pain."

He placed a hand to his heart. "You wound me, Lady Edlind. Have I no amiable qualities?"

She couldn't help but laugh at that, but her smile faltered as reality momentarily set in. The flirty banter was a fun distraction, but it wasn't real.

"You're a prince. By every term the word could encompass." And she meant it. The playful smile slid from his face as he nodded. Both of them understood her meaning. "I think I could use a dip in the cold my-self. Care to lead the way?" It was a courtly deflection. An admittance and a change of subject. One he most likely knew well. His smile was soft and maybe a little sad as he offered for her to follow him.

"Where are we headed to now?" Aleria asked between bites of dried fruit. They had packed up camp and were filling their canteens in a stream not far from where they had slept. The dense trees shaded out the sun, only allowing dappling light through with every whisper of a breeze. The same breeze played with the shimmering lengths of Larkin's hair, making the free and bound pieces bob and sway in the most mesmerizing way. She nearly tripped from staring too long.

Sarding girlish feelings.

"To a village a day or so outside the city walls. Harnick. There's an elder I would like to see. I'm hoping she'll have some insight into this," Larkin said, offering her his hand to step over a fallen log. She snarled her nose at him, but took the offering nonetheless. The strength of that hand beneath hers, that fleeting moment of connection, left gooseflesh in its wake.

Stop it, you. It's a little crush. Act like you've known a man before.

"Harnick." She tested the strange name on her tongue and smirked at him. "Should I brace myself for naked Fae walking around?" The question didn't faze anyone, but it was Zander who answered first.

"Not unless you're into that sort of thing. I'd be obliged to make that happen for you anytime you like."

The following wink made her roll her eyes. "You and your brother are deviants."

"It's one of our better qualities." Zander's smile was so rakish she couldn't help but laugh.

"Being an arse is the only defining characteristic you have," Thea chimed in.

"That too," Zander said, blowing her kiss. Ruke stepped between them in that moment and pretended to be on the receiving end of the imaginary kiss. He wiped it off his face, and he glared daggers at Zander.

"Stop flirting with my woman, boyo, or I will sick her on you." Thea leaned up on her toes to kiss Ruke's cheek before grinning wickedly at Zander.

"And I bite," she added in an equally wicked tone. Ruke let out a husky chuckle.

"All of you are deviants," Aleria said with a laugh as she attempted to match Larkin's stride. "According to Larkin, I'll fit in just fine," she added with a knowing grin. A few good-natured "oohs" followed behind the two of them. Larkin grinned back, shaking his head.

The next few hours of travel were like that, bantering and good-natured teasing. Her favorites were the stories about adventures they had fallen into as young Fae. Strangely enough, Nox and Thea were the youngest of the group. By young, she found out that meant less than a century old. Ruke was the eldest with only a few years separating him and Larkin. Zander fell somewhere in the middle. With all the talk of years and lives lived, her nearly twenty years in her world made her feel like a child. Perhaps in their eyes, she was.

"What about you, spitfire? What sort of mischief does a lady get up to in your realm?" Ruke asked with an easy smile. Aleria found herself smiling back.

"Oh, nothing like fighting ogres and sneaking into a dragon's lair. I'm afraid my life would be quite mundane to adventurers like you." And she meant it. There was nothing she had that could even compare to their tales. Well, besides what she was living out in that moment.

"My cousin Draven was more of the prankster. He was always up to some sort of mischief. Most of my misadventures were spurred by him," she said with a laugh. "You all would have liked him."

"Would have?" Thea questioned, but Nox sent her a pointed stare.

"He...Well, he protected me. He was the reason I was able to get out to the woods where we met. Without him..." She shook her head and tried to smile. "I suppose I'm adventuring for us both. Creator, he would have loved all this."

"I'm sorry for your loss," Larkin said brushing his fingers across her shoulder.

"We all have lost someone. No need to feel sorry. I'm happy to talk about him. It makes me feel like he's still here with me."

"Feel free to speak of him any time you wish," Larkin said with a soft smile as they exited the woods and entered a large rolling field of wheat. It was so golden it nearly hurt her eyes.

"Wow. It's so beautiful," she whispered, taking a step towards it. The sheaths bent and swayed in the light breeze, making it look like the push and pull of ocean waves.

"Oh, you haven't seen anything yet. Wait until you see the fields of Blath Dearg. It's what Harnick's known for," Nox said as they made their way through the glossy wheat.

"What is Blath Dearg?" she asked, walking alongside him.

"Blath Dearg is a flower with healing properties. It's most common use as of late is keeping a Nattmarra bite from transitioning its victim. Without it, there would have been many more losses."

"Oh," she whispered as she came upon what she assumed was Harnick Village. The buildings were made in the same way she had seen Ruke create shelter for them before, but in a much grander sense. Instead of the basic four walls, these homes were all shapes and sizes. Asymmetrical earthen-inspired designs with windows and plants growing both in and out of the formations. It was a gardener's dream and an herbalist haven. Smells captured her senses in every direction. Mint, Basil, Rosemary. Some she was familiar with, but there were others. Warm, earthy, scents that gave her a sense of home and something cooking in a hearth fire. Only one word came to mind.

"It's so...magical," she said, knowing the word was not enough to describe the natural beauty of it all. Larkin chuckled and tugged her to him.

"Let's put your hood on, hm? Though the people here have no great love for my grandfather, he has his spies everywhere. I'd much rather you meet him on our terms rather than his."

Aleria nodded as he slid her hood over her head and into place. Again, another intimate gesture that left her a bit breathless as his storm grey eyes caught hers. A small smile tugged at his mouth before he let go of the hood, his fingers brushing the strands of her hair. How did even the slightest touch from him make her body burn and buzz with some unnamed sort of energy?

Blinking away the thoughts, she followed behind Larkin and Zander, Thea, Ruke, and Nox fell in behind her. There was something protective about their formation. Their larger bodies shielded hers from the curious eyes around her. It wasn't until this moment that she quite realized how imposing the group must look to those on the outside.

Leather armor, armed to the teeth, and an air of authority that swept through like a breeze before a thunderstorm. The lovely village's aura was the complete opposite. It was bright, delicate, and full of warmth. A picture of a dreamy spring's eve.

She took in all the beautiful and interesting-looking beings as she stayed within the circle. Some looked more like the Fae she had come to know. Others were nothing short of fantastical. Creatures with greenish toned skin and large almost bug-like eyes. Some in shades of amber and vermillion. Some short, some plump, and the tiniest little creatures with red mushroom caps on top of their heads. They meandered through the street, chatting in a language she didn't quite understand. Some spoke her language though; she wondered what the difference was.

"Why do some Fae speak one language, and yet, you all understand me and speak the same as my people?" she asked as they exited the center of the village and walked towards the outskirts again.

"Before the divide, everyone spoke both languages. Fae and mortals alike. Though, the lifespans of Fae of course, bordered centuries. Those who speak The Old Language are older than time itself and have passed down the language to their kin. Highborns are fluent in both, whereas other Fae speak what their parents spoke. Whatever was passed down through the centuries."

"Interesting," she said as they passed the last row of stone houses. Upon seeing the horizon in front of her, she froze, her mouth dropping open in awe. Fields of stunning dusky pink and crimson blossoms stretched across the horizon. A pathway was open in the midst of them, large enough for one person to pass through at a time. Each of their party members went on ahead as she stared, breathless with the beauty of it all.

She barely noticed as Larkin came to her side. "Blath Dearg," he whispered, leaning down to pluck a dusky crimson flower. Aleria watched in awe as the stem wriggled and writhed before a new bloom grew quickly in its place.

"Magic?" she whispered as he held the flower out for her to see it up close.

"They do not wither; they do not die. The only way to kill them is with fire to their roots."

"I've never seen anything so beautiful. It's enchanting."

Larkin's smile turned wistful and achingly sweet as he placed the flower under her hood and on top of her ear, his fingers brushing ever so gently over the shell and down the length of her hair.

"Enchanting."

Her cheeks colored, and she opened her mouth to reply. Instead of words, a shriek escaped her mouth. She went blind. Her eyes were seeing, but not. She felt Larkin's arm come around her waist as whatever was happening sent her to her knees.

A roaring thrum in her mind crescendoed as light and color whipped around her. Visions flashed in her mind's eye. A beautiful woman with pointed ears and long white-blonde hair. A handsome man with wild auburn waves, reminiscent of Draven. The images swirled and shifted to a field like the one she was standing in. A couple locked in a passionate embrace. They tumbled together in the field of dusky pink and crimson blooms. Blooms that dripped with dew...no...blood. The field turned to blood before her eyes. There was screaming. The clang of swords and sicken squelch of death. A silent scream filled her. Blood, blood was everywhere and a young girl...She was crying. Shoved in a secret door. Hiding with a creature Aleria had never seen before. A beautiful spider woman with many eyes. The snow-haired woman caught her eyes from across the room. Warriors were coming for her. The auburn-haired man bleeding beside her. Clutching a dagger in her hands, she wailed.

"Aon is aon. Fuil le fuil." The ancient words ringing as power slammed through the room. The snow-haired woman plunged the dagger into herself. The shockwave of it hit her, sending her flying back into her body. Trembling, heaving for breath.The woman's ethereal voice echoed again and again.

"Firebrand. Spark change."

Aleria's vision swam as her eyes blinked back into focus. Larkin was holding her tightly, staring at her as if she had gone mad.

"Aon is aon. Fuel le fuel. What does that mean?" her voice barely whispered. Her fingers clung to his shirt for dear life. He blinked at her, eyes full of concern.

"One and one. Blood by blood," he repeated, looking at her like she were something miraculous. After what happened, she would believe it.

"What in the Mother's name happened? You were screaming - "

"I don't know. I saw things. Lovers, a child. This field and blood. So much blood, Larkin. The woman killed herself after saying those words. What does that mean?"

He paused for a moment as if looking for the words. Hope mingled with worry in his tone when he finally answered. "It means this visit to Tiadona was the right choice. Come on," he said, helping her to her wobbly feet. "Are you good to walk, or should I carry you?"

"I'm alright," she said, testing her legs out a bit more. "Exhausted, but alright." His hand still braced her elbow as she took a step forward. "Thank you."

His concerned expression lifted a bit with the corner of his mouth. "Are you sure you didn't come back as someone else? I'm suspicious of you thanking me for anything."

Aleria snarled her nose at him and resisted the urge to stick out her tongue. "I am the picture of politeness and etiquette...when it's deserved," she quipped over her shoulder as they continued down the flora-surrounded path. Larkin chuckled and followed along close beside her.

"And what would one need to do to be so deserving?"

The way he phrased the question made her look up at him.

"Well, that depends. What are you hoping to be deserving of, Prince?" The question was a challenge. A dare phrased as a tease. A chance to acknowledge the strange pull. The unspoken attraction. The kinship. He took longer than she would like to reply, but when he did, shivers scattered like stars across her skin.

"A woman I have no business wanting." The conflict in his voice made her heart sink, but she pressed on. It was still a non-answer. This was a courtly interaction. Delicate deflections.

"And why would you want such a woman if your judgment tells you that you should not?" The roseate hue of the flowers glowing in the waning of the sun, her eyes remained on the field in front of them, but her heart was in her throat.

"Some would say it is the lure of forbidden fruit," he said as if the conversation were about something as simple as the color of the sky. The words hurt her pride. "But I know it is because she is unlike any creature I've had the honor to know. She's brave, beautiful, kind...when it's deserved." Turning to look in her eyes, he confessed, "And sometimes, even when it isn't." Heat coursed through her veins, flooding her cheeks with warmth. A constant state around him, it seemed.

"And why do you not think you deserve her? Why don't you...pursue her?" she dared to ask with bated breath. Oh, Creator help her, this was too much.

"Most likely some of the same reasons she has come up with in her mind. Reasons that are valid concerns. Lines are drawn that neither she nor I can cross without fear of harming the other."

"How in the world could I...she harm you?"

A small, sad smile crept across his face.

"By leaving. Which she is bound to do in one way or another." Aleria didn't refute his claim. How could she? He was right.

"And how could you hurt her?"

He laughed bitterly. "There are too many ways to number. Do you understand the amount of control I need to touch you as I do?" All pretense dropped. The courtly game had come to an end as passion, the enemy of control, washed over his features. His powerful body ate up the space between them. "Our powers are tied to our emotions. One slip of control, whether in anger or even in passion, could hurt or even kill you. An immortal could handle it. Perhaps even enjoy it...but you...you could die. You will die eventually, and I will not, unless it is by a violent end." He was barely a hair's breadth from her. She could almost feel the rise and fall of his chest. The power of him radiating like the same crackling energy before lightning strikes. Static enough to make her hair stand on end. Still, she looked up at him and breathed a reply.

"And what if she isn't afraid?"

A throaty chuckle fell from his lips as he rubbed his hand over his face and sighed.

"I wouldn't expect any less from her. She is foolishly brave, hellishly annoying, and achingly lovely." He whispered, leaning closer, "But I didn't answer your question did I?" She shook her head, feeling the sparks between them brush over her skin. Slowly, carefully, he lifted his hand and slid it beneath her chin. The first touch of his fingers was nothing short of electric. His silver moon eyes locked on her as he leaned in again. "If she were not afraid...I would lay her down in this field and - "

"Hey! You two coming or what? Sun's going down," Zander called from a little way down the path. Larkin let out an annoyed sigh as his hand dropped from her face and flew up in a fowl gesture at his brother. The spell between them broke in an instant, and Aleria couldn't help but burst out laughing. A real true laugh, the fear of the visions before dissipating with that gentle touch of humor. Larkin rolled his eyes and took her hand.

"Come on."

Chapter 15

Mykhal

A week.

Or maybe it was more than a week. He hadn't been counting the days. Most of the time, one moment bled into another. Or even skipped entirely due to the amount of alcohol he and Draven consumed as they mourned.

This could not be how things ended. He wouldn't allow it. This wouldn't be what she would have wanted for them, for her home, her people. A muddled formulation of a plan drifted in and out of his drink addled brain. They would eradicate the beasts that murdered Aleria. Then, they would handle the monster in their home.

It didn't matter that he was his father. Any excuse he could have made was rung from him the moment he found out Aleria was well and truly gone. His father had said that her death was not part of the plan, but the thought didn't ring true to him. No matter how he wished to believe it. The cold numbness running through his veins shut him off from any relational feeling. While part of him felt a deep sense of loss, he was almost thankful for it. The only thing that kept him from falling into the darkness of the emotional abyss was seeing Draven and Aleria every day.

At first, he thought that he might be going crazy. All the times she showed up in his room or in the cell with Draven, he thought that his mind was playing tricks on him. He had met a man once who suffered from what they called "war sickness." The things he saw were not sweet, not like how he was seeing Aleria. The vision of her didn't speak in the beginning, but now...Creator, it was as if she were standing beside him. The only odd thing about it was that she remained how he once knew her. A beautiful young lady on the edge of sixteen and not the woman of nearly twenty whose life was snuffed out like a lonely candle.

Shaking off his dark thoughts, he crossed the courtyard and made his way to the practice field. It was places like these where he tended to see her more often, so it wasn't a shock when she stepped out of the old weapons shed, a huge grin on her face just for him. The cold in his veins melted a little at the sight, and a small smile lifted the corner of his mouth. He had lost his mind, but when she smiled at him like that, he couldn't find it in himself to care.

Her long blonde hair tied back in a messy braid, she sported her usual sparring attire, a white tunic tucked into a pair of dark tan breeches. "Good day, young Lord Howe. How are you fairing this fine morning?" Her voice held a playfulness that made his smile stretch fully from cheek to cheek. He wasn't a fool though, and she knew the rules. He couldn't speak to her so openly in public, lest everyone confirm his insanity or think him possessed. Instead, he nodded his head towards her and walked inside the weapons shed. Draven was meeting him here for a morning session before they started training recruits and scouts. If they were to go out and hunt those creatures, they needed to be prepared with both warriors and hunters alike. Every man needed to wield a sword and know how to use it.

Aleria's spirit leaned against the wall next to the weapons rack as he perused the weaponry, mulling over what they would need to be training with that day.

"No hi, no hug, nothing? Wow, you certainly know how to make a girl feel missed." The words hit him like a fist to the gut, and he cut his eyes towards her. For her to use exact words from the moment he told her he must leave her was more painful than he cared to admit.

155

"Are you here to haunt me?" he asked her without looking in her direction. It hurt too much at the moment.

"You ask me that every day, and every day, I say the same. I wouldn't be here unless you wanted me to be. You miss me," she quipped, crossing from her position on the wall and taking a step closer to him.

"And so the Creator just let you out of the heavens because I miss you?" he joked, but wished that was the truth of it.

"We aren't that loved by Him," her voice was sad as she leaned over his shoulder to watch what he was doing. MyKhal chuckled and shook his head.

"You are loved by Him, and that is the only thing He and I have in common."

Aleria's voice turned wistful as she whispered over his shoulder, "A poet and a priest. I think you chose the wrong profession."

MyKhal shook his head and picked up a sword.

"I'm too unforgiving and too loveless to be a priest or a poet. I'll stick with what I know best," he said, attaching the scabbard to his belt and reaching for a bow.

"You know me," she said with a soft smile, and he stopped his perusal to look at her.

"No actually, I don't think I do...I mean, look at you. This is how you looked when I left. What are you like now?" he asked, but right as the words were out of his mouth, he regretted them immediately. Aleria's spirit body began to decompose right before his eyes. She was missing an arm, and her eyes were grey and lifeless. Her long blonde hair was matted with blood and gore, and claw marks marred her greyish toned skin. With a hiss, he stepped back, drawing his sword on her, not knowing how he would fight such a thing or if he even could. Bile rose to the back of his throat, and he felt as if he were about to retch. Then, in a blink, she was back to sixteen and looking at him with wide innocent eyes, those evergreen eyes that slayed him.

MyKhal let out a series of curses in her direction before he could get a hold of himself long enough to make a coherent sentence.

"You said you're only here because I want you to be, so...I need you to go. You've...you've gotta go." Aleria took a step towards him, and he held out a trembling hand to stop her.

"Go!" he roared, not daring to look at her again. His eyes widened when he saw Draven standing where she once was.

"Sard," Draven's voice cut through MyKhal's horror as he stepped through the door. His hands raised in surrender, he approached like one would a startled horse. MyKhal worked to catch his breath while trying to wipe the image of Aleria's decayed body from his mind. His hands were still trembling as he ran them through his greasy locks. How long had it been since he washed his hair?

"Sorry," MyKhal breathed as he stood up and threw the bow in his hands over his shoulder.

"Nerves are on edge?"

MyKhal murmured a curt, "Yeah," brushing past Draven. He needed to shoot something, do something other than standing there with trembling hands and a frayed mind. Taking his stance in front of the targets, he took a deep steadying breath. There was something about the calm archery invoked in him, the way it cleared his mind and slowed his heart to a crawl of calm steadiness. This had been and always would be his weapon of choice. The thoughts of the magnificent bow sitting idly up in his room made him feel a bit forlorn. Such a magnificent piece didn't deserve to be hung up on a shelf. It was made to be in the fray. And so it would be when he, Draven, and the ragtag group of men they were putting together would seek and destroy the beasts that had stolen something so precious from them both.

Thwack.

The arrow buried itself deep in the red-lined target across from him.

Thwack.

Another landed, and the tension in his shoulder's released a bit.

Thwack.

A girlish, frustrated huff and the sound of his rough laughter echoed in his mind. He shook his head and breathed out again.

Thwack.

The arrow flew forward, and his mind went back to three years ago...

"I'm never going to get this," she huffed.

"You give up too easily." His voice held the barest of teases as he pulled the bow back up and kicked her feet apart. His arms wrapped around her, but only enough to adjust her hold before he stepped back to a proper distance.

"I do not. You give up too easily," she quipped back at him, the simmering heat in her tone making him cock an incredulous eyebrow.

"Me?"

"You," she shot back, keeping her eye on the target and releasing an arrow. It landed, but was far from the inside of the ring. Aleria cursed. He chuckled under his breath, trying to hide his amusement at her frustration.

"We aren't talking about archery anymore, are we?"

Thwack.

"Why haven't you kissed me again?" she asked, lowering her bow and pinning him with an inquisitive stare full of hurt and confusion. He felt his heart shudder and skid before kicking up like wild stallions across dry ground. He wasn't exactly sure what to say, but Creator have mercy on his soul, he wanted to kiss her again. He wanted to do more than kiss her, but that was not what she was asking. Opening his mouth, he tried to find the words to explain.

"That night. You...It was full of...It was traumatic for you, and I wasn't sure...I just..."

Creator, he was sarding this up, and by the look on her face, those were not the right words he was vomiting up.

"You felt bad for me. It was a pity kiss, and you regret it, right?" Her forest green eyes were boring a hole into him, anger and something else shimmering in their depths. Something welled up within him as he locked his eyes on hers. It demanded he clear the air no matter how complicated this made his life. He knew having feelings for this girl would most certainly complicate things. She was wild, opinionated, strong-willed, beautiful, whip-smart, and...absolutely everything he had ever wanted. Someone to challenge him, to push him, to make him a better man than his father. Was that too much to lay at sixteen year old's feet? He certainly thought so, so instead of saying too many words, he settled on one.

"Never."

Erasing the propitious space between them in one long stride, he slid one hand behind her back and the other at the nape of her neck as he pulled her to himself. She gasped a little and looked up into his eyes. All hope and promises of more shining there, drawing him like a lonely moth to the burning warmth of her flame. He whispered, brushing his lips over her in the breathless promise.

"Never will I regret you."

A mumble of words shook him from the memory as another thwack echoed across the training field.

"Hm?" he asked, turning his head to the only person who would dare interrupt his thoughts.

"You're thinking about her again," Draven said with a slight hint of annoyance in his voice. "You told me we can't keep - "

"I know what I said," he interrupted, and then, groaned, and scrubbed a hand across his scruffy face.

"I'm sorry. I was wrong to say that to you because I can't get her out of my head either. Maybe we should keep thinking about her. Remind ourselves what we're doing all this for. Who we're doing all this for."

Draven raised his brow at him and nodded, "She was my family, my best friend, and one of the best humans I've ever known. I feel like trying to push down these thoughts of her isn't doing us any good either. She'd want us to remember her and think of her often. In that way, doesn't that keep her a little bit alive? Give her a toe hold still in this world?"

From the corner of his eye, he saw her leaning against a post of the fence surrounding the practice field. Her long honeyed locks whipping around her in the wind. Maybe that was why she was still here. It was their memories that kept her spirit with them a little while longer.

"Tell me what she was like. How she changed since I last saw her," MyKhal asked softly, staring off into the distance at the sixteen-year-old he once remembered.

Draven rubbed along his scruffy jaw, looking as if he wasn't quite sure where to start.

"I'm not sure what to tell you exactly. I'm sure you and I didn't look at her quite the same."

MyKhal chuckled and shot him a wry look. "Thank the Creator for that."

Draven punched him in the shoulder and added a shove for good measure. "Letcher, you better be glad I even halfway approved of the way you looked at her. If I wasn't certain it was love and not you wanting to get into her breeches, I'd have you drawn and quartered." His smile was vicious, and MyKhal raised his hands in surrender.

"You know I loved her." Still do love her.

"I do," he answered as he walked over to the fence and climbed up to have a seat on top of the large wooden cross-sections. Crossing his freckled arms, he looked off into the distance.

"She was pretty and scrawny when you knew her. Of course, that was a deception because she was fast as lightning and could have a blade at your throat before you could comment on how pretty she was," he said with a chuckle. "But you knew all that," Draven added, casting him a look before picking up his sword and running his hands over it. He tossed it from palm to palm. A nervous habit. MyKhal nodded, his eyes still looking at the girl in the distance.

"She grew up though, as we all do. If you thought she was independent before…," he breathed a low whistle and shook his head.

"She grew into her role here. Balancing the line of woman and warrior better than any I've seen before. She didn't get any taller, but I don't know...She looked..not like a girl as much, you know? Creator, it's weird describing her," he said with a huff. "She had to chop her hair off about chin length once. A prank went bad that had to do with some tar and feathers. Her mother was furious, but Al took it all in stride. Didn't make her any less pretty though. It had grown out about shoulder length before...," his thoughts drifted off, and he quickly wiped at his eyes before hopping off the fence. The sixteen-year-old on the hill aged before his eyes, her shoulder-length blonde hair whipping in front of her face, nearly obscuring her features. All but those green eyes that still staggered him. "I was proud of her. Proud to serve beside her. I should have protected her better," Draven confessed as he stood up straight. Their men were arriving, and there was no more time to speak of her so openly. "I will not shame her memory by wallowing in that mistake anymore. I'm going to bring her honor, glory, and the head of every one of those beasts I can manage. I'll make that offering to her, and hopefully, she'll forgive my sins against her."

MyKhal wanted to interject that she would have already forgiven him. That there was nothing he could have done differently, but that wasn't what he needed. They both needed something to wake up for every day. Something to drive them forward in this life that felt all the more lonely and dark without her ever-present, blinding light. As the girl on the hill looked down at him with a soft smile and a reassuring nod, he faced the men they had gathered. A wicked, determined smirk pulled across his features. He hoped it came across as inspired and not insane.

"Let's fan some of the flames she left burning," MyKhal said.

The intensity of Draven's eyes matched MyKhal's as he stepped in front of him to address the men filtering in. Some were hunters, trackers, a few soldiers. Some were green boys who didn't know their pommel from the blade. But beggars couldn't be choosers in their situation.

"Brothers of Fayeharrow," Draven started with his arms open wide. "I know you all may think I've lost what little mind I once had. Especially if you've heard the reasoning behind this assemblage of you lot." He looked across the field where thirty plus men had gathered. A small number, for now, was fine. They needed to flush out the beasts and find where their den was first. He only hoped there wasn't a whole hoard of them amassed together.

Some of these men were top of the crop. Former soldiers loyal to Draven, even if they had no sarding clue why he would be working with MyKhal. Their loyalty knew no bounds. The rest was a hodgepodge of trackers, greenhorns, and some who he was certain were as insane as Draven seemed. A wicked smirk crossed his friend's countenance as he continued, "Maybe I have lost my mind. There are some days I hope it will be true, that my cousin would still be here. I'd much rather be seeing her running over that hill, ready to take a piece of any one of you in that ring." A couple of men chuckled and nodded their heads. Part of him felt slighted, even these men knew Aleria more than he did now. "But when you see the bloody truth staring you down in the face, insanity is mercy. Mercy I was not granted! Instead, this haunts my dreams." The men burst into murmurs and gags as he threw out the decomposed head that was half humanoid and half monster.

"These things took my family from me," he growled through gritted teeth. "Anwir is a snake, and I swear to the Creator I will deal with him later, but Khal…" He glanced at him as he spoke. "He loved our lady fiercely. I do not doubt in my mind that he would have laid down his life for her. Just as I would have. Just as she would for Fayeharrow. For you... her people. If she were here today and knew of these creatures, she would be standing beside us, fighting. She would spill her blood next to yours. She would cheer you, inspire you, tend your wounds because that's who she was. And if she were here, she would say the same thing I say to you now." He pulled his sword out and stabbed it in the ground. "We will find these beasts, and we will end them. For Fayeharrow, for Rimeheld! May the Creator take our Lady's blood as an offering...May it water this land to make something better grow!"

Pride and determination swelled within the recesses of MyKhal's heart as he stared at his best friend. There was no way he could do this without him. No way he could face what was to come without his support and determination. They would find these creatures. They would end them, and then, he would restore Fayeharrow to its true lineage. He would see his father brought to justice and an Edlind rule.

Aleria

The elder's cottage sat at the edge of the field of flowers. A small stone home with a thatch roof, a lovely garden in the front surrounded by a stone and wood gate. It's what she imagined a fairytale cottage would look like when she was a child. She wondered to herself if a witch ever lived inside. Maybe one lived there now.

Leading her through the doorway as if they had done so many times before, the Huldra greeted a stunning older woman. In human years, she looked to be in her late forties. Only the Creator knows how many years that must translate to in Fae. Thousands of years? Still, though her appearance was older, she was a marvel to look at. Her skin was a medium shade of warm brown, much like Thea's, with hair the same shade of onyx as Nox. She wondered if they were any relation. When the woman wrapped the twins in a warm embrace, she knew her assumptions were right.

"Nonnie Tiadona, we require your wisdom and your grace," Thea said as she looked in Aleria's direction. "We have a friend who we think can help us with the Nattmara curse, to end the Nattmara curse. We just aren't sure how."

The woman peeked over their shoulder at Aleria and sniffed the air. "A human," she said, turning to Thea in shock. "Well, this is a surprise. Come, child, do not hide yourself away. I remember the days when we used to live side by side. I know your kind."

With a reassuring squeeze of her hand, Larkin pushed her gently toward the Fae woman. Something about her set Aleria's nerves on end. There was magic in this Fae so thick it was like a cloud around her. If Larkin's power crackled like lightning, hers was like thick, heady smoke.

"Who are you, child? What is your family name?" Tiadona asked as she circled her.

"I am Aleria Edlind, Daughter of Philip Edlind, Late Lord of Fayeharrow," she said with her head held high. The woman made a pensive noise as she reached for her hand.

"Show me," she demanded. "Let me see what you have seen, daughter of Edlind. We shall learn together what magic runs in your veins."

Aleria looked to Larkin who nodded. When she looked back at the Fae, the woman's eyes had gone pure white, smoke swirling within them.

"Interesting that I had to ask. I usually do so out of respect, but for you, darling, I had to ask. Interesting."

Aleria closed her eyes and released the walls she felt were always protecting her, bringing to her mind's eye everything that had happened so far. When images of the woman and the curse flashed before her, Tiadona gasped and pulled her hands away.

"That's old magic. Old and forbidden," she said as she looked at the members of the Huldra. "Come. Sit. I'll get some wine. We will all need it."

Aleria looked at Larkin, fear settling in the pit of her stomach at Tiadona's words. He crossed the room in one stride and looked down at her.

"Whatever it is, we will face it together. You're not alone, Aleria."

The words made tears rim her eyes. She wasn't alone anymore. It was almost hard to believe that in such a short amount of time, she would call the Fae warriors friends.

"Thank you," she whispered, afraid that her voice may crack at the words.

Larkin smiled softly and pulled her over to a seat next to a roaring hearth fire. The warmth of it seeped into her, making her relax. In the next room, she heard the tinkling of glasses. That, along with the sweet scent of a simmer pot over the fire: oranges, clove, cinnamon, and something she wasn't as familiar with...The smell reminded her of the autumn celebrations in Fayeharrow. It was homey here. She could see why fairytale children could be lured to a place like this. She would be too.

Tiadona reappeared with a plate of fruits and cheeses, accompanied by wine and, to her relief, water. The lovely woman moved with a supernatural grace as she handed out the libations. When everyone was served, she sat in a large wooden chair covered in lush furs and knitted blankets. She adjusted one of them over her lap and addressed the room.

"You were right to come here," she said to Larkin. "You were always wiser than your grandfather. You are so much like your father was."

"Is," Larkin corrected her. "Do you think Aleria can break the curse?"

"Are you willing to pay the blood debt to do so?"

It was Nox who answered this time. "What is a blood debt? What is this forbidden magic, Nonnie? Should we even be messing with this sort of thing? Larkin is - "

"Hush, child. Too many questions at once. I'm getting there," Tiadona said, lifting her glass to her lips. "Aon is Aon. Blood by blood. The woman in your vision, the originator of the curse, used her life's blood to protect her life's blood."

"That doesn't make any sense," Thea said. "How could she protect and lose it at the same time?"

"Her death would ensure the protection of her line, dear. The blood of her life's blood that runs through her kin's veins," she said, turning her gaze to Larkin. "But as we all know, magic has a cost. Such magic would have a debt to pay to bring balance to the world."

Larkin looked at her, the wheels of his mind churning. "A Fae woman caused this curse? But what could drive her to do such a thing?"

"Love," Aleria whispered. "Someone was attacking the people she loved. In my vision, I saw a child. It was a mother's love that drove her decision."

The group looked at her as if she had lost her mind, but Tiadona nodded, a slight smile on her face. "From what I've seen, it was not only the love of a child, but also the bitterness from the death of a lover. If it were a mother's love, the curse would not have the violent repercussions we have seen. That bitterness, grief, and anger flavored the spell."

"Flavored?" Aleria asked.

"Yes. The old magic is flavored with intention, much like a recipe. Do you know much about the magic that flows through us?"

"Only that emotions are tied to it. That the owners' feelings drive them." She looked towards Larkin who nodded in confirmation.

"Yes, and much like the control one needs to use their giftings effectively, one needs to harness their emotions when using the old magic. Each feeling can be an added ingredient that either strengthens or taints the spell. This spell was flavored with bitterness and rage. Protection that turned to a curse."

"How are we to end it? What are we to do?" Larkin asked with concern on his handsome face.

"It was blood and sacrifice that created the spell, so it must be blood and sacrifice to end it," she said, narrowing her gaze on them both. A shiver of dread sped down Aleria's spine as the urge to run filled her. Blood and sacrifice between her and Larkin. No matter the friendship between them, she knew what the group would choose.

Ruke, who had been quiet this entire time, spoke up. "Is there any way besides death?" His face was grim as he looked between Aleria and Larkin. He was the only one to say aloud what they all must have been thinking.

Tiadona smirked and shook her head. "It doesn't have to be as dark as all that. The spell does not call for death, but a sacrifice of life."

"Taste and claim," Larkin said as if it all finally clicked. His eyes widened, and he looked at her, then at Tiadona. "The Claiming. Joining our blood. But why us specifically?"

Tiadona shook her head with a shrug. "That is the real mystery of it all, isn't it? Why a human and a Fae? Something that was forbidden when the worlds were divided. Something your grandfather would not allow his heir to do," she said pointedly at Larkin.

Larkin opened his mouth to speak, but at that moment, the door to Tiadona's cottage blew open and a bleeding Fae man stumbled in. Soot and dirt covered his face, and his breath came in ragged pants. Immediately, the Huldra were on their feet, weapons drawn.

"They are burning the fields," he breathed frantically.

Tiadona's eyes widened as she grabbed a wooden staff and rushed through the door. The Huldra were quick to follow except for Larkin, who turned to Aleria as she tried to join them. "Stay here." His tone brokered no argument, but when had that ever stopped her before?

"I can help. If we combine our blood, we - "

"You will have no blood if you are dead. I won't risk you."

"We could save people now!" she demanded, but he grabbed her by the shoulders and shook her.

"They are burning the cure. Without it, people will turn. They will outnumber us. Please. Stay here, Aleria. I cannot do what I must if I'm watching over you." He turned her attention to the Fae man leaning against the door frame. "Tend him. I will send more your way. Help in this way. You don't always have to use a sword to help in a battle. Please." It was the please that finally convinced her. The fear and desperation in his eyes.

"Fine," she huffed as she walked over to the Fae male and ushered him to sit.

"I'll return to you when it's safe," he said before rushing into the balmy night air. Aleria followed him to the door and gasped at the sight before her. Half the fields across the horizon were already ablaze. An eerie red glow lighting the skyline. In the distance, she heard the sound of thunder and watched as a fat rain cloud began to gather in the sky.

Larkin could put the fires out, but she couldn't fathom the amount of power it would take to summon such a force. A cold wind whipped at her hair as the rain began to fall. A groan called her back from the front door as she remembered the injured Fae who still needed her help.

"I'm sorry, sir. I was just -, " her voice caught in her throat when she saw the man was laying on the floor, his back arched, his head wrenched painfully to the side, sounds she had only heard once before gurgled up from his gaping mouth.

Oh, Creator have mercy.

Were people able to turn this quickly? They were by the way his smooth skin was sprouting bloody tufts of fur. Swallowing her scream, she looked around the room, frantic for something to defend herself with. There were no weapons.

Sard.

Spying a fire poker near the hearth, she grabbed it and ran towards the door. Did she stay and defend herself as best she could, or did she run? Larkin said he would send others her way for aid. She couldn't let them run headfirst into the creatures they were running from. As if in answer to her question, a few of the tiny red-capped creatures scurried out through the wood outside. Their little voices squeaked in a cacophony of fear as they bounded around her feet.

"It's alright, little ones," she said, dropping to her knees. "I need you to go to the side of the cottage and wait for me. If any others come, call them out to where you are. There is a creature inside. I'm going to take care of it." The little creatures squeaked a reply before holding hands and running to the shadowed area to hide.

She took a deep breath and steadied herself. She prepared to do something she had never done before. Kill an innocent person. This Nattmara had yet to make its first kill. It was only moments ago a Fae who came to warn them. Still, she knew it was kill or be killed in this world of curses and creatures.

Clutching the pointed fire iron in her hands, she made her way past the wooden door frame and into the living area. She didn't expect to find the room empty except for a pool of blood where the body had been. She pressed her back against the wall and assessed her surroundings, trying her best to control her fear.

Do not turn your back on an opponent.

Draven's instructions rang in her ears from training sessions past.

Slow your breathing. Calm your nerves. Let your fear energize you, not drive you.

She took a deep steadying breath as she willed her feet to move forward. There was only one entry that she could see. An open loft with a spiral staircase. A kitchen. A small, dimly lit hallway. Creator knows that's the place the creature would be hiding. Gathering up her nerve, she slowly approached the hall, each step measured, all of her senses on high alert. The worn wooden boards creaked behind her, and she turned, swinging the iron around. The fragile-looking creature suddenly standing behind her squealed and fluttered its long elegant wings, one of which looked to be slightly shredded. At that same moment, a tiny mushroom-capped creature came running. It tugged on the breeches leg of the winged Fae, squeaking something frantic and unintelligible.

"You need to - ," but the words were cut off as something slammed the air from her lungs. Her body went tumbling to the ground. Inhuman hissing and throaty growls came from directly above her. She thrashed beneath the weight of the half transformed Nattmara. Its Fae face stretched and pulled too tight as jowls and pointed teeth reached toward her. With all of her strength, she landed a punch to the creature's face. It stopped hissing in almost a comical way as it pulled back to look at her. It seemed shocked that she could land such a punch. The shock only lasted long enough for her to right the poker and stab it through the shoulder of the beast atop her. She was aiming for its heart.

With a skin-crawling screech, the creature flew back, clawing at its wound before turning its sights back on her. Stumbling to her feet, Aleria braced herself for the next attack. The poker dripped with blood as she held it in front of herself, ready to strike again. Her breath came in raw uneven pants, her ribs were on fire, and a slow trickle of something wet her shirt. Whether it was blood or sweat, she had no idea. She could worry about it later.

The creature paced side to side like a tiger in a cage. It's body hunkered over on all fours as more hair appeared. Its fingers stretched and popped horribly before turning into grey-toned skin. Its back arched as a howl ripped from its throat, and it launched at her again. Aleria struck, but the creature's new claws deflected the first blow in a wild counter, nearly knocking the poker from her hands. She came back at it again, stabbing into the Nattmata's stomach with a sickening squelch. Blood poured from where she had impaled him, but the creature did not stop.

It staggered forward...its long, taloned fingers reaching out to grab her arms, locking them to her sides, and digging into her skin. Pain rocketed through her as she fought the slicing hold, her hands fumbling for the end of the poker. Her fingers grazed it, but she couldn't get the leverage between them to break it free. Instead, she twisted and pushed at the iron, making the creature scream in agony and throw her to the floor.

Aleria groaned, rolling to her stomach and saw movement from the corner of her eye. A mushroom capped Fae was toddling from the kitchen, holding a butcher's knife three times its size. She didn't know whether to laugh or be horrified at the sight of the cute little thing holding such a weapon. She didn't have time to think much more of it before the Nattmarra attacked again, pinning her to her back. The reek of its breath mere inches from her face, its dripping maw opened wide with a victorious yowl.

A squeak sounded beside her. The small creature sliding the knife in her direction. There was only a breath before the Nattmara sank its teeth into the curve of her neck. A scream tore from her as she grabbed the knife and stabbed it again and again into the creature's skull. Blood poured over her face in wild gushes, nearly blinding her. She didn't stop, couldn't stop...until its body collapsed atop her.

With a groan and multiple tries, she shoved the beast off of her and onto the hardwood floor. Clutching her hand to the seeping wound at her throat, she staggered to her knees. The little creature beside her squeaked and came close to her. She looked down at it and smiled softly.

"That was incredibly brave of you. Thank you. Tell the others to come in, but only if they weren't bitten. Those who have bites must stay outside or risk us all."

The little mushroom chirped for an answer, pointing at her throat as if to say, "What about you?"

"It bit me, but I am human. I will not turn. I'll....well, unless my friends come back and happen to have a cure, I could die."

Mushroom squeaked in fear, covering its little mouth in shock as it ran outside. Aleria smiled again as she tried to stand, but the room began to blur and spin. She braced on the chair beside her, but slipped in the blood and her weakness and fell back to the floor. From her position there, she could see the horde of strange and magical creatures at the door. They looked at her as if she were some sort of miracle. If she survived this, they'd be right. Their strange concerned faces were the last thing she saw as the world drifted black.

Chapter 17

Larkin

He found her in time.

The scene that he and the others came back to was as horrifying as it was heartwarming. Aleria was laying on a palette in the middle of the sitting room floor surrounded by doting Fae. Beautiful even in death, the tales of old echoed in his mind as his knees buckled at the sight of her. Blood covered her face and hair so thick he immediately assumed the worst. She was gone, and he could almost hear the crack that split his heart in two. Feeling as if he were walking through mud, he came to her side. From closer up, he could see the slow rise and fall of her chest and faintly hear the skipping beats of her heart. Immediate relief flooded him.

Thank the Mother.

Taking a knee next to one of the Shroomies, he assessed her injuries. A few of the Fae had started scrubbing at the blood on her skin, though they would take much longer to clean her up because of their size. Still, he didn't dissuade them.

"What happened to her?" he asked in the old language.

"There was a Nattmara here. She fought it, and it bit her," one of them said as he crawled atop her to point out the injury. "Here. She said she needed a potion? We do not have any."

"I do," Tiadona said as she joined them from outside. She went to a large cabinet filled with vials and brought Larkin one.

"Have the others search for the Nattmarra and bring any other wounded here," Larkin said as he grabbed the vial from Tiadona. He opened it with hurried hands, letting the liquid pour down Aleria's throat, praying the poisonous bite had not spread too far.

While he waited, watching over her for any sign of distress, his mind raced with the details of the altercation with the Nattmara. They did not fight as he would have expected. They ran. They only attacked the guards who were watching over the fields. It was strange. They didn't seem to want to harm anyone, but rather, the goal was to destroy the fields. The intent behind that chilled him to his bones.

He felt foolish for not making sure the guard who had appeared hadn't been bitten. If he had, then Aleria wouldn't have been on the receiving end of the turning. When the Nattmara venom first takes hold, the victims are wild and unhinged. There always seemed to be a mixture of fear and undeniable thirst that drove them into madness. Aleria was lucky. Well, lucky wasn't the right word; she was still unconscious at the moment.

"I have her from here," he said to the little Fae who bowed their heads. "If I need you, I will call. Thank you."

"Thank her, your highness. She risked her life for us. We will repay the debt."

Larkin only nodded as he scooped Aleria into his arms and walked her to one of the back bedrooms. The slight speeding of her pulse gave him hope that the curative was going to work against the poison in her veins. He should not have left her alone. He thought she would be safe here, but he should have known better.

When he laid her down in the bed, he began pulling aside her clothes to check her wounds. He could imagine what she would say were she to wake and discover him undressing her. A small smile tugged at his cheek. She was...something. That wasn't the right word. Maybe she was everything.

The thoughts that Tiadona put into his mind did not leave him even as he used his storms to put out the flames destroying the fields. A similar storm was raging inside his mind and heart. To break the curse, he and Aleria needed to Claim each other. A sharing of blood that didn't end in death, but a shared life together. The implications of such a thing swirled through him. Would claiming her extend her life or shorten his? Would she be willing to one day leave her home and become his queen? The fact that he was even considering such a thing was insane. He barely knew her.

And yet, the pull he felt towards her now as she laid there helpless and healing was disconcerting. All this time, he thought she was an oddity. Something different that caught his attention and made him curious. He believed it was curiosity that led to a fascination, a fascination that led to attraction, and attraction that led to him wanting her. Mother help him, did he want her, but moreover, he was wrong in what led him to these feelings. His mind had drifted back to that day in the woods, when his fingers wrapped around her throat, he could not destroy her. He warred even then with the feelings she invoked in him.

Attraction was not the most recent development between them. It was the first. Even blood-soaked and half dead, he was attracted to her. The fire and defiance in her evergreen eyes stirred something powerful and deep within him, a slumbering beast nary a Fae woman could wake, even with all their beauty and charms. Never had he met a Fae woman whom he could consider an equal to him. Not in passion, nor in pride or determination, not in will and gall. Nothing like what he found in this woman.

This human woman was a lesson in contradictions. She was a dizzying combination of all things soft and hard, all things fragile and strong. She was changing his opinions on what humans are like and making him question the things that had been ingrained in him since he was a sprig. His fingers reached out to brush a lock of her golden tresses from her face, and he marveled at what he saw there. She was beautiful in all the ways he thought were imperfections. Those kisses of what she had called freckles along her cheeks and nose. They were stars, smattering her skin like the night sky. The thin softness of her flesh like the finest of silks...delicate and precious, requiring great care. Even her scars were like etchings of stories he wanted her to recant to him while she lay in his arms. Mother's mercy, this woman. This woman barely out of girlhood had enchanted his body and soul, and he was graciously lost to her. He closed his eyes and rubbed a hand over his face in frustration and resignation. When he glanced back down at her face again, he was relieved to see her eyes fluttering open. With a sigh, he reached for her hand and squeezed it.

"You have done something few have ever achieved in all my years," he said, wiping at some of the remaining gore on her cheeks.

"Kill a Nattmarra with a kitchen knife and a fire poker?" she groaned, a slight tease with a ghost of a smile.

He grinned at her and shook his head, fighting the urge to lean in and kiss the smirk from her lips. "Yes and no, you brave, ridiculous creature," he said, his smile faltering a bit. "You scared me."

"It was a close one," she sighed, looking him over as she sat up on her elbows. Her eyes shifted to his chest. His shirt was torn open and smattered with the remnants of blood. A few scabbed areas were the only proof of the run-in he had with a Nattmara who tried to stop him from quenching the flames. "Are you - "

"I'm well. I'm more worried about you. I'm beginning to think that there is more than one curse at work here." He couldn't help but tease her. In truth, he had to do something, anything to ease the tension that his newly admitted feelings.

Her face scrunched up in an almost comical way, and she weakly hit his shoulder.

"Don't tell me you don't enjoy playing the part of the savior. You're welcome for the ego boost, by the way, Prince Charming."

Larkin laughed again. It was strange and wonderful how easily laughter came to him when he was with her. His grin turned soft as he bent down and pressed his forehead against hers. He thought he might be imagining things when a small sigh escaped her lips, but his thoughts scattered when she reached up to run her fingers along his jaw. With a trembling sort of breath, she tilted her head so their eyes could meet for a hazy, clouded moment. She was seeking permission, some sort of confirmation that he wanted what she was willing to give.

With a slight nod, he dipped closer to her. Her fingers slid up into his hair and tugged him slowly until her lips were a whisper away. The slight flicker of something in her eyes had him wanting to pour his soul out to her then and there. Before their lips could touch, a disgusted groan came from the open door.

"Bloody nethers! What happened here?" Zander's voice echoed through the room. "The Shroomies said she was in a bad way, but looks like..." He grinned a conspirator's gin and looked between them. "It looks like you've got things well in hand, brother."

Larkin sighed regretfully, "Report." His annoyance was clear from the one clipped word.

Zander's impish smirk faded. "Twelve fields are gone. Only two remain. The ones closest to here. No trace of Nattmara. It's strange. This isn't like a full moon blood lust. It was - "

"Organized," Larkin finished his sentence.

"Yeah. What does that mean?" Zander asked leaning against the door.

"It means we need to break this curse sooner rather than later," Larkin said, looking down at Aleria. "Which means, you and I need to talk."

Zander whistled ominously and turned on his heel. "I think that's my cue. Glad you're alright, spitfire."

Aleria smiled at him before making a small groaning noise as she sat up. "Are there any Fae with healing powers?" A hiss escaped her as she tried to adjust herself on the bed.

"A few, yes. I will direct Tiadona in here when she returns. Her healing abilities are unparalleled. Until then, we need to talk about what she suggested earlier."

Aleria nodded solemnly. "That blood needed to be sacrificed to end the curse."

"Yes, in one way or another."

"The other being…"

"The Claiming."

"Ah," she said, looking anywhere but at him. That wasn't encouraging. Stains of blood still marred her skin and dirty ivory tunic. He felt bad having this conversation after what she had been through, but not bad enough to let it go.

"Is that what you want?" Her question caught him off guard.

"I would do anything I can to end this curse." It was the wrong answer by how her countenance fell.

"And if I refuse…Would you force me?" she asked, gritting her teeth against whatever emotion was filling her at the moment. He shook his head.

"No, Aleria. I wouldn't. Now that I know you…I couldn't do either without your agreement. What I mean to say is that I am willing to do whatever it takes on my part. I will not take your will from you."

Aleria's brows crinkled. "What would it mean for me? Allowing you to claim me, I mean."

Larkin sat on the bed beside her and took a deep breath. "I suppose it would be much like how you described marriage in your world. With the added customs of mine. We would be bound, body and soul for the rest of our lives. As for how long those lives would be, I'm not sure. Perhaps it will cut my life down to the length of yours or expand yours to the length of mine. I have no one to base an educated guess on."

"It could make you mortal or me immortal?"

"Possibly. Though I would be an immortal with a mortal life span, I would think."

Aleria looked up at him in disbelief.

"And you would do that?"

He smiled softly at her. "If they were your people, wouldn't you?" The way she looked at him said it all. With silver lining her eyes, she reached for his hand.

"Speaking of, if I agree to this…Could I go home for a time? Settle things there? I…I know I might not be able to stay, but - "

"I would do everything in my power to make you happy, Aleria. If revenge is on that list, I would set the world ablaze for you. It would be the least I could do to honor what you've done for me."

Aleria huffed a laugh. "A very princely answer." With a deep breath, she leaned back against the headboard of the bed. "And what of your grandfather? Of his laws and way of thinking? Will he even allow this, or will he have me killed the moment he sees me?"

"He has something to gain from all this. I'm hoping that will be enough to make him listen. If not...well...He always called Zander the rebellious one. I guess I would be the one to prove him wrong. As I said, I will do anything to end this curse."

"Even claim a lowly human as your mate?" she half-heartedly asked with an eye roll.

Larkin sat up then and turned to her, his hand coming to her blood-splattered cheek. "A beautiful, interesting, inspiring, human being who has enchanted me from the very first moments we met." Beneath the gore, her cheeks flushed pink.

"Charming, you are just so bloody charming," she said almost as if it were an insult, and he raised a brow.

"Is that so bad?" he chuckled.

"It is when I am not sure of your intentions." She pulled away from his touch. He would be lying if he didn't admit that it had struck him like a blow.

"I'm not trying to manipulate you, Aleria. I cannot lie to you, nor would I want to."

She sighed and ran her hands through her matted hair.

"I know, it's just...I...," she sighed again. "I never wanted an arranged marriage. I spent my whole life trying to avoid such a thing. I wanted to fall in love and be in love with whomever I decided to spend the rest of my life with, and this...It just feels like I'm losing everything I ever wanted," she said, wiping at the tears that started falling down her cheeks. Larkin looked at her in shock, the slight wounding his pride deeper than he would ever admit. As if she suddenly realized how her words sounded, her eyes widened.

"Not that you - You are just - You're wonderful. I mean - What I'm saying is...," She groaned and pressed her hands over her face. "Larkin, you don't love me, and that's...It's okay. I couldn't expect that from you. I mean, we aren't in love, and I'm not saying that you're not loveable - Creator you are! You're kind and handsome and bloody near perfect, and I - I am - "

"Everything." He cut off her words, and she looked at him like he was speaking a different language. His smile grew with her every flustered word.

"What?"

"Everything, Aleria. You're everything I never knew I wanted and everything I'm desperate to keep," he whispered as he crossed the space between them in a heartbeat. Lifting a hand to her face, he stroked over the freckles on her cheeks. He slid his finger beneath her chin, tilting her head up. Forest green eyes locked on his before they drifted down to his lips, a hazy look glazing them over. That was all the permission he needed as his lips captured hers. Begging her to reciprocate, to accept it, to accept him. After a small gasping intake of breath, she let out a moan that danced through every part of him. Then, she opened for him. Her fingers slid to the back of his neck pulling him achingly closer, arching into the kiss with reckless abandon. Holding her was like holding a flame, burning, consuming. Her kiss was a brand upon his lips that marked him as hers, and he allowed the flame to devour him whole.

Before he knew it, she was in his lap, her toned legs draping seamlessly around his waist. The heat of her pressed against him was almost too much for his senses. That, accompanied with the sweet taste of her, nearly undid the beast within him, the part he always kept under lock and key. Mother help her if he let it out of its cage.

"Aleria," he said between fierce kisses.

"Hm?"

"You can't - " But the words were cut off by the slide of her tongue between his lips.

Mother's mercy.

With an inhuman growl, he laid her gently on her back. His lips left hers for only the briefest of moments before he swallowed her little squeak of surprise with another kiss. The girlish noise made his pride swell, and he fought the urge to bite down on that full bottom lip. If her blood was spilled this way, there was no way he could wait until the ceremony to Claim her. Fae did not drink blood as Aleria had once accused him of, but something in their baser nature craved the sharing of blood with their chosen claimed. It was that thought that sobered him as he pulled back.

"Wait, Aleria. What does this mean? Will you - "

"I'll consider it," she cut him off, drawing a finger down from his cheek to his lips. "I do have to say this is the most convincing thing you've done so far though."

His chuckle was low as he bent down to her ear and rumbled his reply.

"I can be far more convincing if you like."

Her shiver inflated his pride and made the beast inside him purr. Sliding his mouth down her neck, he came to an abrupt halt. The bite at her neck was still so fresh, the scent of blood intoxicating. Something inside him pulsed and pulled towards it as a low rumbling growl slid up his throat. His tongue slowly licked over the wound, and Aleria whimpered. Shame and want tangling together in a mess of emotion, he pulled himself back to look at her. The poor thing was still covered in blood, wounded, and conflicted, and here he was, pinning her to the bed and licking her wounds.

"I'm sorry," he said before standing up and putting space between them. Aleria only stared at him, slack-jawed. She must think him a monster. "I'll see if I can get a bath drawn for you. I'm sure you want to clean up," he said stiffly and turned to the door.

"Larkin - ," she started, but he was gone before he heard what she had to say. Embarrassment flamed his cheeks as he went to find Nox. There were no frozen lakes to jump into at the moment, so his giftings would have to do the job.

Aleria

What in the Creator's name just happened?

Aleria laid back against the soft down mattress and pressed her fingers to her thoroughly kissed lips. Everything about Larkin was a force of nature: his touch like the brush of a warm summer breeze; his kiss like a gale, sweeping her away; his passion was like a storm, drenching her to her core. A small, dreamy smile crept across her lips at the thought of his body pressed against hers, at the words he whispered before that all-consuming kiss.

Everything.

Her heart squeezed in her chest. All this was too fantastical to believe. First, there was a world of magic she had no idea existed. Then, she ended up being part of some centuries-long curse. And now, to break the curse, she needed to marry a Fae Prince. It was all too much like a fairytale, except she wasn't so sure it would end happily ever after.

Larkin didn't return after a few moments, so she decided to venture out herself to find something to clean up with. When she stepped out into the hall, she could hear the bustling and tittering of Fae of all kinds. Pixies with sparkling wings flitted across the room, carrying flowers and fruits. The little mushroom capped Fae were bounding around the room, lifting things ten times their size and moving it all outside. Thea was carrying a stack of linens out the door when Aleria stopped her.

"What's going on?" she asked, looking at the hustle and bustle in awe.

"The better question is why are you still covered in blood? Mother's mercy, did you bathe in it?" Thea snarled her nose.

"Larkin went to find me a place to bathe, but he hasn't returned yet. Could you point me in the right direction? I don't want any weird superstitions about humans getting started."

"That wouldn't help the situation, no. The bathhouse is out back. It's just through the trees there, near the garden," she said with a directional nod of her head.

Aleria thanked her before heading outside. She walked past rows of wooden and stone tables, trying not to stare as Fae of all shapes and sizes conjured up seating from winding vines or stones grown from nothing. She wondered again what was going on, but knew she needed to get cleaned up before stopping to ask anyone.

Around the back of the cottage, she spotted the wooden arches. It was next to a stunning garden filled to the brim with vegetables, fruits, and flowers. The large wooden beams were covered in lush greenery and flowering vines. It gave off the appearance of a roof and draped down like floral curtains, shading the inside from view. Light bobbed between the vines, and she saw the shimmer of silver blonde moving in the glow of what looked like candles.

A nervous thrill tickled her stomach as she moved the flowering vines out of the way and stepped inside. Her mouth dropped open at the magic that seemed to drip from every corner of the makeshift room. It wasn't candlelight that flecked Larkin's hair in silver and gold. It was tiny blinking lights that reminded her of stars. Each one moved of their own volition from flower to flower, almost like a dance. When she turned back to Larkin, he was looking at her.

"What are those?" she whispered in awe, taking a few steps towards the steaming copper tub.

"Pixie hearts, or at least, that's what we call them. They're flower dwellers. Both the flower and the creature live because of the giftings the other brings."

"That's beautiful. They're beautiful."

"I'm glad you approve," he said. She could tell there was something he wasn't saying. He seemed tense, and his gaze wouldn't quite meet her eyes. Had she done something wrong? Maybe the kiss was...Maybe he didn't feel as she did. "I had Zander heat the water for you. There are some herbs in there that should aid in your healing and help with the soreness."

Aleria tilted her head to the side and eyed him curiously. "One would think you're trying to win me, Prince Larkin," she teased him, hoping to ease some of the tension between them. He shook his head.

"Not win, Aleria. But I would be lying if I didn't admit to trying to woo you."

A flutter of butterflies took off yet again. So bloody charming. "Well...," she said when she could find her voice again. "I'd be lying if I didn't admit to looking forward to it." His smile nearly stole her breath as he leaned in, but something stopped him before his lips brushed hers.

"I've left you fresh clothes and a towel. Take your time. We're staying for the festivities," he said, pulling back and gently directing her toward the tub.

"Festivities?"

"Fae celebrate everything," he said with a chuckle. "Besides, you have quite a few admirers who wish to share the evening with you." His wink and that showing of dimple were positively swoon-worthy. Part of her wanted to roll her eyes at the unfairness of his attractiveness. The other part wished she dared to ask him to stay, but with things as they were, perhaps it was best he left her to her thoughts. Maybe the waters would give her clarity in more ways than one.

The bath was the exact thing she needed to clear her mind. It was as if the waters themselves were magic. She felt pure, whole, and ready to face whatever would happen next. It had to be some otherworldly sort of magic because who in their right mind would feel so well after the nether-storm she had been through? Maybe it was the denial that kept her sanity intact. Or perhaps, it was something more powerful: hope.

She believed in Larkin. Believed every word from his mouth. Drank it up like a thirsty plant. She needed the hope he brought her and the fragile promise that this might work out in the end. If she were being honest with herself, it was he who kept her hanging on by a thread. One snip of fate's sheers, and she would fall, the descent would be short, and the sudden stop shattering.

She dawned the light blue cotton dress Larkin left out for her, then made her way back to the cottage. Fires and the scent of something delicious made her stomach grumble with a reminder that she hadn't eaten in a while. The days and hours all blurred together in this place. Hours, days, weeks, or even months could have passed; she wasn't sure.

In the distance, the darkness gave way to flickering lights and shadowed silhouettes. Wings reflected in warm rainbow colors as the silhouettes danced around a large bonfire. Fae of all kinds were lounging about, laughing, eating, and enjoying themselves. Strange that they could do that after such a horrifying event. It made her wonder if they were daft or simply used to living with such horrors. Larkin had said the Nattmarra attacks had been going on for longer than a century. Maybe it was that they were happy some of the fields were saved, and as far as she knew, no lives were lost.

Apart from the poor messenger.

A tug on her skirts shifted her attention downward. She beamed at the sight of a little mushroom cap, looking up at her with a bashful smile.

"You saved my life, you brilliant little thing. I owe - " But then she thought better of telling a fairy she owed them a debt. No matter how kind they seem, there were some truths to the fairytales and bard songs. "I owe you a thank you," she stated clearlly, offering the little creature her finger for a type of handshake. The little creature murmured something with a tilt of its capped head before grabbing hold of her finger with a strength she did not expect, yanking her towards the merriment.

"Wow, but you're strong!" Aleria said with a nervous chuckle. "Could you lead me to Prince Larkin? I told him I would join him this evening." The little creature chirped a reply, bounding along the grassy path towards the massive bonfire.

Aleria couldn't help but grin. It seemed as if she made a new friend. A knife-wielding mushroom fairy friend. Creator, how she wished she could tell Draven about all this. He would have loved this world, strange as it was. She could also guarantee he and Zander would be thick as thieves by now... and Larkin. Dray would have liked him too.

As if her thoughts summoned the Fae Prince, Larkin appeared with a gobsmacked look on his face. His eyes moved over in a way that made a faint blush touch her cheeks. His tall, imposing form ate up the space between them until they were standing toe to toe. A tingling sort of electricity danced between them as they looked at each other. He was dry now, his golden blonde hair tied back in a low ponytail. Shorter pieces escaped the leather tie, framing the high points of his cheeks and dusting over the cut of his jawline.

Creator, she wanted to place a kiss right there, wanted to hear those low rumbling noises from before. Blinking, then swallowing hard, she looked up at him. The typical stormy grey of his irises flashed the blinding white of his lightning and dulled to the soft afterglow, much like the moon haloed in clouds. A small, wicked smile teased his lips.

"You're hungry," he said as a statement and not a question. She wondered if it were a double entendre, but she nodded anyway.

"I am. You?" her voice sounding a tad more horse than she would have liked.

"Ravenous actually."

If a heart could do a backflip, hers did, and it bloody well stuck the landing.

Larkin

Ravenous?

Mother's grace and mercy, what had gotten into him? Looking at Aleria's wide eyes and smirking mouth, he knew the answer. It didn't help that her scent right out of the bath was blooming like a flower. It filled his senses with honeysuckle and warm, toasted vanilla. He knew what he was starting, and it gave him no small amount of pleasure when her skin glowed a faint pink. Even more so when she tugged that full bottom lip between her teeth. A small noise tried to rumble up from his chest as he imagined doing the same thing.

Instead of a reply, she offered him her hand. A concession and an offer for him to lead. Bending, he pressed a lingering kiss to the back of her hand. The way her breath seemed to catch in her throat made a rakish grin spread in lieu of a simple smirk. Her twinkling laughter broke the building tension as she playfully pushed at him.

"Now, I see where your brother gets it."

"Should I be offended?" he teased.

"No. It's…"

"Bloody charming?" Mother how he loved flustering this woman.

"Arrogant Fae princes," she sighed with a roll of her eyes. "So... food?"

He nodded and resisted the urge to sweep her into the shadows and show her why he had such confidence. For most of his long life, he had been able to keep his baser instincts in check. Now that he had a taste of her, he felt like a glutton, longing for one more taste.

"Of course," he conceded, taking her hand and leading the way into the revelry. The drinking was already in full swing, and musicians were playing uplifting tunes that tempered a bit of the mesmeric pull between them. At least for a moment.

Aleria looked around in wonder as he led her to a huge cauldron of stew, simmering with vegetables, venison, and spices. His mouth watered more appropriately now. He took the time to describe each dish to her and how they assembled their food. The rice was laid down in the bottom of their stone bowls, then ladened with the stew, and topped with fresh herbs and spices. He offered her a warm piece of flatbread and a wooden spoon before they headed to where the fermented fruit drinks were flowing freely. She didn't say much, but he could tell she was soaking in everything around her. It wasn't until they were seated on large stones that worked as both tables and chairs that she finally spoke.

"Are there any manners or customs I should take into consideration before eating?" she asked, looking at her food longingly. It warmed him that she would even care to ask.

"We say our thanks to The Mother, but you are of a different belief, so I do not expect you to do so. Please, enjoy."

Tentatively, she took the tiniest first bite of the soup and her eyes went wide in shock and delight. A little moan bubbled up from her mouth that sent his mind to other places.

You're being a bloody lecher. You're not a green boy. You're a man. Have some control.

She daintily ate her food. Every move was controlled, almost like a dance. It was evident that she was high-born to have such manners, even in a relaxed situation like this one. The sudden need to know more about her began pulling at him.

"Tell me about your life before this."

She looked up at him with a raised eyebrow before looking back down at her food. Something in her seemed to change as suddenly; she looked very young. He supposed he never thought of her as young because High Fae do not age as other races did. The thought that she had yet to even see her twentieth year was almost a startling revelation.

"It's hard for me to speak of my life before. If you don't want to see more tears, I suggest we change the subject," she answered, her smile tight and her eyes were misty like evening dew.

"I apologize. I didn't mean to bring up painful memories," he said softly, cursing himself for impacting her mood. She shook her head and tried for a smile that didn't quite reach her eyes.

"No, they weren't painful memories at all. They were wonderful. My childhood was wonderful. I loved my family, my life. The painful part was having it all stripped from me in a day." Her lower lip wobbled a little, and she bit down on it hard. She cleared her throat, set down her soup, and took a deep pull of the fermented drink. He wanted to warn her to slow down, that the drink was a bit strong even for his constitution. But she had already downed half before he could get out the warning. When she burped a little and covered her mouth in embarrassment, he couldn't help but chuckle.

"Easy there, love. We don't want you passing out again, do we?"

Sheepishly, she nodded her agreement, and he handed her a cup of water instead. Taking it, she sipped it slowly, thoughtfully, as her gaze shifted to the Fae dancing around the fire. High Fae, Fairies, Pixies, low and high Fae alike flew, laughed, loved around the flames. All of them enchanted to dance to its rhythm. Entranced, she watched them, and he watched her, feeling much the same way. The firelight danced in her eyes, revealing sparks of gold within the verdant green. Freckles, she called them, but in the shade of liquid sunshine. His musings were cut off by the somber timbre of her voice.

"My parents loved to dance together," she said wistfully over the top of her wooden cup. Larkin glanced towards the multiple couples who were dancing joyously, bending and swaying like trees in the breeze. Their bodies pressed tightly together. Their arms draped around one another.

"Mine did as well," he added, noticing the longing look in her eyes. Laying his bowl down, he stood reaching out his hand to her with an encouraging smile. She looked from him to the area where the Fae were twirling and swaying to a cadence of drums, flute, and stringed instruments. He raised an eyebrow at her, a dare he would bet her pride would not allow her to decline. He watched as she considered him and scrunched her face.

"I don't know these dances. I wouldn't want to embarrass you."

It was a poor excuse, and they both knew it.

"Know them? There are no formal steps. Everyone moves of their own accord."

"And if I don't know how to move without knowing the steps?" Her nervousness over something so frivolous was endearing. Leaning closer to her, he slid his hand beneath hers and pulled her up to standing. She looked up at him, self-conscious through dusky lashes, and his heart squeezed. Reaching to steady her, he knew his control was slowly slipping with this girl. He leaned down to whisper.

"Let go a little, Aleria. I'll be here to catch you if you fall."

He had never considered himself a romantic before. Not a poet, nor a writer, nor a singer of songs, but something about her made him wish to be.

"You better not let me fall on my face."

With that signature roll of her eyes, she followed his lead, closer to the fire and amidst the throng of revelers. The light from the flame made her wild golden locks shimmer like wheat in the noonday sun. The flickers of light revealed her lovely face to him as they began to move in the crowd. Sliding his hand to the small of her back, he pulled her close and began to sway her to the gentle rhythm the band was playing. He could tell she was nervous without all her rules and practiced steps. It was then he realized that maybe this was something he could help her with.

There was no shortage of rules when it came to his raising, but he had learned to create some of his freedoms. His Huldra was powerful, structured, and knew of order and how to plan, but when they were not on duty, they knew how to have fun. Rabble rousing and camaraderie were essential if one were to maintain a healthy group. She needed to experience that. Every moment of life could not be one of life or death. Otherwise, what would even be the joy of living?

With a playful smirk and a shout towards the musicians, Larkin encroached too far in Aleria's space making her immediately step back.

"Were you trying to trip me?" she asked, a little annoyed.

"I'm trying to make you a little less rigid," he quipped.

"I am not rigid," she huffed, crossing her arms over her chest.

"Prove it," he challenged, stepping in her space again, making her back up once more. She growled at him as he did it again and again, but this time, spotting her from the small of her back as he walked her backward around the fire. The musicians played a song that sounded much like a wolf stalking its prey. A deadly and desirous tune that perfectly matched how he was moving her around the grassy ground.

She caught on and grinned at him with that spark of fire he had come to adore. He lifted her hand to wrap it around his neck and pull her closer as he led her backward. Her only guide, his hand and the direction his feet were pushing her. When she pulled his hair playfully, he snatched her hand away and used it to spin her out and back, resuming their game of cat and mouse.

When the tone of the music changed, so did his upper hand in this situation. The firelight caught her kittenish smirk as she laid a hand on his chest and circled him to the rhythm of the music. All the while, dragging that hand across his chest, his shoulders, down his back. That hand stopped at his hip, tangled in the hem of his shirt, and pulled him flush against her.

"See? As I said: vixen," he rumbled down at her as the music changed again to something slower, something just as dangerous. Especially with the way her hips were swaying against his. Mother help him, if this song lasted for too much longer, he would lose his mind. Her grin was wide and playful as she tilted her head to look up at him.

"How are my moves?" she chuckled, turning in his arms until his chest was pressed against her back. Mindlessly, his hands drifted from her waist and down to her hips. There were no proper words to fully express how much he enjoyed said moves, so he teased her instead.

"Perfectly acceptable."

She laughed at that, and he did too.

Turning and popping up on her tiptoes, Aleria brushed her lips against his cheek. "Thank you," she breathed, moving along with the music until the song changed again to something more wistful and sweet. He gave in to the pull and moved his head down to brush his lip across hers in the gentlest of kisses, enjoying her and one of the wonders that made life worth living.

When the wine had ran dry, and the music stopped, the two of them still stood staring at the flames that were burning down to embers.

"You should rest," he said into her hair. "All this dancing has probably not been the best way to promote your healing," he added with a guilty look, but she surprised him by shaking her head.

"The bath was as restorative as you planned. I have been healed more on this night than you could ever know," she said, taking his hands in hers and squeezing them. "I have a request to make of you, Fae Prince." Her hands fidgeted with his fingers. Nervous energy was written all over her. Again, she looked so very young, so sweet, and delicate, like a rose at first bloom. How could he deny her anything she asked?

"Go on," he rumbled low, tilting her head up so that she would meet his eyes.

"Stay with me. Wherever it is we are staying. Stay with me." Her eyes were wide and pleading, but he still wasn't sure if it were a command or a request. At that moment, he didn't care. His mind began to race as he reached for that control she had almost shattered with her words.

"Aleria," he choked, his throat a little raw, and her eyes widened in realization.

"I mean, just stay...sleep, I mean...maybe some cuddling...some...oh, sard," she said, slapping her hand over her mouth and trying to duck from his hold.

"Wait, wait. Hold on. What is cuddling?"

She looked at him as if he were speaking a different language when she was the one who threw out the strange word.

"You've never heard of it?"

He shook his head.

"It's - Well...It's holding each other. Maybe some flirtatious touching, a little kissing..."

"Ah, so it's a prelude to - "

'No! It's only those things; nothing more." The pointed tone in her voice was partly hilarious and partly disappointing. If the choice were sleeping alone or sleeping with her curled up next to him, he knew what his answer would be. It would be a true testament to the depth and strength of his control, a challenge he was more than willing to take. Whatever spell she had put him under, he would gladly agree to any of her requests.

"Cuddling, it is."

Aleria's beaming smile was enough to make him do anything to see it again and again.

"Can we start now?" he asked, leaning down for another sweet kiss. The way she pushed up on her toes to deepen it made the beast that lurked inside him claw to be free. His magic sparking in his veins, thrumming with his feelings.

"Where are we sleeping?" she mouthed against his lips as he began walking her backward.

"Tiadona has a guest house a little further back." His hands moved of their own volition to the dip of her waist. When they stumbled over a tree root, he took the liberty of scooping her up and wrapping her legs around his hips. Her squeak and girlish giggle were so enchanting; it made him wonder why he had resisted this pull between them at all. This felt right. She felt right. His mind didn't have much time to linger on the thoughts before she pressed her lips to his throat, and all rational thought flew from him.

Mother help him.

His pace quickened as he raced for the guest cottage a little further into the woods. All the while, her lips lavished kisses up the column of his throat to that tender spot behind his ear. A low growl rumbled from his chest as he stumbled to the front door. Instead of opening it, he took the opportunity for a little revenge, pushing her hard against the door, pinning her body between himself and rough wood. She gasped and looked up at him with passion-drunk eyes, glassy green and fathomlessly deep. His mouth curved upward as he leaned down to brush his lips over hers. A tease and a promise.

"I could get used to this cuddling," he breathed. His fingers slid up the front of her, trailing the length of her neck before finding the curve of her jaw. His thumb slid over her lips as he took her in. Starlit freckles, flush lips, rose-tinted cheeks. She was magic in ways he didn't quite understand.

Magic that had spilled in him deeper than anyone ever had before. "Sweet Enchantress, what have you done to me?" he asked with a small smile, capturing her lips with his. A tease, a coax, mixed with the brush of his tongue. Her arms tighten around him, pulling him ever deeper until there is no semblance of space or air between them. Only heat. A heat that threatened to burn them alive if it weren't quenched, satisfied. His free hand slid from her face to her thigh, inching the soft cotton dress up one pull at a time. He'd never felt so desperate to touch someone's skin. She writhed, her head tilting back against the wood of the door, and he took the opening, a dangerous opening. The beast scratched to the surface, driving him to claim her, to slide his teeth into her neck and make her forever his. It roared at him. His mouth watering a bit as he fantasized what her blood might taste like on his tongue, what the magic of the claiming could do for them both. Her pulse skittered beneath his kiss, and he slowly let his tongue drag over the throbbing, a whimpering growl echoing up from his throat.

She said she would try, not that she wanted this yet. She was still making her decision, and he had to respect that, but Mother help him, it was hard. With a final, lingering kiss to her skin, he pulled back and looked into her eyes. Her pupils were black with desire, golden locks a mess from his worshiping hands.

"Aleria, we should - " Before he could finish, the door to the guest cottage flew open, sending them both tumbling into the room. He barely had time to catch Aleria and then himself before they fell, her legs still wrapped around his waist, his hands braced over her shoulders.

Larkin looked up to see Thea and Ruke standing there with a mixture of shock and amusement all over their faces. Zander's cackle burst out from the other side of the room as Larkin smoothly returned to his feet and offered Aleria a hand. Her face was a deeper shade of red than he had ever seen it. He couldn't help but chuckle, the mood between them ruined.

"We were just - ," Aleria started, but Ruke interrupted.

"Oh, we know what you were just -, " Thea elbowed him in the ribs.

"Ruke, Nox, and I will be staying with Aunnie Tia tonight. We have some catching up to do. We were preparing the cottage for the three of you. There are two rooms to be divided amongst you...however you wish," she said with a knowing look at Aleria.

Aleria pressed her hand to flaming cheeks and nodded her thanks before disappearing into the closest room. The door shut with a near-silent click.

"Larkin," Thea started, but he held up a hand.

"Don't. I know the risks. I get it, but...I care about her, Thea. I want her. She's...This is more than the curse. It's more than the rules of my grandfather. Maybe all this is fate. A way to join our worlds again, but in peace."

Thea sighed, pressing her fingers to her temples. "Larkin. I like her.

We all like her. She's...Well, she could be one of us if she weren't human. We just know the chaos that could come from this. Our worlds have been separated for a reason, and I don't want you to get hurt."

"I'm going to fight for her, Thea. Like Ruke fought for you."

"That's different, and you know it. At least he and I are the same species."

"I wouldn't exactly say that," Ruke added. Thea and Larkin shot him a glare. "Hey, relax, you two."

"How can I relax when I know what his grandfather might do to the girl? To us for even bringing her here!" Thea nearly shouted at Ruke.

"You're right," Larkin said with a nod of his head. "I don't know, and it isn't fair of me to ask you to risk everything for this. For her. She and I will continue from here. Wait for us...and if we don't - "

"Absolutely not," Ruke said, crossing his arms over his chest. Zander who had been oddly quiet for the entire conversation stood and crossed the room.

"We aren't staying here," he added.

"If I command you to?" Larkin dared, and Ruke flinched.

"You'd be a prick," Zander said with a deadpan look.

"Agreed," Ruke added, his stance rigid. Thea, though, stayed quiet. He understood her fear. She had spent most of her life being feared, living a lonely life with only her twin for companionship. She had even left him for a time when her loneliness became too much of a burden on his empathic heart.

Larkin sighed, running his fingers through his hair. "Sleep on it then. I won't force your choice on you either way. You know the risks. I won't ask you to chance them with me."

The trio all nodded solemnly. Ruke patted his shoulder before following Thea out. Zander stayed.

"I don't want to lose you too, brother." Guilt tugged at him. "I want our family back as much as you do, but - " Zander closed his eyes and breathed out hard, "Is this worth the risk? Is she?"

"Yes," Larkin said without question. "I have spent my whole life following orders. I have been a dutiful, loyal, and honorable grandson. If he cannot see past his prejudices and to the heart of the matter, then I do not want to be those things anymore. None of them." He reached over to place a hand on his brother's shoulder. "You don't have to follow in my footsteps, little brother. Your life is your own. Decide how you wish to live it and know that I will love you nonetheless."

Zander didn't quite meet his eyes as he nodded and walked into the spare room. The door closed with a final thud. Apart from the crackle of the hearth fire, the room had gone deafeningly silent. The tension in his body and mind almost an ache as he pinched the bridge of his nose and sighed.

His friends had rarely ever been at odds like this. It weighed heavily on his mind as he turned the knob to the room where Aleria was waiting.

Upon opening the door, he saw her sitting on the bed. She had changed into one of his white shirts and some borrowed leggings. The fabric draped over her form and hung loosely, temptingly over her bare shoulder. The sight would have been bewitching if not for the nervous way she was wringing her hand in her lap, that bottom lip chewed red.

"Aleria - "

"What are we doing, Larkin?" The look on her face was raw, open in a way he had yet to see from her. "Are we kidding ourselves? Are we forcing whatever this is because of the curse? Is all this - "

Crossing the room in two strides, he captured her face in his hands and pressed a kiss to her mouth. He swallowed her words and the shocked noise that came after. Pulling back, he locked his eyes on hers, meeting her vulnerability with his own.

"How does that make you feel?" He ran the pad of his thumb over her jaw. "Aleria, I have felt numb for a very long time. Driven by this one thing. Yes, I want to end this curse, but if you decided against it, I would let you go. I would let go of everything I've ever wanted because I care for you." His words were strong and impassioned. Truth in every one. He swallowed and braced himself to lay his feelings bare at her feet. "And if you left, the worst part of it would be that you took part of my heart with you."

"Larkin…"

"I know there is so much more to be discussed between us. We still need my grandfather's permission. Doing this behind his back would do nothing for our cause." Taking her hands in his, he pressed them to his chest. "I swear to you this is not a means to an end, but a means to keep you."

Aleria shook her head, pulling her hands away. "How can you say that after only knowing me for such a short time? We don't even really know each other - "

"Don't we though?" he answered, reaching out to brush a strand of wild hair from her cheek. "I may not know your father's name, your favorite foods, or how you got this tiny scar at the top of your head…" His smile was warm as he brushed his fingers over the faint mark. "But I know the warmth of your kindness, the strength of your mind and your sword, the courage of your heart. I know the depths to which you will go for those you love. Everything else is secondary."

Aleria sighed shaking her head. "Creator help us both. It looks like we will be having quite the adventure tomorrow." Her voice was nervous as she made room for him on the bed. "We should get some sleep."

Larkin nodded, stripping his shirt off and crawling in next to her. "Try to keep your wits about you, Lady Edlind," he teased her to lighten the mood. She rewarded him with a playful slap, and he smiled at her. "See?

You can't resist touching me. Are all noblewomen from your realm this forward?"

She laughed, then narrowed her gaze at him. "Oh, you wait. You think this world is scary? You've never seen a court lady in heat. They will eat you up," she said close to his face.

He couldn't help but narrow his gaze on her. With a flirtatious lilt to his tone, "They'll have to find someone else to satisfy them." He leaned in a hair's breadth from her lips and whispered, "Because you're the only one I'll be satisfying from now on." The way her eyes darkened stroked his ego, but he couldn't resist the tease. Still, she was right. They needed to sleep. "Goodnight," he added, leaning up to kiss her nose before hunkering down beneath the warm fur blankets.

Her snort of annoyance made him chuckle as she turned away from him and slid beneath the blankets. The space between them was both a cavern and breath, a question hanging in the air. Without a second thought, he answered it, pulling her body flush against him, savoring the warmth of her. Like a contented house cat, she curled in on him, grabbing his hands and tightening his hold around her waist. The smell of honeysuckle and warm vanilla lulled him into the sweetest sleep he had ever had.

Aleria

How long had it been since she slept this well? Months? Years maybe? Who knew that the basic comfort of having someone's arms around you could lull you into such peaceful, dreamless sleep. Blissful and a tad unwilling to wake, she turned around, so she could face the source of such comfort.

Wrapped in the warm furs and lit in the early morning light from the bedroom window, her prince slept. In the deepness of sleep, Larkin's face was much softer. The hard angular lines of his jaw seemed less harsh. Long, lovely lashes graced his cheeks and lessened the sharp gaze of his stormy eyes. His skin was so perfect; it was almost as if he were a dream made flesh. Her fingers itched to trace the line of his straight nose...down to his perfectly arched cupid's bow...and his equally perfect bottom lip.

"It is rude to stare," he mumbled with his eyes still closed. She could see the slight twitch of his lips. With a stretch and a little groan, she cuddled deeper into his embrace, enjoying their moment of reprieve from the heaviness the day would bring.

"Don't get a big head about it," she huffed with a grin of her own before inching closer to him and letting her lips slide over his. His answering noise made her smile broaden, and she pressed further into the kiss. His scent enveloped her, much like the furs around her. Rain and a mist drenched the forest in the spring, refreshing, cleansing. One of his hands roamed into her hair as the other slid behind her back, pulling her closer still until they were completely wrapped around one another. The noise that thundered up from him sent shivers skittering down her spine.

A rush of desire coursed through her veins, begging him to quench the flames he was fanning. Yet, nervousness and uncertainty made her unsure. When his fingers began inching her shirt up, the callouses on the pads of his fingers raising gooseflesh on her skin, she froze. Did she want this? Was it too soon? Could she trust him with...all of her? Sensing her distress, he lifted his head until his eyes found hers. There was a question there. A line he was asking her to cross with him.

"Aleria - "

"Larkin - "

They whispered each other's names at the same time, both starting to say something, but interrupted by the other. Aleria chuckled softly before she motioned for him to go on. Part of her wanted him to say something, anything to give her peace of mind that this was the right time.

His grey eyes were overcast as she watched him gather his thoughts. His fingers moved from the hem of her shirt up to cup her face. The pad of his thumb tracing from the high point of her cheek down to her flushed lips. He looked thoughtful, wistful, and a bit nervous as he finally opened his mouth to speak.

"Aleria...I - "

Without warning, his expression changed. His eyes went wide, his body tense as a bowstring ready to release. In a blink, he was on his feet, yanking her up to her own, but even he wasn't fast enough to fend off what came bursting through the door. Splinters of the door frame pelted the two of them, and Larkin quickly shielded her body with his own.

"Listen to me - ," he started, but before he could finish, all the air felt as if it were sucked from the room. The flame in the small hearth snuffed out, and Larkin's breath with it. Gasping for air, he fell to his knees. Frantic, she was next to him, begging him to breathe.

Another Fae male clothed in black leather armor appeared, leaning against the broken door frame. His hand balled in a tight fist as he looked about the room. When his eyes settled on Larkin, the soldier released his hand and air rushed back into the room. Larkin gasped and glared as he heaved in a breath.

"Grandfather wishes an audience, Prince," his snide voice boomed against the wooden walls of the small guest room.

"I'm certain he does if he sent you here, Helix," Larkin spat, his tone far from friendly.

"If you'd followed orders and not your end-piece, I wouldn't be here." The soldier shifted his stare to her, and Larkin growled at him. Her blood ran cold. This Fae was not like Larkin and his Huldra. This Fae was what the old wives' tales warned of. Beautiful with his black hair and fair skin, but deathly cold. The soldier took a step towards her, his fingers inching ever closer to her face. "She is lovely for a human. Though, I have yet to see a woman turn this one's head in years. I was beginning to think your bell had stopped working." When his fingers brushed over her lips, she did the first thing she could think of. She bit him. He didn't even flinch. Instead, he brought his bloody finger up to his mouth and licked the wound.

"Oh, you like to play rough?...I like that."

"Helix," Larkin hissed. "Stand down." The lustful smile that stretched across Helix's face made her stomach drop to her toes. "I am your commanding - "

"Not for long, Prince. Especially when the King hears my report and sets eyes on that. Perhaps he will allow me to play with her a bit as a reward for my trouble - " His hand reached out to brush down the parted opening of her shirt, and Larkin snatched Helix's finger away, stepping between them.

"If you touch her again, I will singe the skin from your bones."

Aleria shivered at his tone. This was a side of him she had only seen once. In the woods when death rained down like his storm. Helix only smiled and nodded towards the door.

"My men will be escorting your party from here. Mount up! This delay has been long enough. His highness will be most displeased if we do not make it before sunset. He has quite the evening planned."

A soldier appeared with ropes that seemed to glow with a faint aura of gold around them. Larkin cursed as they bound his arms behind his back and led him from the room first.

"Aleria - ," he started, but his words were cut off with a snap of Helix's fingers. She watched as he fought for air, fury rising in her as they dragged him into the living area.

"Stop it," she hissed, and Helix turned to her, closing his fist in a tight ball. His eyes widened as she only stared him down.

"Oh, well, aren't you an interesting little thing?" the black knight purred. "A witch maybe? Is it true humans cook and eat Fae children to gain a portion of their youth and magic? Is that what made you immune to my charms, little witchling?" He stepped forward, and before she could react, he had a golden rope looped around her throat. With a yank of his hand, she was face to face with him. She could smell rot and death on his breath. "Tell me all your secrets, and I promise to make your time left in this world at least a little more enjoyable."

With a pretty smile, Aleria fluttered her lashes and used his hold against him, slamming her head into his nose. A sickening crack echoed in the room as the Fae growled and yanked the rope tighter. Her fingers clawed at the binding as he pulled her close again, blood dripping from his nose to his snarling mouth.

"Keep being so cruel to me, and I might just fall in love with you," he said, leaning in and pressing his bloody lips to her mouth. The way he forced her mouth open while choking her with the rope made her head spin. Vomit fought to come up, but her airway was already too constricted. When he pulled back from her, the rope went slack, as did her legs, sending her to the ground in a heap. Her eyes immediately searched for Larkin, and when she saw him, she screamed.

He was laying on the floor, not moving. She could hear Thea and Ruke shouting from outside. Zander, who must have been sleeping like a rock, stumbled from his room half-dressed. He took in the scene in front of him, and his warm amber eyes heated to molten as flames ignited in his hands. Profanities spewed from his mouth like a broken faucet as he readied an attack, but Helix was too quick. The air pulled, and Zander's flames winked out. He roared with the last of his breath, pushing his power harder. Flames erupted through pockets in whatever Helix's magic was stifling, burning away in patches. Helix balked a little and stepped behind her, pulling out a blade and pressing it to her throat.

"I'll slit her throat, Zee. Don't tempt me."

"Don't call me that," he snarled, his words a struggle.

"Come now, cousin. Don't be such a hothead. Is this human worth all this?"

"She's the key to getting our fathers back, you bloody blighter!" Zander spat.

"You've always been a bad liar, Zee. Our fathers are as good as dead. They are dead to us."

"Dead to you! Dead to grandfather, but bloody alive to me, and she can help us get them back!" Zander argued, the flames all over him sputtering. She felt the blade loosen at her neck. Perhaps Zander was getting to him.

"Come with us now or face the consequences. I don't want to have to kill you for resisting, cousin. But I will." Zander's flames stilled as he gave Aleria an apologetic look.

"Prick," he responded, grabbing a shirt that was draped over an armchair.

"Pot-Kettle, cousin. Rouse your brother and meet us outside," he commanded before yanking the rope around her neck like she were some animal being led to slaughter.

Maybe she was.

Larkin

He should have known his grandfather would have spies here. He should have guessed that as soon as they saw her, they would scuttle back to his feet to lick his boots. All rulers had sycophants, and he was no exception. Helix, his first cousin, was one of them.

This was not how he was intending on presenting the situation to his grandfather. He had wanted to come of his own accord, in a way that showed trust, but he needed proof. The word of a seer, an elder. He would have to listen then. But now, this was not going to work in their favor. Betrayal was something his grandfather did not take lightly. The fact that he not only brought a human into Glair, but also hidden her from his King most likely had sealed their fate. If he were any other Fae, it would mean life as a slave, or for some even less fortunate souls, it meant death.

He knew his grandfather could do neither because he was his only eligible heir to the throne. Zander was - well - he was never trained or even considered a candidate. Helix would kill for the opportunity, but he was technically a bastard because Larkin's Uncle Jericho, Helix's father, was born from a mistress. If it were not for the ward around Helix's neck that protected him from any other Fae magic, he would have already obliterated him. Helix's mother knew of their grandfather's occasional bouts of wrath and had gifted her son with the enchanted item to keep him safe. Though, magic always had a price, and if he were ever to claim his mate, the charm would pass to her, then to his child. Thus, he had never claimed a mate. There was no one in this world he cared for more than himself.

When Larkin came to, he was riding draped across a steed. Hogtied with the thrice-cursed enchanted ropes that fed off his power, both draining him and strengthening itself in the process. Each time he tried to release the floodgates of his power, the ropes would drink it dry. To be led into the palace like this was certainly only the first part of the humiliation his grandfather had in store for him. It wasn't anything he couldn't handle as long as it was only him. Lifting his head, he attempted to look around at the party members, praying silently that the rest of the Huldra had decided to stay out of this. He was wrong.

Ruke was riding behind him with a busted lip, Thea saddled up behind him, and to their left was Zander. Nox was nowhere to be seen. And where was Aleria? Zander caught his gaze and rode up beside him. The guard leading the horse spat out a warning, but Zander only shot him a foul gesture in response.

"We're in deep, brother," he said with a smirk. "Worse than that time we got skunked and pissed right on the throne, thinking it was the privy." Larkin couldn't help but chuckle half-heartedly.

"That was an accidental act of rebellion. This was planned. This... is..." He looked up as best he could to his brother. "Swear to me you'll get her out if you can." There was more he could say, more his brother needed to know, but the fact that he asked his brother for an oath at this moment said it all. "You have the same blood as me you know." He added pointedly, the truth of the words souring his stomach. It really could have been his brother who connected with her; he could end the curse and get the girl. The thought alone made his heart prick.

"I'm not you, Larkin." His response said more than the words.

Realizing he was awake, the soldier leading his horse stopped, cut the ties at his ankles, and let him lead the creature himself. A modicum of respect, he supposed.

The ride into the capitol was quiet. Only the clomping of horses' feet and the occasional whispered direction between guards. It felt like a funeral procession. Larkin's eyes finally found Aleria saddled with Helix, his body pressed tightly to hers. He could tell by the stiffness in her shoulders that she was still trying to pull away from him, to make some sort of space between their bodies. Guilt began gnawing at his insides. She didn't deserve this.

When the large stone doors to the palace slowly came into view, he let out the breath he had been holding. The soldiers standing guard lifted an eyebrow when they beheld the state in which he was returning home. Their prince, bound and escorted. He narrowed his gaze at them, and they shifted their attention to using their earthen magic to open the fortification locks on the entrance. The doors screeched open as the slabs of rock gave way to the main hall.

The group dismounted, handing off their rides to the stable hands. Larkin stole a glimpse at Aleria to see how she was holding up. The focused courtly mask on her face betrayed nothing of what was going on beneath. Her chin tilted high, her posture as fortified as the gates. How could he forget that she had been trained for moments like this too. His brave woman. A queen in her own right.

He expected to be led to the throne room, but when their party steered towards the courtyard, his stomach sank. The courtyard had once been one of the loveliest places in all of Glair. White roses climbed every stone surface as if they had a life of their own. But in the past hundred years, it came to be known as The Blood Yard. So much blood had been spilled on its tiles that the flowers' roots were drunk off of it, turning their white buds the color of dried blood. Dark, crimson death.

The garden gates were made from twisting, swirling vines that slithered back like snakes returning to their holes, and they opened to the sight of his grandfather waiting in all his magnanimous glory. His broad shoulders and striking silvery-white hair were much like Larkin's own. A family likeness passed down from him to all the males in his line. Perhaps that was why Zander kept his so short, to hide away the undeniable resemblance. The scowl on his angular face could have been carved from granite it sat there so often. Though this time, it was much more disconcerting having it directed at him. Zander, Thea, and Ruke pressed in next to him, a showing of support as they walked forward. A united front. Aleria was shoved in front of him, evidence of the crime committed.

For a long moment, his grandfather glared down at him. Urion was always one for drawing out sentencing in the name of justice, but Larkin knew it was a power play, lording his power over those he deemed beneath him, making them realize their place. It was all an intimidation tactic that served the King well. Too bad Larkin had been tutored under the man for more years than he could count, so such devices fell flat. He would wait though, to speak when spoken to. The last thing he needed to do was further agitate the King.

After a long moment of silence, his grandfather's wizened voice tore through the tension like a physical slap. It took everything in him not to flinch at it.

"What have you done, child? You dare stain Glair's soil with this creature?" The patronizing tone of his voice was not lost on him, but he knew the older man was looking for a reaction.

"She's stained more than soil, Grandfather. Good luck marrying him off after when I walked in on," Helix chuckled, and Larkin wished for the first time in his life that he could kill his cousin.

King Urion's roar was enough to shake the room as he turned his attention back to Larkin.

"You did what?!?"

"Forgive me, my Lord Grandfather, for not coming to you sooner. I swear to you that things are not what they seem. If you would only permit me a moment to explain before I receive my punishment - I implore you - this is for the good of Glair. I would not betray you."

His grandfather only glared at him.

"As you well know, actions speak louder than words." The elder Fae narrowed his eyes at him, then turned his gaze to Aleria. Larkin's heart thudded to a stop in his chest. Aleria, to her credit, tilted her head up in quiet defiance.

"I do not care why this creature has been brought here. What I do care about is that you feel as if you are above the law of this land. That you would not only bring a human into my realm, but whore yourself with it - "

"I did not whore myself - "

Larkin knew that if he did not choose his words carefully, then everything he'd risked to get his father back would be for nothing. "This human fell into our hands during a battle with the Nattmara. Something about her blood and mine turned the creatures back to their Fae forms for a time. She is a gift from the Mother to help us finally end this war. She is key to ending this curse."

The smoky grey color of his grandfather's eyes landed on him with so much force it could have pushed him back a bit. He did not dare look away.

"The only key to this curse is to eradicate those vermin from this and every other realm."

No! The key was breaking the curse, so his people could come home. Under the skin of those beasts beats the heart of Fae males and females. They were someone's wife, someone's mother or sister. Nattmarra were his blood. They were his sons.

"What about Father?" he dared, hoping the remembrance of his grandfather's sons would bring out some sort of compassion in ancient Fae, but he should have known better.

"They died long ago. There is no coming back from their fate, and it is your childish whims that have put me in the position where I have to make an example out of my heir."

"I accept the full brunt of your wrath, my King. The only thing I ask is the release of the Huldra and the human. They had no part in my actions. I am their leader, and they are commanded to follow me to a fault. They were following my orders. Permit them to return her to her home from whence she was stolen."

His grandfather laughed. It echoed of compassionless cruelty and sent a foreboding shiver down his spine.

"Noble. A trait that while admirable makes that bleeding heart of yours even more of a liability. If they are as loyal to you as you say, then their punishment will be to stay as a witness to yours." With a nod of his head, the ground in front of him split open. Vines and branches intertwined, making a post of sorts, wrapped in thorns and waist high. He did his best to quiet his insides, finding a spot in his mind to withstand the pain he knew was to come.

Helix smirked at him as he walked forward. Coming face to face with him, he smiled. "You're lucky our grandfather loves you. Even more, that the girl has his required pound of flesh to give in your stead." Larkin's stomach dropped as his eyes shot to Aleria. In the blink of an eye, she was being dragged towards the whipping post.

No.

Shoving past Helix, he ran to her. Ruke called his name, and he could hear the sound of flames lighting in his wake. They would make their stand, and he had made his choice. A skirmish broke out, but it was short-lived with Helix cutting off the breath of his companions with a snap of his fingers.

"Grandfather, she is innocent. She didn't have anything to do with - "

His words were cut off along with his air as Helix stepped behind him. Vines shot up from the ground, wrapping around his arms and legs. Forcing his face upward to meet the shimmering depths of her green eyes. He was less than two strides away from her. She whispered his name as the thorns moved to wrap around her wrists, pinning her to the post like an altar. Her hands balled into tight fists, knees to the ground. The smell of rot and coppery rust filled his nose. He wanted to say something, anything. Apologize, beg her forgiveness, but the words were robbed from him.

His grandfather's disapproving stare drifted from him to Aleria, and the blood lust in the King's eyes sickened him.

Aleria

    Aleria's breath raced as thorns tangled around her wrists, their sharp barbs piercing her skin. She had been part of noble houses long enough to know what this was and what it meant for her. Having once seen a man's flesh ripped from muscle, she could only imagine the pain that was to come from her non-human captors. There was a large chance that she would not survive this. After everything she had been through, the threat of death had been the only thing that had been constant for her. This was no different. At least, that was what she tried to tell herself.

    She dared to look up at Larkin as they ripped the back of her shirt open. She shivered at the invasion and the cold burst of air that hit her skin. Larkin stared at her hard and unwavering. The typical silver of his eyes rolling with storm clouds, blackening ever deeper the longer he stared at her. Devastation pooled in her stomach like hot led as she realized he could not save her from this. Tremors rocked her as she grasped at the vines, even though they bore thorns. An unsteady breath pushed from her lungs. That's when she saw it. His jaw clenched, and there was the slightest twitch in his eyebrow. It was enough to give her hope.

She glanced at the other members of the Huldra, all bound to the ground in a similar way as Larkin. Zander's flames bit at the vines, but every time he would burn free from one, two new bindings would encroach in its place. Ruke kept his eye on Thea, seemingly willing her without words. A silent conversation that Aleria was not privy to, even they could not help her.

In her last moments, she thought of home. She thought of the shores of Fayeharrow. The forests and the fields. The cliffs and the valleys. She thought of her childhood home, of her family, of the love there. She clung to it as desperately as vines in her hands.

Crack.

The first brutal sting of the thorned vine tore a roaring scream from her throat. The Nattmara bite had been painful, but at least it was soon followed by the numbness of the venom. This was stinging, ripping pain that flashed and then burned in ways she had never imagined. She barely had a chance to take a breath before the next strike came like the wicked bite of an asp.

Crack.

She gasped and choked, but wouldn't give them the pleasure of wrenching another scream from her.

Crack.

Her breath and flesh were ripped from her, and warm wetness trickled down the fiery chasm that was her back. Her fingers were numb from their bloody grip on the vines, but she held fast. It was the only thing that kept her from slipping down the dark hole of hopelessness. This couldn't be how things would end for her.

Crack.

The last strike caught her around the ribs and hit so hard that it flipped her over. For the first time, a sob broke free as she struggled back to her knees to at least have something to brace herself on, but there was no reprieve.

Crack.

The whip hit her stomach and sliced through fabric and skin alike. For the first time, she saw the blood pooling around her and wondered for a moment how she hadn't died yet from such loss. The thought was banished with another strike of the whip, ripping more flesh from her abdomen and then, her hip. Her vision began to swim as she tried yet again to reach the post. To brace herself, to have something in this world to cling to. The lashes kept coming, and she knew from the sticky wetness pooling beneath her that it would all be over soon. Blessedly, the darkness would take her, and pain would be a fleeting memory by the Creator's side. Or...would she go to the Mother who Larkin was always on about because this was her domain?

The snap of the thorny whip stopped and was replaced by footsteps coming in her direction. She could not see, her vision was spinning, but the voice was that of Larkin's grandfather. If she believed Anwir to be cruel, then she had no proper word to describe the vileness that this male exuded. How such a person could raise someone like Larkin or Zander was beyond her. There wasn't any form of strength left to resist when they released her. They drug her limp body and threw her to the ground in front of Larkin. She tried as best she could to meet his gaze.

"See the mess you've made?" the elder Fae asked before kicking her in the ribs and making her skidder and slam into Larkin's knees. Her body splayed like a broken rag doll before him, and she couldn't help the brutal and broken noise that blew from her. It was a death knell, and so was the trembling that had taken over her entire body. She had seen it once while working with some healers in the infirmary. Shock, they called it.

"You will stay here until it is finished. Then, you will clean up the mess you've made," echoed the older man's voice in her ears as her vision swam. "Helix. See that it's done. I leave them all in your care."

The sound of footsteps on stone met her ears as she tried to look up at Larkin. From her angle on the ground, she could see his head hanging down, tears dripping from his lovely cheeks. Each drop hit her face like the gentlest rainfall. Her bloodied hand reached for his. Her breathing trembled, her body shaking with the effort.

"Precious," Helix whispered as he came to peer down at her. If she had the strength, she would have spit on him. "Oh, cousin, if she had been Fae, she would have made such a formidable bride for you. I mean, Ophelia is lovely, but there is something special about this one, isn't there?"

Aleria couldn't even fight him as he yanked her up from the ground. Her body was limp as he forced her to her knees right in front of Larkin. "Would it help if I allowed you a good-bye kiss? Something to cling to when she's gone?"

Ruke and Zander threw out curses, but with a squeeze of his hand their voices cut off.

"Rude. You're wasting their precious last few moments together. Tell me, cousin, what will you give me for one last kiss?"

Aleria bit down on her lip, drawing the smallest bit of blood. Larkin's eyes widened, catching her thought as if she had spoken it aloud.

"Anything," he whispered brokenly. "Anything you want."

Helix chuckled.

"Mighty Prince Larkin, how far you have fallen...but I am not without pity. I accept your offer. Shall we seal it with a kiss?" he mocked, pushing Aleria's face forward, allowing Larkin right within reach. She watched as his fang pierced his lip, the tiniest bead of blood budding there before he closed the distance between them.

Bittersweet.

The moment his blood laced lips pressed against hers, she lacked the strength to open her lips to his, but the fleeting touch was enough. Power from the combining of their blood was like an electric current, sending a shock wave of energy. The rippling effect of it lighting his veins and electrifying his giftings, begging to burst from his skin. He held tight though, still needing her to do one thing for him before he could show his hand. Aleria looked up at him, a bit more lucid than before, and he pressed a kiss to her tear-stained cheeks.

"Listen," he whispered as Helix pulled her back and away from him. Larkin glared at his cousin, the fire in his vein threatening to boil over. "You may have the upper hand at the moment, Helix. But if it weren't for that charm around your neck, you and I both know you wouldn't last more than a second against me." He watched as Aleria turned her gaze up to Helix, her body limp.

With a whimper, she caught his attention, begging, "Please. I don't want to die. I'll...I'll make you a deal."

Larkin gaped at her. Her human lore had gotten some things right. Fae loved a good binding oath. Everyone in the courtyard knew the power and the danger in oaths. How some of the more wicked Fae couldn't resist the lure of them, the magic that bound promises and required a price for their fulfillment. And punishment for the broken ones.

"Oh, now, that is an interesting offer," Helix purred, looking over her to Larkin. "She's smart and brave to make an oath to a strange fairy."

"Aleria! Don't!" Larkin shouted, but Helix's power struck him mute.

"Hush! She doesn't have much time left. I suppose grandfather would allow her to stay alive if she became my pet. A whipping girl of sorts. Mmmmm. Yes, I like that idea. A never-ending punishment for you and a new plaything for me." Larkin's magic flared beneath his skin. He was barely holding on. "Deal. Shall we seal it with a kiss?" Helix said with a wicked grin as he leaned down to make a show of their humiliation.

His tongue came out first, tracing the line of her lips, and Larkin felt the first crackle of lightning in his palm. He watched, holding his breath, as Aleria's hand braced itself on Helix's chest. Helix chuckled low as his hands pressed into her wounds making her cry out in pain. With a scream, she reached for the dangling pendant at his chest and pulled. There was a snap in the heartbeat of silence that followed, then a boom of thunder. The pendant tumbled to the blood-soaked ground, followed by a drop of rain, piercing the bloodstained gore soaking the stone floor.

Larkin's bindings snapped at his wrists, the vines falling away like dead leaves. Helix fumbled for the charm, but Aleria shoved it out of reach. With a growl, he reared back to strike her, but Larkin caught his wrist. Unhinged electricity rolled from him in waves, and the skies crackled and hissed.

"We made a bargain," Helix stammered. "You said you would give me anything. Well, I want - "

"Anything encompasses a lot of things, cousin. You've always wanted my power? I'll be happy to give it to you." The rumble of thunder boomed. Rain pounded down around them. Larkin sent a bolt of lightning to the base of the roots holding his companions captive. Zander was at his side in a flash, scooping Aleria up in his arms. Larkin gave him a thankful nod before turning his attention back to his cousin. He felt the sting of Helix's power, but it was not enough to dampen the roaring inferno that was his own.

"I will tell your father you did not die a traitor. Not for your sake, but for his. Perhaps if you had more time with him, you would have become a better man."

Lightning shimmered from the sky, arching and bucking in wild excitement as it dove towards its mark. It struck with enough force to rattle the stones lining the courtyard. Helix's scream of terror turned to ash on the wind. Along with the rest of him.

Larkin turned without another look at the ash shadow staining the ground. He knew he should feel guilty, but he could not bring himself to. Helix was his blood, but not his family. Family was a choice, a life lived together, blood spilled together. His family was now looking at him, ready to move with him and for him, however he decided. But in this case, he wanted them to choose for themselves if this was the path they wanted to follow.

"I release you all from the oaths to the crown." His voice was booming like the thunder and lightning taking over the skies. It was Ruke who stepped forward first, a serious look on his face.

"Our oaths were never to the crown, but to you."

A tight-lipped smile pulled across Larkin's lips as he nodded his thanks. Words were not enough to describe what that meant to him. Looking at Aleria, his heart sank in his chest. She was so pale. Gently taking her hand in his, he rubbed at the wounds already closing in his palms. The pressure reopened them so he could drip his life's blood her wounds. The flash of power between them, was not like it had been before, but hopefully, it would be enough to keep her alive until they reached somewhere safe. He knew a place that could offer them haven, at least for the night.

"You are unleashed, my friends."

The wicked grins that stretched across his companion's faces would strike fear into the bones of any creature.

As one, they turned to Thea. Zander laid Aleria into Larkin's waiting arms. He pressed a gentle kiss to her forehead before nodding in the direction of the main hall. Thea's eyes went wholly black as her obsidian hair began to float on a phantom wind. Black smoke plumed from beneath her skin as it rolled in waves towards the entryway.

Thea's power was not of flesh and bone or wind and fire, but something much more deadly. Hers was an attack on the mind. She was a waking nightmare. A close personal friend of death. The images she could assemble in one's mind were unfathomable horrors come to life. Pain and torture without even lifting a finger. There were few who could shield themselves against her wicked gifting. But they could not shield both their minds and bodies.

The first to fall was Helix's men. Fae of the same ilk and twisted desire for power. The sealed doors to the courtyard flew open, and twenty of them came roaring towards them. Thea only smiled as black plumes of smoke flowed along the blood-soaked stone.

The tendrils snaked towards the soldiers, climbing their bodies and forcing itself into their noses and mouths. The choked screams of the men echoed over his booming thunder. They clawed at the smoke, at their faces, but it was too late. Thea whispered in the old language, heightening their worst fears.

There were some whose hearts gave out without a fight. Zander and Ruke handled those who weren't as affected by Thea's curses.

His grandfather's men came next, sounding an alarm. The soldiers created a barricade between them and the exit. Larkin shouted to his companions, "Hold. Those are our brothers."

Smoke, flame, and shards of earth cocooned them as they stood ready for attack.

The captain of the guard, a Fae by the name of Leonois, stared him down, sword at the ready. He was a good person, an honorable person and because of that, Larkin would offer him one chance.

"Our quarrel is not with you. Let us leave. Now."

There was room for argument. The threat was as tangible as the crackling of his gifting in the atmosphere. The guards did not move, though some cast their eyes in the direction of the captain. It was his decision to make. Larkin hoped for their sake it was the right one.

"If you leave with that thing, you know we will hunt the both of you down," Leonois warned. With pity and caution in his voice. "From the looks of her, she will not last past the doors. Weigh your options, highness."

Larkin laughed, bitter and hateful.

"Your King forced my hand by striking out at someone I care about. She is innocent, human or no, and I'm ashamed it took me this long to walk out of these doors. Now, this is your last chance. Move!" Larkin's voice echoed off the stone. Zander's flame burned hotter, and Thea's smoke inched closer to the soldiers holding the line.

The captain's sword dropped as he stepped away from the exit, the other soldiers falling in line with him.

Not letting down their guard, the group left the bloody court and rushed through the main hall and out the doors. He would have taken longer to savor the moment, but Leonois was right. Aleria did not have long.

Still, he wished to leave his mark. Something his grandfather could not misconstrue. As they exited the keep, Larkin looked at Zander. "Leave our grandfather a parting message, will you, little brother?"

With an evil grin, Zander faced the fortress and lit it like a wildfire, spreading a moat of flames around the castle. To add insult to injury, he scorched profanity in the old language into the castle gate.

"I hope that's clear enough for him," Zander said, shaking the bit of flame from his hands as he rejoined the group. Larkin could only manage a nod as he counted Aleria's shallow breaths.

"Hey. She's going to make it," Zander said.

Larkin sighed as he looked down at her. "I made you a promise. Don't let me break it," he whispered as they headed towards the stables.

Aleria

Darkness.

The flutter of her lashes on her cheeks.

Bleary movements and muffled sound.

Fire and Light. Shadow and Screams.

The rush magic. The brush of lips against her forehead and cheeks.

"Stay, Aleria. Stay," Larkin's voice pierced the dark like a beacon, but she could not hang onto the light. It slipped through her fingers like a fine mist. Deeper she fell, but his voice chased her into a chasm of night.

"Love."

The word sending ripples of something through her, shimmers of stardust and wild flecks of hope. Creator, all she ever wanted in this world was a love like the fairy tales told of. One that beat the odds, ended curses, and lived on through happily ever after. If she had learned anything of love in her short life, it was that love was not like the stories had told. Love was hard-fought. Love meant sacrifices. Love was selfless. Was that what she and Larkin had?

"I would let you go."

Sacrifice.

"I wish to woo you."

Selflessness.

"Touch her, and I will singe your flesh from bone."

Fighting words.

"Aleria!" Larkin's voice rang out again in the fog of her mind. "Stay, love. Please stay."

Opening her eyes, she took in her surroundings. Wherever she was, it was warm and comfortable. It felt like home. Though, the pain shooting through every part of her was a reminder that she was nowhere near home.

Rising to a sitting position, she groaned as the barely healed wounds stretched and pulled beneath the bindings. The world spun a bit and the blood rushed to her head. Either that, or it was the blood loss, and her battered body had still yet to refill her veins. Looking around the room, she took in the comforting surroundings.

Colored pieces of glass hung in beautiful designs all over the room. The slightest movement of wind sent them tinkling in almost a hypnotic sort of melody. It calmed her bruised spirit at the sound. Too bad it could not quell the fear and desperation in her heart.

She turned her body to hang her feet off the soft bed. Part of her wished she could stay a bit longer, to enjoy being wrapped in its finery and furs. But she could not bear to stay in this world a moment longer. Could not stay cooped within this deceptively comfortable room.

Steeling herself, she got to her feet. Painstakingly, she made her way to where she heard low whispers mingled with the crackle of the fire. A warm herbal scent hit her first. It mingled with a strange sort of smoke like what she saw priests burning in the local church - maybe sage or some otherworldly cousin of it. As soon as she passed under the door frame, all eyes shot to her. The Huldra was there, along with a Tiadona. Concern and shock lit most of their features.

Larkin shot to his feet as soon as her eyes met his, the tension between them palpable. Echos of his words from whatever fever dream she was having before played on repeat in her troubled mind.

"Where are we?" she asked, bracing herself on the doorframe. Larkin was the first to speak.

"Somewhere safe," he comforted her, reaching out a hand to brush it over her cheek. He took a long moment to look her over, relief and affection sparkling in his eyes. She wanted to pull away. "How are you feeling?" His voice was raw, tired. She huffed a bitter laugh.

"Like I was nearly beaten to death." Her tone intended to learn towards levity, but fell flat from the bitterness flavoring it. Larkin flinched. "Can we talk?" She looked around the room at the range of looks focused on her. Pity, concern, guilt, and relief. "Alone," she amended, nodding towards her room.

Larkin nodded, slipping his hand beneath her arm to steady her. As soon as the door shut, his eyes and hands roamed over her as if checking that she were there and not some apparition. His concern should have made her feel something, but at that moment, all she could feel was the pain, something she had become akin to in this world that was not her own.

Slowly, she pushed his hands away and looked up into his silver eyes. His normal countenance of all-knowing arrogance and intense focus was nowhere to be found. It was strangely unnerving. Cocky know-it-all Larkin she could handle. This side of him, she had no idea where to even start.

Creator, this was going to hurt.

With a deep breath, she closed her eyes, rallying every bit of resolve she could. Her hands squeezed into tight fists at her sides.

He broke his promise. He lied to her. Of course, in fairy tradition, he did not directly lie, but he left out a pretty important detail.

Her mind drifted back to hearing, "What about Father?" His father was Nattmara, and his grandfather didn't give a sard. If the king didn't care for the return of his son, what difference would a cure make? They were doomed from the start, and it didn't matter that Larkin had saved her in the end. She couldn't trust him, his judgment, and it was time for him to uphold his side of the bargain. She had given enough. Rung dry of giving...broken in more ways than one.

"I want to go home."

You would have thought she physically slapped him by the way he flinched. His eyes went wide as he shook his head in confusion.

"What?"

"I want to go home," she repeated, that mask of calm cracking a bit as tears clearly formed in her eyes. For a moment, he fumbled with his words, landing on another one-word response.

"Why?"

Her answer was to cock her head to the side and cast a knowing and yet disbelieving glare in his direction. He shook his head at her and took a step forward. "Aleria - "

She cut him off with a hand held up between them in a warning for him not to come closer. It was another blow, and the way it landed on him made her heart crack. It was as if he suddenly didn't know what to do with his hands. The shock washed over him first before resignation settled, and he stepped backward. "Aleria, please," his voice was low, pleading. "I'm so sorry."

"I know you are, but I can't - ," she choked on her words. "I can't do this. You lied to me. I can't trust you, and I don't want to die here, Larkin. I want to go home, to my people and my life. I'm done fighting for something that is not my own. Giving my life for a world that is not my own. I want to go home."

"I never - "

"Your father and your uncle are Nattmara. When were you going to tell me?"

"Aleria - "

"When?!?" she shouted on a broken sob.

"Aleria, I know you've been through - "

"You have no sarding clue what I've been through. Creator, Larkin, this is just...sard. Maybe this has finally made me realize my mortality, something you have no way to fathom, by the way. I will have sixty, seventy more years if I'm lucky, and the way my luck has been here, I may not reach twenty. Twenty years, Larkin. Twenty to your - What is it? - hundreds? I only get one life and a rather short one at that. I don't want to die here."

"I told you I would not let you die here. We made a deal."

"Well, I want you to hold up my end now. Call me a coward. Call me anything you want, but I cannot stay in this place a moment longer. I want to go home. Please, Larkin, take me home."

Part of her wanted him to stop her, to make more promises that no harm would come to her, that she could go home...that he would come with her. But when that courtly mask slipped over his wounded features, she knew she had drawn a line, and he would not cross it. Whatever had been between them shattered in the dust.

"Fine," he growled, the mask now like a fortified wall between them. "As soon as you are well enough to travel."

"No, tomorrow will be fine. I've traveled worse."

He growled and strode towards the door, yanking it open so hard the hinges whined. He started to say something, but only growled again and slammed the door shut.

Aleria clutched her stomach as she allowed all the emotion she had been holding back to surface. It threatened to devour her, body and soul. Her hand flew over her mouth, muffling her sobs as she slid to the floor. It had to be this way. Still, her heart writhed in a shattering pain she didn't expect to rival all the others.

Larkin

Crying was not something Fae did often. Even Fae babes did not cry, They made little noises that signaled different needs, but rarely ever did they cry. If they did, it was because of intolerable pain or sickness. Rarely, because death was rare, did they even cry over the loss of a loved one. Even more rarely did they cry in liquid form as he had seen Aleria cry on multiple occasions, whether from physical pain or the pain in her delicate heart.

A heart he had come to cherish.

A heart that he had unwittingly betrayed and undeservedly broken.

He couldn't explain or understand how deeply her cold words affected him. He would have never described her as cold. No, she was fiery and bold. Her temper struck like an asp, igniting like that of flint on stone. Always ready to put up a fight or die trying...but this version of her...He had no idea how to combat it, nor did he know how to fight off the slight moistening of his eyes, the prick of something that made his face tingle in the worst ways. As he made his way back to his comrades, he didn't dare blink for fear the telling liquid would tumble down the high peaks of his cheeks.

Clearing his throat, he sat down next to the hearth fire and picked up his previously abandoned glass. Part of him wanted to drown himself, unwanted feelings and pain alike, in the drink. Though, he knew that such a thing was folly, especially if they were to head out the next morning as Aleria demanded.

Thea looked at him in a way that made him think of his mother, soft-hearted compassion with the slightest hint of disappointment. She reached out a hand to try and comfort him. He didn't reciprocate. A human girl opened up wounds and left him here to bleed out; it infuriated and devastated him to no foreseeable end.

"And yet, you did the same to her, only in a literal sense," his conscience threw at him in accusation. Part of him agreed, thinking himself a horrible person and understanding where her ire was coming from. She had been beaten nearly to death, all for a cause that was not hers.

"I'm guessing it didn't go so well in there?" Zander interrupted his thoughts.

"Don't pretend the lot of you weren't listening," Larkin huffed, taking a deep pull from his glass.

"Oh, we tried, but Tiadona seemed to have enchanted the glass in the safe house. All I heard was a little clinking." The obvious disappointment was written all over his face. It made sense now why the decor was hanging in every room. It wasn't just for art's sake; it was protection.

"You don't seem well, Larkin. Is there anything we can do? Perhaps I could speak to her?" Thea's offer, though kind, was not something he thought Aleria would take well to, and he didn't want to push her any farther away. That and his wounded pride would not allow him to beg anyone to stay who wanted to leave.

"She wants us to take her back home," he repeated Aleria's words. It poked a finger in the wound she had already caused him.

Thea stared back at him, mouth agape.

"But what about the curse?"

"She wants to go home."

There was nothing but silence in the room and the crackling of the fire as his words settled on everyone. He wasn't sure what was running through their minds, but he was certain that one, if not all of them, were as disappointed as he was. The silence continued for a long while before Zander pushed himself off the wall and nodded his head in a silent request for Larkin to follow. With a sigh, he drained the last of his drink and followed after his younger brother.

Drizzles of rain pelted the overhanging bit of the roof on the front porch. Thunder rumbled in the distance. When his emotions tended to overflow, his powers did the same. It was a curse that all gifted Fae had to learn to control. Perhaps that was why Fae tended to not be overly emotional; it was all part of the Mother's plan. As if in answer to his thoughts, the rain swelled and came down in sheets upon sheets of water, a veritable waterfall in reflection to his emotional state.

"You'll flood this place if you don't get ahold of yourself." Zander's voice was barely heard over the cascade of rainwater.

Larkin ignored his brother's attempt at levity. Sighing, Zander ran his fingers through his longer bit of bangs. The mist from the rain dampening it and making it stick out wildly in all directions. He crossed his arms over his chest and leaned against the building as he spoke.

"You took a risk and came up short." Sparking up a flame in his palm, he stared into it, gathering his thoughts. "I've seen how you look at her, brother. I've never seen you look at another that way, and yet…you risked her." He shook his head as if the memory might have popped into the front of his mind. The flame in his hand burned brighter, richer in color. "I get why she wants to go home. She has no skin in the game." He shook his head and snuffed out the flames. "Okay, maybe that is a bad choice of words."

Larkin shot him a look that, if he had Zander's gift, would have set him on fire.

"What are you trying to say?"

"I'm saying you've been careless. You knew this could happen. You knew what would happen with grandfather, and yet, you still brought her here, thinking he would understand. When has he ever seen reason?"

Zander had turned to face Larkin. Each of his words hit like an anvil. A growl reverberated in Larkin's throat as thunder rumbled in the skies. He didn't know what was making him angrier: the words, the accusations, or the fact that his brother was right.

"And what would you have done, baby brother? Please bestow your vast wisdom upon me."

Zander groaned and shook his head before leaning back against the wall. The only noise within their silent standoff was the clap of lightning and the rolling boom of thunder. Zander was the first to break the silence.

"You're in love with her."

Larkin's eyes shot to his little brother. The words sending a jolt through him, trading his frustration for shock. Lightning struck a tree.

"I'm not - "

"You are. I don't know why the two of you are pretending otherwise."

Larkin huffed a frustrated noise and leaned back against the cottage wall. The rain and wind whipping about.

"What good would it do admitting it now? She wants to go home," Zander huffed.

"Take a bloody moment to think about it from her perspective. She just spilled her blood for your cause. She very nearly died for it, and for what? It doesn't seem like there is much hope in this world. All she has left is hers. We have no idea what it is like to fear death. She does. We've been fighting this war for a century. She does not have an extra hundred years to spare."

The rain slacked up as he ran a frustrated hand through his hair, the length of it nearly soaked. "How can I fix this?"

Zander took a deep breath and sighed,"First, you have to decide whether or not she's it for you. That she is worth crossing worlds for. That she's worth more than getting Father back."

Larkin closed his eyes as he focused on the answer to that question. If a heart could talk, his would have screamed a resounding yes. He almost laughed at his obliviousness.

"And if the answer is yes?"

"Then, you take another risk. Take her home, but don't let her go."

Larkin huffed a half-laugh, leaning his head against the wall. He was right. Mother help him. He didn't want to let her walk right out of his life. He had to do something to make amends. She was worth the risk. With a conspirator's smirk, he turned to his brother, the rain fading to a mist over the soaking earth.

"If I admit my feelings for her, does that mean you're going to stop flirting with her?"

Zander returned his smirk."Oh, absolutely not. Not until you've laid claim to her and all my chances are gone. You better be glad I respect you, or I'd tell you to sard off and take her for myself."

Larkin chuckled, shaking his head. "Using her people's words now are you?"

"It's a good word. She's taught me a few of them."

He laughed and patted his brother on the back before turning to head back inside. The warmth of the room and the crackling of fire would have made for a picturesque evening with his family were it not for the suddenly glaring missing piece to the puzzle. It wasn't the same anymore without her.

The sound of her chamber door opening made him shoot to his feet again, hope swelled in his heart, only to have it dashed when Tiadona walked out, carrying a tray full of bloodied bandages. The sight was another jab to his already slowly bleeding heart.

"How is she?" His voice was hesitant and pleading.

"I put her to sleep for a while. It was unacceptable that she wanted to travel in the morning and ruin all my work. Stubborn little thing. Her back is barely hanging together by threads of skin, and she wanted to trek through the woods? I've never seen such ridiculous pigheadedness. She'll be under for at least three days. I'll tend to her; don't you worry."

He had the urge to hug the woman.

"Your kindness knows no bounds, Tiadona. You have my eternal gratitude."

"It's she who should be thanking you. It was you keeping her tethered to this world all that time."

The bargain.

"Ah. Yes, I was hoping that would help," he said, sitting down and taking the fresh glass of hot herbal tea Thea offered.

"Not just the bargain, prince. Her affections for you. Your fates are tethered and tangled, youngling. She should be thankful for that. Well, I suppose you both should be."

Larkin only nodded as his thoughts swirled around her words. Three days to decide how to tell her of his feelings. Three days to decide where fate would take him.

Aleria

"A week!?! I was out for an entire week!?!" Aleria's screech made the glass ornaments around the room ding in protest. Thea flinched at her outburst.

"You don't realize how close to death you were - "

"I realize plenty, Thea," she snapped, narrowing a glare at her. How dare she say that? As if she didn't know what happened to her. As if she didn't relive every strike. Or the sound of her flesh ripping from her body. Or the darkness that tried to drag her under.

"Obviously not if you planned to travel so soon," Thea fought back with hurt and offense woven into her tone.

"I need to go home before I die here. My people need me." It was true, but it was also a deflection from all the feelings still swirling beneath the surface. She needed to get away from them. From Larkin. From this world of magic and wonder before she succumbed to their spell again. While she still had the resolve to leave. Thea's solemn nod and restless hands sorting things in the room made her feel a little guilty. In the courtyard, Aleria had seen the desperation in Thea's eyes. She saw the fire in Zander's and the way Ruke refused to look at her at all. They cared for her, and that was not helping her resolve.

"Is everyone ready to leave?" she asked, blinking back the emotions that threatened to give.

"They are. Larkin arranged for use to travel on horseback. It's not our typical way, but he wanted it to be a bit easier on you. You're still healing after all."

"How kind of him." Her words were almost snide as she walked to the door.

"That isn't fair. He wasn't the one who hurt you," Thea said, stopping her in her tracks. Aleria spun to face her, all courtly control went as she stepped toe to toe with Thea.

"Didn't he? You said it yourself he knew this would happen. He knew his grandfather would try to kill me. He lied to me about his reasoning for wanting to break the curse. Not directly, no, but don't you think it matters that his father is under the spell? That all this time he was fighting to get him back, and yet, he decided to keep that from me? He told me he could not lie to me, but lies of omission are fair game? Fairy tricks of twisted words and crooked deals. I'm done with them all."

"Aleria, that's not - "

"I'm done!" Aleria shouted, and Thea's eyes flashed to black. Ruke was suddenly in the room with them, the broken door still hanging by its hinges.

"What in the nethers is going on here?"

"Nothing. Let's take the human home," Thea hissed. She didn't look back as she walked past him and out the door. Ruke gave Aleria a confused look before following after his lover. Aleria could hear him questioning her about what happened, and guilt gnawed at her as she headed outside.

Carrying her pack in her hands, she made her way to where Zander had told her Larkin was preparing the horses. Each movement felt like a wave of pin pricks all over her back and down her sides. If it weren't for the steady stream of herbs Tiadona pressed in her hands, she would be barely able to walk. The older Fae woman had warned her to be beyond gentle with herself. Careful to the utmost. Otherwise, the wounds could split back open and would take even longer to heal. The tight pull of scabbed cuts made it obvious that her words were true. She hadn't taken a moment to look in the mirror and see how bad the damage was. Part of her didn't want to.

She wouldn't call herself vain by any stretch of the imagination. But when she was younger she took some pride in her looks. It was more the power it granted her in some situations really. In her heart of hearts though, she hoped one day to marry and that her husband would find her beautiful. Pristine. Without blemish. The Rose of Fayeharrow. These things men seemed to hold in high regard, according to the standards of beauty. Until that time came, if it ever would, she would rather not know how monstrous her body must look now. She knew it must look horrid beneath her tunic and thick wrappings. There was enough pain to deal with already without facing down her reflection, something these stunning Fae creatures could never understand.

Clearing her throat to announce her presence, she stepped up to the stables. Standing amongst the Fae warriors were the biggest, most fantastical horses she had ever seen. Each one was massive, saddled, and standing like soldiers ready for battle. Fear of controlling such beasts settled in her stomach, making it churn. Larkin, and his annoying ability to read her body like a book, dared to smile softly at her.

"They are intimidating, aren't they?" he said, patting down the mane of a majestic white stallion.

The bloody perfect Fae prince rides a white steed. Of course, he does.

"Which one is mine?" Her tone brokered no hint of friendly conversation.

"You will be riding with me."

"I most certainly will not."

"It takes years upon years for Fae to be able to control Rayshires. There is no way you would be able to lead one, so you will ride with me."

Aleria stared at him with fire in her eyes. There was no way in the infernal depths she was going to travel with him. Next to him. Pressed against him. Her mind scurried to find another option. Nox would not even look in her direction, Zander would work her nerves to no end, Ruke was staring daggers at her. That only left…

"I'll ride with Thea." Everyone's eyes shot to her including Thea who raised a curious eyebrow at her. Larkin looked at her for a moment, hurt evident there for but a moment before he cut his eyes to Thea.

"Fine."

"Fine," she echoed as she made her way over to Thea, who was still looking at her curiously.

"I wish you would not put me in the middle of your lovers' quarrel," she said as she helped Aleria up onto the black beastial horse with the utmost gentility.

"Larkin and I are not lovers." Aleria could have been imagining it when she saw Larkin flinch slightly. What she didn't expect was for the words to wound her heart too. "And I chose you because I think you are the only one who couldn't care less whether I stay or go. I know you aren't fond of me, but you will be free from me soon. Just endure my presence a bit longer," she added as Thea looked up at her, those typically stoic features betraying the shock of her words.

"What makes you say - "

"I heard you that night and every other night I was a topic of discussion. Though my hearing is not as good as yours, I'm not deaf, nor am I stupid."

Black flickered in Thea's eyes, and Ruke put a calming hand on her arm.

"You'll ride with me," Ruke commanded, leaving no room for an argument.

Without a word, he climbed up behind her and gently adjusted the space between them. He even took a moment to place a folded blanket between her backside and his front, so their bodies wouldn't touch. Part of her wondered if it were because he couldn't deign himself to be close to her or if he didn't want to put pressure on her wounds. She wouldn't ask, he wouldn't tell, and the silence suited her just fine.

Larkin

Larkin and I are not lovers.

The words echoed over and over again in his mind as they made their way to the crossing. It was a profession and a warning, as was her choosing Thea of all people to carry her home. It hurt, and he knew that was the intent of the words. The countenance of his companions also pulled at him and burdened his spirit. He had never once seen his Huldra so solemn. Each member kept a silent vigil as they passed the hours of travel with nothing but the sounds of nature to comfort them.

His thoughts raced around every moment they had together, trying to pinpoint the moment everything had changed for him. Then, his mind drifted back to how perfectly she fit in his arms. How she soothed his mind with her humor. How she stirred his passion with her fire. She was...the only woman who could turn his head. The only women who understood what it meant to have the burdens of their people on their shoulders. He had to tell her. Mother help him, he wanted her to stay.

Upon reaching the mirrored image of the waterfall that hid the crossing between worlds, each member of his Huldra dismounted. They lead their nervous steeds through the water and mist. There was no need for purification this time. Glair was pure...or so he had thought all of his life up to now. His home would forever be stained with her blood now, a permanent blemish his little black sheep had left on this altar that changed him forever.

Thea passed through first. Then Ruke, Zander, and Nox, but Aleria remained, staring at the entry as if she were facing down a nightmare come to life. Perhaps she was. Larkin wasn't sure what to say to help or if his help would even be wanted. Still, she had to pass through if she wanted to go home.

Coming to her side, he laid a gentle hand on her arm. "Remember," his voice was a whisper of a breeze, "the only torment it can bring upon you are the things you refuse to face. You have faced everything in this world without fear. You can handle this too."

She did not turn to him. She stepped through the entry, her back straight, her resolve unflinching. The woman he had fallen for.

He waited a few moments, hoping the silence therein was a good sign before starting his passage through. The darkness was all-consuming apart from light beaming down on the Elysian. Its presence like solidified smoke, whole and yet not. Moving and yet contained. The Elysian was strangely quiet as he led his Rayshire into the foggy darkness. It only observed him, tilting its head to the side and staring with that beautiful, eyeless face. The creature cooed and made a pitying sound that rubbed him the wrong way. Turning his face away from the creature, he could have sworn he heard it chuckle.

The rush and crash of water called to him, guiding his way from darkness into the cool mist of waning dusk. The Human Realm was an odd combination of warmth and wildness. A reminder that, in many ways, their worlds were reflections of each other. Stoic silence met him, just as he had endured for hours, and it was beginning to grate on his nerves. Pressing his heels into his Rayeshire's side, he spurred it forward. They only had an hour more daylight before they needed to set up camp for the night.

Less than a day and a half before he had to watch her leave.

That moment would wound him. He couldn't imagine letting her go. Fighting the urge to turn to her that very moment and offer her whatever she wished, he focused instead on what his final words to her might be. He could do as she wished and give her a simple goodbye, but everything about that felt wrong. He imagined her walking away from him without ever knowing the true depth of his feelings. That thought alone made regret form a tight ball of pain in his gut. There was only one way to go about this, one way to let her know he was serious. It wasn't about the curse anymore; it was about her.

Aleria

Everything about this trip was off. The group was oddly quiet. It was as if all the laughter in the world drained away, and it left them all shells filled with nothing but melancholy. She hated it. What she wouldn't give for Zander's unabashed flirting or Ruke's playful banter with Thea. It was her bloody fault. She was leaving them and dashing whatever hope they had in breaking the curse on their people. Her departure would force them into a life of fighting their kin and watching the neverending destruction therein. Guilt tore at her insides with each passing thought of how her decisions were affecting them all. By the time Larkin called for them to dismount, she was so deep in self-inflicted guilt she barely heard Ruke ask if she would mind filling the canteens.

Aleria nodded in response as she trudged her way through the forest and to the creek she had seen them pass no too long ago. The only sounds were the gurgling of the water, the occasional chirps, and the buzzing of birds and bugs alike. With a sigh, she sat on the edge of a rock that jutted out just over where she could easily dip in the skins. The cool water slid over her fingers like dancing silks. It beckoned her to dunk herself in hopes of washing away the sadness that seemed to clung to her like a parasite constantly gnawing at her. If only the waters here had the same healing powers as in the Fae Realm. Maybe then, she could let her bitterness and hurt wash downstream and return to the group with a fresh attitude...but things in the human realm were not so easily healed.

The popping of twigs from behind her drew her attention. As quick as a blink, her hand flew to the borrowed dagger at her side, her senses on high alert. When her eyes settled on who had come, her posture only barely relaxed. There Larkin stood in the dusk of the day. All six feet of a beautifully carved male, standing stock still, watching her. She gulped and resisted the urge to take a drink of the recently filled skins, but instead, she leaned over the rock again and tried her best to ignore him. She didn't speak. In all honesty, she couldn't find the words to.

"Aleria," her name rolling off his tongue in that deep rasping baritone made her entire body react immediately. It was a siren's call, and she gripped the stone to keep herself from succumbing to it. "Please look at me."

The desperation in his tone nearly made her whimper. She was pathetic. Drawing on her shaking resolve, she swallowed hard, took a deep breath, and set her features before she faced him. Moving the water skins aside, she gripped the edge of the stone to keep herself from trembling. If she stood, she knew her legs would not hold her, so instead, she slid to the edge as if the stone were a throne of her making.

When he reached her, his presence dwarfed her own, but she refused to be intimidated. Rolling her shoulders back and lifting her chin, she looked up at him defiantly. Rulers, facing off.

His fists clenched and unclenched a few times before he bent at the knee. Slowly, deliberately, he lowered himself to the ground. The sunset sky darkened further as the gentlest sort of rain began falling from through the canopy of trees. One knee pressed into the ground followed by the other until he was below her. Wide-eyed shock took hold of her as she shook her head at him. Even in her court, for a man to kneel before a woman was nearly unheard of. Except for an offer of marriage. This otherworldly prince was kneeling before her. With a deep breath, he bent further down and placed his forehead on her knees. A complete and total showing of supplication that knocked the breath from her lungs.

"Larkin," she gasped, not knowing where to place her trembling hands. He didn't reply, but his hand gripped the backs of her calves as if he were trying to ground himself or hang on. Large rain droplets splashed around her, but she barely noticed.

"I am so sorry." His apology hit her like an arrow, straight and true to the dead center of her aching heart. The tears swelling in her wide, unblinking eyes mimicked the puddles of rain droplets. "I am sorry for not being careful with you or with your affections," he mumbled into the open air between the ground and her feet. "I am sorry for believing my grandfather could be something other than he is." When he moved his hands to her knees, tilting his gaze up to meet hers, she found herself in awe of what she saw shimmering around the icy grey depths of his eyes. "I am sorry I did not save you from him. I'm so desperately sorry, Aleria. I had hoped - "

One glistening drop of liquid silver threatened, and then, fell. It hovered teasingly over the slope of his cheek, and Aleria couldn't resist the pull of it. Her breaths were shaky as she slowly inched towards that glittering rarity. With the barest brush of her lips against his cheek, she kissed it away. His body stiffened, and his hands clawed into her knees. His forehead pressed against hers.

This was a prince who deemed her worthy enough to lower his pride and give her more than promises and broken oaths. It was enough to make her fall even more in love with him. But was it enough for her to forgive and - more frightening still - to trust him again? Her mind warred with her heart as she searched for what to say. For a long moment, they stayed there, the rain soaking her to the bone, warm, but cleansing.

"Forgive me. Please," he whispered next to her cheek, his hands still planted firmly on her knees. "I beg you to end no other curses besides the one of my own making. Please, Aleria. End my torment." He breathed a feather-light kiss to her ear. A brush of his lips over her neck, then into the curve between her neck and shoulder where he rested his head.

For a long moment, Aleria considered his words. He wasn't asking her to stay for the curse; he was begging her to choose him. To stay for him...but what did that even mean? Maybe it meant that he would come to Fayeharrow with her. She was willing - Creator help her - to face whatever was before them, but not because of oaths or broken promises. She would do it because they each cared deeply for the good of each other. Because that's what people do when they are falling in love.

Tangling her fingers in his hair, she pulled until his face lined up with hers. Her eyes met his, her truth dangling from the tip of her tongue.

"I never wanted to play the damsel." Aleria couldn't remember a time where her voice had ever sounded so small. "I never wanted anyone to do the saving beside me because that would prove my weakness. And yet, there I was in a situation where I could not save myself, and I unfairly placed the responsibility on you. I signed up to be the savior here. Even if we were not forced to the palace, I would have gone because I wanted to be your savior."

She pulled back to look him in the eyes, her own brimming with tears.

"I wanted to be the heroine in my own story, not the victim. Break the curse, save the prince, win his heart," she said with a tearful laugh as she stroked her fingers over his jawline. "But the truth of the matter is neither of us is the hero or heroine when it comes to love. It's not a competition, a passing of blame, or a prize we set out to win." She tried for a smile as her eyes caught the weight of his stare, the curiosity, the hope. "Love is waking up every day with the person who makes you passionate about your calling. Love understands when to be the heroine and when being a damsel is perfectly fine. Love is fighting beside someone to reach not only your goals, but theirs. It's sacrifice, it's hard work, it's trust and forgiveness. And Creator above, when you find your someone, it's worth every bit of it."

The words tumbled from her in a river of expression, jagged, raw, and wet. Larkin stared at her, hanging on her every messy word. With a watery smile, she pressed her forehead against his and whispered, "You're worth it, every bit of it."

He held her gaze for a long moment before the tension between them snapped like a thread stretched too tight. All there was in her world was him and the way he was looking at her. There was an awkward cautiousness to how his hands found their place on either side of her face. His thumbs brushing away the stream of tears and drops of rainfall alike. She was getting soaked, but she couldn't find it in herself to care. His eyes were searching her face for something else, a question still lingering there between them that gave her pause.

"Tell me what you're thinking," she whispered, afraid of the revelation. All she knew was that there could be no more secrets between them if this were going to work. Another lie or veiled truth would surely break them both.

"I'm wondering if this is real," he said with a little self-conscious laugh. A Fae prince, self-conscious, because of her. "I'm wondering if I'm being presumptuous in assuming you feel the same way about me." Pulling back, he tilted her chin up, searching her face for the answer before voicing the question. "Do you love me, Aleria Edlind, Lady of Fayeharrow?"

The question made her gasp. She had asked for this, and yet, standing here on the precipice of it scared her out of her mind. Images of MyKhal flashed for a moment, and she banished the thought away. Larkin wasn't MyKhal. No love was the same, and to compare the two would be unfair. She knew her answer, but the fear of giving it life by voicing it was nearly choking her. She tried to say the words a few times, but her mouth wouldn't quite cooperate. So, instead, she said one word.

"Yes," her voice shook. He swept her rain-soaked hair away from her face. His smile revealed the rare glimpse of his dimples before he let out a breath tinted with a chuckle.

"Allow me," he breathed, sliding one hand behind her neck and the other on her hip. "Allow me to show you the depth of my love for you, Aleria Edlind." She could barely nod once before his lips were upon hers. Electric-like lightning, singing her down to her very soul. Creator, he was burning her alive. Thunder rumbled around them. Warm spring rain poured over them in gentle, soaking rivulets. The warmth on her skin and the heat of his lips against hers were a blur of sensation all their own. Larkin's passion was a tempest, and it was her pure delight to brave it.

When his gale had tempered, and they both were desperate for breath, he slowly pulled away from her. His thumb ghosted across her lips. Aleria's legs felt like jelly as he supported her against his chest and tilted her head, so he could brush the tenderest of kisses against her forehead.

"If you still need the words, I love you, and I would lay the world, either world, at your feet, were you to wish it so."

Aleria couldn't help but laugh at that.

"You absolutely would not. You are far too noble to do so, and I love you enough to never ask such a thing."

"Which is why I knew I could trust you with such a powerful thing as my undying affections," he teased her gently as he kissed her cheek, her nose, and her lips again. The rain around them slacked to a light mist.

"Creator help anyone who opposes us now."

"Indeed," he chuckled, breathing in her kiss once more. When a chill began to settle in her bones, she looked up at him and shivered, pointing in the direction of the camp.

"We should probably go back. "

Kissing her lips one more time, he nodded and locked his fingers with hers. She looked at him curiously.

"They all know anyway. I won't hide this, not from anyone. Never again."

Her heart fluttered, and she nodded as a faint blush heated her cool cheeks. Her fingers tightened around his.

He should not have come out tonight.

It wasn't the fact he'd been drowning himself in drink lately. It was that any type of revelry felt like spitting on Ali's grave. It was all part of Dray's idea to build comradery within his merry band of misfits. The truth of the matter was they hated MyKhal, and he bloody well didn't blame them for it.

He made training worse than the nethers for all of them. If they were going to war, there was no point in pussyfooting around. After seeing the creature's bloodied remains, he wasn't sure why any of them had even stayed. Those that had stayed after the gory revelation of their assemblage were either desperate or completely insane. Draven tried to convince him it was loyalty to the Edlinds that drove most of them, but he did admit that there were a few who were completely mad.

MyKhal had laughed half-heartedly at that. If he were honest, he knew that he couldn't say a word about their mental stability. He was still seeing the ghost of his dead lover both day and night. At least when he was around other people, her presence stayed away. Sometimes, she would watch from the other side of the room. Sometimes, she would disappear entirely. He hated himself for missing that presence. It's the only small piece of her that he was still blessed enough to keep.

Tonight though, she was nowhere to be seen. While the sane part of him knew it should be a relief, it also made him uneasy and paranoid. Guilt and self-loathing were the only two things that never left his side.

When he walked into the rowdy bar, it took everything in him not to turn right back around and head out. If not for Draven calling his name from across the room, he probably would have. With a forced half-smile, he meandered towards the group of men who took up half the pub. Some offered up their drinks in salute, others hooted after him, but a few gave him glares that he knew all too well. Those were the men who had known of his father's injustices and similarly suffered losses. He wouldn't be surprised if one of them tried to run him through. Creator knows, he would if he were them.

Quite literally pulling him from his thoughts, Dray grabbed him by the back of the neck. He pulled him down into the seat next to him with a laugh.

"Bout' time you showed up. I was beginin' to think I was gonna have ta' drag your arse out here." He was already sloshed.

"You can't even drag your arse out of here," he said, flagging down a waitress and ordering a pint. "I'm not holding your hair back while you worship the chamber pot later. Just so you're aware."

"This stomach's made of lead. The only deity I'll be worshiping this evening is that goddess right over there."

MyKhal didn't even look in the woman's direction.

Before he drowned his sorrows in drink, he made the mistake of drowning them in women. It was always when someone reminded him of Aleria. But no matter how intriguing the woman, how lush the body, how high the bliss, it always came crashing down on him that it wasn't her. He remembered the first time he had slept with a woman after Aleria's supposed betrayal. It was rough, angry, short, and shameful. From that moment on, he felt numb, always chasing the things he felt when he was with her. It took him longer than he would have liked to understand that no amount of pleasure could satisfy him. It wasn't about pleasure. It was about loving her.

"Be careful with those goddess types. They will smite you where you stand," he teased as a lovely blonde sat a few glasses down on the scratched wood table.

"Sounds like you've been burned, handsome," the barmaid said with a sweet smile. "I'll tell you the cure is not in the bottom of these, that's for sure," she said, pushing him a drink anyway.

"There is no cure for what ails me, darling," he said, tilting his glass towards her in thanks. The blonde leaned over, propping an elbow on his shoulder before leaning in to brush the words over his ear.

"I bet I have a few things that could ease your ache." She smelled like ale and something warm and earthen. Good, grounded, but not his taste. Not wild-grown honeysuckles and toasted vanilla.

"I doubt that." He didn't want to wound the girls' pride, but the words fell out of his mouth nonetheless. She balked and rolled her eyes before scooping up some coin Draven tossed down and sauntered away.

"Eh," One of the larger men at the table directed at him, "You outent hurt a lady's pride like that. Ya shoulda taken what she offered ya. Unless ye a flit. Then, well, guess that would make sense."

Draven choked on his ale and nearly spit it on the table. MyKhal narrowed his gaze on the big mouth brute. His meaty hand clutched the large mug and nearly swallowed it whole. MyKhal smirked. This was a distraction he could get behind.

"Just wasn't interested. That's all," MyKhal said, giving the oaf one more chance to shut his mouth, though part of him revelled in the idea that he wouldn't. The brute, he thought his name was Henric, took a deep swig of his drink and eyed him over the rim. Draven had moved on from the conversation and was instead flirting with his aforementioned "goddess."

MyKhal could tell Henric was weighing his words. Deciding if what was mulling around in his tiny brain was worth whatever would happen next. When he set his drink down, MyKhal knew the idiot had decided to press his luck.

"Yeah, a cultured Lord's boy like yourself only has a taste for the finer things in life. Speaking of, how was the Lady Edlind? Rumor has it you're the blighter who took 'er flower."

Rage like no other flashed inside of him before the onset of cold rushed through his veins. A killing calm that narrowed his perception and pulled a cruel, wicked, smirk across his lips.

"Not as good as your sister. I can tell you that." MyKhal took another long pull from his glass as Henric stood, shouting profanities. MyKhal held up a finger to him as he drained the last of his drink and set the tankard down. The cup had barely hit the table before that meaty hand was flying towards his face in a fist. The first hit split open his lip and snapped his head to the side so fast he felt his neck crack. That euphoric sensation of pain and the copper tang of blood lit him like a bomb. The slow turn of his head...like a long fuze. He smiled broadly. Trepidation ghosted over the oaf's features as MyKhal stood and faced him down.

"That wasn't as good as your sister's either." This guy was too easy. Henric took on the color of a freshly pulled beat as he shook like he was about to combust. He reached across the table to grab MyKhal by the throat, but with a slight turn of his body, MyKhal dodged, reaching up to snatch Henric's wrist.

Draven suddenly caught back up to what was going on and tried to intervene. "Bloody Creator's bollox, the sard are you - "

But Henric used his other fist to land a second punch to MyKhal's jaw. Draven cursed and reached for his ale. "Sard," he said, rolling his sleeves up. "Promise me you'll use your daddy's money to foot the bill for this," Draven said as he took his ale and stepped back to give them some room. MyKhal nodded his head with a broad grin. That was all the permission he needed.

Without another word, MyKhal drug the brute from their table and further into the pub. Jeers sounded around the room, but all he could focus on was the pounding of blood rage in his ears. It felt good. Sard, it felt too bloody good. Wiping the blood from his mouth, he stood to his full height. The room went silent as the two stared each other down. Henric stood a little more than six feet tall, broad, and as meaty as his fists. MyKhal was nearly as tall as him, but half the mass.

His structure was more coiled muscle, compact and sculpted by years of mercenary work on Brennan's shore. It was true he was a Lord's son, but he was nothing like the young man that had left this place. The first year had very nearly broken him. His first kill even more so. Then, he had lost Aleria, and all hope and kindness he had possessed disappeared in the darkness of death and debauchery.

He waited for Henric to move again, something he learned in year two. Your opponents would show you where to strike,   what their weakness was within the first few moments of a fight. As Henric stepped forward, cocking his fist back again, MyKhal noticed the way he favored his right side. The strength that came from there. The room slowed to a crawl for him as the fist flew at him again. He sidestepped it, using Henric's momentum against him and shoving him into a table behind. The oaf stumbled around, gaining his footing again as he turned on him like a raging bull. MyKhal smirked at him. Another thing year two taught him, anger made you foolish when it was not contained. Striking out in anger only made you open for an attack. Just like Henric. When the brute flew at him again, MyKhal ducked the blow, shooting up with a punch to his throat. Henric gasped, gripping his neck as he fought for breath. The blow was a bit childish, MyKhal thought, but the prick deserved it for provoking him with Aleria.

When Henric could breathe again, he had very nearly lost his mind, striking out wildly, attempting to take him to the ground. MyKhal met him blow for blow, slamming his fist into Henric's face before taking a fist to his guts. The air rushed from his lungs, and he panted a laugh. His grin, stretching across his face, split his lip further. This. He needed this.

"Why are you laughing, you sick blighter? I'll give you something to laugh about," Henric growled as he launched at him again. MyKhal laughed harder when his fist crunched into Henric's unprotected nose. The spurt of blood that covered his hand made his vision swim in red. The levity and invigoration of the fight lost in a single smattering of blood. The smile fell from his face as a cold calm settled over him. Blood, so much blood flashed in his mind's eye. His entire body was covered in it. Metallic, rotten, swallowing him whole.

He didn't even flinch as the next hit came and the next. He only stood, his vision narrowing, rimmed in red. In a blink, he was moving, forcing Henric first into a table, then flipping him over and onto the ground. The red in his vision pulsed, begged, drove. He landed his next punch to Henric's face, and the next, and the next. The cheers in the room switched to worrying noises, shouts of his name. He hit again, the blood spattering on his face, his hand, wet with it.

"Khal! Enough!" Draven's voice called him, but he didn't stop. Sets of hands pulled at him, yanking him off of Henric's motionless body. Concern, calls for a healer, shocked silence, all of it met his ears that thrummed with the beat of his pulse. Shaking off their hold, his mind began to slowly right itself, and the eyes that met his first were Draven's, full of concern and a twinge of fear. "What in the Creator's name happened to you?"

MyKhal didn't answer as he turned and left the pub with a slam of the door.

He should not have come out tonight.

Mykhal

No one came for his head in the middle of the night, something he honestly expected. Maybe that meant that Henric had survived. He had been too much of a coward to seek him out or even ask about him this morning. Part of him felt ashamed, but the more disturbing part of him felt elated. Living in death and destruction for so long, it changes you. Most of the time, he felt like two people shoved in one body. One held who he was, and one kept a hold on everything he had become. The monster who lurked in the shadows and the young Lord who pretended the monster didn't exist. Last night, he was a monster, and today, he would be the young Lord, running his dead fiance's family home, pretending it wasn't driving him insane.

It was strange though how things had fallen into this odd routine that made him feel like this was his home. Truthfully, Fayeharrow had always been more like home to him than Wimborne had ever been. Coming back here simply reminded him of all the hopes he had of ruling at Aleria's side.

He had followed her father around like a lost pup. He asked him question after question, preparing before he even knew he would ask for her hand. That day had been one of the most nerve-wracking clusters of chaos he had ever been a part of, and yet, she had said yes. Shouted it, actually, and he doesn't remember ever smiling so hard. With an exasperated chuckle, he put his missives on his desk. He wondered if he would ever stop thinking about her.

Movement in the corner of his eye drew his attention, and he groaned. This ghost of Aleria made herself known with a soft smile and even softer looking hair and skin. Always standing within reach of his hands. So real he had reached out once only to pass through her like fog on the forest floor. He had summoned her yet again with his reminiscing. Creator help him; it was beginning to get too bloody hard to tell her to go.

"What can I help you with?" he asked, knowing that it was he who had invoked her visage and that she knew it too.

"Question returned, young Lord Anwir," she replied, her eyes scanning the bookshelf, fingers trailing the spines as sensually as one would a lover. He reminded himself that those fingers would not even stir the dust from their pages, nor would they be able to pluck her favorite from the pile and begin to read it.

Standing from his desk and walking to where her fingers lingered over one of her most cherished tales, he took one from the shelf and laid it open on the table before her. He was losing his mind.

"We are making progress in tracking the creatures." It was almost pathetic how much he wanted to impress her. For her to know they were going to avenge her death. For her to know how much he still cared.

"How did you manage that? Certainly, the trail had gone cold by the time I was found." She reached up to tuck her shoulder-length blond hair behind her ear. The urge to reach out and assist with that one errant wave at her cheek was maddening.

"It had, but it seems as if they hunt around these parts and close up to Wimborne and Illian Falls. We've found tracks, leftover carcasses that look nothing like what an animal of these parts can do. They are cautious though; they never leave a trail back to their hoard. I think what is most disconcerting about these things is their intelligence. These aren't mindless beasts, and that makes them all the more dangerous. "

Aleria looked at him and tilted her head to the side, considering him and his words.

"I hope you and Draven know I do not need a sacrifice from either of you. If this is a threat to either of your lives, you should stop now. I don't want to have to kick both of your backsides from joining me far before your time."

"We aren't - It isn't - I mean, we want you to rest, and this is only the first on the list of things you deserve. You didn't deserve this fate, and we only want to make it right."

Aleria sighed and turned away from him, pacing the length of the room while tying her hair back in a low bun.

"If you want to make it right with me, support Draven's rule here. Get rid of your father, get him out of my family's home, and stay. Stay to support my cousin because he will need you in the coming days. He did not train for this, but you did. The two of you could take care of my people. It's the only thing I've ever wanted to be done in my name. Take care of Fayeharrow, Khal."

His smile was soft as he nodded to her and went back to his spot at the desk.

"I will do all those things, love. I swear it to you."

"Thank you," she said quietly, as she came to sit on the edge of his desk. She was so close, and he swore he could smell her signature scent of honeysuckle dancing between them in the air. Her fingers lay splayed next to his, less than a touch away. His own unconsciously twitched towards her.

"I miss you so much," he confessed, voicing the words that suffocated him day after day. Her fingers shifted close, and his breath hitched. "I would set the world ablaze to hold you in my arms again," he groaned and leaned as close as he dared, nearly breathing her in, a hair's breadth away from brushing his lips against hers. "My gift and my torture alike, what I wouldn't give to kiss you again." As he neared her, she dissipated and reappeared farther from him.

"And that is why we could never be. Our love was too wild, too selfish. We wanted each other so desperately, and if not for the interference of your father, we would have never grown up."

He shook his head.

"I don't believe that for a second, and neither do you. We were good together. We were different, but we balanced each other out. I'm the stone to your fire. You can burn atop me, singe me, but I will forever be your grounding and your strength. I would never dream of quenching you. I would have held you aloft for the world to see and be as inspired as you made me feel."

"Poet," she whispered with a twitch of her lips.

"Only for you," he whispered, taking a step closer. He leaned in with a tilt of his head, but all he felt was cold and the morning mist.

Quick rapping on his chamber door broke the tension and snapped his mind back to attention.

"Come in," he said, reorganizing the missives on his desk and looking through the week's payroll. His father had dropped the mundane and financial parts of running Fayeharrow in his lap only a week after his arrival. He didn't mind it though. At least in this way, he was doing as Aleria had asked, taking care of her people. If his father had his way, he would have cut everyone's pay already, saying the Edlinds were far too generous.

MyKhal recognized the soldier who entered swiftly with urgency written all over his face.

"Sir, excuse me for the interruption, but there has been an attack."

He shot up from his desk and began strapping on his weapons, excitement and trepidation alike racing through him.

"Where?"

"Near Harion's Glade, off the King's Road. Two miles north."

"Commander Edlind?"

"I sent Kai to inform him."

"Good. Ready the others. Meet me at the stables. We are going hunting tonight."

"Yes, sir."

Once his weapons were strapped on, he turned and saw the Whitewood bow leaning in the corner of his room. Something inside him felt the anticipation in the wind. Purpose. As he grabbed the bow and strapped it to his back, he felt everything he wanted to give to her and for her rushing through him. Tonight, he would be her avenger. Tonight would be the first step in setting her free.

Chapter 31

Aleria

It was strange how things had fallen into this odd routine that made her feel...at home. The first words spoken when they returned to camp were lude comments.

"There are other ways to - , " Zander started, but Larkin cut him off with a spark of electricity shot his way. His brother deflected with a flame and laughed. The tension that was there disappeared as quickly as the smoke of his flame.

Aleria knew she needed to clear the air further; there was no sense in putting it off. Addressing the group, she took a deep breath.

"I'm sorry for how I acted before. To all of you, especially you, Thea. I'm sorry."

Thea gave her a harsh stare as she stood up. Aleria felt nerves settle in her stomach at her approach. She deserved whatever tongue lashing was coming.

"You were wrong," Thea said. "I do care about whether you stay or go. You...you've become my friend, and I don't have many."

Aleria blinked, a small smile forming on her lips.

"Aleria, I don't want you to go. This curse..."

"Thea," Larkin's deep baritone cut her off as he shook his head. Aleria felt the sting of his command as Thea withdrew and nodded.

"Thea, I have to go home at least for a while. You are fighting for your people, and I understand that, but I have my people too. I've been away from them long enough." Her shoulders slumped as she took a step forward and placed her hand on Thea's arm.

"I get it. I do." Thea moved quickly to the other side of camp where Ruke was preparing the food. It was a dismissal, and she knew it. With a sigh, she looked up at Larkin, who seemed just as torn. The two of them still needed to talk about all of this.

"I need to get those wet bandages off your wounds and rewrap you with dry ones. We don't need infection setting in."

"Thank you." Her returning smile was tight-lipped as she followed his nod in the direction of her tent.

She reminded herself apologies and forgiveness were the hurdles of every relationship, the blind jump that could have you catching your toe and falling face-first to the ground. Compromise, on the other hand, was a fork in the road that could lead you away from the race entirely. Whatever was said in this tent would determine both their paths and whether they could run them together.

No pressure there at all.

Her hands pushed back the flap, and she ducked inside. A chill rolled through her as she quickly opened her pack and pulled out another tunic and leggings. Exhaustion then made itself known, bogging down her movements and weighing her eyes. Larkin approached her. He reached out, gently tugging the sopping hem of her shirt.

"May I?" he whispered, and she swallowed hard.

"Why are you always trying to get me undressed?" she teased.

"Because I can not get enough of you." His teasing whisper was rough as he pulled the dripping fabric over her head and threw it in the corner of the tent.

"Shameless flirt." The playful banter was a deflection. A way to tamper the myriad of feelings racing through her as his fingers ghosted over her bandages. His only response was a wink as he handed her a blanket and directed her over to the makeshift pallet. With a grunt of discomfort, she splayed the front half of her body out and braced herself. His breaths were deep, even, and controlled as he used a small blade to cut away the binding that wrapped around her. When the final binding was cut free, his sudden intake of breath made her flinch. For a long moment, his fingers did not return to her skin, and her insecurities rose tenfold. For a perfect creature like himself, easily healed from every wound or scar, she must look like a monster.

"I'm so sorry." His voice broke a little on the words.

"I already forgave you."

"I know. Aleria, I - "

"Please, don't do this. We have other things to deal with, and I don't want to talk about this part anymore."

There was a pause. A tension. Then, a release as a soft cloth dipped in some sort of fiery astringent wiped over the lower parts of her wounds. She bucked, biting down on her lip to keep in a groan.

"I'm sorry. I have to clean them. I'm not as adept as Tiadona at the healing arts. Did she give you some herbs to take?"

Aleria nodded and pointed towards her pack. "First compartment. In the small bag." She thanked him as he handed her a ball of the herbal concoction and gagged as she swallowed it whole. When he swept the cloth back over her wounds, she placed the blanket between her teeth and bit down. The herbs would take a while yet to set in.

"I'm so - "

"Don't dare say that again in this tent," she growled. "We are delaying the - Ow! - inevitable."

His only response was a hum of acknowledgment and a hiss when he made her jump again. So he wouldn't be the first to bring it up. Fine. She needed a distraction from the pain anyway.

"I still want to go home," she started, and to his credit, his hands didn't stop their tending. "It's not because I don't believe in you or trust that you care for me. It's just - do you want to be tied to me? After everything? Your grandfather - "

"Is a racist monster who needs to be dethroned."

Aleria flinched a bit, not expecting such a confession, but the words gave her a bit of hope.

He chuckled a little at her reaction.

"Did you think I would side with him on this? Aleria, the moment I ran towards you, I challenged him. Now, it's all about whether or not you wish to stand there with me. We have an idea about the curse. We can - "

"I have an idea if you will hear me out," she interrupted him. He had reached the center and most tender part of her back, and her hands clenched so tight the blue and green of her veins nearly glowed beneath her skin.

"I'm listening." His voice was as calm and focused as his hands, and it made her feel a little more at ease.

"Come with me to Fayeharrow."

She waited for him to combat her, but he only whispered, "And do what?"

"Help return me to my home."

"Done. Anything else?" His hands moved up to her upper back, and she groaned.

"Jus - Mmmmm. Ow. - Just like that?"

"Were you expecting me to deny you when you well know that to deny you anything is beyond me?" he teased her lightheartedly. "Knowing such a thing makes you quite the powerful creature now."

"It does, doesn't it?" She buried her smile in the blanket. "Well, then, I guess I have one more request."

"Ask it," he whispered, leaning down to kiss her ear.

"Stay with me," she whispered, her heart on her sleeve. "You and the Huldra could have a home with me until we figure out how we can help your people. We can do the Claiming on my side of the crossing, away from your grandfather's interference. I swear to you, I will do everything I can to help you end this curse, and when it ends...your people...if they wish it...will have a safe place with me in Fayeharrow. We can bridge the gap between our people...and - ," she tried to turn to face him, to see how he was reacting, but he tisked at her, pushing her down gently.

"It's a beautiful offer, love. But if I know anything about humans, it's that we won't be accepted as easily as you believe we will." The sound of a jar being opened filled the silence after his words. The bittersweet smell of ointment filling the air before the sting of it hit her wounds. "Everyone fears what they do not understand, and that fear can easily turn to hatred and violence. You and I both don't want that for our people."

"I understand the risks, Larkin. But I can also see how promising the future could be. Will you take some time to think it over?"

The herbs were beginning to take effect now, her eyes feeling heavy, her body tingling from head to toe.

"Can you sleep like this?" he asked instead of answering her question, and her heart sank a bit. "I think it would be good for your wounds to air out a bit, at least for a few hours."

With a deep sigh, she nodded and turned her head away from him. She wouldn't have expected it to be easy convincing him, but that he wouldn't hear her out at all...

"I will come with you. As for the Huldra, they'll have to make their own decisions. There is much at stake here, and changing both our worlds is a bigger decision than the two of us. "

With a deep sigh, she nodded again, burying her face in the blankets. His echoing sigh was more of a deep groan as he kissed the back of her head.

"I will seek the counsel of the others on the matter and see where they stand. I'm not saying no, Aleria. I'm simply admitting that I don't know what to do. Nonetheless, I will return you to your home with you." Her heart picked up its hobbled trudge and sprinted into a full and giddy gallop.

"Thank you."

His tone was nowhere near as giddy as her hers when he said, "You know as well as I do this love between us can never be entirely selfish. We are rulers down to our very soul, and understanding that, I hope you also understand that the lengths you are willing to go to save your home are the same I do for mine. Please don't expect something from me that you could never offer yourself. We are too much alike in that way."

Turning so she could look him in the eyes, she gave him a tight-lipped smile. "I understand. We have to share each other with the world... well...worlds."

"Indeed, we do," he whispered as he kissed her forehead. "Now, rest a few hours. I'll bring you something to eat before I take the first watch."

"Thank you," she managed as a strange feeling began to overtake her. Perhaps it was the herbs, but the strange feeling plagued her even as she slept. In her dreams, she stood at a fork in the road.

Larkin

"She wants me to come with her."

It would have been comical how everyone's brows rose to their hairlines if he hadn't been serious. When she asked, his instinct was to say yes. To tell her again that he would give her anything she wished. Mother help him. He wanted to be with her, but it wasn't that simple.

"I've promised her I would help reclaim her home. Then, from there, we need to decide our paths." Looking them all in the eye, one at a time, he made his thoughts known. "You swore an oath to go where the crown called, and I released you from it. Every step you take from now on will be of your own volition. I will bear you no ill will if you choose not to follow me where I go."

The silence that followed was long and difficult to bear. He had known them all since childhood. To have them walk away from him now would be a blow that was difficult to recover from. He meant every word he said though. He wanted them to be free to make their own choices. Zander made a move towards him and slowly took a knee in front of him.

"I have followed you this far, brother. I will go wherever your winds carry us next." Holding his hands out in offering, he set them alight. "My power is your own to use however you see fit." Larkin felt that strange prickling sensation in his eyes as he reached a water-drenched hand out to his brother and clasped it, creating a puff of steam. When Zander stood, Thea and Ruke took his place.

"As we belong to each other, together, we offer ourselves to you. Our power is yours to use however you see fit." Larkin fought to hide his smile as he nodded and gripped their wrists in a warrior's handshake. Nox stood with his arms crossed. The flame and shadow of the fire danced around his features. Something had been off about him since their return to Tiadona's.

"Nox?" Thea prompted, her words a question and a prod for him to follow.

"I can't do this," Nox said, fearful and nervous. "Not in good conscience can I follow you. Not when - " His voice caught in his throat. "I sent for Helix."

Larkin flinched as a stab of pain shot through him as raw and violent as an arrow to the chest.

"What do you mean?" His voice was hard as he took a step forward. Thea slid between them and placed a hand on his chest. "Larkin, please," she begged him, knowing the danger in provoking him. Ruke was close beside her, ready to intervene if he must.

"I turned you in. I sent for the guard. I didn't expect...I was only trying to protect you. This was a fool's errand, and you see how it all turned out. I thought...I thought it best that she - "

Thunder boomed around him as the wind began to pick up. "You thought it best?!?" Larkin shouted, trying as best he could to reign in his giftings before he hurt someone. The storm raging inside him threatened to swallow him whole.

"I thought it would release you from whatever spell she'd cast. You were blind to the realities of our world. I had no idea she had a cure in her blood, not until Tiadona. I'm sorry. I thought it was unfair that you were risking us all for nothing."

Larkin growled at him over Thea's shoulder, "She is everything. You know that. You can feel it. And yet you still tried to kill her."

"Larkin," Thea begged, but he stepped back from her, the wind dying down.

"You've made your choice, Thea, and your brother has made his. He made it the moment he betrayed me, betrayed us all." He glared at Nox. "Go home. You felt as if you could make a decision for me, and now, I will make a decision for you. I wish to break your oath. Leave."

Nox looked as if he were about to wretch as he glanced around at the members of the group. Thea reached for her brother, but Ruke pulled her back. She looked as if she didn't know whether to smite him or collapse on him in tears.

"Do you see what she's already caused?" Nox said with a wrinkled brow.

"Your betrayal was what did this. Not Aleria. Use her name. Perhaps that would make you see that she is a person you allowed to be tortured nearly to death. I wish you had been there to feel her pain." Narrowing his gaze he said, "You were right on one part. I foolishly risked us. I foolishly risked her, and I will not do so again. I will protect my family, and I claim her now as part of it. If you cannot do the same, then leave."

Nox looked from Thea to Ruke to Zander, and finally, to Larkin before shaking his head and saying, "I do not claim her. I won't risk my life for her."

Larkin felt a strange mixture of pain and acceptance at the confession. He would not force anyone to join him on this new journey. "Then, I wish you well on your journey back home."

There would be no brokering of an argument. No changing the other's mind. Nox huffed a sigh and started to say something else, but thought better of it and turned to leave. Thea ran after him, wrapping him in a hug, tears running down her cheeks. Ruke followed after a moment, leaving Larkin standing there with Zander at his side.

"Well, sard," his brother sighed, crossing his arms over his chest.

Larkin did not have the words to reply. The ache in his chest and the anger of Nox's betrayal still fresh and oozing. A cut that hurt him deeper than he was willing to show. Nox had been the heart of this group for so long, and Larkin hated the idea of going on without him. Though, he was right when he said they had both made a choice. His was Aleria, and he would do whatever it took to keep her safe from here on out.

Nox said his goodbyes and saddled up, not wasting a moment, leaving them behind. The rest of the evening was spent in somber reflection. Food was prepared. They ate in silence, and then, headed to their respective tents. Zander took first watch, though Thea tried to convince him to let her do it. Larkin didn't envy the choice she made. If he were in her shoes, he would have done the same. He loved his brother dearly, but he would let him go his own way if he chose to do so.

Filling a bowl with some stew, he took it to Aleria's tent, honoring what he had said before about waking her before he took the second watch. He hated to wake her. But if she were to go waltzing back into her old life, she needed to be fed and as rested as she could be. He worried about her mobility were things to come to blows. From what he had learned of the vile human who had taken her home, he was a coward and a snake, both of which could be easily dealt with by either a quick beheading or startling him back into his hole.

Pushing the tent flat back, he smiled as his eyes fell to her sleeping form. His human woman was warm like herbal tea. Her skin glowing with soft honeyed cream tones in the light of the fire from outside. Setting the dish on a small side table, he leaned over and brushed a wild golden lock of hair from her cheek.

"Bewitching little thing," he whispered, leaning down to graze his lips over her forehead. She moaned and mumbled something he couldn't quite understand. Chuckling, he moved his lips to her cheek and then her nose. She mumbled profanity at him loud and clear. Laughing at that intended insult, he kept kissing her playfully until she swatted at him. He dodged it and caught her wrist, pulling it to his lips and placing a kiss there that was far from playful. Her sharp intake of breath made his pride swell a little. Her forest green eyes met his, and he knew he finally had her attention.

"You're a dirty fighter, Fae Prince," she mumbled, still half-asleep as she tried to rise, all while keeping her modesty intact. It was silly, but he would respect her choice nonetheless.

"And you're a wicked temptation..." He watched as she blushed prettily and sat up, motioning to her pack.

"I'm guessing that smell means food and your first watch?"

He nodded and leaned in as he handed her pack to her. He took longer than he should have to breathe the same air as her before pressing the gentlest of kisses to her lips, sudden vulnerability overtaking him as he basked in the warmth of her.

"Happiness has always been something that frightened me. Too many times it's been snatched away..." His lips brushed hers again before he pulled back to look her in the eyes. "That fate would have me fall for a finite woman could have been seen as cruel. But it has only affirmed the idea that I should bask in this happiness for as long as I have. You make me happy, you delicate, perfect, human, and I will not waste a moment of it."

He was helpless, and she was breathless. He swooped in, Claiming her lips, and relishing the happiness between them. His fingers brushed her cheeks, her neck, her collar bone. Lightly touching her, he continued down her sides to the hem of her breeches where he hooked in his thumbs. How he wanted her. All of her. But not like this. Not with her wounds as they were. Not in a camp where every noise could be heard and commented on at a later time. No. She deserved more than a lust-induced romp in a tent in the middle of the woods.

Regretfully, he pulled back and kissed her forehead, taking the initiative to slow things down before they went too far.

"Let me bind your wounds, and you need to eat something and get some rest before we finish the trip. You're less than a day from home; you need to be prepared."

Aleria sighed and rested her head against his chest.

"You're right, but...Larkin...I..." She looked up at him, flushed, and bit down on her bottom lip again. His attention on the rosey flesh of it was snatched away as a sound rumbled low in the distance, a crack that perked his ears and snapped his head in its direction.

Panting.

Fire crackling.

Slow controlled steps.

Snap.

A low growl.

"Stay here," he commanded before he released her from his hold and was out of his tent and into his own in seconds. He could hear her questions on the wind as he grabbed his weapons. His magic pulsing beneath his skin, adrenaline and fear alike danced along with the sparks lighting his veins. A building of pressure, primed, ready to be released.

Upon stepping out of his tent, the scent hit him like a raging steed.

Briony.

Burning briony was like releasing a magical gag. If a Fae breathed it in, they could no longer reach their magic. It was typically used for medicinal purposes or surgeries. The fact that it was now encompassing the perimeter of their camp only meant one thing: this was a trap.

Since when were the Nattmara conscious enough to set traps? Ripping a strip of fabric from a sheet, he wrapped it around his nose and mouth before tying it in the back. He should have been more careful. Nattmara did not attack like this, not without the driving of the moon. Something about all this was like it had been in the fields. This was planned. He cursed as he looked around the campsite that was slowly filling with Briony infused smoke. Thea and Ruke stumbled from their tent, coughing and tying their makeshift masks around their faces. Zander was nowhere to be seen.

His heart lept to his throat when he saw a Nattmarra. It was at least two heads higher than him, dragging a gagged and tied Zander into the center of their camp. Fury and electricity sputtered, like a guttering flame. He called to the light inside him, but it trembled and shook, slipping through his hold. His breath became ragged as he called to the winds and the rains from the depths of himself, smoke choking him and his efforts.

The Nattmarra pinned him with a glare and intelligence he did not expect from that side of the beast.

It spoke. Its words grave and deep, a mumble without lips to cut the syllables and oversized teeth that made each word have the remnants of a hiss.

"Come with us, prince. You and your human girl. Come peacefully, and we will leave the others be."

Larkin stared, dumbstruck for a moment. It was talking. It had consciousness. Larkin looked to Thea and Ruke, who seemed to be trying and failing to reach their powers. Briony had done its job. Still, they were far from helpless and even farther from bargaining.

"Would you call this peacefully done, beast?"

The Nattmara retorted with a rumbling growl. Larkin glanced towards Aleria's tent and saw the open flap rippling in the light breeze. In the back of his mind, he hoped she had fled or at least was hiding until everything was over. She was in no condition to fight, but that was not who she was.

As if his mind had conjured her, she stepped behind him and slid her hand into his. It was warm and wet and for a moment; the feeling startled him. Then, realization settled over him, and he glanced back at her. A moment of understanding passed between them as he looked down at the fresh wound in her palm. A promise that he would not be alone in this, that come darkness or drowning rains, her hand would not leave his. Turning his attention back to the Nattmara, he grinned wickedly.

"How about we settle this like Fae?" he whispered before releasing Aleria's bloody hand for a moment and sliding his over his blade. The slice of metal on his skin was uncomfortable. Still, he knew the rush of magic between them would burn away any residual pain. His eyes didn't look away as a pack of Nattmarra appeared, two by two, then four by four. He counted twenty in the shadows, but he knew there were more. This was going to be a bloodbath.

His heart pounded in his chest as the tension thickened. His powers were dulled, but his senses were acute. Glancing towards his companions, he smirked at Thea, who already had her bow drawn; Ruke with his massive glaive; and Zander who was staring at him, begging to be set free. Releasing his brother would be his first task. Casting one more glance at Aleria, he slipped his hand into hers and chaos reigned as curse-breaking power sparked between them.

Larkin

It was as if everything were moving in slow motion. His hand, dripping in blood, slid into hers, and like a clap of lightning, power ricocheted through her entire being and burst outwards. She watched as the hoard of beasts roared, rippled, and transformed before her eyes back into their original forms: Fae men and women, painted for war. They shook themselves, stretched, and groaned. They were not completely naked like the first time she and Larkin had turned them. No, this time, their bodies were covered in furs in their most intimate places. Leather straps wrapped around their chests and backs, holding their weapons until they freed them.

They were expecting this. They had prepared, and she and the Huldra had lost their edge. Squeezing Larkin's hand, she pulled her borrowed blade free. With a roar, she and Larkin charged forward, setting their sights on what mattered most: Zander.

Fire and energy crackled through her veins as she attacked, slicing through skin and muscle alike. Her blow sent the Fae female in front of her to her knees where she shrieked and held her injured side. An angry Fae man charged towards her, his eyes flicking to the injured woman before connecting with hers. He flew at her. His wicked-looking daggers arching in an eviscerating attack. Larkin yanked hard, pulling her away, sliding in with his weapon.

The deafening crack of metal against metal made her ears ring. Aleria steadied herself and swung in for the assist. Slicing her blade in an upward arch, hoping to disarm the Fae warrior, her sword caught one of the duel weapons and sent it flying off into the darkness of the wood. Larkin drove his sword home in a nearly lethal hit beneath his opponent's ribs. They didn't have a moment to breathe as three more descended upon them. Larkin parried the strike of a sword, ducked the swing of a glaive, all while pulling her along with him. Each step was a dance, and she was learning to step in rhythm with him.

They moved as one across the campsite, switching the position of their hands as needed, nevermore than a finger's length away from each other. Her back pressed to his as her fingers laced tighter around his own. Their breaths synced, and pressing back and forth against each other's back, they had almost made it to Zander, who was trying desperately to invoke his magic. Hot rage bubbled around him, and if it weren't for the Briony smoke, she imagined he just might burn the forest down.

As Larkin backed her up until she could reach Zander, a nagging thought entered her mind. Something was bothering her about how the Fae were fighting. There was something off, and her mind could not slow enough to decipher what it was. Releasing Larkin's hand for a moment, she slid her sword behind Zander's back and sliced the ropes binding his wrists. With a growl, he ripped out his gag and ran towards the Fae who had dragged him in. With a brutal kick, Zander dropped the unsuspecting Fae to the forest floor.

Reaching her bloodied hand towards Larkin's again, she had barely touched his fingers when something slammed into her. The force sent her sprawling violently across the understory. Her body stopped abruptly as a weight pressed atop her. Her vision swam. Her breaths became ragged and labored as it pressed her into the craggy, rooted ground. She cried out as her wounds stretched and cracked. Warm, wet heat soaked the back of her shirt, and she cursed. Scrambling, she reached for her sword that was just out of reach. Digging her fingers into the moss-covered ground, she grabbed for it, but a hand pressed over her wrist and another on her throat. The hands were morphing into even larger claws, the tips of which felt like sharpened silver bearing down on her skin.

A shout shook the small battlefield, and her captor howled in what she thought sounded like victory. The leader spoke again in panting, slurred syllables.

"Come with us, or the girl suffers."

Aleria's heart hammered in her chest. Larkin did not do ultimatums. Bred rulers like him knew when to sacrifice for the greater good. It's what he thought he was doing when he risked her coming here. Nausea rolled through her as her body began to shake at the memory. Creator save her, if his grandfather did such things to her, what would these creatures do?

"Release the others," Larkin spoke through gritted teeth. "Release them, free her, and I will come with you. Alone." Careful resolve in every syllable.

"You and the human are what our queen desires. We can't risk letting the others go. They will hunt us."

The leader yanked Aleria up from the ground; the claws of her captor had left bloodied red lines on her throat. They stung as she swallowed hard and stared at Larkin in wide-eyed fear. The creature's hot breath sent shivers down her spine as flashbacks began. How much torment was she able to withstand? How much could her soul bare before it broke?

"Fine."

The word echoed like the crack of that Creator forsaken whip, and her body began to tremble. She wasn't sure she could take this. She wasn't sure her mind would survive it this time.

"We will come with you if you free the girl now. Let me tend to her. Tend to your own wounded, and we will go."

Aleria felt her knees buckle beneath her in shock, relief, and sudden all-encompassing exhaustion. The Nattmara supported her weight until Larkin appeared at her side, scooping her up in his arms and walking back towards his tent. He nodded his head in the direction of the Huldra who all seemed a little worse for wear. Ruke, Zander, and Thea looked as unnerved as he felt.

"We have a fragile accord, Prince. Do not shirk our kindness," the creature called to him. Larkin didn't even nod as he ducked beneath the tent flaps and sat her down on her backside. Thea, Zander, and Ruke sat down on the pallet settled in the corner of the large tent. Aleria was still shaking.

Panic. Sheer panic consumed her as the uncontrollable trembling overtook her. Her throat felt like Nattmara claws were still wrapped around it. She couldn't breathe. She couldn't cry, though the fear and desperation clamping her mind and body in a vice made her wish she could. Curling in on herself, she dropped her head between her knees and tried to control her ragged breaths. The world blurred around her. Larkin's questions and assessment of everyone's injuries blurred into mumbles. The world tipped and bent. The next thing she knew, Larkin was shaking her lightly, saying her name again and again.

"Tell me what's happening. Aleria, can you hear me?" His hands were all over, searching for wounds. Overwhelming her. She fought them off, unable to say what she wanted. What she needed.

"Aleria. What are you doing? Let me - "

"No!" she screamed at him scuttering away to the corner of the tent, drawing her knees to her chest. She begged her mind to calm, to make it stop. Out of control. She was out of control. Her fingers pressed against her chest. Larkin reached out a hand, and she held up hers for him to give her a moment. The hurt and confusion in his eyes made her feel guilty.

"I don't…," she attempted, her chin wobbling as the feeling ebbed into something else, a weight that felt bone-deep.

"I don't know…what's…what's happening to me," she choked.

"Please let me check your wounds, Aleria."

Aleria couldn't contain the whimper that escaped her throatas Larkin came to her side. Creator, she was a coward.

A mess.

Ridiculous.

What was happening to her?

She was still trembling when his hands pulled up her shirt and revealed her reopened wounds to the cool night air. He tended her gently, cleaning, treating, and binding another piece of her that never seemed to heal. When he finished, he left her side. The blurry outline of him moving about the tent made her dizzy. She smelled blood, could almost taste the coppery tang of it on her tongue. She thought she saw a flash of a wound on Thea's thigh, the glint of a needle in someone's hand. Her hands shook as she held her head in them, trying to pull her vision back into place, to make the pieces fit. They fell in slowly, but were misshapen and forced together in places.

Tension and fear gripped her mind as she stared off without really seeing. The weight on her chest was ever-present. Her arms and legs felt as if she had run across the country barefoot while carrying a barrel of ale.

When Larkin returned to her side, she continued her blank stare off into nothing. It was easier than seeing the hurt and confusion on his face.

"I am sorry," her voice a broken whisper. " I -, " her voice wavered, and she shook her head. Larkin reached over and slid his hand beneath hers. He didn't say a word, just held her hand for a long while until she found the will to speak again.

"Something is wrong with me."

"Nothing is wrong with you…apart from being human," he assured her, pressing a kiss into the skin of her palm. "This is my fault. You've had so much taken from you, and I swear to you I will do everything in my power to not let that happen again. I will not leave you to anyone's will, nor will

I ever impose my own upon you. I am sorry I wasn't prepared for this. I'm sorry I have no idea what tomorrow will bring for us all, but know, I will fight."

Aleria sighed as his arms wrapped around her and carefully pulled her closer. The weight on her chest so heavy she felt it pulling her under, beckoning her to sleep. Her answer was the barest nod as she laid her head against this chest and let the weight sink her.

The sun had barely begun to dip over the tops of the trees when their party made its way into the Dark Wood. Energy and adrenaline sparked in electric currents between them all, anticipation and nerves alike. The hunting party was small. Their intention for tonight was not to kill the beasts, but follow them back to their lair. They would look for weakness, scout their numbers, and finally, send for reinforcements. Though MyKhal and Draven both were chomping at the bit for bloodshed, there was no reason to do something so foolish as barreling in there unprepared.

No more than ten men accompanied them, each separated in groups of two, fanning out the expanse of the wood. MyKhal kept his ears acutely tuned to everything around him. His bow in hand, arrow notched at ready should anything try to surprise them. Beside him, Draven mounted his crossbow with a bolt tipped in silver. Some legends tell silver is the key to kill beasts. Though neither one of them was a believer in superstition, they couldn't deny the merit of at least having something of the sort in their arsenal. Just in case.

Each of them moved in silence, relying on hand gestures and vocal cues that mimicked local bird calls, each with its own meaning. If these creatures were like any other wild beasts, they had acute hearing. The slightest snap of a twig, an uncontrolled breath could give them away.

As they made their way deeper into the wood, a howl echoed in the distance, sending a shiver down his spine. It stopped him and Draven dead. Casting a look towards one another, they picked up their pace, sprinting like wraiths through the dusky wood. The smell of pine and the sharp bite of autumn wind rushed over his skin as he ran from tree to tree, seeking cover. Rumbling growls and shouts bounced around the wood, making it seem as if the creatures were everywhere and yet nowhere. MyKhal pressed his back against a massive oak tree and carefully turned to the clearing ahead.

Nearly a hundred yards away, Wolven looking creatures of nightmares stood in front of what looked like humans. He couldn't tell who had the upper hand from this vantage point, but they looked to be talking. He needed to get closer. His hands formed a few signals to Draven before crouching down and making his way towards the creatures. All the while, he kept his hand on his whitewood bow.

Fifty yards, and he could see everything more clearly, though he could scarcely believe his eyes. There was a camp in the glade, smoke rolling from the ground and up into the air in wicked curling tendrils. Within the grey veil, the humans had their massive weapons at the ready. He strained his ears, listening intently for some clue as to what was happening when a clap like thunder echoed through the wood. Gasping, he dropped to the ground as a wave of something passed through him so hard he nearly lost his footing completely.

Righting himself, he gazed towards his companions to make sure they were all still with him. When he turned back to the glade, a full-on battle had broken out. The roar of the beasts turned to battle cries as the sound of clashing weapons filled the space. The creatures were no longer monstrous wolves, but long, lean men and women covered in furs and not much else. Draven whistled, throwing his hand up in a silent command to hold. MyKhal's nerves itched to join the fray, but it was a wise decision on Dray's part to wait it out.

Instead, he focused his attention on the fight. The way the creatures moved, grace and power like nothing he had ever seen before. Their massive weapons swung with an ease that did not make any sense compared to their visual weight. Skin tore, blood-splattered, and he should be horrified, but instead, he was enthralled. Until his eyes caught on a small figure moving in chaos.

The look of her gave him pause. A wildflower among goldenrods of wheat. She was a regular-sized warrior...and what warrior she was. Her golden hair lit like molten gold in the reflection of the fire. She moved like water over the rocks of a stream. Fluid. Carving out a path with understated strength. For some strange reason, her hand was in constant connection with another warrior in the group. A strange way to fight, but it didn't seem to slow them down. If anything, watching the two of them move together was enthralling. Her golden flame to his cold calm. They were mesmerizing.

He glanced back towards Draven; he was staring wide-eyed at the blonde. Awestruck.

Something in the back of his subconscious ticked. Familiarity. Like the snip of sharp shears, the threads in his mind that began to unravel... The girl...She looked like Aleria.

Shouts tore through the air, snapping his gaze from Draven and back to the battle at hand. A large man tackled Aleria's doppelganger to the ground, pinning her there with his body weight. Her companion roared as he fought to get back to her. A sudden howl ripped through the air, and the fur-clad warriors erupted with snarls and fur. Arching their backs, their noses lengthened, turning to snouts. Their skin fell away, and their bodies contorted to reveal the same grotesque wolf creatures as before. From the corner of his eye, he saw Draven move towards the fray. Murder and hope alike sparking in his eyes as he prepared to dive headlong into the chaos. Idiot. He would get himself killed.

Racing across the distance between them, he nearly tackled Draven to the ground, wrestling him back behind a tree.

"What the bloody nethers are you doing, Anwir?" Draven hissed. His eyes locked on the scene playing out in front of them, thrashing against MyKhal's hold. "It's Ali down there!" Draven growled as MyKhal doubled down on his efforts to hold him down.

"You don't know that for sure, and I won't let you rush to your death over a look-alike that could get you killed. Think of Fayeharrow," MyKhal tried to reason with him as the two of them rolled around like boys in a schoolyard tussle. Certain death was fifty yards away, and they were wrestling.

The sudden lack of noise caught his attention, and he stopped, looking up towards the glen once more. A beast held the girl in front of itself; blood stained the front of her shirt. She was trembling.

Creator. She looked just like...

Draven had gotten to his feet and had lifted his crossbow, aiming it at the beast that held Aleria's double. It was too far. The shot would miss. The girl was too close. Without a second thought, he shoved Draven, making the bolt release into the air. It ricocheted off a tree and hit the ground with a crack and a thud.

"They're going to kill her!" Draven growled, shoving him back. "If she dies, I swear to the Creator, I will kill you." The threat was out of desperation, but still, he didn't doubt those words.

"If they wanted to kill her, they already would have. They are holding her hostage. Look," he demanded, turning Draven's head into the direction of the glade once more. From this angle, he could see the back of the girl's shirt was soaked with blood. A deep dark pit of emotions swirled in his stomach as he watched the beast handed the girl over. When she disappeared with the others inside the tent, the creatures prowled around the camp, sniffing out their wounded and seemingly trying to mend them. He watched in awe and horror as the beasts' bodies shimmer and cracked. Bones arching through furred skin, tufts of hair falling like rain, they were almost in those semi-human forms again. In the distance, he could see Aleria's ghost shimmering in the dappling moonlight, a translucent replica of the girl that had disappeared within the tent. The ghost tilted her head, a soft pitying smile played on her lips.

"We need to reconvene with others," Draven whispered through gritted teeth as he stared at the tent in the distance.

"It may not be her," MyKhal refuted him. It couldn't be her. He would not dare to hope, not when her ghost had been so present. So real. If she were alive, what did that mean for him?

"She's my blood, Khal," Draven growled into the darkness, interrupting his thoughts. "I have to know for sure."

Chapter 35

Larkin

The smell of Briony and blood still clung to the musty air of the tent as Larkin began mentally preparing for what was to come. They were captives about to trek into the wolf's den to be presented to the Nattmara queen. The rumored "first cursed," the spawn of Fae and Human that wove the world of the Fae into chaos.

His hold tightened on his mortal love, still deeply asleep in his arms. He wondered what the first betrayers of their kind had felt. Was it like this? Was their love worth turning the world upside down?

A barked order came from outside the tent, and he couldn't help but make a fowl gesture in the guard's direction. Pressing his lips against her forehead, he whispered for her to wake. It had only been a few hours, but it seemed their captors' patience had run out.

A soft whimper slid from her lips as she stretched and yelped when the remnant pain caught up to her. As his hands helped her up, he wished there were something he could do to help her heal faster. The poor thing was well past exhausted, and his worry for her only grew when she didn't say a word as they exited the tent. The comforting presence of his Huldra steadied him. But something about Aleria's countenance felt off. Her glassy emerald eyes stared off into the nothing. Her posture slouched, like an invisible weight pressed down upon her shoulders. When his hand brushed the tips of her fingers in a silent request, her reaction was slow, a sort of caution that only deepened his concern.

"We will take the horses. The girl is in no shape to travel," Larkin said as they walked to where their steeds had returned after the battle. They were trained to do so, even against their initial fear impulse.

The hulking beasts growled at him, but they did nothing to try and stop him as he lifted Aleria onto the saddle and slid in behind her. There were no idle threats about what should happen if they were to run. Instead, each of their mounts was flanked by Nattmara, guarding their every step. Larkin's mind ran wild, weighing his options. He could kick the horse into a full gallop, and they could make it away. Though, he wasn't sure how Aleria would fare with such a brutal ride. Her wounds were still seeping a trickling flow.

Solidifying his worries, Aleria's body swooned and tipped over. His hands wrapped around her waist, and he fought to urge to pull her against him. Adjusting her slightly in front of him, he leaned down and whispered in her ear, "Rest on me, love. Help me turn you around, so I can hold you."

Lifting her head slightly, she obeyed. Swinging her legs side saddle first before making the full turn to him. She didn't even look him in the eyes before she laid her head down on his chest and wrapped her arms around his waist. Larkin wasn't sure how to take Aleria being so immediately compliant to his words. There were no questions, no quirk of an eyebrow, not even a huff of resignation. Something was indeed wrong. At this moment though, he would not question it. Instead, he kissed her forehead as they rode off to the Nattmara encampment.

They rode deeper and deeper into the lush, overgrown wood surrounding what he imagined would have been Aleria's Fayeharrow. The sound of a sniffle met his ears, and he realized he wasn't the only one who noticed.

"So close," she murmured into his shirt as her body began to tremble and shake with barely controlled sobs. The wet warmth of tears soaking through the fabric and onto his skin tore at his heart.

"I'm so sorry, Aleria. Don't lose hope. All is not lost yet."

She choked a little and shook her head as the dreary processional ambled on until the sight of an abandoned stronghold came into view. Vines climbed the stones like living bindings, pulling the building deeper into the darkness of the woods that was attempting to claim it. Lights flickered from behind a large wooden drawbridge, slatted with one window. A Nattmarra howled, and the gate clicked, slowly lowering itself with a grating noise that signified its old age.

Aleria looked up at that. Her eyes went wide as she took in the fortress. Sliding her feet around again, she gaped and looked back at him.

"This place...," she whispered. "I know it." Her voice was cut off by the sound of a busy courtyard. The scent of baked bread and seasoned meats filled the air. Fae men and women rushed about, handing out food and laughing by the fire. Children ran and chased each other along the path. No Fae within these walls was in their Nattmarra forms. This was certainly not what he expected. As they made their way through the throng of people, they were not spared a second glance. Their presence, neither noted nor feared. What is the Mother's name was happening here?"You know this place?" Larkin echoed her previous statement.

"It belonged to my family. A stronghold...nearly a century ago. Everyone said it was haunted, that people disappeared in these parts," she gaped, still wide-eyed. "I suppose, in a way, they were right."

Larkin only nodded as they were led up to the castle entry and told to dismount. The grand entryway was rustic, but not falling apart or overgrown like the outside of the castle. No, there was something warm about this place. A sense of home and family that he had never once felt within the halls of Glair. A pit of nervousness opened in his stomach at the thought. His father could be there. His father could be within these walls. Nerves and excitement alike trilled through him as they walked through the Foyer and into the Great Hall. Entering this room was nothing like entering the cold, golden perfection of his grandfather's castle. If there were two complete opposites in feeling and design, this was it.

The walls were stone and worn, but rich tones of wood covered the floors. The sconces, aged brass and flickering with sunny flames that danced all across the room. Hanging from the ceiling there was a chandelier made from intricate woven bits of wood, bone, and antlers. It arched gracefully, and perched on each tip was the flame of a candle. There was no grandiose throne atop the dais. Instead, a simple high-backed chair draped in furs and cushions stood amongst a half-moon of others. It was slightly smaller, but still a comfortable looking seat.

Larkin looked to his companions who were taking in the room with the same attention to detail, if not more. Ruke had most likely counted every entry and exit point, while Thea had pinpointed every face and assessed each of their ranks. Zander, well, he was most likely identifying the most flammable substances in the room. The five of them stood in front of the gentlest throne room he had ever seen, and a howl echoed off every wall.

Aleria jumped a little beside him, and he would be lying if he said the sound didn't rattle him as well.

A group of Fae men and women entered through a side door, circling a woman he could barely see in the middle of them. The group took standing positions at their chairs, each one casting a glare in the direction of him and his companions. All except for a tall, golden man with eyes like a moon drenched sea. His heart leapt to his throat, and Zander took an unsteady step forward. Larkin reached a hand out to stop him, unsure of how things would move forward. The fifteen-year-old royal orphan in him wished to run to his father, desperate to be welcomed into his embrace. But the man he was now held suspicions and old hurts that would not allow him to even acknowledge his father's presence.

As the circle fanned out, it revealed a very human-looking woman. Shorter than Fae, though a bit taller than Aleria. Her eyes, a glimmer of golden tones made all the more shimmering by the rim of black coal lining them. Her skin betrayed no signs of aging, and yet, she held herself with a confidence and grace well beyond the appearance of her years. When her eyes fell on them, he felt a shimmer of recognition. Something that tugged at him and gave him more questions that needed answering.

"My dear children, forgive the way I have brought you here. We are not ones to waste precious time."

Larkin did not respond, nor did he show any kind of reverence to her station. That she would call them her dear children irked him to no end.

"I'm sure you have many questions, but first, I have one of my own, and it is of the utmost importance you tell the truth. Well, I suppose telling is not exactly what I'm looking for. I need you to show me." Her voice was gentle as she slowly stepped down from the dais and pulled a dagger from her belt. Larkin and the entire Huldra moved as one. He slid Aleria behind his back, Thea, Ruke, and Zander flanking him, their powers sparking with energy.

"Peace, princeling. I only wish to see what powers you and the human girl conjure together." Her gaze peeked around his shoulder to Aleria who was looking up at her in wonder and quiet assessment. "I am Hathra. What is your name, child? I am sure you would much prefer to be called by name rather than that of your race."

His nerves frayed when Aleria placed a hand on his arms and stepped towards the Nattmara Queen.

"My name is Aleria Edlind, Daughter of Phillip Edlind, Lady of Fayeharrow." The assurance and pride in her tone made his heart swell. His brave woman stared the queen down and reached for the dagger. The queen balked a moment at the mention of her name before a wide grin overtook the harsh lines of her face.

"Well met, Aleria Edlind. I trust you will not stab me with the dagger as soon as I place it in your capable hands? An accord between two power-ful women?" The mirth in her tone and obvious slight towards him did not go unnoticed.

"An accord," Aleria said with a slight smile. "Though, I would like to know why you wish to see this power yourself. Surely, your people have told of it."

Larkin watched as a haunted look passed over the queen's features before a melancholic smile took its place.

"I too would like to feel this temporary freedom you have brought to my kin."

Aleria looked to him, trepidation and unease in her eyes. Still, she reached for his hand. "What do we have to lose?"

Her eyes locked on him as if she were looking for an answer, confir-mation that she was doing the right thing, but the truth of it was he wasn't sure. They could see the bond of power and decide that spilling of blood would be the only suitable offering to the curse. Looking towards his father, he tried to get read on what he was feeling, an inkling that this was the right choice. What he saw shining in those moonbeam-like eyes was hope and barely held restraint. From what, he wasn't so sure. Still, he opened his hand to hers and watched as she sliced first his palm and then hers. With a deep breath, they twined their fingers together as the now-familiar shock of magi-cal energy spiraled through the room.

He watched as the queen closed her eyes for a moment. She breathed deeply and gasped before her golden eyes shot open. Wiggling her fingers, a flame began dancing at her fingertips. and she let out a choked sob mingled with wide-eyed glee.

"Hector! Edwin! Look!" she said, turning to her council. A small flame danced from finger to finger as she walked towards them. "See for yourselves!" The Fae behind the queen closed their eyes and giftings of all kinds burst from them. None were the full kind of power that he and his Huldra, but more like that of a child's, coming into their own for the first time. Small flames danced. Water appeared out of thin air; branches and stones shot up from beneath the wooden floors.

He did not expect that. Warring within himself, he made a split de-cision and released Aleria's hand, snatching the dagger from her. In a heart-beat, he had the blade pressed to the queen's throat.

"Larkin, stop!" Aleria's voice broke through the popping of skin and bone and raging snarls echoing across the entirety of the room. The crack-ling of fire, smell of decaying smoke, and shifting of earth echoed behind him. His Huldra was ready to move whenever he gave the command.

"Stand down," the queen ordered the transformed Nattmara. The group had begun to prowl around them, hissing and snapping their teeth in fury. The Huldra had closed in as well, an inner circle of protection. Aleria crossed the distance and laid her hand on his, wrapping her fingers around the hilt of the blade.

"They don't want to hurt us, Larkin."

"At least one of you has a modicum of discernment," the queen hissed, arching an unamused brow at him.

"Then, explain to me the attack in the woods," he snapped, but Aleria was quick to retort.

"Do not be like your grandfather. Allow yourself to listen to what they have to say before making a snap decision. Give her a chance before drawing blood."

Her words landed like a blow. That she would even compare them in the same breath was...

He looked at her pleading gaze and at his blade pressed against the queen's throat. She was right. Mother's mercy. Larkin looked towards his friends for some sort of backing, but Aleria pressed her hand to his cheek, directing his attention back to her.

"Trust me." Her words were the barest of sounds, but as powerful as an anvil slamming into his convictions. He did not want to release the blade. Old hurts, fear, and anger raged beneath his skin. Aleria did not drop her eyes from him. She held firm, sure of her instincts, her feelings, where he was not sure at all. With a warning glance to the Nattmara and a lingering gaze at Aleria, he slowly lowered the blade and released the queen. He did trust her. He could only hope she was right. The Huldra slowly powered down their magic and backed away a few cautious paces, giving them a bit of breathing room again.

The proud Nattmara queen took a few steps back as well. Righting her clothing as she nodded her head to Aleria in thanks.

"Your companions may go and find rest and refreshments in the adjoining room. There is something I must discuss with the two of you, alone." Larkin looked toward Ruke who shook his head, crossing his arms over his chest. Thea stood resolutely beside him. It wasn't until his father spoke up that anyone dared to move.

"We have quite a bit of catching up to do, don't we?" His father's voice was gentle, unsure, and full of restrained emotion as he looked from Larkin to Zander. His baby brother was the first to step forward. A bit unsure, but with the same sort of fragile hope he saw shining in his father's eyes. Larkin sighed and looked towards Ruke, resigned. "We will be alright. Go with Zee."

Ruke growled a bit and took Thea's hand in his, following after Zander and their father. Only two of the seven members of the council remained, hulking beasts, who snarled at him in barely contained contempt. Larkin met the queen's gaze and growled his threat.

"If any harm befalls them, a knife will be the least of your worries."

The Queen only smiled as she gestured for them to follow her. "Your care for them is admirable, princeling, but you do not need to fear me. Besides, I think your father and uncle will be the most hospitable guests. Along with the rest of my closest companions."

Larkin froze mid step at her words. His father and uncle were on her side. Companions. They were her council. How? How could they betray Glair in such a way? To aid in their hunting and attacking of their people? It was insanity. Pure, aching madness that threatened to tear him apart. He had always thought that his family were prisoners here, wrapped in a cursed skin with no other choice but to serve. His world was fading into a strange tone of blurred grey as he weighed what this all meant. A scathing retort tingled on the tip of his tongue, venom ready to spew because of his pain. Still, he was no novice in the world of politics. He would not allow his emotions to be so easily revealed. Let her believe he didn't care; perhaps he shouldn't.

The corridor her highness led them through was as warm and welcoming as the throne room. Paintings and ancient weaponry lined walls. Worn and well-loved wood draped in tapestries that told legends of old. Fae legends. Histories of Glair and the Mother. Some were of humans and animals...fairy tales, he realized. One was a beautiful rendering of a woman who looked as if she were pure sunlight and a man as silvery as the moon, both entwined in a loving embrace.

"That one is one of my favorites, but it is a tale for another time," Hathra's voice echoed through the hallway. "I have one that might interest you both in my sitting room, one which I have tried to decipher for one hundred years."

The doors to her chambers opened to the sound of another crackling hearth fire. It and the slight echo of rain outside were the only noises from within. Still, his every nerve prickled with tension. His back was straight, and his hand was never far from his sword. This could not be so simple. They could not be so welcoming. Something was wrong.

His wildly alert thoughts stuttered to a complete stop as he beheld the massive tapestry hanging from ceiling to floor. He heard Aleria breathe in sharply as she slowly approached the vivid work of art, Hathra at her side. The piece depicted a man and woman embracing in a field of flowers. The dusk and crimson of the blooms like shimmering streams of blood pooling at their feet. The Blath Dearg crept along their bodies, entwining them together. The moon above casting them in ethereal light and shadow.

"There are more than Nattmara here," the queen whispered, staring up at the art piece with unmasked admiration. "There are creatures of all kinds who find refuge within these walls. Creatures who found refuge with my family long before I was even born."

Larkin drew his eyes away from the piece and watched the queen warily. He knew there were many creatures not allowed inside Glair's walls because of their appetites or their dark and mysterious powers. This. This could be what he sensed was amiss.

"The being who created this piece is called Spindel. She weaves stories, histories, and even futures. She was my mother's handmaiden and very best friend before...," the queen's voice hitched as she lovingly traced the intricate patterns of the piece. Her face turned hard as she returned to him and Aleria. "Before her father sent Fae Warriors to murder her in cold blood."

The words sent a chill down his spine. The animosity he had expected upon their first meeting shown in her amber eyes, alight with barely restrained rage. He could not fault her for it in this respect. He could not imagine what kind of monster would murder his kin. The queen's glare narrowed on him as a small snarl pulled her teeth back. A wolf assessing its rival.

"Would you like to hear the story prince? The truth of which your precious Glair has hidden? Why its walls are so high? Its King's heart like the same cold stone?"

Larkin bristled. A blistering retort primed on his tongue, but Aleria, who was still staring at the tapestry, cut through the tension in a barely audible whisper.

"I am sorry for your loss." Her words were gentle and reverent as she turned to face them both. "I would like to hear it. All of it."

Hathra's snarl retracted into a soft and genuine smile as she turned to reach a hand out to Aleria.

"Come. Let us sit. I'll have something to eat brought in. Perhaps something as sweet as you, child," Aleria chuckled and nodded her head for Larkin to follow.

"I will stand. Thank you," he answered, though he did move closer. The queen only rolled her eyes and said, "Suit yourself."

Aleria

This was not what she imagined it would be like in the Nattmara's fortress. It was warm, lived in, and comfortable, much like her own family's estate used to be. Hathra's chambers were something her mother would have adored, a gorgeous mix of femininity and history. Whimsy and warmth. Fresh flowers with amber-colored glasses of all shapes and sizes decorated the room, the scent of them reminding her so much of home it nearly made her heart ache with the familiarity of it. Wood and soft furs echoed the same atmospheric warmth that permeated the near frigidness of her anxiety-ridden soul. All she wanted to do was curl up in one of the soft blankets and sleep for hours upon hours. No matter how foolish the sentiment might be. Maybe this was all a farce to lure her into a false sense of security, but at the moment, she honestly couldn't care less. Especially when the scent of freshly baked cinnamon pastries soaked the room further into an overwhelmingly comfortable ambiance. Hathra plated a cinnamon roll for her and one for Larkin, who was still glaring from only a few feet away. She couldn't help but smirk a little as he eyed the pastry like it would jump up and bite her.

"Would you like to test it for poison first?" Aleria's mouth quirked in a teasing way. Larkin only huffed and murmured something about being able to smell it if it were poisoned. She could understand where he was coming from. Creator knew she had seen first hand the kinds of horrors the Nattmara could reek. But then again, she had first-hand experience of the cruelty a Fae ruler could invoke as well. Villainy is in the eye of the beholder.

As much as she wanted to believe Hathra was not the villain in this story, she still waited for her to take a bite as a showing of good faith. Hathra only smiled as she plucked up the pastry and took a large and very unladylike chunk out of it. Aleria couldn't help but chuckle as she echoed the move and moaned her appreciation as the buttery cinnamon sugar delighted her senses.

Larkin rolled his eyes, but she saw the small smile tug at his lips. Hathra smiled as Aleria stood and handed him a plate before pressing a quick cinnamon flavor kiss to his mouth.

"Does your grandfather know the two of you are…," Hathra began as Aleria walked back to her seat. Aleria's back stiffened as flashes of the heartless Fae haunted her.

"Yes," he replied sharply. Aleria felt his eyes on her back and did her best to relax as she sat back down. The constant ache that plagued her every move somehow felt more prominent.

"Interesting," Hathra whispered as she took a deep drink from her teacup. "Perhaps this story will be even more impactful than I originally believed. Are we ready to begin?"

Aleria nodded her head. A pang of anticipation rolled her stomach, though not enough to keep her from taking another bite. Larkin, though, sat his plate down on the wooden end table next to her. Hathra cupped her tea in her hands and peered into it as she began, almost as if she could see the scene reflected in the amber liquid.

"Nearly two hundred years ago, my mother was forced into a Claiming ritual." Aleria flinched as she looked towards Larkin who had paled considerably. She remembered that conversation in the woods. How disgusting and destructive such an act was.

"She was the firstborn to a noble household and, thus, was commanded to have a proper mate for her to breed with. Someone who would add more power into their line. My mother refused the arrangement for she would not be bound to a man with whom she was not in love. Her father had no understanding of love in his heart, so he had her led to her the Claiming in chains after beating her unconscious. Her ceremonial dress of ivory was fully crimson by the time she reached her intended." A low growl rumbled from Larkin and tears pricked her own eyes at the brutal imagery.

"When her bridegroom saw the shape she was in, he outright refused the ceremony. He claimed that he would not be bound to a woman who was so close to death. It was postponed until the next evening, but Spindel could not stand to see my mother go through such torment. She and my mother escaped through the Crossing and into the human realm that very night, though my mother was barely healed enough to make the passage. She collapsed on the rocks at the base of the falls." Hathra smiled as she looked towards the tapestry hanging above the fireplace. Aleria followed her gaze and noticed the depiction of a beautiful silver-haired woman and a handsome man with fiery red hair.

"That is where my father found her. Twas a love story for the ages, I suppose. Though, in my case, it was one with a tragic ending. My grandfather did not think my mother would have gone so far as to cross over. It was forbidden to come into human lands, even more so to sully one's self with a human lover. He sent a hunting party to find them. When they did...," Hathra cleared her throat and shook her head.

"My father and mother fought for us. But even with elven steel and my mother's vast powers, they were no match for the warriors who came for her lover's head. As well as to destroy any proof of their union. Her mutt, as they called me." A low growl reverberated in her throat. "When her people stabbed my father through the heart, it broke something within her. I remember the look in her eyes. The way she looked at me. The desperation. The heartbreak and true unending love. She gathered all of her power unto herself. Every drop. She poured out her lifeforce to protect me...and to curse those who would try to harm me. Such magic demands a price in return. Her life was not enough to balance the shift of power. So at that moment, the full moon high in the sky, I became what I am, and the very first blood lust set in." She took a deep breath as she stared Larkin in the eye.

"I killed every one of them. I was barely a girl of thirteen. I woke naked in the forest. Spindel was the only one left in our household. The only person I had left in this world." Setting her cup down, she rose to her feet and walked to the fireplace. Each move radiated power and grace, just like the creature that laid buried under her skin. Her lithe figure was a lean muscle. Coiled, controlled, and deadly. If she wished, Aleria knew Hathra could cross the distance between them and snap her neck without breaking a sweat, her appearance echoing the horror of her words.

"I learned to control it. The hunger, the urges, all the while running from the men who were sent again and again by my grandfather. I did not want to kill any of them. It was my restraint that made me realize I could turn others into creatures like me. You have to realize how lonely, how lost, how angry I was. It is not an excuse for turning people against their will. Your father and uncle were among those ranks, and because I was the first, that gave me a certain amount of control over them."

Aleria watched as Larkin's stormy gazed iced over into cold rage. Sard. This is about to get ugly.

"You kept them as your slaves. You forced them to kill their people. You took my father from me. From my mother, my brother," he growled as he inched forward, a predator about to tear into another who entered his territory. Hathra only straightened her shoulders and nodded her head.

"I did, but only for a year, Larkin. I could not in good conscious hold them here when I learned about them. When I learned about you, your family. My mother would have been ashamed of me. So I let them all go."

"Liar!" Larkin snarled, and Aleria stepped between them. "My father would have come home if that were true," he spat.

"I did go home, Larkin," a deep baritone echoed across the room, and everyone stilled. Aleria could have sworn the fire even guttered. She slid her hand into Larkin's, knowing from the wide-eyed look of recognition and heartbreak in his eyes, who the voice belonged to. Larkin squeezed her hand so tightly she could feel the bones grind together, but she didn't cry out. She would be his grounding, no matter the pain of it. The tall and achingly handsome Fae man made no move forward. He stood inside the room as if waiting for permission to come further into the chamber. His golden mane of curls shimmered in the firelight, pooling around his shoulders. Similarly tied in leathers like his son's.

"Leif. You don't have to - "

"It's time, Hathra. It's long past time." The gentleness of his voice reminded Aleria so much of the way her father used to speak to her. The warmth and affection of a family. Larkin's father took a few steps further into the room until he stood between Hathra and Larkin. The look in both their eyes made her heart ache.

"I went home, Larkin. To your grandfather. I told him of what had happened to us, the curse. He responded that we should have died. That it would have been better for us to be dead than to live as we are. That we and all others like us were now mongrels needing to be put down." The growl that shook his words was nothing short of animalistic. "He tried, but soon found that we were not vermin to be exterminated." His eyes softened as he looked from Hathra to his son. "I tried to come for you, for all of you, but, Larkin, life was not always this way. Your grandfather didn't stop hunting us. Then, he trained you and Zander to hunt us. I couldn't...I couldn't bear you looking at me like I was a monster. So I never showed you my face again."

"But you hunted our people. Attacked us. You've been murdering - "

"We can't control that. Not when the blood lust sets in every full moon. We've tried. We've tried shackles, magical barriers, putting everyone on lockdown. Nothing worked."

"It is the curse. The price of magic is only quenched by blood." Hathra cast a lingering look at both Aleria and Larkin. The words of the curse began churning in her mind, everything clicking into place.

"One and one, two of the same.
Blood by blood. Taste and Claim.
Peace to soothe the hunger pangs.
Peace in knowing we are the same."

Aleria repeated the words aloud as tears fell down hercheeks.
"Where did you hear those words?" Hathra whispered.
"Tiadona and the Blath Dearg -"
The images she had seen in the field flashed before her once again. The silver-haired woman, their field of flowers, the man. His fiery red hair. Edlind hair. Her mouth fell open as she looked up at the tapestry of Hathra's parents. The emblem on the sword belt of the man. Of the man whose red hair reminded her so much of her father's, of her uncle's, of Draven's.
"You are an Edlind," Aleria whispered.
Hathra's smile was wobbly as she took her in as if she were seeing her for the first time.
"As are you," her voice wavering.
The profaniies that slipped from both their mouths were far from fitting for women of their station.

Edlinds.

She and the Queen of the Nattmara were both Edlinds. Certainly Edlinds with nearly a hundred years between the lines. An Edlind she had never heard of. An Edlind whose life ended young and had no other children besides Hathra. Creator have mercy.

Hathra and Leif were still staring at her, then glanced towards the field of Blath Dearg, the field of blood. Perhaps they were considering murdering her now. But still, there was one piece of the curse she did not understand. How did Larkin factor into all this? Was it because he was Fae or…

"Hathra, what Fae bloodline is your mother from? Who was her father?" Leif and Hathra shared a look before turning their attention towards her and Larkin. It was Leif who responded first.

"Ours. Hathra's mother…She was my sister," his voice cracked a little as his eyes met his son's. "I didn't know. I had never met her. I didn't put the pieces together until after returning here. Until Hathra trusted us enough to tell us the whole story."

Larkin only stared at them for a long moment before shaking his head and walking out of the room.

"Larkin," Aleria whispered and turned to go after him, but Leif placed a gentle hand on her shoulder.

"Let me. I need to talk to my son."

Aleria looked up at him with a soft but cautious smile before reassuring him.

"He's been fighting all this time to get you back. That's why he even bothered with me. It was all to get you back," Aleria added as a bit of encouragement. She thought that perhaps Larkin's pride would not allow him to admit it.

Larkin's father smiled slightly and tilted his head to the side in a way that made him look like Larkin's twin.

"I highly doubt that was the only reason." It was a light tease, and a flush of understanding crept across her cheeks. She watched him leave before turning back to Hathra with a solemn expression.

"Blood must be spilled and combined to end the curse, but we think that instead of our deaths - "

"The Claiming. Mother help us. Of course, it'd be the bloody Claiming."

Hathra looked from her to the tapestry and nodded her head. "One and one, two of the same. Two of the same bloodlines. My mother's and my father's."

Aleria nodded. "Taste and Claim. If Larkin and I claim each other, we would be joined by blood. The curse will be broken," Aleria said as Hathra crossed the room to her, reaching a hand out to hers. Aleria hesitantly took it, but when she felt the warmth of her touch, she relaxed into it.

"We will not force you into this, Aleria. That's not what my mother would have wanted. That is not what I want. If we have to live this way for all eternity, I would never force you to make such a choice."

Aleria smiled softly and resisted the urge to hug her. "Larkin and I have already come to that decision together. We are willing."

Hathra's jaw dropped as happy tears filled her eyes. She stammered for words for a moment before clearing her throat. "Then, I suppose congratulations are in order. When - "

"He wanted his grandfather's blessing, but after what happened…"

"You know, tradition dictates it is the male's father who officiates the Claiming ceremony."

Aleria smiled softly. "That's a wonderful tradition." It was very similar to the idea of a father giving his daughter away, something she knew she would never get to experience. Tears pooled in her eyes, and she tried to blink them away.

"Perhaps we should all retire for the evening," Hathra said, linking their arms and walking her out into the hallway. "I'll have a healer sent to your room to see what they can do about your wounds." Aleria looked up at her in wide-eyed curiosity. "I can smell blood and infection on you, child. I do not know how you received such grievous injuries, but I can guess. I will have a healer sent to your room with more food and a bath drawn as well. Wash up first."

Aleria almost had to fight the urge to say, "Yes, mother" at the tone of her voice. Instead, she simply nodded and whispered her thanks as Hathra led her to her quarters.

"What about my friends?" Aleria asked as Hathra opened a chamber door in the long hallway.

"My circle is incredibly hospitable. Do not worry about them. If I had to guess, they're in the middle of a drinking game," she said with a light chuckle. Almost on cue, a burst of laughter echoed through the halls, and Hathra grinned, "I know my people well. Go clean up and prepare for the healer. I'm sorry to say you are in no condition to join in the revelry."

Aleria sighed and then gave in to the yawn her body couldn't hide.

"Thank you, Hathra. Just - could you let Larkin know where I am? I want to give him time, but I also don't want him to worry."

"Of course." Her smile was soft and knowing as she bowed her head and headed towards the joyful sounds still bouncing off the walls.

Aleria

A few hours later she was bathed, fed, and under the gentle yet painful ministrations of Hathra's court healer, a faerie creature she had yet to see before. The healer's skin was a light green almost pastel in its coloring, as were her large eyes. Her face was lovely but sharp in its angles, only emphasized by deep brown markings along the high points. Aleria didn't dare to ask what manner of creature she was. She wasn't sure what might offend her. Nonetheless, she was too grateful to care much about it. Well, grateful wasn't quite the right word to use when someone was scraping infection from wounds. She supposed that was better than being ill, or well, dead. Sucking a hiss between her teeth, Aleria bit down on the pillow to muffle the bellow she was trying to contain. The metal tool dug into her wounds for what felt like the hundredth time.

"So sorry, Ma'am. I'm almost done with ya. Got some strong liquor for ya too. It'll help ya sleep. Though I suggest you stay on yer belly most tha night. We wanna have no pressure on these babes for a bit," the healer said as she began packing the wounds and laying what felt like a wet, squishy fabric across her back. "The poultice will make ya feel worlds better by morn, but ya have to endure. If you need anything, I'll be back to check on ye in a bit."

"I'll watch over her," a velvety smooth voice answered from across the room. She raised her head to greet him, but the little creature shoved her head back down on the pillow.

"Not finished yet, and you, Sir, should not be in here with a half-naked woman unattended."

She could almost hear the slight chuckle, the roguish taunt in his reply.

"It's not anything I haven't seen before, is it, love?" Aleria couldn't help but roll her eyes as she felt the other side of the bed shift with his weight. Turning to face him, she smirked.

"He has certainly seen everything I have to offer," she confirmed, her words taking on a heaviness, a sort of self-consciousness as she reached for the flask the healer was dangling in front of her face.

"Have it yer way then. Just..no funny business. You know what I'm sayin'." Aleria couldn't help but chuckle as the healer exited the room in a huff. Larkin cast a sidelong glance at Aleria, and she chuckled again as she took a deep but awkward pull from the flask.

"You heard the lady. No funny business, Prince Larkin," she teased, offering the flask to him. "This tastes like piss and burns like fire. Fuice?"

Larkin chuckled and took her offering, knocking it back with barely a grimace. "That's how you know it'll work."

For a few moments, they just passed the flask between them in the silence of the room. The occasional laugh or off-key shouting of bard songs would seep through the stones, pulling a slight smile to both of their mouths.

"You checked on them?" she asked after a while.

"Oh, yes, they're having a grand time. Miracle of miracles. I don't even know what to think about this place, its people. For so long, I've been...," he growled, running his hands through his hair and staring up at the ceiling.

"I know. You don't have to explain it to me. I understand," she whispered, nudging his arm with the flask. It began to taste less like piss and more like nothing. A nice warm feeling, heating her from her stomach outward. "I know it's foolish to ask if you're alright. How could you be? But... how did things go with your father?"

Larkin took the flask and another long pull before he spoke again.

"I couldn't speak to him. All this time, everything I imagined I would say, and not a single word came. I just...stood." He took another pull from the flask before handing it back to her.   "There is so much I wish to say to him. But I'm so...angry. Mother help me, I am, and I know it's not entirely his fault, and yet, I'm still angry. I'm angry at him. I'm angry at my grandfather. I'm angry at myself."

Aleria took the flask from his outstretched hand and then laid it against the headboard. It was mostly empty by now. "You have every right to be. You have every right to take your time in deciding what to do. Though, I do have a word of advice from a girl who is just recently father-less." She slid her hand into his and squeezed it gently. "Don't wait too terribly long. Fate is a cruel mistress, and I would hate for you to have any regrets."

Larkin's gaze softened as he slid closer to her side, his hand reaching out to stroke along her cheekbone, down her jaw, and across her lips.

"No funny business," Aleria whispered with zero conviction. Larkin only huffed a little before leaning in to kiss her forehead. Their faces so close they were breathing each other's air. His fingers made their way into her hair, lighly rubbing her scalp and untangling the still damp pieces as he whispered.

"And what did you and Hathra speak of?"

Aleria sighed and closed her eyes, relishing in his touch. "The Curse and the Claiming."

"And..."

"She knows everything, and she told me of an interesting tradition." Opening her eyes, she looked upon his face. The way it fell made her heart hurt for him. "You wanted your father to be the one who did the ceremony."

He nodded.

"Let's do this. Here. Tomorrow. Let's end this curse, and then, take back my home and yours and - "

"Aleria - "

"Larkin, don't tell me it - "

"Would you let me finish before you make assumptions, woman?" His playful tone made her press her lips together, fighting a smile. He smirked, shaking his head as touched her cheek.

"What I was going to say was I love you. I am committed to loving you until the darkness takes us. I want you, Aleria. Curse or no. If there were no pressing issue, perhaps I would have waited a while, courted you. But as things are now, I would claim you this very moment if you'd allow me," he whispered, leaning down to place a kiss on her lips, her chin, her throat. "I am forever yours, Aleria Edlind, and I want you to be forever mine." Tears pricked her eyes as her heart felt like it very well may explode with happiness.

"But I want you to be prepared," he added, pulling back from her, and she almost whimpered with the loss of him. "I want you to learn what will happen during. What the ceremony is like, what to expect afterward. I want you to enter this relationship with your eyes and heart wide open. Are those agreeable terms?"

Nodding her head, she threaded her fingers with his and beamed at him. She wished she was not on her stomach, so she could adequately express her appreciation. Larkin leaned down to kiss her knuckles, her wrist, the inside of her elbow, before draping it around him as he slid closer, tilting her slightly on her side. She noticed how his eyes flickered to her complete bare chest before snapping back up to her face. His silver-toned eyes were positively slate as he stared at her. Sucking his bottom lip into his mouth, he let our low rumbling groan that did horribly wonderful things to her lower half.

"Ask me all you wish to know. I could use a distraction from...the funny business," he said with a self-deprecating chuckle. If she were honest, she could use a cold bath, not a simple distraction.

"Will it hurt?" she asked, and he barked a laugh at that and kissed her forehead.

"Ah. Well, yes, a little. It is a bite after all, but because a Nattmara has bitten you, I say it would be a pinprick in comparison." He nuzzled her nose and kissed it next. "Nothing my fierce woman couldn't handle. Besides, some quite enjoy the experience," he murmured as he leaned over to nip at the shell of her ear. Aleria fought the urge to purr.

"And..mm..what will happen after? You'll bite me; I'll bite you. Blood everywhere, and boom...Claimed?" His laugh was the most sultry thing she had ever heard as he pulled away from her ear and kissed her cheek.

"How about I walk you through the whole thing, hm? From the ceremony to...the end."

"Please," she answered with a pained groan, Aleria lifted from her position and moved the short distance to lay on his chest. He raised an eyebrow, and she only shrugged.

"I'm still on my stomach."

"And my chest...with your chest...are you trying to drive me insane?"

"I thought it was pretty easy for me to do that," she chuckled, and he groaned. "Play with my hair and walk me through it."

He snarled playfully at her, but acquiesced to her request, sliding his fingers into her hair.

"First, there will be a party. Food, drink, music, and dancing. Our intendeds wear a dress of ivory, something flowy and lovely. The men wear something similar. And ivory tunic and lightweight breeches."

"Why ivory?"

"Well, this may sound strange to you, but the blood shows up best on that color. A symbol of the Claiming. At the high point of the celebration, the couple will slip away to a tent or chamber. It is there that the Claiming will take place. The couple will share in a few words and..." He stopped for a moment as if he were considering leaving out the next part or maybe how he should say it.

"And?" she parroted.

"The couple consummates the marriage. It's different for everyone. Remember how I told you the bite could be pleasurable?" Aleria nodded, blushing down to her toes. "Some couples wait until the moment of completion to claim one another. I'm told it heightens the moment. Makes it all the more pleasurable."

Her mouth went completely dry at the images he was creating in her head.

"Oh," was all she could say as her body tightened in response.

Larkin cleared his throat. "Then, after both have...come down...they return to the revelry. Bloody and sated. The parties tend to last all night, though the couple tends to disappear again well before the others do."

Creator, she understood why. The thought of being with Larkin in such a way made the comfortable warm room suddenly unbearably hot.

"And what about us? How will it change what we have? I'm human, so what does that mean for us?"

"Perhaps that is something we can ask Hathra? I honestly don't know."

She turned her head to place a kiss on his still blood and mud-covered shirt. Guilt settled in her heart as she realized he was still in the clothes they had brought them here in.

"How about you have a bath? I'll ask you more while you clean up. I'm sure someone would bring you some clothes if you peek your head out the door. You could even stay the night if you like..." His grin was positively feral, and she felt the heat of it to her toes. "To talk and sleep. The healer said - "

"No funny business. I know," he groaned, sliding out from beneath her and leaning down to press a kiss on her bare shoulder. "Believe me, I find nothing about this funny."

Her chuckle followed him out the door and into the hall.

Larkin

Hours.

They had spent hours in each other's arms. The questions were put on hold when sleep claimed Aleria, her body pressed as tightly against his as possible. Something about having her here like this made the chaos of his mind slow and settle on thoughts of forever. Perhaps it was because she was half-naked, and he was only a man, or maybe it was that he had meant every word he said to her. He would claim her this moment if she would allow it. Aleria had not been the first woman to turn his head, but she had been the first to claim his heart.

Brushing his fingers through her hair, he thought of what it might be like for her to be his. For the two of them to be joined mind, body, and soul. There were still things they needed to talk through before the ceremony, but he was willing to bend for her. He was willing to do whatever he needed to for her to be happy. If anyone deserved happiness, it was her.

Knock-knock-knock.

It was still the middle of the night when a woman poked her head in, mumbling apologies.

"The Queen wishes to see Lady Aleria. She said it was something she might wish to see for herself."

Larkin sighed, but nodded. "Tell her we will be there momentarily." He hated the idea of waking her from such a sound sleep. Tomorrow, he would request for the two of them to not be disturbed as they prepared for the ceremony.

Leaning down, he pressed a kiss to her temple. "They need you," he whispered, but she only groaned in answer. He couldn't help but chuckle as he kissed a line from her temple down to her shoulder. Taking a moment to nuzzle her neck playfully, his mouth watered at the thought of sinking his teeth just there and claiming her as his own. Mother help him, he wanted that. When she groaned again and pushed up on her elbows with a death glare in his direction, he grinned at her.

"You look lovely."

"I feel murderous."

"Why do I find that incredibly attractive?"

"Because I'm still half-naked."

Larkin chuckled as she groaned loudly and pressed her face into the pillow. Painstakingly, she rose to her feet, taking the blanket with her.

"Will you remove the poultices?" she murmured, reaching for a tunic that was laying on the nightstand next to her. Without a word, he slid behind her and slowly began removing each strip. To his surprise and relief, the wounds had fully scabbed over. In some places, it had even begun to close completely. Still, her severely mangled flesh tore at his heart. When he was finished, she slipped the linen fabric over her head and slid into her boots.

"I wonder what is so important they couldn't wait until morning."

"Hopefully, Zander didn't burn anything down in his drunken stupor."

Her soft chuckle warmed his bones. "Let's hope not." Pulling her hair back and tying it at the nape of her neck, she turned to him, "Ready?"

"Almost." With one stride, he was across the room and pressing his lips to hers. He cupped her backside with one hand and pressed her fully against him. His other hand found its way to the side of her face to pull her back and brush his lips over her forehead.

"Now, I'm ready."

Hand in hand, they walked into the throne room. The room was thick with tension, though only a few people were in attendance. Hathra stood at the dais in front of two figures, bound, hooded, and on their knees in front of her. When she and Aleria's eyes met, there was concern there. Concern and a wariness made him instantly alert and Aleria's body stiffen.

"Lady, these men were found trying to find a way into the stronghold. Strangers are typically dealt with by my guard, but they mentioned your name. That they were looking for you, and I thought it best for you to decide their fate. Aleria's hand tightened in his as she took a step forward.

"Remove their hoods," she said, and when the two guards stationed at the dais did so, Aleria's legs gave out beneath her. As quick as a breath, he caught her, but her eyes were glued to the two men on the floor. One with dark hair and a scowl, the other with hair that showed like heated copper in the firelight. His were the eyes that held shimmering tears. His was the mouth that choked her name. Pushing against his hold, Aleria scrambled to her feet and rushed towards the prisoner, flying across the room and latching her arms around his neck. For a raw, purely male moment, jealousy lit his bones to fire and ash as she buried her face in the other man's neck.

"Let them go. For Creator's sake, let them free," she sobbed, her hands on the red-headed male's face. "Dray?" He heard the love there. The joy. And it hurt more than he could say until he remembered the name. Dray. Her cousin. He smiled then, shaking his head at his foolishness.

When the two men were freed, the dark one stood to his feet and assessed the room in quiet calm while her cousin threw his arms around Aleria and sobbed into her shoulder. Laughter bubbled up between them through the tears as they helped each other stand, each brushing the tears from each other's faces before hugging again.

"You have no idea the cluster sard you just got yourself into, cousin," she said with a delirious laugh.

"I want to hear all of it," Draven replied, squeezing her hands.

Finally taking a moment to look towards the dark one, Aleira stilled. All the joy drained from her face as her posture tightened. Larkin felt something radiating from her, but he wasn't sure what it was until she ran forward. Her arms reached out to the dark stranger, but then, she stopped. Before she could reach him, she seemed to catch herself and think better of it. The tension returning to her body, caught in indecision. The stranger took a step forward, his eyes wide like he was seeing a ghost materialize from thin air.

"You're alive. You're - you're here. Ali - ," he started, reaching a hand out to trace her cheek in a lover's gesture. Larkin's skin prickled as something raw and fiery ignited beneath his skin. When Aleria didn't move, the pulse of magic beneath his skin began to pound like a war drum. He watched as the stranger slid his hand behind her neck and pulled her flush against him. His mouth claimed hers, and pain like none he had felt before wretched in his chest. The flare of his magic nearly knocked the breath from him as thunder boomed in the throne room. Lightning cracked in his clenched fists.

The boom of sound was the breaking of whatever spell the stranger had worked around her. She returned to herself in a breath. Shoving the dark-haired one back, Aleria unceremoniously slammed her fist across his face with a brutal right hook. The jealous rage shifted immediately into smug satisfaction before fierce protectiveness took hold. Larkin was instantly moving, ready to step in to defend her, but the man, to his credit, only turned his hard stare back to her. Draven smirked, seemingly pleased with the way she was handling the situation. Taking a cue from him, Larkin stayed back and watched the scene unfolding in front of him.

Blood dripped down the dark one's lip as his eyes locked on Aleria's with an intensity that made his blood boil. He wasn't sure if the stranger were thinking about murdering her or bedding her, and both options made a low snarl rumble in his throat.

"I don't know, nor do I care why you are here, Anwir, but - "

"Ali, it's not like that," Draven said finally as he tried to pull her back and away from the dark one. Anwir. That name sounded familiar too, but he couldn't remember.

"Do you feel better now?" The low timbre of Anwir's voice echoed in the quiet of the hall. Aleria's eyes snapped to his; rage like a burning ember of flames flickered there as she flew at him again. He stepped out of the way of her fist this time, and she hissed a series of profanities at him. "Big talk from a little girl throwing a tantrum."

"MyKhal," Draven warned, but still kept his distance. MyKhal. Yes, he had heard that name before. The name she whispered in her sleep. He felt his ire prickle at that. Larkin had no idea what was happening here, but he did know the moment MyKhal laid a hand on Aleria, he would find himself missing it. Larkin caught Draven looking in his direction and nearly balked when he crossed the distance between them and offered his hand.

"I'm Draven. Aleria's cousin."

"Larkin. My title as well as what is going on here is...complicated."

"So is that," Draven motioned to the area that Aleria and MyKhal were full-on fist fighting now. Aleria sidestepped MyKhal's attempt to grapple her by the waist, pulling her knee up hard in an attempt to slam it into his groin. MyKhal anticipated her attack and dared to smirk at her. Aleria's growl of fury stirred some of his wildness until Draven continued. "But they both need this. It's best for us not to interfere unless things get ugly."

Larkin looked at him with a curious stare and then back to Aleria who had been knocked to the ground. Larkin cursed and stepped forward as she writhed for a moment. He knew her injuries had to be screaming from the hit. Draven's fingers clasped over his forearm, and Larkin's eyes sparked with electricity. To his credit, Draven didn't even flinch. His eye widened a bit, betraying his shock, but still, he kept his hold.

"He's not going to badly hurt her. Trust me. He loves her." The words hit him as brutally as Aleria's kick to MyKhal's legs.

"You're certain?"

"If you don't want her to kick your arse next."

Larkin huffed at that. Then, he noticed Hathra had left the throne room. It was only the four of them now. Larkin watched as MyKhal and Aleria met each other blow for blow. It was as if they could sense which move the other would use next.

"Who is he to her?" Larkin asked after a long moment. Draven raised an eyebrow at him with a slight smile.

"The better question is who are you to her? Though, if I had to guess, the answer is the same as him."

"Astute," Larkin huffed, crossing his arms as MyKhal deflected another blow. He wasn't hitting her. The man was tiring her out.

Aleria

Rage.

Out of all the things she felt when she saw him again, the rage was the loudest. A rage that was both cold as death and as white-hot as the center of a flame. She felt it burning her alive and freezing her heart at the same time. His face. That face she had once loved reflected the same cold she felt. That steel wall slid into place when they wanted to keep their emotions from spilling out all over the floor. It was a wall they had both forged as children in a court where feeling anything could be exploited as a weakness. A wall that each of them used to have the key to.

When her shoulder slammed into his ribs, she knew she had him. Wrapping her fingers around his throat, she sat across his chest. He stopped fighting her.

"Fight me," she growled.

"No."

"Fight back!"

"No. You've won." His warm brown eyes were absolutely molten as he stared up at her.

"I could kill you," she panted, her hands tightening around his throat.

"Do it then."

She squeezed tighter, but her hands began to shake. Tears threatened to fall, and she released her grip as if he had burned her. Stupid, sarding prick and her stupid, sarding heart. She wasn't a monster. She wasn't like him. Wasn't like his father. She wouldn't give in.

"Prick," she echoed her thoughts, rolling off him and stomping off in the direction of Draven and Larkin. The two of them simply stared at her with equal looks of concern and pride.

"What?" she snapped at them, still fuming. Narrowing her gaze at Draven, she pointed her finger at him and tapped his chest. "You better have a bloody good reason for bringing him here, or I swear to the Creator I will kick your arse from here to Rimeheld and back."

Draven only shrugged, but Larkin's eyes widened a bit, a slow smile pulling across his mouth. Those dimples showed in their full glory.

"What?" she snapped at him again, and his smile turned predatory.

"Has anyone ever told you how stunning you are when you're furious? Mother help me, I want my turn in the ring."

Draven choked on a laugh, and she tried to fight the blush creeping across her cheeks.

"Shut it, you."

Her attention snapped to Draven.

"Come to my quarters, so you can explain to me what in the Creator's name you are doing here. Bring Anwir too. I don't want him out of my sight. Larkin?" Her tone softened as she said his name. "Can you find us some liquor? I have a feeling this will be the kind of conversation that needs a bit of lubricant."

Larkin smirked at her before leaning down to press a kiss to her lips.

"Only if you promise me a match later."

She couldn't help but chuckle as she pushed at him playfully. "Cad."

Draven only gave her a knowing look as she led the way.

"It's none of your business."

"The nethers it isn't," Draven shot back. Aleria couldn't help but grin as she linked her arm through his.

"I've missed you."

"And I you, Al," he whispered, kissing the top of her head.

Aleria

"Sard," Draven whispered as he pressed his third glass of whiskey to his mouth. Aleria couldn't help but chuckle as she still nursed her first.

"That about sums it up, yes." She felt heavy and so very tired after telling the entirety of the tale. Her emotions raw and ragged, her nerves frayed. She had glossed over the moments in Glair's throne room. The moments in which she would have almost rather give up and die than continue in the pain and darkness of her body and mind. Draven would be ashamed of her...Moreover, he might try to kill Larkin for allowing her to go through it. Even worse, he might blame himself, and she wouldn't dare belittle the sacrifice he made for her.

"And what of you, Cousin? How did you and Anwir join forces?" She wouldn't dare call MyKhal by his first name. That name she had whispered between passionate kisses. That name she called out when nightmares had plagued her sleep. The name she had cursed on the wind. The name that still floated through her dreams at night no matter how desperately she wished it weren't so. No, she needed to remind herself that he was her enemy. He was his father's son through and through. So she'd say his name like she would spit a curse, and she knew she wasn't imagining it when he flinched slightly each time.

"Ah, well. Let's just say Lord Anwir is as he always has been, a bell-end with an agenda. He kept me alive to hunt your friends under the guise that they were the ones who killed you. Khal here knew something was off the entire time. Through some of his findings - well, let's just say that once we were finished with this monster hunt, we'd head out to kill the real one," he said tipping his glass towards MyKhal. "Anything you want to add to that, brother?"

Aleria cringed at the term of endearment, but turned her gaze towards MyKhal. He met her cold stare with one of his own and shook his head.

"That about covers it," he murmured, looking back at Draven with a warning glare. Draven groaned and leaned up to brace his elbows on his knees.

"Listen here, you little shites. I'm not going to be your go-between anymore. You got something to say to each other, then bloody well say it. If you want to spend the rest of your time hating each other, that's between the two of you, but I'm not choosing. Neither will I be listening to you curse each other's names either. So be honest or agree to disagree because we are grown arse adults who have much bigger things to deal with than your hurt feelings."

Aleria's jaw dropped open, and she swore she heard Larkin snort through his nose. She dared to look in MyKhal's direction, but he would not meet her eyes. Draven was right. Still, she wished he would just tell her what he wanted her to know instead of having to face MyKhal alone.

Part of her didn't know if they could even exist in the same room without coming to blows. She was more comfortable hating him than knowing whatever truth they were keeping from her. But was that unfair of her? Would she be able to live with herself?

"Perhaps you're right," the low rumble of MyKhal's voice broke through the tense silence of the room. Her heart stumbled in her chest.

"We have much bigger things to deal with right now." He locked his eyes on hers and nodded once. "All you need know is I'm on your side, as I always have been. I always will be. Your family has always been closer to me than my own. I want to help you avenge them, no matter the consequences."

Aleria felt her throat close up as she let the words sink in. She made herself look at him, really look. Three years abroad had taken its toll. The markers of a warrior's life were written all over him. His hair long and tied back, with unruly chestnut curls falling across his brow and cheekbones. There was a scar through his upper lip that had not been there years ago, and his skin had been bronzed from days upon days in the brutal Brennan sun. His eyes though, so dark they were nearly obsidian, fathomlessly deep and so very sad. She didn't dare linger on the thought too long. If what he said were true, then, of course, he would be sad. He finally understood that he was sired by a monster.

The words were like saltwater in her mouth, tough to swallow and necessary to spit out. "Fine. I suppose you're right...That's all I need to know." The words sounded bitter even in her ears. A final nail in the coffin of whatever they once had. It was dead and needed to be buried. MyKhal's only response was a slight nod before murmuring that he needed to see about their sleeping arrangements. Aleria didn't dare allow her eyes to follow him as he shut the door behind himself.

Draven let out a long sigh and leaned back in his chair. "You don't have to be so cruel to him, you know. He beats himself up enough as it is." Aleria snarled at him before standing from her chair and moving over to the fireplace.

"Don't you dare guilt me when you have more information than I do and refuse to relay it."

"It's not my place."

"Neither is guilting me."

"Somebody ought to when you're over there kicking beaten pup."

"Pup, my arse. That man is a wolf, and you and I both know it."

"He's not his father."

"That is yet to be seen."

"I've seen it."

"Well, I bloody well haven't, so either spill what you know or shut up about it," Aleria hissed over her shoulder. She felt anxiety creeping up inside her blood. Her heart racing and stammering, tears pricking her eyes, swallowing hard, she shoved her trembling hands into her pockets and turned back around. Larkin met her gaze with a concerned one of his own.

"Are you alright?" he asked, taking a cautious step towards her.

"No," she whispered, and he reached out a tentative hand to her. She gave his hand a quick squeeze before putting hers back in her pocket. Something about this moment made the idea of being touched too much. She could not risk falling apart. Not now. Not ever again.

"So," Draven's voice cut through the fog of her emotions, "this Claiming business. It's like getting married, right?"

Creator help her. Larkin was the one to answer before she could.

"Aleria mentioned the same concept, and I suppose in a way it is, but the...connection is deeper. She said human marriages share lands and wealth. While this is true with Claiming, we share our bodies, our minds, and our lives. There is no separation option, as there is with humans."

Draven raised a brow. "I don't understand."

"To be honest, neither do I," she added with a shrug.

Larkin sighed deeply in that way he always did when he was being incredibly patient with her.

"Imagine being able to see into my mind when you wish. To cross space and time to see where I am through my eyes. To feel what I am feeling. To be able to communicate without seeing one another. To share the very essence of our lives with another, our power."

"Power?" Draven asked, looking between Larkin and Aleria.

"All Fae are endowed with giftings from the Mother," Larkin said, holding his hand out in front of himself. "I have been gifted with control over atmospheric elements." As he opened his palm, water swirled and danced around it. Wind whipped and twirled the water in patterns before he directed it into a glass pitcher across the room. Draven only stared, mouth agape.

"That is a small fraction of what he can do, Dray," Aleria added with an appreciative smile in Larkin's direction. "Thank you for choosing not to soak my bedding with a rainstorm in here instead."

"I figured we wouldn't want to sleep on a soaked mattress."

Draven's eyes narrowed at his words, and before Aleria could explain, he was on his feet.

"The two of you have been sleeping together?" The accusation in his tone annoyed her to no end.

"Sleeping, Dray. Not that it's any of your business."

"The nethers it isn't. Aleria, if you're going to take the throne, if you're going to marry, you know what they will expect."

"Those traditions are completely outdated and entirely unfair."

"It doesn't matter. They will demand proof."

"Well, that ship has sailed, and I will find a way to prove it to them. Even if I have to cut myself and put the blood on sheets."

Draven froze. Larkin did as well, his back stiffening.

"You said just sleeping," Draven said slowly, but Aleria gave him a pointed look, gritting her teeth before she could no longer meet his gaze. "Khal?" She straightened her shoulders. How dare he put her on the spot like this? How many women had he slept with, and yet, her relationships were somehow within his authority. "I'm going to kill him."

"You will say nothing to him about it. You will not shame me, nor my decisions of what I did with my body. I thought I was going to marry him, Dray." Her face tightened as she gritted her teeth and took a deep breath. "None of this is your business. The Claiming, whom I choose to sleep with - you're overstepping your bounds."

"I'm being pragmatic. Your decision in the Claiming affects me. It affects all of Fayeharrow. What do you plan on doing, hm? Bring back this magical Fae creature to help run a very human, very superstitious world?"

He shot a look towards Larkin and grimaced apologetically. "No offense. You seem like a decent bloke, but the truth of the matter is I don't think the two of you understand the repercussions of your actions."

Aleria started to speak when Larkin interrupted.

"I will go back to Fayeharrow with her. I will glamour myself to seem just like your people. No one will know besides us."

Aleria's jaw dropped open as hope and pure admiration filled her chest.

"You..you will? What...glamour?" she stammered completely overwhelmed by this new revelation.

"Remember when you could not see the Sluagh in the woods? I told you it was glamoured in your world so that you could not see it's true form."

Aleria nodded, but still didn't quite understand until he stepped back from her and moved his hands over his ears, his otherworldly eyes, his mouth, all the indicators that he was not from this world. When he was finished, he looked like any other human man. Still breathtakingly handsome, but in all other ways...human. Aleria took a step towards him, wide eyes shimmering with affection. Her hands traced his ears, his cheekbones, his mouth before she could find the words to reply.

"You would do this for me?" Her voice was as soft as his smile as he brushed his fingers over her cheeks.

"I would. Happily so. Would that make you happy? Would you allow me to rule at your side? To be your helpmate?."

Aleria sucked in a breath and chuckled as a tear slid down her cheek. "In the human world, that would sound an awful lot like a proposal."

Larkin's grin broadened as he looked towards Draven. "Tell me how to make it an official human proposal."

Aleria choked a laughing sob as she looked at Draven with hopeful expectation shining in her watery eyes. She knew Larkin had asked him, not for his advice, but his blessing. Draven shook his head before letting out the same sigh of endearment and standing from his chair.

"Well, typically you'd take a knee...submitting yourself to the woman's cruel whims." Aleria snatched a book off the mantel and chunked it at him. He dodged it and pointed at her in shock. "See? You sure you want to pledge yourself to that?"

Larkin laughed and took a knee in front of her.

"I love that fire in her."

Aleria beamed at Larkin, then shot a smug glance at Draven, who rolled his eyes.

"The only thing you're missing then is a ring. Typically, a proposal comes with a ring."

Larkin looked up at her a little embarrassed and sheepish as he looked around.

"I don't…," he started, but then smiled as he reached up in his hair and untied one of the longer leather ties from his hair.

"A place holder," he said, reaching out his hand for hers as he whispered the words from before. "My heart's desire is to make you happy, Aleria Edlind. If you find me worthy, would you allow me to rule at your side?"

Aleria's smile stretched from ear to ear, but because she loved him, she had to ask one more question.

"But what of Glair, of your people? I can't ask you to - "

"My father will be restored when the curse is broken. He can take his place on the throne. He can reunite our people. Maybe my path was always destined to lead me here, to you."

Aleria shook her head, unable to believe what she was hearing.

"And when I'm old and grey, and you remain beautifully the same?"

"Do you believe my love is that vain?" he asked with a laugh. "And when I die?"

"I will watch over our children, and our children's children for as long as the Mother allows."

"Children?" she asked with a blush and a wider smile.

"Scads of them." His grin was absolutely impish.

Aleria burst out laughing and started to say something else when Larkin interrupted, "Woman if you don't say yes this moment, I will rescind my offer and - "

"Yes! Yes. It would be my honor to have you at my side."

She had never seen him smile in such a way. He wrapped the leather band twice around her ring finger, down the top of her hand, and around her wrist before tying it in a knot. Grinning, he kissed her palm before shooting to his feet, gently wrapping his arms around her waist and lifting her, so their lips could meet. When their lips parted, he slowly let her slide down the length of him, keeping his forehead pressed against hers. She felt herself leaning in for another when she heard Draven clear his throat.

"Killjoy," she murmured, but turned to him with a bright smile. "Do you have another question?" she teased, slipping her hand into Larkin's, the feel of the woven promise like a beacon of hope for her scarred heart. She wasn't going to be alone anymore. She had Larkin. She had Draven. The Huldra. A family, and hope for the future.

"Only one for now," he said, rising from his chair and walking over to give her a side hug. "What in the Creator's name are we going to do now?"

Aleria took a deep breath as she looked between the two most important men in her life.

"We plan for the future. Then, we go home."

Far from the end

Acknowledgements:

First and foremost I would like to thank my Lord and Savior Jesus Christ, My heavenly Father, and the Holy Spirit. Without their love, kindness, mercy, and gentle guiding hands I would not have ever come this far. They knew all along that they made me with such an imagination and I'm so thankful for the means to share it with all of you.

Speaking of blessings from the Lord, I would like to say thank you to my husband for being the curator for my dreams. My encourager, even if he doesn't quite get what I'm talking about. My first sounding board. I'm thankful for his willingness to allow me to be butt hurt at him when something I've written doesn't make sense and he calls me on it. I'm thankful for all the toddler distractions, the meals cooked, the dishes washed, and the love given in all the best ways. You are my very own Fae Prince made real, Jonathan. I love you.

I would also like to say I love you to all my family right here. Griffin, Courtney, Josh, Jade, Susan, Cam, Chris, Kimberly, Kibbie, Curtis, Faith, Nana O'Dell, Sandy, Wayne, Adam, Donna Kay, Mammaw and Pappaw, Mac, The Underwood Clan (too many to name. Lol) All of you have loved and supported me in the journey and I thank you so much.

Thank you Jessica Howard for listening to me about everything, all day every day. I want the world to know how amazing you are and how blessed I am to call you "bes-fran". I love you.
Thank you Heidi Wilson for your incredible artwork, friendship, food, and laughter. I am better because of you. You are forever the Moon to my Mushroom and I can't wait for all our future projects!

Thank you to the best editor in all the realm, Lady Nikki Wright. Not only is her work amazing but her personality and little bits of humor sprinkled into all of the "fixing my mess" literally have me rolling with laugher and actually looking forward to reading about how grammatically challenged I am. My favorite being, "People will love this, I on the other hand do not." Ha! She's the best ever!

I would like to continue with a list of people who have made this book possible. I want to give a major shout out to my very first beta (from my fanfiction days) Carmen Fritsch. This woman gave me my real start at writing. She taught me, pushed me, and became one of my best pen pal friends. I told her once that I was going to write a novel one day (and that she should too. Oh my word is she a fantastic writer.) and one of my joys will be being able to send her a copy of this with some scenes inspired by our co-writings. Thank you Carmen for everything you've done for me. It has brought me here.

Moving on to beta number 2. Bri McGill. You made me so excited to write. You kept me going when it was hard. Thank you for letting me annoy you 24/7 with "have you read it yet?". You are the best and I couldn't have done it without you!

To my beta number three and my best writer friend. Author Christian Rann (who will be a best-selling author one day. Mark my words. She also did the blurb on the back of my book!) I don't know where to start here and I'm going to get misty-eyed. She was a perfect stranger who took the time to believe in me. She made me believe in myself. She tore my manuscript up and I am forever grateful for it. I live for her constructive criticism, New Girl memes, witchiness, and lyrical writing. I thank the Insta-gods for her on the daily. Love you, girl.

Speaking of Insta-gods, a huge shout out to Laura aka L.P. Savage, aka Newbietonovelist for her invaluable advice in both my book and the writing world. Talking with her is so fun and encouraging and I can't wait to hold her own work in my hands! So thankful she is on this journey with me and I'm so humbled to be on hers!

C.A. Farran you are one of the best people I've ever met and I'm so thankful for your energy, your kindness, your critique, and your friendship! Fan-fic Friends for life.

Staying on the Insta bandwagon special shout-outs go to Autumn Krause (my dark heart twin), Ashlynn Crow, Stella B James, Skye Horn, Sara Em, Raylynn Fry, Megan Davies, Kara Weaver, Jess Pearl, S. Escobar, Kate Argus, and all of my #writingcommunity friends (there are so many more and I'm sorry if I didn't name you specifically!) I am so thankful to have met all of you!

Thank you to all my Instagram, Bookstagram, Booktok, and Facebook buddies for being a part of this journey. You all are so wonderful!

And last but not least, thank you to you. The reader. I hope you loved this book as much as I do. I hope it gave you all the feels. And I hope I see you again soon fellow Inkdrinker.

Brandi Gann has always been a fairytale girl in a small town Georgia world. Her weirdness and search for where she belonged have led her to a collection of degrees. Fashion Design, Cosmetology, General Studies with Specialization in Creative Writing. All of which have aided her in not only her day job as a quirky Elementary and Middle School Art Teacher but on the journey of self-publication. She has always loved telling a good tale, much like a magical creature would spin over the dying embers of a fire. That is why she has dawned the title of Brandi Gann -Teller of Tales. Magic is her goal. To tell a tale that makes you feel, makes you think, and makes you dream big dreams. Her purpose in writing is to share a little bit of magic with those who are willing to see it.

For more magic visit https://brandigann-telleroftales.weebly.com/
Or check out her Instagram @brandigann.telleroftales
For Character Inspiration Boards and sneak peeks check out her Pinterest brandi-ganntelleroftales.

Printed in Great Britain
by Amazon

59625224R00177